Fuzzy

Brown

Dog

Nancy T Whitesell

DEDICATION

This book is dedicated to all of the mentors

Who share their time and expertise

With the next generation of professionals.

Especially to my main mentors,

With profound gratitude,

David E. Thoma, D.V.M.

Roy A. Coolman, D.V.M.

ISBN: 978-1-7178-4846-8

Thank you Brad Coolman, D.V.M., Amanda Hilliard, D.V.M., and Lisa Christlieb, R.V.T., for the cover photograph.

CONTENTS

ACKNOWLEDGMENTS

Thank you to all the amazing people and pets that I was privileged to work with throughout my career. The veterinarians, technicians, staff, owners, and pets taught me everything I needed to know about veterinary medicine AND about the way I wanted to live my life.

Thank you to the awesome people who helped me tell this story, supporting me on a wild adventure. To my first reader, Lenore Perry, my deepest gratitude; without her outstanding assistance and constant encouragement I could never have completed this project.

I also want to thank my extraordinary expert advisors: Allison Clark, Ph.D., ABPP; Brad Coolman, D.V.M., M.S., Diplomate ACVS; Sharon Riek, Attorney at Law; and Collin Whitesell, Attorney at Law. Any mistakes that might have crept into the story are mine alone.

I so appreciate the Fuzzy Brown dog pack, devoted pet people and committed readers: Nancy Wermuth, Phyllis Bush, Donna Roof, Laura Carrico, Allison Clark, Ph.D., ABPP, and Jamie Stover, D.V.M.

A huge thank you to my beta readers extraordinaire: Michelle Pittard and Sharon Riek, Attorney at Law. I'm in awe that you both would work so hard and provide such valuable insight to a stranger, and I'll be forever grateful.

Chapter One

Yesterday may have been one of the worst days of my life, a fitting conclusion to a spectacularly horrible year, but I wasn't going to let anyone or anything interfere with my enjoyment of this day. Because on this day, if my courage doesn't fail me, I'll walk through the hospital doors in front of me and be what I always wanted to be: a practicing veterinarian.

I stepped through the entranceway, smiled with confidence and started to speak to the woman behind the desk, but as soon as I said, "I'm the new," the receptionist waved me in and then pointed to the hallway and finished my sentence, "intern. Head to the back, they're doing an emergency C-section with more than twelve puppies so it's all hands on deck."

As I reached for the indicated door, the intercom system paged similar instructions, "All available technical help to treatment. All available help report to the treatment area Main Hospital."

I entered the treatment area just as the other doors to the large multipurpose room swung open and people in various colored scrubs or white lab coats jogged in and formed up in a loose semicircle around the swinging double doors leading to the surgery suite. A beautiful young black doctor closest to the door called out, "I'm the puppy doctor!"

The woman next to me briskly rubbed her hands with hand sanitizer, made her hands dance in the air to dry them, then grabbed a clean towel and announced, "Ready for puppy," as the rest of the waiting helpers echoed that statement. I chimed in last as I scrambled to get ready, finally cupping my hands under a towel and holding them ready in front of me. I whispered to the woman beside me, "Emergency drugs?"

"Center table, next to the oxygen and the bulb syringes," she replied as the first transport tech rushed out of surgery and practically threw puppies at people and then rushed back into surgery, turning sideways to pass the second transport tech with her precious cargo on her way out.

I reached out with my towel covered hands and grabbed my first puppy. He was already moving and I rubbed him vigorously to stimulate his breathing, wiping his nose clear then moving over his body, suctioned him with the bulb syringe, and then rubbed him again, gently tilting his nose down to help the fluid run out. I was happy to see no one was swinging the puppies like they used to do in the old days to remove the fluid; it was certainly done with good intentions but since it was found to create a problem like shaken baby syndrome in rare cases, the profession had been trying to get the word out to quit reviving pups that way. My automatic assessment of their care made me realize that I wasn't the only one being judged this year.

The pup was doing so well I called out, "Incubator?"

The puppy doctor replied, "Wouldn't turn on so we're getting the old one out of storage. Wait a minute."

The transport techs jogged through the doors simultaneously and quickly ran out of empty waiting hands. I couldn't see where they were putting the puppies as we waited for the incubator, so I quickly tucked my top into my pants and popped the wiggling pup down the front of my shirt where he was held securely in my bra, keeping him warm by skin to skin contact, and where I could feel him moving or heaven forbid feel it if he quit.

I took another pup. This one wasn't moving or breathing and I quickly rubbed, suctioned, rubbed, and kept it going while walking to the center table where others had moved with their more fragile puppies. I saw the towel lined box with the more vigorous puppies but couldn't stop working with my second puppy long enough to deliver my first puppy into that space. I tried to pull up a touch of a respiratory stimulant one handed, but the bottle was just big enough I couldn't hold it and the syringe and the pup. The tech next to me managed to keep rubbing her pup with one hand and still hold the bottle for me with her other hand while we awkwardly managed to perform the docking of needle and bottle and draw out a newborn dose. I administered it to my pup as another tech held the oxygen tube over to him. He was now breathing but still maintained a lavender color, half way between the dreaded blue and the desired pink. I continued my rubbing and suctioning and holding his nose in the oxygen until the puppy doctor took him from me.

One of the transport techs handed me two wiggling pups and said, "Sorry to double up," as I tried to hold on and rub and suction both of them at the same time. I found space at a counter top to help control the pair, their vigor both blessing and curse since while they needed less help from me, their seemingly random movements were surprisingly strong and threatened to pop them out of my hands.

The tech next to me placed her pup into the box and took one of my pair just as a technician came back with the portable incubator and ordered, "Doctors, take care of the cords and get the pups into the incubator."

I reported to the center table, took a long piece of suture and did a hand tie on the cord of my pup, and then cut the cord and removed the clamp, then repeated the procedures as the techs around me presented their pups. I looked up at one point, while the activity swirled around me, true controlled chaos at its very best, and caught one of the staff doctors staring at me. I had never seen a face so absolutely devoid of expression in all my life. My own personal blessing and curse in life is how well I can read others and how easy to read I am, but I couldn't pick up any hint of negative or positive emotion from her. She held my gaze until someone asked her a question and never once gave an indication of what she was thinking, but I assumed I had made some kind of mistake. I did notice that the other doctors were doing instrument ties instead of hand ties but I thought that it was a doctor's choice kind of a procedure. Old insecurities tried to rise up and overwhelm me, but I just took a deep breath and resumed tying off cords as pups were presented to me.

One by one the pups were placed in the incubator, except a sad case of a tiny deformed pup that had failed to take even a single breath. Just as the puppy doctor joined the techs that were situating the pups in the incubator, the surgeon strode out of the surgery suite, pulling off his cap and mask and dramatically rubbing his head with his hands held like stiff claws. He looked out at all of us like we had only gathered to admire him, and I have to admit he did look good with his broad shoulders and narrow waist shown to advantage in his tight fitting scrubs. As I looked closer, it dawned on me that it looked suspiciously like those close fitting scrubs were worn uncomfortably snug to do just that, which wiped out any earlier admiration I might have had for his physique. After the year I had just lived through, I had no use for men who had become stuck in the look-at-me stage of their childhood development.

"Ahhh," he said stretching dramatically, "did medicine manage to get all my pups up and running? Surgery team was perfect; if you don't have fifteen happy and hungry Labradors in that incubator, it wasn't our fault."

"We lost one," the puppy doctor replied. "It was the tiny deformed one; he didn't really have a chance."

"I was worried about that one," he casually admitted. "So, fourteen then?"

The tech hunched over the incubator straightened up and announced, "I have thirteen pups."

"Count again," the surgeon demanded angrily as the puppy doctor immediately did her own count.

"Thirteen," she said quietly.

"What the fuck?" the surgeon snapped. "It's bad enough to lose a pup to medical problems that we can't control, but we don't just lose, fucking misplace, puppies in MY hospital. Find it!!"

For a second I stood there frozen, I had never heard one of my Professors swear inside the clinics, much less directly at a group of his or her colleagues. As I turned to check the used towels for a forgotten pup, the puppy in my bra shifted and I gasped out loud and then half shouted, "I have the other puppy!"

The crowd turned my way in unison, like a team of synchronized swimmers, as I slowly reached down my top and pulled the puppy out. I tried to walk with some small modicum of dignity over to the center table and rapidly take care of the cord. I then took a deep breath and coolly walked over to deposit the puppy in the incubator as the prolonged silence around me became even more excruciating. The entire assemblage was soundless; no one moved except to follow my progress with their eyes as they waited for the surgeon to speak. I couldn't swear that anyone was even breathing, although I certainly would have known if anyone had dropped a pin.

The surgeon walked over to me and stood there looming, just staring down at the top of my head. When he finally spoke his voice shook with emotion, "Where the hell did you do your training, some boondocks cow barn? Or were you trained at all? And just who the hell are you anyway?"

"I'm the new intern," I answered softly.

"You were the new intern," he snapped back. "I don't put up with that backwoods bullshit. We do high quality, medically correct, evidence based treatments here."

I twisted my neck awkwardly to look up at him and said, "The incubator wasn't available so I made the next best choice. I made sure he was breathing well and his color was good, then it was vital that I found a way to keep him warm."

"Is that correct Stretch?" The surgeon asked as he theatrically spun and pointed at the blond doctor on the other side of him.

The tall young intern looked back at him calmly and replied, "Yes, that's correct."

The surgeon moved into the center of the gathered staff and flicked his fingers forward at them in succession to move them into a circle around him. He then yanked me into the center of the circle with him and demanded of another young doctor, "What about you, Quickcut? What would you have done?"

"If the puppy were stable enough to go down my shirt, it would have been stable enough to be put in the box and been warmed by the piling effect of the littermates," the pudgy doctor replied rather haughtily as he tried to stretch his neck to lift his head up far enough to literally look down on me as he gave the strong impression that he was for sure figuratively looking down on me.

The surgeon spun again and pointed at the puppy doctor, "What do you think?"

She gave me a quick sympathetic glance and then said, "I think it was an acceptable choice under the circumstances."

"How about you, Dr. Photographic Memory?" the surgeon fixed his glare on the blank faced staff doctor. "Will you lower yourself to participate in an intern training exercise?"

She stared right back at him and replied completely impassively, "Torturing interns is not now nor will it ever be training," and then turned and walked out, pausing halfway across the room to say, "I like her hand ties," without even turning back to face us while speaking, and then she continued out of the room.

The surgeon shrugged melodramatically and stuck his tongue out at her back while she was opening the door, and then attached his large claw hand on the top of my head and made my head shake back and forth, while he spoke for me in a falsetto, "No Doctor, I will never ever put patients down my shirt or let clients in my pants."

As soon as he made the comment, I went white hot with a mixture of anger and humiliation and jerked away from him, and then brought my hands up in a classic defensive stance as if to block an impending blow as I faced him. The reaction might seem overly dramatic but I had let people hurt me for a long time, with the events of this last year culminating in betrayal so complete that I had lost everything. But the one thing I had not lost was the dream of being a veterinarian and working in a profession that mostly attracted good hearted people who cared about the animals and their families. It wasn't proven yet if I would still let people hurt me in my private life, but I had no doubts I would protect myself from letting anyone touch that dream and treat me unprofessionally here. I did however fervently wish I hadn't just reacted physically to a verbal assault!

The surgeon instantly threw his hands up and shouted, "I give up! I went too far! I am soooooooooooo sorry," and then dropped to his knees and clasped his hands together in front of him and begged, "Please, please forgive me."

I let my hands drop down to my sides and smiled nervously at him but couldn't imagine what I was supposed to say or do next. I was rescued when a short round woman in street clothes bustled up, took his arm and said, "Enough fooling around Doctor, I have patients waiting for you, get yourself out front for your appointments," as she started physically propelling him towards the door.

I gave a last look at the mass of squirming puppies in the incubator and made my way out of the treatment area. When I passed Stretch, the tall blond doctor, he gave me a small smile and whispered, "Did they forget to warn you that our brilliant surgeon is insane?"

The short round woman hustled back in and told me, "I have everything ready for you upstairs, we need to make you official," and motioned me to join her and then turned back around and added, "I'm Molly."

Then she almost ran through the door to the back stairs and with surprising athleticism bounded up the stairs two at a time. I followed at a more careful pace, afraid to fall and break my neck before I was official, whatever that meant.

It turned out making me official was a long drawn out undertaking involving licenses, accreditation, malpractice insurance, taxes, health insurance, OSHA warnings, and an introduction to a long and detailed employee handbook. The only problem came when Molly asked me what name I wanted to use professionally. She explained that they had multiple pairs of veterinarians with the same names so they had to get a bit creative. For example, they had a father daughter pair that, to keep misunderstandings to a minimum for the clients, were known as Dr. Tom and Dr. Nikki instead of both being called Dr. Lane. Adding to the confusion, other doctors shared first names or had been known by their last names for such a long time that they were reluctant to make a switch to first names now.

"But you're free to choose," Molly said. "You're our only Katya and our only Nikolova, so you're free to pick either one to be used by the front desk for the clients and to be embroidered on your lab coats and scrubs."

I froze again; I was new to subterfuge and yet my troubles were no one's business but my own. I honestly didn't think I could survive if I had to talk about any of it here at work. I had a sudden vision of the black ooze of my personal life squeezing under the door of the beautiful bright clean hospital and contaminating everything and everyone here. I desperately needed this place to be my sanctuary away from all of that.

Molly looked at me quizzically while I struggled and finally I blurted out, "May I be known as Dr. Kate? I'd really rather just start fresh here."

"Sure," Molly said with an accepting smile, "lots of people use nicknames."

I thanked her profusely while I tried on sample lab coats and scrubs, looking for that perfect fit. I wanted them somewhat loose so that I would still move in them easily when I gained the weight back, but I certainly wanted to look sharp and professional in the meantime.

She gave me some used uniforms to wear until mine came in and then looked at the clock and said, "I hate how long that takes, but at least now you're official: covered and protected and ready to work. The day shift is almost over so no reason to start today. But let's walk down to the treatment area so I can introduce you at evening rounds and then you can start bright and early tomorrow morning."

"Thank you, Molly," I said sincerely, with a sudden burst of deep, heartfelt appreciation. After my harsh senior year, I found myself almost overwhelmed with gratitude at any tiny kindness or consideration that a new acquaintance showed me.

Molly smiled and, attempting to tug her gray streaked red curls into some kind of control, said, "My title is Complex Manager, but everyone calls me Molly-Mom because I believe that if I take good care of everyone who works here, they'll be better able to take the best care of the patients and clients."

"I truly appreciate it," I replied simply and followed her back downstairs.

The group gathered in ICU was in either colored scrubs or in street clothes covered with white lab coats, and I was thrilled to see that all the uniforms were embroidered with their names and titles. It's hard enough being the newbie and starting later than the other interns, but to do that at a place where everyone used nicknames made it close to impossible. But at least I'd be able to use official names until I caught up. Now I knew that the beautiful black intern with the constant smile was Dr. Taren, I just had to find out if it was her first or last name.

Molly clapped her hands a couple times to get everyone's attention and then simply announced, "This is Dr. Kate, our fourth and final intern. She'll start with an introductory week observing in each department and then she'll join the regular intern rotation. Everyone, especially the other three interns, must check their new schedules meticulously because they've all changed."

Rounds progressed from cage to cage as doctors and ICU technicians from both the leaving day and arriving night shifts discussed each case. I paid close attention to the details of the cases as well as the way the interns were periodically put on the spot to answer questions about various details of their cases. I patted the pocket sized notebook that I had crammed with vital facts and formulas throughout my four years of veterinary school and thanked God again that it had been in my pocket when everything else that I depended on, including my computer, had been ripped away from me. I realized that without my computer and books, I would need to do all my after hours studying here at the hospital. Thank goodness I had seen a wonderful library and separate computer stations dedicated to the interns' use on my hospital tour, so I should be able to manage. But during the expected daily crises when I had to react quickly, it would be that mangy looking notebook that would let me respond with speed and accuracy; it was my most priceless professional possession. Rounds wrapped up rapidly and everyone moved off; the night ER staff to the front for incoming patients, the daytime staff to various desks to finish up their paperwork before they could call their long day done. I gathered up my uniforms and tried to leave quickly before anyone could see me head off across the back field on foot instead of climbing into my nonexistent car.

Chapter Two

The walk back to my apartment was awkward as I had to wind my way through the multiple buildings and parking lots that made up the campus of the sprawling Hamilton County Veterinary Hospital. Then I had to figure out the way across an abandoned field full of weeds and pot holes, and sneak down a thoroughly spooky alley to the huge Victorian house that contained my new home. Usually the four interns shared a different apartment in the modern complex next door, but other arrangements had to be made for me when I came so late to the position that the fourth intern room had already been rented to one of the residents. Luckily I was pleased to be by myself and loved the feel of the old house.

I used my ornate skeleton key on the vintage front door, entered the small lobby, and noticed that the caretaker/manger Mr. O'Sullivan had already put my name on one of the antique postal boxes in the hallway. He had told me last night that the owner of both our converted house and the huge apartment complex next door allowed him to indulge his love of antiques here as long as he kept the complex sleek and modern. It reminded me of my grandparents' house in upstate New York; although my grandparents hadn't collected antiques so much as their furniture and accessories had been in the family for so long that they had become antiques just sitting in the same position they had always been.

Lost in my memories, I startled when Mr. O'Sullivan leaned out of his apartment door to call out, "Hey, Katie girl, did I remember to tell you about Thursday night house dinners at my place?"

I turned to grin at him and admitted, "You sure did! I've been looking forward to it all day, but I still feel bad about not bringing anything."

He grinned back and replied, "We take our dinner details very seriously so I couldn't make such a big decision by myself; your contribution will have to be properly discussed and maybe voted on."

I laughed and said, "I won't be late because I'm starving, and I want to meet my other housemates!"

I used a second more normal looking key in the modern deadbolt lock on my apartment door. Last night, exhausted and terrified after my final family confrontation, I had been relieved to see security favored over historical correctness in the choice of door materials. Tonight I closed the solid steel door behind me and threw both the dead bolt and security bar, and then breathed a huge sigh of relief and looked around my sanctuary. Feeling physically safe somehow made me feel protected from further emotional pain, even though I knew it wasn't really true.

The main living area looked larger than the square footage would predict because of the high ceilings, tall thin windows, white walls, and varnished carved wood moldings. The kitchen was tucked into one corner and was separated from the main living space by a peninsular countertop of modern multi-toned granite. It was mounted on a dark cherry base that looked like a piece of furniture, in fact looked a lot like the Victorian buffet downstairs in the entranceway. The appliances were stainless steel but somehow they still fit with the traditional cherry cabinets. I don't think I've ever had a decorating style, but I loved it, like it had been designed just for me. There were two cherry high back bar stools with black leather seats at the counter that Mr. O'Sullivan confessed to buying for the unfurnished apartment simply because they looked like they exactly belonged there. I agree they're perfect but more importantly they keep me from having to sit on the hardwood floor. Last night, tossing and turning trying to sleep on the carpeted floor in the bedroom, I certainly regretted telling Molly that taking an unfurnished apartment was fine with me. I don't know what I was thinking since I had no furniture and furthermore had no way physically or financially to get any.

I hopped up onto the stool and rested my head on the cool counter as my stomach growled uncomfortably. I resisted even looking at the only food in the apartment, a huge container of brownies that my best friend Lainey had instructed Doris, her Mom, to give me. I'll never forget Doris's face when she drove up on me pitifully stumbling down the road, dragging my suitcase, and juggling the huge quilt my Grandmother made me along with my big fluffy pillows in their matching shams. At that time my poor shocked and overwhelmed brain hadn't been able to formulate even the simplest of plans but, after a series of panicked phone calls between Lainey and Doris, they decided the priority was to drive me straight to my career saving internship in Noblesville without delay.

I accepted the ride to Noblesville, but refused all offers of financial or other practical help. When we got to the house, Doris unloaded everything that she was supposed to deliver to Lainey for our weekend together, and I don't know why but I tried to decline those things as well. Doris had refused to take no for an answer, begged me with tears running down her face, to let her do this one small gesture, and insisted that Lainey would never forgive her if she didn't leave these things with me. So now my worldly possessions consisted of my purse, my quilt, my pillows, my suitcase packed with enough clothes and supplies for a weekend trip, a container of brownies, a ridiculously bright pink shaggy throw rug, a roll of quarters and a huge bottle of laundry detergent.

I lifted my head off the counter after realizing two important facts: it was still unwise to spend more than a fleeting minute thinking about my problems, and I had no idea what time it was. My Uncle claimed ownership of everything of mine that had any value when he kicked me out of my own home, and I let him. With no phone, computer, or clock, I was in trouble. It probably wasn't seven o'clock yet, but I didn't want to be late to dinner so I decided to just go downstairs now and hope that it wasn't considered too rude.

The door was cracked open so I knocked as I let myself in and called out, "Hello, Mr. O'Sullivan! Am I too early?"

"Katie girl," he replied, "come on in and please call me Phil! Ethan and I are in the kitchen. Feel free to join us whenever you get home on Thursday nights."

Phil's apartment was wonderful in a very masculine version of the Victorian era furniture and accessories in the rest of the house. I mentally named it Victorian high tech décor; he had a huge flat screen TV above an ornately carved mahogany mantle and his computer station with two 17" screens sat on the most gorgeous antique inlaid wood desk I had ever seen. I walked through to his kitchen which was a larger, more elaborate version of my own.

"What a wonderful home, Phil!" I exclaimed. "Each part I see is more perfect than the one before."

"Thanks, Katie," Phil said with a smile. "I'd like to introduce you to my nephew Ethan."

I shook hands with the very slightly built twenty something young man and said, "Very nice to meet you."

"Very nice to meet you, too," he replied, and when I smiled he returned my smile.

"I particularly like your computer set up," I said, hoping my blue eyes weren't turning green with envy as I spoke.

"Ethan did all the hard work," Phil said proudly. "He's a wizard with anything technology related."

We happily chatted about computers until a petite Asian woman, with straight black hair to her waist, walked in.

"Hello, Mei," Ethan said as he bowed to her and she returned the greeting. "Mei, this is Kate and Uncle Phil calls her Katie girl. Dag, hurry up and meet Kate."

My final house mate walked into the kitchen, and after a year of being shocked and astonished by the bad behavior swirling around me, I reacted with equal intensity but all in the positive to my first sight of Dag. Tall, dark and handsome sounds so trite but does not even begin to describe him, and I was not only impressed, I was stunned. I couldn't begin to guess what his mixed heritage was, but somehow it had combined to form the most beautiful man I had ever seen.

He came towards me with his right hand extended, and luckily good manners let me shake his hand and say "glad to meet you" while staring into his strikingly bright blue eyes as I struggled to shake off whatever strange reaction I was having. I had always been proud not to be such a superficial person that I was unduly influenced by a person's looks, but Dag dazzled me before his first word.

"Nice to meet you," Dag said, pushing his jet black hair out of his eyes and smiling warmly.

I grinned back and then turned around to Phil and asked, "Anything I can do to help?"

"Why don't you and Ethan set the table, and Dag can help me with the pasta," Phil replied as the three men said together, "It takes a big man to handle a big pot," and laughed out loud like that was the funniest thing anyone had ever said. It was so typical of the stupid, not really funny, family jokes that my brothers and I had laughed at for years. I was simultaneously happy to be a part of the warm family atmosphere and stricken that my own family was now completely shattered.

I took a couple focused breaths, not sure if anyone had caught my weird reaction, but both Mei and Ethan were watching me so I smiled reassuringly at them. I continued my deep breathing and tried to ground myself by concentrating on the delicious aroma of the food.

The meal was fabulous and the atmosphere continued to be easygoing; the conversation chased around the table and ping ponged between people and, without knowing how, I managed to fit right in. Phil's contribution was the cornerstone of the meal, and he always made pasta; today he served rotini and his not only homemade but also homegrown marinara sauce. Mei made an Asian inspired sesame cabbage salad and the other housemates bragged that she had never brought the exact same salad in the three years she had been coming to the dinners. Ethan always brought dessert, chocolate chip cookie bars today, and Dag's responsibility was the bread. I ate like a pig, more than the men did, but I wasn't sure when I was going to get another real meal with my first paycheck a full two weeks away.

Phil hadn't been joking when he said that the decision about my weekly contribution to the meal was a big deal; the discussion did get heated in a friendly way. Ethan was worried that I might have trouble getting to dinner in time to cook since I could be held at work with a sick animal, but they finally decided that I should plan to bring a fresh vegetable but could keep some microwavable vegetables in Phil's freezer as a backup.

I was touched that they cared about making my contribution as easy as possible for me, but I only had a week to figure out how far away the closest grocery store was and how much of my cash the fresh vegetables and frozen backups were going to use up. When you only have a twenty dollar bill, two singles and a roll of quarters, there should be a more dramatic word than budget to describe your situation.

I must have looked worried as we left the apartment because Mei asked, "What's the matter?"

I suddenly remembered that I had a much more pressing problem to be worrying about, and replied, "I wasn't prepared to start work this week, and I don't have an alarm clock."

Ethan pulled out his iPhone and said, "Your phone has an alarm, I can show you how to use it."

"I don't have my phone," I said with a grimace, "so I can't have someone call me either."

"I'll set my alarm and then knock on your door," Ethan offered. "I'm reliable, aren't I, Mei?"

"Yes, you're very reliable," Mei agreed with a smile. "On grocery night you always knock on my door at exactly seven PM."

I looked up at her with hope or interest or something that gave me away and she added, "Would you like to go with us to the grocery store next Tuesday?"

"I would," I replied happily. "And thank you, Ethan, for offering to be my alarm clock, but I have to get up at seven. Wouldn't that be inconvenient?"

"No, I get up at seven every morning. Just because I work from home doesn't mean I don't keep to a schedule. I'll put my robe on and run right upstairs," Ethan offered.

Dag passed our little group clustered in the entrance way and said, "I have a travel alarm clock that I don't use. I'll get it for you."

He headed out the front door while I looked questioningly up the stairs, and asked Mei, "Isn't his apartment upstairs?"

"Yes, but he has a separate entrance outside," Mei replied.

"Where the fence is?" I asked. "Does he have a dog?"

"Yes to the fence, but no to the dog," Mei replied. "Absolutely no pets allowed here."

"Oh," I said unhappily. I still grieved the loss of my Golden, and even though I couldn't afford a pet right now it was something to daydream about.

"So I'm not your alarm clock?" Ethan asked sadly when Dag jogged back in and handed me the clock and two new batteries. "I really wanted to be your alarm clock."

"Well, it's my first day of work and I can't be late, maybe you could check that the alarm worked?" I replied.

"Yes!" Ethan agreed with a big grin. "I'll knock on your door at five minutes after seven so the alarm clock has time to work. See you then."

Later that night, lying wrapped up in my precious quilt on the fluffy pink rug, I had an odd feeling in the pit of my stomach. It was mainly composed of this year's twin companions of pain and fear, but for the first time it was dotted with tiny bits of hope. And it felt really good.

Chapter Three

My first week of work as a veterinarian passed in a blur of new paperwork formats, computer programs and meeting a boatload of new people. Sadly, I still felt like a senior student because I wasn't fully in charge of any patient care; at the same time, it was hard work to learn all the new practical details. For example, it was easy to figure out what blood work I would recommend medically in each case, but knowing which 'package' of blood tests would give me the tests I wanted for the least cost to the client, and when each of those results would be available, was a mind boggling mystery.

My first day as a real vet would be at the primary care hospital but I wanted the comradery and assurance of meeting with the other interns before I started, so I headed to rounds at the big hospital. Sometimes we moved from cage to cage as we discussed the cases, but today I arrived just in time to join the circle forming up around Dr. Vincent, the intern coordinator and the crazy surgeon that had so charmingly introduced me to the practice, as he started rounds in the open treatment area. My guess is he was trying to include the ER docs who were still working on early morning patients on both of the treatment tables.

Dr. Taren, the puppy doctor from my first day, stood calmly next to me cradling a huge armful of charts. She was petite, truly beautiful, and everything about her was round: face, eyes, figure, mouth, and best of all her constant smile created beautiful deep round dimples on both sides of her face. Her skin wasn't just mocha colored; it was the most gorgeous caramel mocha shade a person could be. She was as outgoing, confident, and charming as she was beautiful, and I was a little bit in awe of her.

Dr. Vincent clapped his hands and, nodding at Dr. Taren, said, "Take it away, Squash."

She didn't frown in response to the nickname as much as her face relaxed and her awesome dimples disappeared. But she spoke evenly as she described the status of her cases. There was absolutely no indication that she needed my protection or support, but my nature immediately made me frown and lock eyes with Dr. Vincent.

"What?" he asked crossly, leaning toward me, then caught himself and relaxed. "You do know why I call her that?"

I shook my head, angry at myself for making things worse for Dr. Taren.

"I got looking at Dr. Taren and Dr. Lars at rounds one day and realized what a study in opposites they are," he explained. "I nicknamed them Squash and Stretch since they looked like they had both been printed on Silly Putty and then Taren had been squashed and Lars had been stretched."

The two ER doctors laughed while I just said, "Oh, that's interesting," but I was a little offended for both of them. Although guiltily, I had to admit the description did fit them perfectly.

Lars grinned and shrugged; he didn't seem to mind his nickname but maybe when your parents name you Lars Larsen you have a different frame of reference. Lars was, in his own way, as good looking as Taren, but in a tall and lean way, with white blonde hair, much lighter than mine, pale blue eyes and extremely fair skin. This past week he had given the impression of being cool and calm and didn't grin or laugh out loud much, but if you paid attention, you could tell he was often amused, and I swore his eyes would actually twinkle. He loved to whisper little comments and puns to Taren and me during rounds, and we took turns getting dirty looks from our superiors for laughing while he escaped reproach with his quiet angelic demeanor.

"No cases today," he reported.

"Dr. Melanie?" Dr. Vincent prompted.

Melanie gave an even better deer in the headlights expression than my classic response, and said defensively, "What?"

"Do you have any cases in the hospital?" he asked with a loud sigh.

"I don't," she said frowning, as if it was somehow her fault that she didn't have a report to give. Melanie's looks were average, maybe below average if I weren't being nice: medium brown hair and eyes, medium height and build, but she had a stunning smile that really lit up her face. Except she always seemed so desperate to do everything right and know the exact answer to every question that she rarely shared that wonderful feature.

"I'm just checking in before heading over to primary care," I explained, before he even had to ask.

"Well, aren't you special," he said sarcastically as he turned his back on me, and I slipped away quietly.

I headed to the smaller 'family' practice building. My first rotation on my own was scheduled to be with the primary care practice, the so called regular veterinarians, terminology which led to jokes that the board certified specialists and ER veterinarians working in the big building were somehow irregular veterinarians. Of course, it's what most of us doing internships wanted to do eventually, so there was more than a touch of sour grapes to the jokes. Dr. Blackwell, a primary care veterinarian with thirty plus years of experience and my mentor for this rotation, met me with a warm smile and waved me to the back of the clinic.

"This is the heart of our hospital," Dr. Blackwell said as she swept her hand around the little lounge. "Here's the water cooler, coffee machine, bulletin board announcing continuing education opportunities and clinic social events, and the place for any treats brought in to share. Get a drink and a snack if you like and then we'll head up front for morning appointments."

"Thank you," I said, taking her up on the offer. I had been seriously hungry all week, and while the hospital treats were often unhealthy, they had so far provided the calories I needed to keep going.

"You're an athlete," a cute blonde technician said as she passed me in the hallway.

"Excuse me?" I asked in confusion.

Dr. Blackwell and the tech laughed together companionably and the tech continued, "Dr. Blackwell is going to tell you that you're an athlete, and you must treat yourself as one!"

"I try to subtly work my lectures into random conversations, but since you called me out, Amelia, you can give the talk this time!" Dr. Blackwell said with a grin.

Amelia grinned back and said, "Veterinary medicine is an intellectually, psychologically, and physically demanding profession," dramatically clutching her chest and then continued, "and you'll be bombarded by the wants and needs of your patients, owners, colleagues, and technical and lay staff. If you're a typical veterinarian, you love animals and you're a people pleaser so that all sounds perfectly reasonable. That is until it's an hour past closing, you've been on your feet for twelve hours straight, you're trying to give a dog a pill and while wrestling the dog your best technician accidentally elbows you in the mouth!"

Dr. Blackwell looked at me and asked, "And?"

I looked back and asked, "And you'll need to set limits?"

"Good one!" Dr. Blackwell said while shaking her head and pointing at my cookie snack, "But no! It WILL happen no matter how many limits you set! You need to eat healthy food, and drink lots of water, and treat yourself as an elite athlete! You need the stamina to get that dog treated!"

I nodded ruefully, and replied, "I'll try to be better," knowing that it was going to be difficult until I was back on my feet financially.

"Now, Amelia, how about feet?" Dr. Blackwell asked.

"Practice is a series of daily sprints AND a career long marathon, if you want to survive the race you had better and most importantly take care of your feet!" Amelia replied enthusiastically.

Everyone looked down at my shoes and Dr. Blackwell nodded approvingly at my cross trainers and said, "Good start! Now, your first client is a good friend of ours. She breeds Yorkshire Terriers and Doberman Pinchers, and we do lots of litter work for her, but when she's going to keep one of her puppies or buys a new puppy to add to her bloodline, she treats them as if they were her only pet. This means she wants a full puppy talk and individualized attention, and she always asks for the newest techs and interns for the talk and the exam."

"Why?" I asked incredulously.

"She says it's good training for the puppy AND the intern and technician, and keeps her up to date on all the latest research and thinking from the University," Dr. Blackwell replied. "Whatever you do, don't give her a shut up answer."

"A what?" I asked.

"Don't just make up an answer to shut her up so that you can get on to your next patient," she replied. "Maisy won't just call you out on it; she'll make a formal complaint against you. If you don't know an answer, admit it and say you'll get back to her about it. Then make sure you do it; look it up or talk to one of us and then call her back or send her the information in the mail."

I nodded but was suddenly nervous about doing 'just' a puppy vaccine.

"You'll want to go in and listen to the tech give the puppy talk this time," Dr. Blackwell continued. "Purdue is an excellent school, but you'll need to learn how to take the huge load of information you've been taught and condense it down to practical, manageable lessons that you can give to new puppy owners in a reasonable amount of time."

Amelia walked into the exam room first and said, "This is Dr. Kate," and then continued, "And this is one of my favorite people in the world, Maisy Cruse, and her eight week old Doberman, Roman."

Once again I blessed my parents for teaching me every day manners so that I could shake her hand and tell her how nice it was to meet her, at the same time I was dealing with her appearance. She looked exactly like June Cleaver from Leave it to Beaver, from her heavily sprayed perfectly flipped blonde hair to her single strand of white pearls to her pink shirtdress with matching pumps. All to take her puppy to the vet? Her eyebrows were plucked nearly to oblivion, a single surprised line above blue eyes with matching blue eye shadow, and of course pink lipstick that matched her dress. And worst of all she spoke with an odd high pitched little voice. Maybe she wasn't June Cleaver; maybe she was a Stepford wife?

The puppy talk and visit went well. Maisy did seem to know and care for her puppy, even though he was one of many at her home, and we plotted out a vaccination schedule individualized to this puppy's needs. She asked about genetic testing for the puppy, which is one of my areas of special interest, so I started chattering away about all the new tests now available, especially for the bleeding problems common in Dobermans. Even as I spoke, it dawned on me that as a modern breeder she had to already be testing for Von Willebrand's disease, the cause of the bleeding problems, so I abruptly stopped speaking and asked what the status of her breeding program was. She answered me with a knowing smile; it turns out she was one of the breeders who helped geneticists develop the first test, and both of Roman's parents had tested negative for the bad gene. But she was interested in some of the new genetic tests for heart problems so we had a good discussion about them, and I wrote down the name of a couple of websites for her. By the end of the visit, I realized I no longer cared that she looked like she had escaped from a 1950's sitcom and talked in a mousey voice; she was a sharp and committed owner that loved her puppy. And that was all that was important to me.

As I finished up, Maisy took a picture of Roman and me for his scrapbook, and then promised to download it to our website so I could have a copy too. It gave me a funny feeling in the pit of my stomach, thinking about Dr. Blackwell and wondering if she remembered her first puppy examination from 30 years ago. And I was pretty sure that having his own scrapbook was an important clue about how this puppy would be treated in this household!

I thanked Maisy wholeheartedly and she responded, "I like you, Dr. Kate, I can tell we're going to be friends. Roman and I are glad you're going to be part of our lives."

I went to the rest of my appointments with a light heart, and met lots of nice people and pets there for routine wellness exams and vaccines. I only saw one or two people in an hour while Dr. Blackwell saw three or four, and none of mine had surprise lumps or broken teeth or bad ear infections like hers did, but I still managed to get behind. Everything just took so long to explain, and about halfway through my explanation, the owners would get a glazed look in their eyes and I knew I had lost them. If I tried to shorten the explanation, it felt like I wasn't telling 'the whole truth and nothing but the truth.' If anyone had told me about this in school, I didn't comprehend what they were trying to say; this preventative medicine was way more complicated than I expected.

Explaining titers and modern vaccine schedules caused me the most trouble; too many veterinarians were stuck using old fashioned schedules and giving every vaccine yearly when not all of them needed to be given that often. I don't know why some hospitals haven't updated to the new schedules, but I had always assumed it was fear, fear of failing to protect precious pets from lethal viruses, or less admirably, fear of making less money. But after today I wonder if what is most terrifying is having to explain the switch in detail to hundreds or thousands of owners. One day of giving the explanation, and I was worn out and feeling guilty for making people wait while I did it.

By the end of the day I was bone tired and couldn't wait to get home. I met Dr. Blackwell at the back door and my eyes must have had the same glazed over look that my clients had earlier in the day. She laughed at me, shook her head grinning and just said, "It gets easier!"

Chapter Four

The walk home gave me a chance to relax and I, more than anything, wished there was a hot meal waiting for me at home. I'd forgotten to leave my lab coat at work, but I was too tired to turn around, and besides it would give me a chance to wash it. Quarters for the washing machine could be used for food instead so I had been washing out my clothes in my sink. I had to make it through one more week before I would see my first pay check, and my money hadn't stretched enough for two weeks of food. I had to spend a big part of my lonely twenty dollar bill on a head of cauliflower and two big bags of frozen vegetables for my contribution to our house meals, and then I barely had enough to buy milk, eggs, rice and dried beans with the rest. I was pretty happy with my economical but nutritious food plan; I had tried to look at it as a fun game instead of a hardship.

But then in the car on the way home with Mei and Ethan I realized I didn't even have a pan to cook any of it in. I hadn't eaten anything but a few clinic snacks the day we went shopping, and my pride and determination to handle my problems on my own slipped away as my hunger overwhelmed me, so I reluctantly asked to borrow a pan from Ethan, just until my stuff arrived. He and Mei didn't seem to look down on me or disbelieve my story at the time, but at the end of Thursday's dinner all of the leftovers were packed up and sent home with me with no chance for refusal. So they must have suspected something; they probably all exchanged pitying looks behind my back the whole time I was busy shoveling food into my mouth as fast as I could at dinner. I took a deep breath and tried to push the thought away. Before all of Justin's character assassinations last year, it would never have occurred to me to wonder what people were thinking or saying behind my back.

Too bad I finished the last of this week's lasagna leftovers, but my wishful thinking did remind me that I needed to return those containers to Phil. A hopeful thought occurred to me, maybe he'd be cooking something, and he'd force me to join him. I jogged the rest of the way home, bounded up the stairs to get the containers, and then knocked on his door.

I heard a funny thumping sound, but he didn't come to the door, so I knocked again and called out loudly, "Phil, you home?"

I heard another noise, and something just didn't feel right to me. Phil was a big bear of a man with a loud booming voice; if he were yelling for me to wait from anywhere in the apartment, I should be able to hear him easily. I tried the door and it was unlocked so I yelled, "I'm coming in," and pushed it open slowly. Looking through the living room, I could see Phil sprawled out on the kitchen floor, lying unconscious in a spreading puddle of blood. As I bolted over to him, I could see the blood continuing to pump from a laceration on his temple.

Without even thinking about the gloves in my pocket, I knelt down beside him and pinched the spurting artery between my fingers, and then urgently looked around to see if I could continue to hold on while stretching to reach his phone. It wasn't in the charging dock and then I spotted it on the floor near the open refrigerator door, next to a spilled bottle of juice. Phil's body started to twitch on the floor like a cell phone on vibrate, and I couldn't decide whether I should let go long enough to grab the phone. I didn't know if his seizure was from head trauma, the blood loss or from some other cause?

I've never been someone who automatically exclaims when I hurt myself, or screams when I'm surprised, so it took a minute for me to realize that if I needed to get one of my housemates to help us, that screaming was oddly my only logical choice. I screamed wordlessly a couple times until I could hear stirring in the house, and then I kept yelling "Help me! Help me!" to let them know where we were. Ethan flew in first, with Mei right behind him, but then they both froze.

"Call 911, Ethan," I said. "Now!"

Ethan could barely speak as he gave the address, and then looked at me wide eyed when I asked, "Is your Uncle diabetic? Does he use Insulin?"

"Yes," he finally answered me, then shook his head and said, "No," in response to something the dispatcher said, and then handed the phone to Mei in confusion.

"Ethan, get me honey or Karo syrup," I ordered.

"No," he said.

"Yes!" I said emphatically. "Do it now!"

"Glucose is better," he replied, staring at me intently.

"I don't have any glucose," I replied. "Mei, get me honey or Karo."

Ethan said "No," in a panicked voice and moved towards his Uncle's jacket hanging over a chair and patted the pockets. He exclaimed "Here!" and handed me a tube of glucose gel.

I fumbled with it one handed, then handed it back to him and said, "Rub a small amount on his gums, carefully. I don't know if he can swallow. "

Ethan knelt down with me and gently lifted Phil's lip and rubbed the glucose on his gums. He was meticulous and focused on his task and slowly Phil quieted between us. As my pinching fingers started to cramp and a feeling of panic about being able to hold on crept in, the faint sound of sirens became louder as the front door was banged opened and heavy boots pounded to the door.

"What happened?" Dag demanded aggressively. "Who did this? Where are they?"

"I don't think 'a who' did this," I replied, shifting my weight uncomfortably, now my knees had started to scream at my awkward crouch. "I think he had low blood sugar and fell and hit his head."

"Oh," Dag said, looking less angry, then he turned and said as he jogged back out again, "I'll direct the medics in."

The Paramedics were spectacular; efficient and professional and soon had Phil's head bandaged, his blood taken and an IV started. There was a brief delay on our part trying to decide who would go in the ambulance, but Dag took charge, jumped in and directed me to go with Mei and Ethan. It wasn't a long drive to the hospital, but it seemed to take forever.

The ER was a surreal experience as I concentrated on being the 'client' with my patient; they had so many more people and equipment than we did in our ER, but everyone's distress seemed similar. And while my mind wanted each doctor, nurse and technician there to be busy working on my friend, my heart just wanted them to stop working and come tell me what was happening instead. Everyone stared at me sitting there in my white coat; like they were angry I wasn't helping them, so I removed it and held it in my lap. Ethan was just as bad; he tried to ask questions of anyone wearing a uniform that walked by our area of the waiting room, but when that tactic failed he appeared to just shut down. He sat practically motionless in his chair and gave single word answers when we tried to engage him, so I started to worry about him too.

When we were allowed to go in to his room Phil looked pretty much back to himself, sitting up in the bed attached to his IV and monitoring equipment with a much smaller bandage on his head and a partially eaten meal in front of him on the tray.

"Katie girl! They told me you're my hero!" Phil exclaimed while poor Ethan burst into tears and threw himself over his uncle. Phil continued, "Ethan, my favorite boy! I'm fine."

"I'm fine now that I see you," I said with a smile, along with the tears filling my eyes.

We chatted about the incident, each one sharing our part of the story, until Ethan recovered enough to join the discussion. I was basically right about what happened; Phil had given himself an insulin injection but then had received an annoying phone call and had been distracted from eating. When he got sweaty and started feeling dizzy, he headed to the refrigerator to get some juice, but that was the last thing he could remember until he came to in the ambulance.

Ethan gave a small smile and said, "The first thing I heard was Kate yelling 'Help me, help me,' like she was in some horror movie!"

Dag and Phil laughed out loud and Mei agreed, "I heard her scream first, but then it got a little creepy!"

I shook my head laughing, and said, "Okay, okay, I guess I'm not a very good screamer. But I'm a pretty good judge of character because I knew with all my heart that if I could just make myself heard, you would all come running to help, even if you thought someone was being murdered!"

"That's pretty cool," Phil said pensively, and we all nodded our agreement.

Chapter Five

My four week rotation at the primary care practice went by way too fast, the Doctors and the staff generated such a warm helpful atmosphere that it made it easy to work hard, learn lots and still have a great time. There were certainly sad days when we had to make the decision to share final goodbyes with a beloved pet. But most days there was a nice balance of the slightly overwhelmed puppy and kitten owners with their adorable but obnoxiously energetic youngsters on their first wellness exams and the owners with their stately geriatrics just looking for a little extra time. Those and other routine visits were interspersed with enough medical mysteries to keep my brain fired up, and peppered with enough comic relief to keep me well entertained and humble.

So I went to my last set of afternoon appointments with a gloomy attitude. I had a long time goal of becoming a board certified veterinary surgeon, but this month working in the primary care practice had stolen my heart. I loved working with the pets and clients and being included in their everyday lives, but I did wonder if each rotation was going to be my 'most favorite.'

My first patient was an older Golden Retriever that was having trouble getting up, and I just hope that when my senior time comes, I will have as much class as he had dealing with the harsh changes that so often accompanies aging. He sat next to Mr. Emerson, looking back and forth between his owner and the rest of us in the room, sweeping the floor with his tail every time that his owner patted him or said his name. The other dog in the room, a younger female black Labrador Retriever, was giving the owner a lot more trouble. In the first two minutes she wrapped her leash around his legs and almost brought him to his knees, and then the minute she was untangled, she jumped up on my tech and knocked her glasses askew and gave her face an exuberant licking.

"Dizzy is just here for her heartworm test and to get her nails trimmed," Amelia said. "Why don't I take her to the back and give you and Jiminy some peace?"

"Great idea," I agreed, and knelt down beside him to do his exam.

When I asked Jiminy to get up so I could watch how he moved, he reached over and licked my hand and looked expectantly into my eyes, hoping that being adorable would talk me out of making him move. I told him he was a sweet boy, but then asked him to come again, and he dejectedly gave a big sigh and looked at his owner for confirmation. When Mr. Emerson encouraged him, he started the struggle to rise, throwing his weight forward and rocking back and forth, finally getting one back leg under him and then hitching himself up. He panted with the effort but wagged his tail and cooperated as best he could with the rest of my exam. Mr. Emerson didn't expect an easy answer; he had lived through cruciate knee surgery with Jiminy a few years ago and some hip arthritis had also been diagnosed then, but he wasn't ready to accept there was nothing more to be done to help his old friend. He and I decided to do some blood work to make sure that another health problem wasn't changing Jiminy's ability to deal with his arthritis and agreed that it was time to add anti-inflammatory medicine to his regime if he passed those tests. Mr. Emerson also agreed to keep Jiminy on his special joint diet, but wasn't sure he wanted to try physical therapy or the underwater treadmill.

"I'm a little worried about teaching this old dog new tricks," Mr. Emerson said with a worried expression.

"I hear you," I replied. "But in my short career I've been shocked at how well these old timers do adjusting to all sorts of things. It makes me a little ashamed of myself sometimes!"

He laughed and asked, "So maybe I'm the old dog that needs to learn the new tricks!"

"Why don't we discuss it again at the recheck in two weeks?" I answered grinning, and then grimaced when I realize I wouldn't be there in two weeks. "I'll be in my emergency rotation then, but I'll make a note in his chart about what we've discussed. Maybe I'll get to see Gentleman Jiminy in my rehab rotation!"

Mr. Emerson laughed and said, "He IS such a gentleman! His sister's only a few years younger but she's always been a real hooligan compared to

Mr. Jiminy!"

I watched them walk out with sudden great affection for both of them. Dr. Blackwell talked a lot about balancing the needs of the patient and the needs of the owner, but in this case they were the same. Mr. Emerson was interested in buying good time for Jiminy, and I sure hoped that we wouldn't diagnose additional problems and that the medicine would help give him back a great quality of life. Accepting Amelia's help with Dizzy, the two seniors walked out together slowly. They paused to gawk at a woman and a scowling teenaged boy carrying a wire cage full of wriggling yellow, brown and black puppies. I happily realized that these were the Lab puppies delivered by C-section on my first day here, in for one of their de-wormings. I laughed at Mr. Emerson and Jiminy, the two of them had matching expressions on their faces, half fascination and half dismay at all the noise and smells and mindless activity emanating from the large cage.

I didn't have a patient scheduled so I went into the room with Amelia to help her with the chore, and of course to get my chance to play with the puppies. In quick order we had an assembly line going, weighing and dosing them, but we had to put the pups that were finished down on the floor instead of back in the cage to make sure no one got missed or double dosed. Amelia had warned me to shuffle my feet so I didn't step on anyone, but she didn't warn me about how slick the floors were going to get as excitement caused every pup to pee or poop almost as soon as they were set free. As I was congratulating myself on how great we had done, I took an awkward step toward the sink and lost my footing. In that split second I knew I couldn't land on one these vulnerable little puppies, so I threw myself back over to the table and awkwardly stretched and grabbed on with one hand. Grossly overextended, I couldn't pull myself up and couldn't see if there was a puppy under me so I hung there flailing until I could get shifted around. I finally carefully lowered myself onto a spot that was free of the precious puppies. It wasn't in any way free of their contributions, however, so I immediately felt the wetness seep through my clothing.

The teenaged boy, dressed entirely in black and liberally decorated with tattoos and piercings, had been leaning sullenly against the back wall of the exam room, but suddenly laughed out loud at my dilemma and continued laughing until he started making snorting noises. Only when I started laughing with him did Amelia and his mother join in and the puppies mobbed me as I defenselessly sprawled out on the floor, laughing too hard to get up. I had puppies everywhere, biting at my hands, chewing on my shoelaces, jumping on my stomach, slobbering in my hair and snuffling sweet puppy breath all over my face. The boy whipped out his phone and took my picture and I continued to laugh helplessly until Amelia offered me her hand and pulled me up.

I thanked the family for my most memorable visit so far, and as I left I heard the boy tell his Mom, "I like her! We have to ask for her every time we come!"

After a quick run to my locker to change into a pair of scrubs and a clean lab coat to finish office hours, my next appointment was Maisy with Roman for his twelve week vaccine.

"Hi Dr. Kate!" Maisy said happily, dressed much the same way she had our first visit but in a different shade of pink today. "Roman's doing great."

"Good," I said and got right into my exam. I didn't find anything out of the ordinary; he was growing well and his behavior was age appropriate. "Do you have any questions today?"

"Just one," she replied with a grin. "Isn't he the cutest puppy you've ever seen?"

We exchanged smiles as I replied, "He's the most handsome Doberman puppy I've cared for today!"

I gave him the vaccine and then, looking up at the clock, I asked, "We were so quick today I have some time left, may I take him for a get acquainted tour of the hospital? I sure hope he never needs to stay with us or visit radiology, but I'd love to give him an early positive experience."

"What a great idea!" Maisy replied. "Here are his special good-boy treats."

Roman and I had a great time visiting the different departments, and I let everyone we encountered give him a treat. The hardest thing I asked him to do was lie down quietly on the X-Ray table, but he seemed to know the command "settle" so that helped. When he managed to lie there, I gave him a treat and let him down, praising him profusely. Then I sold it by acting equal parts happy and excited.

It was worth playing the fool to see how happy and engaged Roman was, until Dr. Drama, my new secret nickname for our crazy surgeon, came in, glared at me and sarcastically asked, "If you're done performing your obviously vital lifesaving procedures, can we use Radiology for our anesthetized surgical patient?"

I mumbled, "Sorry," and escaped with Roman back to Maisy and our exam room.

I saw a couple more predictable appointments and then went into a room containing a small fuzzy black dog. She was accompanied by her entire family squeezed into the room, on the schedule for her routine yearly exam and vaccinations. Amelia had written down an unusually long list of problems and questions in the chart, and I had a distinct feeling that this visit wasn't routine or about vaccines. The list was too long, the children were too quiet and well behaved, and both parents were there looking way too somber, but I didn't know how to ask what was really going on without being insulting.

I decided honesty is always the best policy, and asked, "There seems to be a lot going on today. What's your biggest worry?"

The family looked at each other nervously and the young daughter blurted out, "Do we have to put Belle to sleep?"

I was stunned by the question, and stumbled through an answer, "I don't think so. We can help most problems, but first we need to figure out what the problem is."

The family all nodded and I continued, "We're going to postpone vaccinations for now, but maybe we'll want to do some blood work. First I need to look her over really well."

"Is it because we're a couple weeks late for vaccines?" the daughter asked apprehensively.

"No," I replied confidently. "I don't know what's going on yet but I do know that it's not that."

The whole family looked relieved, and Amelia put Belle up on the table for me. As soon as I lifted her lip and saw how pale she was, I became concerned and then became even more nervous when I heard her racing heart. I looked at the parents and said, "I'm quite worried about Belle, but there are more questions than answers at this point. I want to send her with Amelia to draw some blood so we can have our first answers as quickly as possible, okay?"

The daughter started to cry, but Mrs. Presley stopped me and said, "Oh, she has a rash too. I'm sorry; I forgot to tell you about it. It's on her tummy."

I started to explain how unimportant a skin rash was compared to the problems I was considering, but decided it would be quicker to just go ahead and peek at it. Amelia gently held Belle up so I could see her abdomen and there were multiple dark red bruises across the entire area and hidden up under the hair as well.

I stifled a gasp and explained to the family, "Those are bruises and a vital clue," and then told Amelia, "It may be a clotting problem, be careful with the blood draw. Hold off until you're positive she's stopped bleeding."

"Bleeding?" the father asked gruffly. "She isn't bleeding."

I wanted to explain that bruises were 'bleeding', and answer all of their other questions, but my priority was getting more information so I said, "We're going to take great care of Belle and I'll explain everything but I must ask a bunch of important questions first, okay?"

They all nodded, and I started my interrogation, jotting down notes as I got answers until Mr. Presley cried out, "Ticks and rat poison and the color of her poop? I don't understand what that has to do with anything."

"Each answer provides another important clue," I answered as Amelia returned with Belle. "Diagnosing a problem is about solving a mystery. Now I need to go to the lab and look at her slides; meanwhile Belle needs to be kept safe and quiet. Do you want to hold her for a few more minutes, or do you want us to get her into her cage now?"

They all cried out at once, some variation of the incredulous question, "Belle has to stay?"

It shocked me that the parents at least didn't realize that Belle was going to have to be in the hospital to fight for her life. Then it dawned on me that maybe they didn't even understand yet that it was going to be that kind of a fight. I didn't want to panic them or cause them to lose hope, but I needed to say something. But say something quickly.

Amelia rescued me and said, "To help Belle, Dr. Kate needs to get right to work in the lab, but I can tell you what she's worried about and give you some idea of what treatments might be needed. But Belle is seriously ill and will need to start treatment in the hospital."

I turned and heard Amelia bring up the cost of basic and intensive care treatments, and I realized I had forgotten to discuss that too. I was worried about Belle and every fiber of my being was telling me to focus on getting answers so that treatment could be started as quickly as possible. But I was obviously having trouble dividing my attention with the other important parts of providing care for the family.

As soon as the lab tech handed me Belle's slide and I sat down at the microscope I immediately felt better, more focused and less insecure. I had a professor who called what you could see in a microscope 'the unseen world,' and I just loved the information that I could glean from my view of that world. The lab would soon give me the vital numbers I needed, but I wanted to see the cells and platelets for myself. Except that I couldn't find a single platelet to look at. I rescanned the entire slide; especially the edges, but I only found a rare platelet to examine. Amelia excitedly ran up waving the lab print out because the machine agreed with me; Belle didn't have any platelets to help her clot her blood and her red blood cell counts were low as well.

I went back into the room and carefully explained what I knew and what I still didn't know, i.e. why Belle's platelets were low, and we made a plan for further diagnostics and treatment. The family seemed to have recovered from the worst of the shock and understood that Belle would be transferred to ICU and be cared for by the internal medicine department. They were thrilled beyond measure that I would be over there tomorrow in my new ER rotation, and I was almost as happy to be able to be there for Belle and the family and to be able to follow her recovery.

After the Presley family left, Amelia and I finished Belle's transfer; I had missed evening rounds so I had to find the ER doctor and the ICU technician that would be caring for her overnight. I felt like I was leaving Belle in good hands but hated the fact that I didn't have a phone to be called if something changed. I decided that finding money for a phone and service was my number one financial priority; I could eat rice and beans and sleep on the floor for the whole year if that meant that I could have the peace of mind that being connected would bring me. Interns weren't paid very much in salary; Dr. Drama loved to say that we were paid with a priceless practical education, but I needed somehow to be in contact with the hospital. I made a plan to run home, take a shower to wash away the evidence of my earlier enthusiastic puppy mobbing, and then come back and spend my evening at the intern computer station reviewing all the information I could find on platelets and anemia. At least that way I'd be within shouting distance if Belle had any problems.

By the time I returned, Belle had settled into ICU well and seemed to be feeling a little bit better already. The ER, however, seemed to be just as busy as when I left, both Dr. Drama and Dr. Tolliver, the Radiologist, were running around with their interns like crazy people, and there were surgeries going on in both operating rooms. Since there didn't seem to be any way to get up to speed fast enough be able to help without getting in the way, I escaped upstairs in part to study and in part to stay away from Dr. Drama.

There were two cute kids at the intern computer station, in the ten to twelve age range I'd guess, but they immediately closed out of their game and stepped away from the area around the computer.

"Hey," I protested. "You didn't need to stop."

"Rules," the pretty girl with an elaborate pattern of braids across her head said with a smile.

"I'm Kate," I introduced myself and shook their hands with the girl as she replied, "Lyssa," and then with the younger boy who said, "Sam."

"Well, I need to review the causes of anemia, then I'll just be here killing time so maybe we can all play some computer games?" I asked hopefully. I seem to get along better with children than I do with adults, or at least I seemed to understand them better without having to work so hard, maybe because they are naturally more open and honest. Probably the same reason that animals make more sense to me as well!

"We'll get our homework done while you work," Lyssa said as she turned to her brother and pointed to the nearby table and their gear.

"I'll race you!" I said and jumped into the computer chair and started to madly type.

Sam and Lyssa laughed as they tore into their backpacks, scattering their supplies a bit but then quieting down so that soon all I could hear were the scratching of their pencils and the little noises from my computer. I readily lost myself in multiple articles and discussion boards on causes and treatments for canine anemia and startled spastically from my deep concentration when Lyssa and Sam shut their books with loud claps.

"You won!" I announced with a grin. "But I'm done too, just need to make a couple more notes."

"What's your patient's name?" Lyssa asked.

"Belle," I replied.

"That's a great name," she declared, looking at her brother and then at me. "What game do you want to play?"

"It's been so long since I've played that I don't even know any games," I replied, "so you'll have to choose."

34

They exchanged looks and wordless nods, started a game, gave me minimal instructions and then the hilarity ensued. They were so much better than I was; it almost hurt my feelings except that they were so encouraging, seeming to be equally happy and despondent in turn as any of us succeeded or failed. I had so much fun, never even gave a moments worry about my real life problems like my upcoming ER rotation. It was the most fun I'd had in a very long time, and I was sad when the intercom summoned them to their ride home. I stuck around another hour, and thank goodness Belle continued to do so well that I felt free to walk home. To be more precise, after making my way slowly across the rough terrain of the empty lot, I alternately jogged and sprinted to make myself less of a predictable target for the odd assortment of people hanging out in the alley that night.

Chapter Six

Day one of my emergency rotation was a lesson in absurdity. I'd been told that daytime ER duty during the weekdays, when all the regular veterinarians were open, would be a lot like police work; ninety-five percent routine calls interspersed with five percent pure terror. Only today it wasn't a single terrifyingly critical patient, or even a mass causality incident with multiple patients from something like a fire or car accident; it was some kind of weird synchronic influx of every kind of case that threatened to overwhelm every department's ability to respond. Not only were all the cases serious, they all needed multiple diagnostic tests, multiple stat treatments, and immediate transfer to one of the specialty services and/or ICU. And worst of all, the cases just kept coming.

The technician in charge of appointments directed me to a room and said, "It's just an ear infection. Get in and out of there quickly, I need you and I need that room for more serious cases."

I walked in and the enormous fluffy white mixed breed dog was standing in the middle of the room trembling, with an expression of absolute abject misery on his face, and when he moved his head slightly to look up at me, he winced and froze in position. The room tech had to gently slip a muzzle on before I could even lift his ear flap to look. But as soon as I lifted it, the odor engulfed me as thick yellow discharge oozed out of the swollen canal. I turned and got gloves for both of us; anything that smelled that bad was always going to be a bad thing to be exposed to. I took a quick sample with a cotton swab, rolled it out on a microscope slide and turned to go to the lab to stain and examine the slide.

I turned back and asked the tech, "What was his temperature?"

She winced, not in pain like the dog but in regret for skipping that important step in the craziness of the day, and shook her head no.

I took my hand off the doorknob and told the owner I needed to do a couple things before I looked at the slide, and then knelt beside the dog and completed a full physical, which I should have done before I zeroed in on his affected ear. His temperature was a concerning 104.5 degrees, his pulse was rapid, and his skin tented when I pulled it up, indicating serious dehydration and impending shock. I felt around the affected ear, comparing it to his other side, and the entire right side of his face and neck were hot, swollen, and intensely painful. This had stopped being a simple ear infection days ago; this was a massive infection that had overcome the body's defenses and invaded into the surrounding tissues. One of my Immunology instructors had served in the Army and often talked about the immune system and any infectious agents as opposing forces, complete with primary missions and defensive and offensive strategies. There was no doubt in my mind which force was winning the battle today, and I knew I would see hundreds of ear infections before I saw one this bad again. I also knew Bear would need to be added to today's group of patients needing multiple diagnostic tests, multiple stat treatments, and immediate transfer to one of the specialty services and/or ICU.

I excused myself and as I left the room the appointment tech hissed at me, "What's taking you so long in there? I told you I needed the room."

I whispered back, "You also told me it was just an ear infection. I had a professor who said the hair on the back of his neck would always raise when he heard someone say 'just something' like 'just a torn nail' or 'just vaccines' because it was going to be used as an excuse to do a shoddy job. That dog is seriously ill."

She looked back at me through angry squinted eyes, but I turned away and went to deal with my slide. Dr. Blackwell was standing in the lab, waving a slide in the air to dry it, and looked at me quizzically.

"I just saw the worse ear infection I have ever read about, much less seen, and the plan I made is going to stress everybody out," I explained.

"Really?" she said grinning. "They were absolutely thrilled when I brought over a dog with an adrenal tumor in full crisis."

"They were?" I asked naively.

"No," she replied laughing out loud. "But just give everybody a little time to adjust and everything will work out. Just focus on this patient and then worry about the next patient."

"Okay," I said doubtfully.

"So why did this ear infection get so severe? Is the organism that's causing the infection just that powerful, or is there something else suppressing his immune system so he can't fight it, or did the owners simply wait too long to come in?" she asked.

"I don't know," I replied.

"Right answer! It's always easy to leap to one conclusion or another but you can't afford to make a mistake. Collect your facts and then make your diagnosis," she said moving to the microscope with her slide. "And if it's as bad as you say it is, get the poor dog a pain shot before you do anything else."

I took my turn at the microscope and my patient's slide was wall to wall bacteria and cells, so I made my plan of attack quickly. I strode toward my exam room, grabbed the first technician I saw and gave instructions to get the suffering dog a pain injection stat.

I had my hand on the exam room doorknob when the ICU technician tapped my shoulder and said that Belle was vomiting blood and the internal medicine clinician was busy with the adrenal crisis so she needed me stat. I dashed back to ICU, and thank goodness Belle was still bright and alert, and it was just a few flecks of blood, so I added medication to stop her vomiting and another to protect her stomach and jogged back to my exam room. I could have started those medications earlier, but the owners had begged me to keep their bill as low as possible.

I slipped back into the exam room before anyone else could grab me and said to the owner, "Bear has a bad bacterial infection involving his ear and the right side of his face and neck. He'll need to be treated and monitored in the hospital, maybe for a couple days, maybe for longer. He's seriously ill."

"I knew it!" the lady owner replied and burst into tears. "I told my husband it was bad, but he kept saying it was just Bear's allergies, and he'd get better if we kept him indoors. And then when Bear stopped shaking his head, I thought my husband was right."

I handed her our box of tissues and said, "He stopped shaking his head when the discomfort in his ear deteriorated from an intense itchiness into excruciating pain."

She sobbed harder and turned her head into the corner. I immediately knew I had messed up; this wasn't the right time to be educating her on ear infections so that she could make a better decision next time; it was time to let her know what we were going to do solve the problem.

"We're going to get him help right away; in fact here's the technician with Bear's pain shot now. I'm not even going to touch his ear again until that has a chance to work," I explained.

When she looked up at me, I smiled reassuringly, patted her arm and said, "We'll take great care of him."

The technician and I were awkwardly bent down giving Bear the IV injection that would bring him the relief he so richly deserved when loud screams of "Poison! Help him! He's been poisoned!" blasted into the exam room through closed doors, and at my nod the technician bolted out of the room. I reassured the owner that Bear would respond soon and followed the tech into the waiting room.

Maisy was holding Roman tight to her chest in a blanket and was now screaming gibberish, or some language I had never heard before, and didn't respond to my attempts to question her.

"What happened, Maisy?" I asked again. "What did he get into?"

She turned wild eyes to me and replied, "Nothing. There's nothing to get into."

"Why are you saying poison then?" I asked.

"Look at him. He's poisoned," she replied incredulously, like if she weren't being polite she would have added "you stupid idiot."

"I can't even see him, Maisy, let's move into the exam room," I said guiding her to the empty room at the far end.

She resisted moving into the room and looked at me again like I was making no sense and said, "This is the eye exam room."

"And it's empty," I replied, now really concerned that there was something wrong with both of them. I added carbon monoxide to my list of concerns, but Maisy didn't have that characteristic bright pink color, in fact she looked uncommonly pale.

She followed me into the room, and when she unwrapped Roman's swaddling and placed him on the table, his legs held him for a minute then went out from under him in super slow motion. I had enough time to shove my hands under his chin to prevent his head from crashing down onto the tabletop.

Maisy stared down at the large stain covering the front of her dress and exclaimed, "The urine is just running out of him."

I pulled a bunch of paper towels out of the dispenser for her, bent to listen to his heart and then he slowly pushed back up into a wobbly stance and threw up chunky brown material in a cascade over the side of the table that landed with an audible splash. Then he collapsed back down onto the table again. A technician rushed in with a couple cleanup towels, but I stopped her and told her to save samples for testing first.

"Maisy, start at the beginning," I said slowly and serenely. "What happened?"

She was still breathing rapidly, distractedly brushing the front of her dress with the paper towels, and looked at me like now I was speaking a foreign language.

"Maisy, Roman needs you to take a couple deep breaths and then tell me what you know. I'm sending Roman with Becky; she'll start an IV and get a full blood and urine workup while we talk, okay?" I continued speaking as calmly as I could.

Maisy nodded yes and grabbed Roman one more time and tenderly kissed his face before Becky took him to the back. Then she sat down suddenly as if her knees had just given out from under her.

"When was the last time Roman was normal?" I asked.

"He was fine when I left for the store," she replied. "I was gone about two hours."

"And where was Roman?"

"He was in an outdoor pen but he had water and shade and it's not even hot out today," she replied.

"So you came home and found Roman what? Collapsed?" I asked.

"My son was supposed to be working in the kennels, and he was nowhere to be found so I went looking for him. And then I found my kitchen had been completely trashed from one of his silly baking projects so I was distracted and didn't check on Roman right away. When I looked out the kitchen window, Roman was lying down in such an awkward position that I knew something was wrong," Maisy answered.

"Is the food you feed that dark brown color that Roman threw up?" I asked.

"Oh, God, NO!" Maisy exclaimed. "Brownies! Lawrence was making brownies! But he knows better than to ever give a dog something chocolate. He knows it's toxic for dogs."

"You saw nothing in the pen?" I asked.

"Nothing," she replied miserably. "Do whatever it takes to save him first, but then find out what was given to him. I don't care what it costs. I don't think it's the brownies, I think it's something that one of those juvenile delinquents that hang out in the alley threw over my fence. Drugs. I think it's drugs."

"I need to go to Roman now," I said.

"I'm going home to make sure the other dogs are okay," she replied, now sounding like she was back to herself. "And then I'll come back and wait here for news."

As I stepped back into the hallway I heard Bear's owner loudly calling for help, and I rushed back into that room. Bear was lying down in a relaxed position and making a mild snoring sound, not an uncommon occurrence when the relief and sedative effect of the pain injection works for a patient.

"What's wrong?" I asked anxiously.

"Look at him!" she replied even more nervously.

"Oh," I said sheepishly. "I'm so sorry. This response is actually what I was hoping for from the shot we gave, but I didn't get a chance to warn you and I should have."

"Oh, I didn't know," she said. "I'm just so worried, I thought he was dying."

"We're going to take him in back now that he won't mind moving," I said with a smile. "We still have lots to do for him, but he's feeling better now. I'd better warn you though; he'll walk like he's drunk."

"Thanks, Dr. Kate," she said with shy smile.

A receptionist wearing a phone headset met me at the door and said, "Mr. Emerson is on the phone about Jiminy."

"I can't take the call right now," I said reluctantly. "Can you ask him what's going on?"

She spoke into the headset, then nodded as he answered, and said, "Thank you for letting us know. I'll tell Dr. Kate right away."

"Well?" I asked as she started to make notes on the chart.

"Jiminy is doing great with the new medicine, even chased Dizzy in the backyard today!" she replied with a smile.

I wished I could have spoken to him, but jogged to the back and was met by the ICU nurse and the technician holding Roman. They started speaking together, and then the ICU nurse yielded to Roman's technician.

"Do we know what he got into?" she asked.

"I don't even know if he did get into anything," I said walking toward a treatment table. "I need to see all his results and do his physical."

Roman didn't show pain anywhere; his color was good and his bloodwork was within normal limits, but his heart was racing and he alternated between being depressed and being agitated. And he was definitely incontinent; he had peed on both technicians who were working with him. I think he did get into something, or was given something, but Maisy's history wasn't giving me the important clues that I needed.

I tried to figure out what tests to send out to the reference laboratory, I needed to include all the illegal drugs that Maisy wanted checked for, but I wasn't sure what juvenile delinquents she was so worried about. The alleyway behind her house was the same alley I walked through to get to the hospital, and the kids that hung out there certainly had a different fashion sense than Maisy but I wouldn't want to be put on the spot to admit which one I preferred. And they never seemed to be under the influence of drugs or up to no good. There were some older odd characters that were there some days that were more worrisome; but they seemed more down on their luck than they seemed like some fearsome drug kingpins.

The intercom announced, "Dr. Shoe, main floor hallway. Dr. Shoe, main floor hallway."

Most of the people in treatment paused to look at the bottom of their shoes. I continued to look around in confusion until Becky the ICU tech said, "You were up front."

"And?" I asked, sure my bewilderment was evident.

"Dr. Shoe means check your shoes, someone is tracking something around the hospital," she replied.

I pulled my foot up to check the bottom of my shoe and the evidence was clear that I was the offender just as Dr. Drama walked up to us and sarcastically said, "Nice job, great way to make a bad day worse. Clean it up immediately! And don't you dare say you're too busy."

"What are your orders for Roman?" Becky demanded with a frown.

"Now!" Dr. Drama insisted.

Becky moved closer and stared at me intensely as I grabbed a spray bottle of disinfectant and paper towels and started cleaning off the bottom of my shoes as I said, "Fluids at double maintenance rate, vitals every hour and recheck blood on the I-Stat machine in four hours."

"Toxiban?" Becky asked.

I had just knelt down to start wiping up the floor and mumbled a swear word under my breath and then looked up and replied regretfully, "Yes. Sorry. That's what I came back to tell you. Without knowing what he got into we're going to need to use the charcoal. It's as close to a universal antidote as we have."

Becky smiled and nodded. She hadn't really been getting angry with me so much as being a persistent advocate for her patient.

As I cleaned up, tracking backwards to the room I had been in with Roman, the technician working with Bear tracked me down, handed me his chart and asked, "How often do you want Bear's medications to be given? You didn't write it down."

I opened the chart and the receptionist walked up and said, "Maisy's back and wants to speak to you," at the same time the ICU nurse walked up and asked, "Can I give Belle a couple bites of a bland diet?"

I struggled for a minute to remember who Belle was and looked at the ICU nurse blankly until she continued, "The platelet dog. She hasn't vomited again and seems interested."

"Yes," I answered as my heart dropped. How could I have forgotten which one Belle was? I had always assumed that forgetting names was a sign that one of my professors hadn't cared enough to learn their patient's name, but I absolutely cared, more than I would ever want to explain. It was like I was a computer, and I had too many applications open and had to close a couple of files before I was able to access an earlier one. It made me feel awful but I took a deep breath and said to the ICU tech, "Let me finish writing up Bear's orders, then I'll see Maisy."

The deluge of serious patients continued, so I felt like a pinball being sent flying one way and then being shot over to another maze to tackle until I was shot back to a different challenge. And there was no one to help me because they were dealing with their own messy pinball games. I heard Dr. Drama bellowing for Stretch multiple times and was thankful I wasn't in the surgery rotation with him at least. But when no one had time to take their regular lunch breaks, Molly ordered in pizza for the entire hospital and nothing tasted as good as that hot food except maybe the donuts and coffee that Maisy brought in later in the afternoon.

Somewhere in the middle of my horrible senior year of vet school, when I was being taunted and mocked by my classmates, and hadn't yet learned what my supposed fiancé was saying and doing behind my back, I had reacted to the hurt by exerting tight control over my pain and sadness. I found something, no matter how small, to be happy about every single day, and I hadn't shed a single tear, even in those last heartbreaking months as his treachery was revealed in an excruciating piece meal fashion. I didn't cry when I learned that he and his new girlfriend both got internships at Michigan State, even when he announced it to our class without warning, even though my shocked reaction made my public humiliation complete. But oddly tears welled up at Maisy's simple kindness because it was offered in the midst of her own traumatic circumstances. It represented the absolute antithesis of being selfish, which I guess is altruism, but there should be a more exceptional word for being able to think about another's feelings and needs in the middle of a personal crisis. I shook my head to dispel those tears when I took the presented coffee, and when Maisy urged me to take the special donut with extra icing, I grinned at her and did just that.

Chapter Seven

I didn't ignore my obnoxiously early alarm nor did I launch the offending clock across the room, so I was feeling exceptionally virtuous as I trudged across the badlands, my new nickname for the huge vacant lot. I arrived early enough to see that all my patients were doing significantly better as well as to run upstairs and grab left over pizza for breakfast. After that I was filled with joy and satisfaction, to have patients responding and a full stomach was almost more than I could have dreamed of. As I was finishing my last piece of pizza, Dr. Drama arrived with warm homemade breakfast burritos for everyone and I ate two of those as well. Now I was markedly overfull, but it felt good after last week's short rations; I had been afraid to spend much money on food until I had paid my first full month's utilities bills. And while saving for a phone was my number one priority, I would have trouble working the long hours required in my emergency rotation without getting enough to eat, especially when I couldn't scrounge up something mid-shift to sustain me through the twelve hour days. One of the surgery techs had gotten an activity monitor for her birthday and had racked up way more than ten thousand steps on her first day wearing it at work, and I think I was more than exceeding that number every single day.

And while I try hard not to think about my looks, besides wanting to look clean and professional, I sure do miss having curves. I know there are freakishly lucky girls that can lose weight and have super flat stomachs and still have womanly boobs and hips, but I can't. I need a little bit of fat to soften my athletic figure into any kind of an hourglass. I accept that I'm as emotionally broke as I'm financially broke, not ready for any kind of a serious romantic relationship, but I would love, just once, to have Dag look at me like I was a girl, or at least with as much interest as he showed in his spaghetti! I giggled to myself at the thought and headed to the bathroom before rounds to be sure I at least looked clean and professional, i.e. without pizza or breakfast burrito on my face.

With my hand on the door, I heard Dr. Drama call me, "Hey, Dr. Kate."

I turned back to him, and he came up right next to me and asked, bending down to speak softly to me, "You're not going in there to throw up, are you?"

"No," I responded, horrified. "Why would I?"

"You're skinny as a rail, but every time we bring food in you eat like you're going for first place in a hot dog eating contest," he replied gently. "We can help you if you have a problem; we have lots of resources to call on."

"No," I replied and thought that this is what I get for trying to be less than open and honest. Right or wrong, people will make their own best guesses. "I have cheap healthy food at my apartment, but I never get home to cook it. I can't afford anything more portable."

He stared at me thoughtfully, then nodded and said, "We can help with that too."

"I don't want to seem ungrateful, but I think if I took charity at this point, it would cause some kind of a nervous breakdown. The pride of fighting through it is the only thing holding me together right now. I've made it a game, a challenge; how tough can I be, how much nutrition can I get for the least amount of money?" I replied, in a quiet, matter of fact tone of voice, in direct contrast to my emotional words.

He nodded again and turned to leave, and then said, "But consider this: it would make people who remember how it feels to be hungry happy to help you."

I nodded and he straightened up and strode away, back to his full dramatic self, and yelled back, "Move it; you're going to be late to rounds!"

Dr. Drama was on fire for morning rounds, spinning and pointing at people when he had a question and if one of the overnight people wasn't reporting quickly enough, he would start snapping his fingers to hurry them up. Stretch had all the surgery cases ready to go and was giving great concise updates, but when Dr. Drama started snapping his fingers at him anyway, he sang his last report, sounding like a Kyrie in church, or maybe I'm thinking of a Gregorian chant? Dr. Drama stopped in stunned silence to raptly listen, then applauded loudly at the end and wouldn't stop until we all joined him and Stretch took a bow. And that brief unexpected interlude would bring me flashes of enjoyment all day long, I'd chuckle out loud every single time I remembered it.

Belle was doing great; her platelet count was climbing up, and she was eating well so we could start her switch to oral medication, a necessary step before we could safely send her home. Bear's response was practically miraculous; he was bright and alert and his pain was so well controlled that he had started scratching at his ear. That meant that he would have to wear the Elizabethan collar, the so called cone of shame, to prevent him from tearing up his ear and face. But if he ate his breakfast and kept his pills down, he'd be able to go home later today. I couldn't wait to call both owners and tell them the good news.

Roman was doing better, but he still wasn't normal. His racing heart had slowed down, but he was still acting out of it and the ICU staff had a difficult job keeping him clean overnight; some pretty ugly diarrhea had joined his urinary incontinence, made even worse by the black Toxiban making its way out. Maisy was not going to be happy about that. I picked Roman up in a towel and held him while they cleaned his cage once again. At first he was responsive and looked up at me with interest, but then he seemed to zone out and stared into the distance at nothing that I could see. Becky stopped to talk to me on her way to feed Belle, and Roman brightened back up and almost jumped out of my hands trying to get his head into the bowl.

"May I give him something to eat?" Becky asked.

"He can have a small breakfast, but better make it the low fat bland diet," I replied. "Let me know how he tolerates it."

I sat at an empty desk and looked at the three charts in front of me. I really wanted to make the fun calls to the owners that would get good news, but I knew the right thing was to start with the owner of my sickest patient first.

When I called Maisy, she answered laughing and said, "I just walked in your front door!"

I laughed with her and said, "I'll be right there."

"Roman's stable and is getting some breakfast right now," I told her before she could even ask a question. "But he's developed some bad diarrhea. He's not himself yet mentally, so he'll need more time in the hospital."

She nodded, looking remarkably composed compared to yesterday, and said, "He hates being dirty; he's a bit of a prissy boy, but at least I'm spared the yucky cleanup chores. Do we know what he was given yet?"

"Not yet but we should get some preliminary reports late today or early tomorrow. Everyone else still normal at home?" I asked.

"Everyone's fine, and my son and husband swear that they didn't give him anything or leave him where he could have gotten into something," she replied.

"I'll call you when the tests come back or if anything changes," I told her with a smile. "Were you hoping to visit?"

"Not if he's eating," she replied and turned to leave.

When I returned to the back I spoke briefly with the ER staff hoping to make today run more efficiently than yesterday, and then negotiated with the other services to divide up the extra staff that had been called in. And then we all sat around and waited. And then we waited some more. Not one emergency case called or showed up. I tried to keep busy, but all I could think of was how did this happen? Yesterday we had a workload beyond anything that we could reasonably handle and not a single case today? It didn't make any sense or feel at all fair, but the more experienced people shrugged it off and told me that it wasn't that uncommon. Sitting around doing nothing made me feel extraordinarily anxious after the day we had yesterday, but there was nothing I could do to change it on either day.

Late morning Dr. Blackwell found me upstairs and asked, "Do you like Sweet and Sour Chicken?"

"I love it!" I replied enthusiastically. "Why?"

"We're having a weekend Lunch and Learn over at the primary care hospital, and we miscalculated the order so there's an extra lunch," she replied.

"Great!" I answered thankfully.

"You'll have to come to the presentation," she added. "Not fair to buy lunch for someone who won't come and listen."

"What's the presentation?" I asked.

"Flea and tick control!" she replied.

"Oh, since I just graduated, I'm pretty up on the new products and the latest parasitology research," I replied disappointedly.

"No problem. You'll be able to ask good questions then," she replied. "We need all the information we can put our hands on before we decide what products to carry for next year."

"Why don't you carry them all?" I asked naively.

"We need to buy enough of fewer choices to get the best volume discounts! That way we can keep the price as low as possible and more people can keep their pets and families protected year round," she answered pointedly.

"That makes sense," I replied.

"Come on over in about a half an hour and earn your lunch," she said with a smile.

"I'll try but I'm pretty sure the interns and techs and the lay staff at these meetings aren't the ones making the purchasing decisions!" I said laughing.

"Right! It's like people who get angry with our receptionists over our fees," she agreed. "Really never their job to set fees!"

"Who does make those decisions?" I asked.

"We're such a large practice we have committees for everything, but in general it's the owner doctors," Dr. Blackwell replied.

I filed the discussion away to think about later. Did I sleep through all the practice management lectures in school? Or did I not have the right frame of reference to understand the points they were trying to make until I worked as a Doctor in a real world practice?

The meeting was actually pretty good. I won a candy bar for answering a flea life cycle question correctly and made a funny fearful face at Dr. Blackwell, as if I was petrified that I would be unduly influenced to buy their product by a free Snickers bar. But I did ask some good questions so I felt useful. I was mainly glad that I wasn't the one who had to make the final decision!

At the end of the presentation, Dr. Blackwood handed me a huge bag full of the lunch leftovers that no one wanted. I don't think anyone ate their soup or white rice so I had multiple containers of those, and then a smaller assortment of spring rolls and Crab Rangoon, which I was extra excited about. I stored it in the upstairs refrigerator and felt rich as I went back to searching for something productive to do.

Sending Bear home late afternoon to his ecstatic family was the highlight of my day and I watched him leave with pride and pleasure. He wore his cone without concern and his big white plume of a tail was held high, waving gracefully as he trotted out. I'd have to wait four or five more days for his culture and sensitivity results to tell me which bacteria had caused the problem and what medications would kill it, but I was pretty sure we already had him on a winning combination.

For once everyone was on time for evening rounds, but the day's odd schedule wasn't done with us yet. After sitting around twiddling our thumbs all day, the decision was made to take the adrenal tumor patient to surgery. The tumor was producing a flood of hormones that was making the poor dog dangerously ill and, since medication had already been tried and failed, the only way to stop the production was to remove the tumor. But those exact same hormones were making him medically unstable for the surgery; it was a true dilemma. I swear I heard Dr. Drama argue both for and against immediate surgery, but Quickcut, the surgery Resident, was practically frothing at the mouth during the debate and claimed every second wasted was a travesty of good care. In contrast, Dr. Melanie seemed overwhelmed during the heated discussion, stressed beyond her ability to cope and afterwards I found her back in the laundry room crying. When I asked what was wrong, she had trouble answering me, but she seemed to be saying that everyone thought she was wrong to recommend waiting one more day to continue prepping the patient for surgery. I told her I didn't think that there was one completely right or wrong answer, and sometimes practicality had to be considered, like the fact that at this moment in time all the personnel and equipment was available. Melanie was probably the brightest of all the Interns, or maybe just the most well read, but she seemed to be the most distressed all of the time. I hadn't seen her smile in the past couple weeks, and it was her best feature.

I stayed to watch surgery, and it was personally an eye opening experience for a multitude of reasons. Most importantly is that I saw Dr. Drama in a completely different light. He started off his typical self, firing questions and demands to anyone and everyone who came into his sphere of influence. After he had all his equipment and instruments arranged to his satisfaction, and had made his midline incision and placed the retractors to open up the surgical field, he changed into a calm focused unexpectedly quiet version of himself. Then when he was meticulously working to remove the tumor that was wrapped around the vena cava, the largest vein in the body, he was doing the most dramatic work I had ever had the privilege of observing. Yet his personality was the most subdued.

When the surgery started, I was disappointed that I wasn't scrubbed in and able to assist, but it turns out that I had the advantage of being able to move around and watch every step from multiple viewpoints. When Dr. Drama was at the most critical point of teasing out the tumor tentacles, that if left behind would start the hormone flood back up again, from around the huge blood vessel, which if compromised in any way would start a flood of blood that would be immediately disastrous, he was beyond amazing. At that perilous point I changed my position more than once but could still barely see, but Dr. Drama continued pressing forward, working carefully but confidently, and I couldn't tell how he was doing it, if he was feeling his way or using his vast experience to know where to cut, but it seemed to me that he was using magic.

When he pulled the tumor out, I had tears of respect and awe in my eyes. And when he saw my eyes glistening above my mask, he said quietly, "Pure drama." I nodded my agreement, but then my chest tightened as I had the realization that someone must have told him about the new nickname I had given him. I was suddenly afraid of what he was going to do to me in response, or even worse, what he was going to call me as punishment.

The second thing I realized was about me, or maybe I didn't so much figure something out as I understood that there was a very important topic that I needed to ponder about my future when I had some peace and quiet. Many of the veterinarians I admire most as human beings, now unexpectedly including Dr. Drama, were board certified Surgeons. I think I wanted to be a surgeon so I would belong to that group of people, but maybe not necessarily be perfectly suited to do the actual job. I was drawn to being a part of the pets' and their families' lives on an ongoing basis, while most specialty surgery patients returned to their regular Vets for all of their routine care as soon as they had healed. Of course, my Uncle always insisted that I couldn't be a surgeon, and in my own quiet way I had always followed my strong urge to prove him wrong, so pigheadedness might have equally influenced my decision. And I may have simply chosen that field of study years before I had any clear idea of what the job would actually be like and how happy I would be doing it. Sadly, I would need to apply for my specialty residency in a few short months and I was afraid I wouldn't have enough time and experience by then to make the right choice.

Chapter Eight

With a quick prayer for the patient and the ICU staff, I headed home. Dr. Blackwell reminded me to bring the lunch leftovers with me so I bounded upstairs and repacked the giant bag. It was going to make my walk home awkward, but it would be well worth it over the next few days.

I stopped to readjust the bag when I made it to the alley, trying to turn it into a backpack by slipping my arms through the handle openings, but there wasn't quite enough room to get it to fit across my back. I so much wanted it to work that I stood there messing with it for way longer than I should have, but carrying it by the handles was killing my hands.

"Excuse me Ma'am," a deep voice said from behind me, startling me into jumping straight up and then spinning to face the speaker. "Can I help you carry that?"

I smiled at the older bearded man, who was dressed in dirty jeans, a faded flannel shirt and oversized gray hoodie, and replied, "I'm okay. It's not that heavy, it's just uncomfortable."

He bashfully looked down and said, "I'm one of Dag's friends."

"Nice to meet you," I said reflexively, before I realized I hadn't actually met him yet.

"He told us to watch out for you," he continued.

"That's so nice of him," I replied. "And nice of you too! I'm Kate."

"I'm Jim," he said staring longingly at the big bag of Chinese food.

With a split second decision I offered, "One of the Doctors gave me all the leftovers from our work lunch, and it's mostly the soup and plain rice. I didn't want to hurt her feelings but I really don't like them either."

"You don't?" he asked hopefully.

"I don't and I already ate everything that came with my lunch," I said, not outright lying but not telling the whole truth either. "Do you want them?"

"I do," he said shyly. "And I could share with the guys. We have a fire already going with the night getting so chilly."

"And I won't have to carry it any farther!" I said as cheerfully as I could, as I pictured my favorite Crab Rangoon disappearing with the lesser offerings.

"Thanks," he said and looked at me full in the face for the first time. "The guys will be so happy."

"Cool!" I said as I handed him the bag.

"See you around," he said as he turned to leave.

After I left Jim speed walking down the alley the other way, exhaustion overcame me in waves with every step so that I was scarcely able to put one foot ahead of the other by the time I got to the house. I didn't know if it was from yesterday's long physical exertion, my early wake up time, or todays more emotional expenditure of energy, but I was completely wiped out.

The guys, Phil, Ethan, and Dag, were sitting on the wide front porch when I shuffled up and they all spoke at once, asking multiple questions of what was wrong.

"Long days," I replied and Phil finished, "short nights," and we all laughed companionably.

"Katie girl," Phil said sympathetically, "I know exactly what you need. I'll make us all some pasta, and we'll eat it out here watching the sun go down and you'll tell us all about it."

"Thanks, Phil," I said gratefully. "I promised Dr. Blackwell I'd check in on her cases tonight, but I had to get out of there for some kind of a break."

Ethan, Dag and I leisurely swayed in the porch rockers and chatted about inconsequential things while Phil cooked. Dag told a hilarious story about the three of them eating at the Cracker Barrel restaurant in Indianapolis and deciding that they had to buy and somehow transport the six rocking chairs home that same night, all without renting a truck. By the time we finished Phil's huge bowls of spaghetti with his famous homemade marinara sauce, I was a new person. The warmth and comradery, along with the simple hot food, had banished my fatigue and I felt fresh and reenergized.

Dag was the first to leave; he stood up, stretched and announced, "I'd better get my run in before it gets so dark that the local homeowners lose whatever wits they have and call the police on me."

Dag's my friend and I trust him. I had never seen him be anything but helpful to Phil or respectful to Mei or kind to Ethan, but if I came up on him running in the dark, I think I'd be afraid of him too. At least once in most conversations I had with Dag an odd reaction would occur. My friend would be there and then in a split second he would shift; his body language would adjust like a wild animal alerting, his eyes would alter, like his focus had changed and he was no longer looking at the same world that I was, and it would be apparent that he was someone or somewhere else. And each time it happened it made me wonder; should I be afraid of him or for him? And then he'd shift back, and he'd be our Dag again.

Plus he'd never give a straight answer about his job; he'd say he was in sales and laugh, and I heard him telling stories about working at a bar, but all I knew for sure was that he was gone odd hours of the day and night. It would bother me more if Phil were bothered; Phil wasn't evasive about what his occupation had been before managing the apartments. He was a proud New York City Police Officer until he was disabled on the job, and then he moved to Indiana when he inherited some property in Hamilton County. I couldn't believe that Phil would put up with someone living in the house doing anything too illegal.

I knew I should get back to the hospital, but first I ran upstairs for a quick cleanup and change of clothes. The walk back in the pitch black was sure to be spooky after listening to Maisy's stories of puppy poisoning druggies marauding in the back alley so I clipped all my little LED jogging lights to my jacket. A flashlight would have been so much more helpful, but all I had were my little blue and yellow fairy lights. I didn't see anyone at all in the alley, superhero or villain, as I moved quickly across its smooth surface, but I paused when I got to the empty lot, or as I liked to say, the badlands. It was always strewn with potholes and large rocks but the most dangerous obstructions were the haphazard illegal trash piles that randomly appeared.

I plotted my usual route across the obstacle course, congratulating myself for my ease until my toes ran into something and abruptly pitched me forward. I twisted midair and landed on my right knee and shoulder instead of face planting right there, but before I could at least feel glad of that, I heard a sharp cry and then rough breathing. I moved my legs off a soft pile of what smelled like garbage, and felt around in the dark until I felt wetness on my hand and, too late to avoid it, braced myself for the crushing pain of a bite. But there was no bite, just a flash of pink in my little light halos and another lick on my hand. It made no sense to me; wounded animals, wild or domestic, usually bite if injured because it's such a strong natural protective instinct, their thinking brains not even engaged enough to know if it was friend or foe, but at the time I was simply grateful.

I stared at the pile in front of me in the low light and honestly couldn't make out what kind of creature it was until I scooted over as close as I could get. It was a young dog with floppy ears and a longish matted coat of some dark color. As I gently patted over it I reached the poor thing's back and my hand squished into something soft as it cried out in pain again. I immediately stopped and wiped my hands off on my pants. I really shouldn't be messing around trying to diagnose anything out here in the dark; I needed to get this dog help as quickly as I could. I awkwardly jumped up, but then groaned as I tried to bear full weight on my right leg. Removing my jacket and covering the dog's back, I bent over and gathered the suffering dog up into my arms and with great effort managed to stand up straight again. I took one painful step with my precious bundle and tripped forward, landing painfully on both knees, but I managed to squeeze my charge tight to my chest and didn't let go. We both let out little cries, and I clumsily shifted around until I was sitting with it in my lap, legs hanging off both sides. The suffering pup sighed and rested its head on my arm.

I knew I should leave the dog where I found it and go get help. Without the extra weight I certainly could hop, hobble, or crawl to the hospital, but I didn't want to leave it. Someone had dumped this living, feeling, suffering creature out like trash. On the exact day that it needed help the most it had been cruelly abandoned, the betrayal more complete than anything that I had ever faced. Until it was absolutely proven that I had no other choice, I would not, even temporarily, do the same thing.

"Help me! Help me!" I screamed out, but no lights in the neighborhood or at the hospital lit up in response, no doors opened to investigate, the 'guys' eating my leftovers didn't hear me and come to help.

I pushed with my legs and scooted my bottom across the ground, and then kept repeating the movement until we were both breathing roughly and I had to take a break. I repositioned the pup and did discover this sweetie was a boy; I liked thinking of him as a him and not an it.

Then I called out again, "Please help us."

Again no response, so I inch-wormed a few more feet and then heard a faint, "Katie, call out."

"We're over here, Dag," I called back. "We're over here."

A bright flashlight beam coursed over the field, finally settling on us, and Dag quickly made his way straight to us.

"I found an injured dog, but I fell and now I can't carry him," I said weakly.

Dag reached down under my arms and lifted both of us together up to a standing position, then scooped the dog away from me into his arms. I reached over to grab the dog's mouth during the transfer but he made no move to defend himself, even with Dag's sudden move. Was he just that sweet of a soul or was he too weak to even snap?

"Hang on to my shirt if you need support," Dag said. "Where are we going?"

"We'll head for the back door. I have my keys," I replied and pointed to the closest entrance.

We slowly made our way across the field and after the first couple steps I did have to hang onto Dag's shirt to steady myself. I unlocked the back door and Dag strode straight through into the treatment area and loudly called out "Corpsman up!"

One of the techs pointed to a treatment table and Dag deposited the pup on it. I had just enough presence of mind to call out, "I found an injured dog, and I'll take responsibility," but then I was struck speechless at the extent of the dog's injuries that were now visible under the bright hospital lights.

Techs and Doctors circled around me and Dr. Drama, with his jacket already on and clearly ready to leave, stood directly behind my right shoulder but didn't speak, indicating I was the one running the emergency. Everyone else looked at me expectantly, but I was still frozen until Dag patted my back and nodded when I looked up at him.

That implied agreement with me, to what I don't know, animated me and I started my list, "I need vitals, full blood work, an IV started, pain shot…" until Dr. Drama interrupted quietly, "Is everyone protected?"

"Gloves and gowns for everyone," I ordered as I held up one finger to Dag and then hurried to the locker room. I changed into scrubs after disinfecting myself and then found a large scrub top for Dag. I jogged back and handed it to him, but before I could point out our changing area, he snapped his black protective gloves off one by one directly into the trash, and then pulled his T-shirt off over his head and sent it sailing into the same trash can. He rinsed himself off with straight alcohol, waved the scrub top in front of his chest to speed up the drying and then slipped the scrub top over his head. And while we all stopped what we were doing and stared at him through the entire procedure, he didn't seem to notice or care. And he didn't seem to care whether we were admiring his incredible muscular physique and defined abs, or if we were checking out the massive scar snaking around his side. I finished putting on a gown and gloves, to protect myself now and the rest of the hospital from contamination when I was done. The protective gear would be disposed of before we left this spot, instead of traipsing around the hospital in contaminated clothing or heaven forbid even dragging contagion home.

I carefully examined the suffering puppy, trying to be gentle and kind but still thorough, at the same time staying out of the way of the techs working on him. The technicians were always amazing in critical cases like this, and they smoothly worked together in a dance as complicated as any award winning musical routine, their mission to get everything done in as little time as possible. As soon as the pup received the pain relief injection, he relaxed completely and melted down onto the table, but his eyes continued to follow my every move.

"Do you need a ride to the hospital?" Dag asked. "Should I go get my car?"

"No, I'm just bruised and battered," I replied. "I'll be okay."

"I'll come back and pick you up later," he said firmly.

"No, thanks. I'll be staying here tonight," I answered with an appreciative smile.

"Well, then, can I bring you a change of clothes in the morning?" he persisted.

"Yes," I accepted gratefully, tossing him my keys. "Thank you, Dag, for everything."

Dr. Drama hitched his backpack strap over his shoulder and then came over to Dag with his hand extended, "Hi, I'm Dr. Vincent. Thanks so much for helping Dr. Kate."

Dag shook Dr. Drama's hand and replied, "Nice to meet you."

Dr. Drama continued, "And you are?"

"I'm Dagger," he replied with a small, possibly amused smile.

Dag was short for Dagger? It had never dawned on me to even ask, and he sure didn't seem to be a guy who'd use Dagger as his nickname.

Except that Dr. Drama leaned in rather aggressively and said, "Dagger?" in a decidedly skeptical tone of voice and suddenly that typical Dag shift occurred, and as Dag's body language morphed Dr. Drama took a hasty step back in response. And right then Dag did seem like a guy that would be called Dagger.

But Dag relaxed, turned to me and said, "I'll see you in the morning, but call me if you need anything," and he was back to himself. He slid his hand under the back of my scrub top and left it warm on the small of my back for a minute before patting me a couple times and walking away. My heart skipped a beat and I couldn't tell if it was from Dag's touch or the stress of the situation with the pup.

Dr. Drama smiled, but it didn't completely reach his eyes, and he told me, "I'll do the pup's first debridement surgery tomorrow if he's stable. "

"Thank you, Dr. Vincent," I said with true gratitude.

"And you may need to give him plasma, large burns can cause a dangerous protein loss," he added.

"Burns?" I asked doubtfully.

"I've seen burns in that pattern, a large wound along the back and then stripes down the sides, when something hot is dropped on them like frying oil or boiling hot coffee, and it runs down their sides," he explained. "Often right after the initial trauma, not much can be easily seen through the fur and people think there was no harm done from the accident until the skin starts to die and slough off days later."

"I thought it was a really bad infection like a flesh eating bacteria or something equally horrible," I said.

"I can't prove it yet, but to me the pattern doesn't fit primary infection," he argued. "Plus, I think he smells like coffee."

"Disgusting coffee," I agreed nodding. "But he's just skin and bones; wouldn't not eating be more a symptom of infection?"

"You're assuming he was fed and chose not to eat," Dr. Drama explained grimly.

"Oh," I said unhappily as I got what he was saying. In the world I wanted to live in, you were able to assume a suffering animal was at least offered food.

"But the pain and secondary infection might have made him anorexic," he continued. "Just don't assume anything."

"Thank you," I said again.

"I'm out of here," he replied as he walked away.

I pulled a chair over next to the treatment table and plotted out everything I wanted to do for the pup, and then studiously numbered each task in order of importance. The technicians clipped off large expanses of matted hair and then started gently rinsing the wounds, and as unidentifiable debris and rotten chunks of skin washed off and fell through the grate down into the tub below, it ripped my heart apart. And then with every passing minute, my stomach rolled and tightened and I had to move the trash can next to me in case I couldn't control my visceral reaction.

But it wasn't the wounds or falling debris that were making me sick to my stomach. After years working for a vet in Fort Wayne and four years of Veterinary school, I truly didn't get disgusted working with any kind of wound or infection or bodily fluid. But I was in no way immune to the suffering of an animal, especially knowing how long it must have been going on. My chest tightened as the cleaning process continued, and then my head began to throb because I couldn't stop thinking of the people who did this terrible thing. The degenerates who neglected and abandoned this helpless pup were far more disgusting than any wound I would ever care for. They may wear an outer mask of a regular person, but underneath they are ugly repulsive rotting corpses pretending to be human. They weren't like Bear's owner who made a mistake in judgment; we all make mistakes and she had been doing her best to take care of her dog with the facts that she had at the time. I had attended long years of school, and I made a mistake when I could have prevented Belle's stomach ache by starting her medications earlier, but I was trying to keep costs down and thought she wouldn't need them. But the people who so repulsed me had to have seen how horribly their pup was suffering, chose to do nothing to help or comfort him, and solved their problem by just throwing him away.

I shook my head, trying to shake the thought away and told myself that those kinds of thoughts weren't going to help the puppy, or me, feel any better. I moved closer to my sweet pup and stroked the uninjured top of his head, speaking to him gently, telling him what a good boy he was. He gazed lovingly up into my eyes and gave a couple weak thumps of his tail.

Then I looked up at the technicians around the table and confessed, "He's a better person than I am. If I'd been through what he has, I'd never trust anyone ever again; much less trust the very next person I met."

Chapter Nine

Stabilizing the puppy was an all-night battle, and by the next morning I'm sure I looked like it had been won with some kind of hand to hand combat. But the puppy's temperature was down to normal, his glucose was up into the normal range, and his electrolytes and proteins were stable by sunrise so I celebrated by taking a shower. Dag hadn't arrived with my clean clothes so I had to put on a set of ill-fitting scrubs from the emergency pile. The pants in particular were at least twice as big as they needed to be, and I not only had to cinch them in as tight as possible, I had to roll odd looking cuffs so I wouldn't trip on them.

Dr. Drama arrived early for rounds with a huge cup of fancy coffee for each intern; mine was enhanced with lots of sugar and milk and hopefully would give me the good caffeine and calorie kick start I needed. He examined the pup, reviewed the chart with me and then said, "I think we'll do him last, surgery in the late afternoon, so you can offer him a bite of food now if you want to."

"Thanks," I replied. "I'd like to know if he'll eat."

"Only one other important question," he stated rather gruffly, but his eyes gave the joke away as the corners crinkled. "What are you going to call him?"

"I had a flash of brilliance, or possibly insanity, at four in the morning and decided his name is Maximum Courageousness because of his attitude," I replied. "And I can call him Max."

"Good one," he replied as he turned to check on his post-op adrenal tumor case. "I expect you to scrub in on Max's surgery. When I'm ready for him, you can switch responsibilities with Stretch."

"Thanks, Dr. Vincent," I called out and then turned to the ICU technician and asked, "Becky, I'm going to give Max a few meatballs now, but if I get called away, can you take away whatever he doesn't eat so that he can have surgery later today?"

"Sure, Dr. Kate," she replied with a smile.

I took a small amount of the bland diet and rolled it up into bite sized pieces, dropped them into a small bowl and put it in Max's cage. We, the bowl and I, were greeted with a couple tail thumps and then Max looked at the food, and then looked at me, and then continued looking back and forth. I told him he was a good boy and encouraged him to eat, but he made no move to put his head into the bowl even though he kept sniffing the air around it. I swung the cage door open wider and sat on the edge, picked up one small meatball, and offered it to him. He took it from me gently, using mostly his lips almost like some horses do. He looked back at the bowl, and I gave him another one, and he took it the same way, so I just hand fed him the rest of the tiny meal.

As soon as I stood up, the crazies started. A receptionist walked in one door and announced, "Your family is here, Dr. Kate. They have food for you, so I put them upstairs in the lounge."

"My family?" I asked in disbelief.

"That's what they said," she replied smiling. "Three gentlemen and a lady?"

"I'll be right there," I promised, as Becky approached with a printout from the reference lab while Dr. Drama rushed past me and out the door toward the stairs.

"Roman's toxicology report is back," Becky said with a rather amused expression on her face.

"What?" I asked, but she just waved the report at me and as soon as I took it she returned to ICU.

I moved toward the stairs while reading the information, a positive test for both theobromine and THC. Chocolate and marijuana? How did that happen?

I looked up, caught Becky watching me and called out, "What???"

"Pot brownies?" she replied laughing. "Not the first time we've seen it."

"Who would be so stupid to let that happen?" I asked.

"Duh? People who have been eating pot brownies?" she asked, still laughing at me as I tried to wrap my brain around the concept.

I reviewed the general supportive care that we had been giving Roman and realized we were already providing the proper therapy; it was just going to take more time to flush both long acting toxins out of his body. Since Roman was on the right treatment plan, I decided I could postpone the dreaded phone call to Maisy until I had seen who was upstairs waiting for me.

I bounded up the stairs to find Dr. Drama already entertaining Phil, Dag, Ethan and Mei, acting like he was their new best friend.

Dag gave a chuckle as he stared at my supersized scrubs and pointed to the street clothes and clean smock hanging on one of the cupboard knobs, "I think you need these!"

I smiled and said, "Thanks."

"How's the puppy?" Ethan asked, obviously greatly concerned. It seemed unlikely, but maybe I've finally met someone more sensitive than I am.

"Max is stable," I replied and, looking over at Dr. Drama, continued, "And he just ate a couple meatballs for me."

"Good," Dr. Drama replied as he turned to leave. "You better hurry up and eat too; Monday holidays are always a wild ride!"

My 'family' urged me to sit down and eat the still warm omelet and perfectly fried hash brown potatoes, and then presented me with a huge travel cup full of coffee. I might be sleep deprived, but I would be very well fed and caffeinated today!

"We made you lunch, too," Ethan announced proudly. "And Phil already put it in the refrigerator, is that okay?"

"That's great," I mumbled with my mouth crammed full. I wasn't sure when I was going to get pulled away, and I was determined to wolf as much as I could before that happened. "Thank you so much."

As soon as I was done I jumped up and asked, "Do you want to meet him? I can sneak you into ICU for a minute."

"Sure," everyone replied together as they jostled each other to grab my plate and clean up the area. We walked downstairs, and the moment I opened the door into treatment you could hear Max's tail start to thump as it reverberated against the sides of the stainless steel cage.

"Aw," Phil said as he realized what it meant. "He knows you already."

We stood in front of the cage speaking softly, and Ethan asked, "What kind of dog is he?"

"I don't know," I replied. "But I'm guessing he's an Oodle."

"An Oodle?" Ethan questioned.

"Half poodle," I replied laughing. "Like a Labradoodle or Schnoodle."

Everyone laughed and Phil asked, "How old is he?"

"His teeth say he's about four months old," I replied.

"Then he's huge for his age," Dag replied. "He must be half Irish Wolfhound. An Irish Woodle!"

"Maybe," I answered with a smile.

"He's adorable!" Mei said.

"He is!" I agreed. "And he's the sweetest boy ever."

Dag grabbed his chest taking mock offense and incredulously asked, "Sweeter than me?"

I shook the hanger with my clean clothes and replied, "Just barely."

We laughed together companionably until Dr. Drama strode by us in his 'I'm all business' mode and, exchanging quick looks, my family immediately turned to leave as I called out, "Thank you all so much."

I went to the locker room and changed into my street clothes and white smock, keeping the scrubs ready for later. I wish I had also asked Dag to bring my clean scrubs; I'd be stuck wearing this gigantic set for Max's surgery.

As soon as I was dressed, I sat down at the quietest desk, arranged my chart and lab reports, pulled the phone closer to me, took a sip of coffee, rehearsed what I was going to say to Maisy, took a couple deep breaths, and then took another sip of coffee. I finally punched in her number and braced myself.

"Hi, Maisy," I said in an upbeat tone of voice when she answered, "Roman is feeling good and his diarrhea is much better."

"And?" she asked expectantly.

"And his lab results are back and he was exposed to chocolate and marijuana," I replied calmly.

"Marijuana???" she screamed, her mousey voice transformed into a lion's roar. "How did that happen?"

"We don't know, but our best guess is something like pot brownies, but we," I started to reply.

"Pot brownies?" she roared again. "No, it can't be. I'll call you back."

And then she hung up on me without giving me a chance to reply or even finish my sentence. I wasn't sure what to do next. I decided I should warn the receptionists in case Maisy showed up in an emotional state again. And I'd better let them know that I did want to talk to her further, to assure her that we were already doing all the right things for Roman. And that he might even go home pretty soon as long as he didn't start any new problems, even though a part of me wanted to keep him in the hospital until we knew how he had been exposed to the toxins. But I reluctantly accepted that I may never learn the truth.

Belle was taking all her medications by mouth with no more stomach problems, and her platelet numbers had climbed even higher, so she would get to go home today. I quickly made that phone call and her owners, the entire family seemingly, gathered around the phone on speaker mode to talk. And they not only didn't hang up on me; they vigorously resisted ending the call at all. I was slowly recognizing that emergency practice was a constant study in extremes: extreme medicine, extreme behavior, and extreme emotions.

The rest of my morning went well; I saw mostly urgent care cases like bladder infections and torn toe nails. While the patients definitely needed help, their cases didn't carry the stress of the more complicated, life threatening emergencies. I was able to get them comfort and care without hospitalizing them and without having to quote high bills for complicated treatment. It made life a lot easier and much more pleasant.

In the afternoon I was asked to see a patient whose owner was demanding to see Dr. Vincent; however, he was in the middle of a surgery so that was impossible. I was happy to help, and had no ego problems telling the owner I would have Dr. Vincent double check everything I did since she had such a strong preference for him. The patient was an overweight, middle-aged Labrador retriever, and Dr. Vincent had already repaired a ruptured cruciate ligament in one of his knees so it was easy to guess what might be causing lameness in his other leg. But I wouldn't be fooled into jumping to conclusions; I would do a full exam, of course!

When I walked into the room and introduced myself, the rather severe looking woman didn't even smile or respond except to give me the briefest nods of acknowledgement.

"Tell me what's been going on with Rex," I said with another smile.

"Rex tore his right cruciate, and Dr. Vincent needs to do surgery right away," she stated imperially. "I have a trip planned and I won't delay it."

"Okay," I said, looking through the chart for a referral letter from her primary care Vet. "Did Rex already see his regular Vet for this?"

"No," she replied. "It's obvious what it is, and I'm not going to pay someone to tell me to come see Dr. Vincent."

I started, like I start all my exams, by listening to his heart. Mrs. Kaye cleared her throat emphatically a couple times and then stated, drawing out each word like I was having difficulty comprehending her spoken words, "It's. His. Right. Rear. Leg."

I smiled at her, but it was harder to do this time, and replied, "He needs a full physical to diagnose the problem and to be sure he's well enough to have anesthesia and surgery."

"I told you what the diagnosis is," she snapped, obviously frustrated.

I went back to my physical; I thought she was going to glare holes in me while I was looking inside his ears. What would be worse than having a ruptured cruciate? Having a ruptured cruciate and an undiagnosed ear infection.

She let out a huge sigh of relief when I started examining the back legs, but when I reached for the left leg first she snarled, "Right leg."

I couldn't make myself explain that I always saved the affected area for last, for lots of reasons. For one so that I didn't get distracted by the problem and forget to do a complete exam, and two because it's nice to have felt the normal side for comparison to the affected one. It was a good thing that Rex was so nice because Mrs. Kaye wouldn't help me at all. She wouldn't even hold onto his leash so that he would stay in my vicinity, so after I crouched down to work with him, I had to duck walk after him as he moved around the room. And while he did have an odd wide legged stance and gait, he was bearing full weight on both legs and moving much faster than I could duck walk.

When I called a tech into the room to hold him on his side so I could check his knees, the owner was almost beside herself with impatience. Both knees felt stable, and Rex showed no pain with my manipulations until I moved my hands up his leg to feel his hip area, running one hand on the inside and one on the outside of his leg, and he suddenly lurched away from me with a little cry of pain. We got him situated again, and I raised his leg, looked up into his groin area and saw that the skin was bright red and chafed raw. I gently felt around the area, finally palpating his testicles and he lurched again, and cried out even louder. I waved the tech off and let

Rex get up and away from me.

I turned to Mrs. Kaye and said, "I know where Rex's problem is, but we'll have to give him some pain relief before we do any more testing to find out what it is."

"What did you do to him? There was no reason to hurt him," she said forcefully, with her face turning red. "Take his pre-op blood, get his X-rays taken and schedule his surgery for this week."

"It isn't his knee," I countered calmly. "He has an infection or tumor in his testicle, and it's causing him a great deal of pain so he's walking funny."

"Oh, my God," she fumed, as her face turned a more brilliant crimson color. "You're an idiot! And you don't know what you're talking about."

She picked up the leash and jerked Rex to her, and then flung open the door to the reception area. She stomped across the floor as I followed behind, pleading with her to stop, "Please, Mrs. Kaye, please let me keep Rex in the hospital. He really needs help. I'll double check everything with Dr. Vincent. I won't do anything until he agrees."

She stomped another couple steps as I tried to explain, "There's almost no pain worse than pain from a swollen testicle."

"You're a dirty girl!" she shouted at me.

"Please let me get him some pain meds at least," I begged.

I looked up at the crowded waiting room and realized there were a disproportionate number of men, and big rough looking men at that, waiting there; the impression compounded by their motorcycle gear and matching jackets. I caught the eye of one of them and he leaped up and walked like the dog with an exaggerated wide stance and said, "Nothing hurts worse, Ma'am; you gotta let Doc help him."

Four more of the group jumped up and started limping around or, regrettably, grabbing between their legs and grimacing in make-believe pain, and Mrs. Kaye ran the rest of the way out of the waiting room. But then she paused at the door and turned for one more parting shot, "You're a dirty, dirty girl."

Dr. Blackwell came up next to me and whispered, "Let's step to the back," and then raised her voice to speak to the entire reception area, "Gentlemen, thank you so much for helping, but we're going to scare the pets, so let's sit down and let them all relax."

Everyone sat down, led by the group that appeared to be a motorcycle gang, and I saw the receptionist take her hand off the alarm button.

Dr. Blackwell and I walked to the back and she asked, "Was that Mrs. Kaye?"

"Yes, it was," I replied and tried to think how to explain how that visit went so wrong, but Dr. Blackwell waved me off before I could speak.

"She's always a firecracker; don't worry about it," she said with a tolerant smile. "I'll call her husband and arrange for him to bring Rex back."

"I'm sorry, Dr. Blackwell," I apologized. "Thanks for rescuing me."

"You're welcome," she answered with a smile as she walked over to a cage and was greeted by an exuberant white puffball of a Bichon. "I better get Fluffy back to her family before there's an act two in the waiting room."

"That's the motorcycle gang's dog?" I asked incredulously.

"Yes, and don't sound so surprised," she said with a sharp edge to her voice. "They love this dog and take great care of her."

"Sorry," I replied. "I didn't mean to assume."

Dr. Blackwell nodded and left with Fluffy. I took a couple of deep breaths and wondered if I was going to make it through this day. One of the ICU techs waved me over and told me that Max was up next for surgery, so I helped her give his sedative and held him as he got sleepy. Stretch came over while I was sitting on the edge of the cage with him and I caught him up on all the ICU patients he'd be taking care of while I was in surgery.

My heart beat a little faster when the surgery department told me they were ready for Max, but as soon as he was clipped and scrubbed, and we all moved into the procedure room where Max was hidden by surgical drapes, my anxiety finally abated. Dr. Drama kept up a running monologue about wound care, burns, prepping for future reconstructive surgery, and a hundred other topics, and then fired questions at me whenever I started staring at Max's monitors or giving other clues that I was starting to worry.

"Max may only need a couple of surgeries total," Dr. Drama said thankfully. "We'll remove all the dead tissue and clean everything up today, then when he's grown plenty of beautiful, healthy granulation tissue we'll do his reconstruction."

"Sounds good," I agreed. "But if he had received immediate care?"

"Less tissue would have died, that's for sure," he said nodding his head. "But we still would have had to do surgery in stages. We tease Dr. Blackwell because she always tells the owners that burns 'have to declare themselves.' She insists you have to explain that concept very well to owners, or they will freak out when what looks like a little road rash turns out to be a friction burn and the whole area slowly turns black and falls off."

"Makes sense," I said. "I can't help thinking about how much better it would have been if he received care right after it happened."

"I agree," he replied, looking grim. "I know how difficult this is for you, but you'll have to find ways to cope or you won't last long in the profession. I like to look for silver linings; it doesn't mean I don't know they come with big black clouds."

"I know," I agreed. "I'm usually all about the silver linings."

"The other thing I do is take some solace in the science," he continued. "I think about how we're going to help, not about why we have to help."

As we cleaned up the wounds, I did get a sense of power as we removed the damaged tissue. But then disaster struck, but it wasn't with Max, thank goodness! After dealing with the biggest wounds at the front of his body, I was concentrating on re-draping the wound on his rump. I walked back and stepped on the unrolled cuff of my oversized scrub pants, and then awkwardly moved forward and partially tripped. I was, of course, also wearing a sterile gown and gloves, so I couldn't grab onto anything that wasn't part of the designated sterile field. So I held my hands up out of the way and kind of banged my belly into the drape covered table to stop my fall instead. I was fine, and I didn't compromise sterility but the awkward movement managed to jerk my huge scrub pants down which then fell and pooled around my ankles. My modesty was intact since I was covered by my gown, but I couldn't safely move with my pants shackling my legs together.

I looked at Dr. Drama with my best deer in the headlights look, but he smiled reassuringly and said, "No harm, no foul."

I shook my head and asked, "Can I have Tracy come help me?"

"Rob's right there," he replied, pointing at the male technologist just a couple feet away from me, mystified that I'd want to call someone else in from the prep area.

"I have more of a Tracy problem," I explained grimacing. "My scrub pants have fallen down and need to be pulled up."

Dr. Drama looked down to verify my preposterous statement, then cracked up. He laughed so loudly everyone came to look in the windows to see what was going on, and he just kept laughing, so much so that when he tried to ask Tracy to come in, he wasn't even able to speak. Oddly enough he effortlessly proceeded with his surgical responsibilities, such as securing the new drapes and putting a new blade on the scalpel handle, so his hilarity didn't impact Max in any way. But it did start to impact my dignity!

Rob figured out what Dr. Drama was asking for and got Tracy. She handled my crisis like the true professional that she was, reaching up under my gown from the back, pulling my pants up and out of my way, and securing them with the old hemostat that she usually used for her blood draw tourniquets. She nodded at my quiet thank you, and I was really happy with the way she was downplaying the whole incident. That is until I saw her gather a big group of people in the prep area and tell an animated story. Which I assume was all about me and my pants.

Dr. Drama settled down and said, "Thank you. That was way better than finding a measly silver lining! That's the kind of entertainment I can laugh at for years to come."

Part of me wanted to die of embarrassment, and I could only imagine what his letter of recommendation might say about me if I did apply for a surgical residency, but deep down I did think it was freaking hilarious. I smiled up at him with true appreciation of the humor and said, "It's a day neither of us will ever forget."

Chapter Ten

I stayed with Max until he had recovered from the sedative and was sleeping serenely in his post-op cage, which meant I didn't stumble home until after midnight. Then I had thrown myself down on my sleeping spot and dramatically switched off like a shutdown robot. When my alarm rang in the morning, I hit the snooze button and tried to grab a couple extra minutes of sleep, until the exact second it dawned on me that something could have happened to Max overnight, and nobody could have called me. I catapulted off the floor, flew into my clothes, and ran most of the way to the hospital.

Max was noticeably feeling so much better! I grabbed a couple of slip leads to take him outside for a little quality time before the day got too busy, and as I opened his cage door and was messing around with the leash loops, he tried to stage an escape. He was moving in slow motion and stopped when he was barely a few steps away from me, but as soon as I stepped towards him, he spread his legs apart and lowered his head down in a much abbreviated play bow in my direction. I couldn't believe it! What a resilient individual!

As Becky finished arranging the cage above Max's, I belatedly realized that Roman wasn't in ICU and with a terrible feeling in the pit of my stomach, I anxiously demanded, "What happened to Roman?"

"He started feeling too good overnight and had to be moved to one of the wards," Becky replied with a smile. "He was too loud and rowdy for the sicker patients."

"Great news!" I said. "He'll get to go home today; I'll call Maisy after rounds. I finally received a message from her late yesterday, but I never was able to speak to her."

Rounds were a circus; everyone seemed to take exception to something that someone else said. It was obvious that some drama must have happened between Quickcut and my Intern cohorts, but their bad attitude had spilled over to involve their departments as well, since technicians tend to be protective of their doctors and defensive at any implied criticism of their team. Somehow I had been totally left out of the disagreement. I guess not having a phone has some benefits, but I didn't know if I was part of the underlying problem or not. But I didn't dare say a word about anything to anybody for fear I'd be chiming in on the wrong side of whatever the argument was.

At least Max was a safe subject. Dr. Drama was thrilled with how great his back looked so we started joking around with each other about what words we would eventually be able to spell out on his back using his potential scars. One of the most common reconstructive techniques to close large wounds is called a Z-plasty which can leave a z shaped scar, so we were concentrating on z words, which taxed our brains and led to inexplicable hilarity as Dr. Drama randomly called out nicknames for Max that started with a z.

He started with "Zippy!" then tried "Zither," drawing out the z sound then "Zen Master!" and Max wagged his tail and looked up into Dr. Drama's face with enthrallment at each pronouncement while we two humans laughed like maniacs.

I agreed, "The Zen Master!" and we chuckled together pleasantly.

But when Quickcut and Dr. Taren started snapping at each other over a patient at the other treatment table, Dr. Drama lost his sense of humor and harshly demanded, "What the hell is wrong with all of you?"

Dr. Taren looked up, for once without her trademark smile and adorable dimples, and tried to answer without actually saying anything relevant, "We're so sorry. No problems here. We'll be quieter."

"Quickcut?" Dr. Drama asked with an intense look.

"We're fine," Quickcut replied. "Harsh week."

Dr. Drama glared at them, then shouted across the room at Dr. Tolliver, the blank faced Radiologist that he sometimes called Dr. Photographic Memory, "Hey, are we busy this weekend?"

She answered him without asking any questions, "We're free Saturday night."

"We're taking the interns and Quickcut out to eat," he said, making it sound more like a punishment than a reward.

"Okay," she replied blandly. I couldn't get a read on her, and I didn't understand why Dr. Drama and she were or weren't busy together.

"I'll text the kids," he continued. "Can you notify the other interns and free up their schedules?"

"Sure," she replied and sat down at a computer station.

I was stunned. The two of them are together and have kids? There couldn't be a more unlikely couple. Although it did certainly explain why he had been so darn nice to her kids the day they had been dropped off here after some school event; at the time I thought it was out of character for him to encourage someone else to be the center of attention. I really liked their kids; I still remember playing video games with them as one of the most entertaining evenings I have had here. We did have lots of fun together playing those computer games, but I sure hope I hadn't said anything rude about their Dad that night.

He walked away laughing to himself, and I couldn't stop myself from wondering what he was imagining. I may have a perpetually whirling brain, but he had an even busier mind and his thoughts went places that I may never be able to follow. I put Max away, the whole time just cherishing the positive emotions I was having, confused and conflicted perhaps, but in general they were wonderful warm feelings. Six weeks ago I had no family and now I had two, my hospital family and my house family. I maybe didn't fully understand either one, but I was feeling incredibly blessed to have them both.

Roman was back to himself and feeling great, but when I called Maisy to have her come pick him up, she wanted to delay his release until she could have her son come with her. She wanted me to counsel him about the dangers of chocolate and marijuana. I couldn't decide if she was implicating him in Roman's intoxication, or if she just wanted me to do a general, scary, drugs are bad talk?

Dr. Blackwell set me up to see Mr. Kaye with Rex for an appointment late morning, and I was really worried about the visit. For absolutely no reason it turns out, he was the nicest man I'd met so far. He apologized for his wife, agreed to my entire plan to work up Rex's problem, including approving all the tests and leaving Rex with us until we got some answers. I almost hated to bring up the final important questions, but because one of the possible causes of a swollen testicle could cause disease in humans too, I would have to 'go there', even if he reacted like his wife.

"Has Rex been used for breeding?" I asked, trying to keep my tone matter of fact.

"I was considering it. He's such a nice dog, but I never got around to it," he replied just as blandly, as if we were talking about the weather.

"Has he ever been in a situation where he was around breeding animals or bitches that may have just had pups?" I asked.

"I've boarded him at his breeder's farm, but I don't think they let him run around where he could have gotten into trouble," he replied.

"Have you or your wife been sick recently, especially with a fever?" I asked, holding my breath.

"No, we've both been fine," he replied, and I could breathe again.

"Well, hopefully it's something else, but we'll be taking precautions in case it's a zoonotic disease, which is an animal disease that can effect humans," I explained.

"You're going to go all hazmat on him?" he asked with a smile and then explained, "I'm the Hazmat Officer at work."

"Yes! I'm going to use special precautions, and I'm going to let you scrub your hands or use some special hand sanitizer before you leave," I replied. "I'll have some answers today, but some of the other tests will take longer, so we'll have to take precautions until we know."

"So he'll be tested first, but then his treatment will be some kind of medicine, not surgery?" he asked with his apprehension evident.

"Well, we may have to do surgery to treat it or maybe even to get a final diagnosis," I replied regretfully. "But the good news is surgery stops the pain quickly."

Mr. Kaye nodded and I continued, "Dr. Vincent will be working with me on Rex's case, so don't worry; we'll come up with the best plan for him."

He smiled and said, "I trust both of you."

I left Mr. Kaye and the tech finishing the paperwork and got ready to meet with Maisy and her son. I printed out information on both toxins. I wanted to be able to answer any questions either one of them had. Looking at the LD 50, the dose that will kill fifty percent of the patients, and then doing some quick math, I had the terrible thought that if one of the tiny Yorkies had eaten whatever Roman had, the outcome could have been a fatal incident. It was an odd silver lining thought to have, but it might be an important warning for the family to hear.

Maisy smiled at me when I walked into the room, but her son just gave me a rather cool, calculating look. He was dressed in an old fashioned preppy style; if you saw someone dressed in the same light colored slacks, pastel shirt and brand name sweater in a movie, you would automatically assume the character was a spoiled brat rich kid. I didn't want to prejudge the kid, since I had learned to like and respect Maisy despite her odd fashion sense, but his half pouty, half arrogant expression was like nails on a chalkboard to me, way too reminiscent of my Uncle's face every time he tried to explain his superior logic about how my money found its way into his account. I smiled at both of them and admonished myself to keep my personal reactions out of the professional setting.

"Dr. Kate, I'd like you to meet my son Lawrence," Maisy announced proudly.

We exchanged equally pleasant "Nice to meet you," greetings and shook hands, and I'm sure we both looked normal as we did, but there was something about him that struck me as off kilter, and it wasn't just because he was obnoxiously popping his gum as I spoke.

I opened up the discussion by asking, "Have you found out any new information about how Roman was exposed to chocolate and marijuana?"

"Tell her," Maisy prompted.

"I don't know anything, Dr. Kate," he said in what I'm sure was supposed to be an open manner. "But I have a concern. There was a misunderstanding with some of my classmates, and I'm afraid someone might have tried to punish me by tossing something over our fence."

"Tell her the whole story, honey," Maisy encouraged her son.

"Some boys were talking about a party that I wasn't invited to and complaining that no one could bring the brownies, so I said I could run home and make some. But when I got to the party, they were angry that they weren't 'enhanced' brownies," Lawrence explained, looking down as he spoke but flicking his eyes up to check my reaction after every few words.

Maisy patted his arm and added, "They pushed him around, hit him with the brownie pan, and then chased him. They could have followed him and found out where he lived."

"I have the complete lab reports for the police," I said.

"My husband is afraid the boys will take it out on Lawrence if we call the police, but we're going to upgrade our security in the kennel and yard," Maisy said.

I went over the pup's discharge instructions with them and asked the technician to get Roman, but then remembered to warn them about the Yorkies.

"Oh, I did want to add that the same dose that made Roman so sick could have killed one of the Yorkies," I warned, and to my horror the quick look that Lawrence gave me was one of glee, like I had just given him the best idea of his life. It flashed across his face, and then disappeared before I could be absolutely sure of what I'd seen. Maisy thanked me profusely and turned her attention to Roman as he wiggled his way into the exam room.

When Maisy started to leave the room, she turned back and asked, "Did I hear you rescued a puppy about Roman's age?"

"I did," I answered grinning. "Roman and Max were in ICU at the same time but were too sick to meet each other!"

"Are you going to take him to one of the puppy classes over at the training center?" she asked.

"I'd love to, but I don't know when Max'll be medically ready for that," I replied.

"I hope we can get the boys in class together," Maisy said. "And it would be our honor to give you the classes as a gift for everything you have done for Roman. It has meant so much to us."

"That's so nice of you, but you don't need to do anything for me," I replied.

"For Max!" she insisted.

"Well, let's see how his recovery goes," I said. "Thank you so much for the offer."

"When do you get to bring Max home?" she asked.

"I'm not sure, depends on how he responds and heals," I replied as I ushered them out of the room. "Bye bye, Roman. You're such a good boy!"

I took about five steps down the hallway toward the treatment area when a thought exploded in my head, and I abruptly spun around to flee upstairs where I could be alone. Oh my God, no pets at the house. Take Max home? There's no home to take him to. What am I going to do? All joy and hope drained out of my body, my knees went wobbly with the loss, and I dropped unceremoniously into the closest chair. What could I do? The apartment was provided by the hospital; I didn't know if I was allowed to move if I could even find an apartment that allowed pets within walking distance? And I didn't want to leave my new house family. More than that, I didn't think I could make myself leave them. And I couldn't leave Max; that was not going to happen. I caught myself hyperventilating and consciously slowed my breathing down before I had to find a paper bag to breathe into. Oh my God, I couldn't see a way out.

"Dr. Kate has an appointment," the intercom broadcast behind me. "Dr. Kate, appointment, exam room four."

I took a deep breath and steeled myself to go back downstairs, determined to lock this terrible thought away to keep it from interfering with doing my job. Last year had been like being out of control on an icy mountain toboggan run, a long terrifying ride down with a ghastly crash landing at the end, but now I found myself on a rollercoaster where the alarming ups and downs came on rapidly and unpredictably, yet I seemed to be heading to an even more spectacular traumatic finale. I never quit and I seldom ask for help, but choosing between this pup and my house family might be what finally breaks me.

Like flipping a switch, I locked my own concerns away, read the chart, and then walked into the room with a smile. There was a grim looking couple with a cat in a carrier on the table.

"I don't want to see it again," cried the woman. "The leg is just flopping."

"Do you know what happened?" I asked gently. "Was your cat outside?"

"No, he was inside," she replied, looking at the man. "He must have fallen."

"I heard a thump," the man said gruffly.

"Can you estimate the height he fell from?" I asked.

The woman shook her head but the man said, "Six feet?"

"And the surface he landed on?" I continued trying to figure out what the chances were that the cat had internal injuries as well as the reported dangling leg.

The man glared at me like I had reached his limit for questions, and the woman just stared at the ground until he spit out his one word answer,

"Tile."

I explained what we were going to do next, including that I would take the cat to the back to do the exam. Maybe rescuing a severely abused pup was making me seeing the negative in people, but the male owner was creeping me out. And the lady seemed strange as well, although maybe she had just gotten grossed out by the injury. She had extremely dramatic makeup on, more appropriate for the stage than daytime wear, which made me wonder if she were a performer of some kind, but I would swear it was applied so thickly to camouflage a black eye.

The sweet little tuxedo cat, a black cat with white markings on his chest and legs like he was wearing formalwear, did have a broken femur, the big bone in his back leg. But good news, I didn't find any other significant problems; he wasn't in shock and he was bright and alert. I made my plan and went back in the room to present it to the owners. I expected resistance to the charges required for an orthopedic repair, but the woman signed the estimate and thanked me while the man continued scowling at us both. He stomped out of the exam room, slamming the door as he left, almost hitting the woman as she tried to exit behind him.

Sheesh! This is definitely one of those days when the dogs and cats seemed like the much better species compared to their humans. I just wanted to get home and make some real food that I could eat before it was stone cold, like a normal person, and not interact with any more people. But as soon as I got little Oreo's protective bandage on and got him settled into his cage, a Boxer with cardiomyopathy arrested in the cage right next to us. As soon as we had the Boxer stabilized, the surgery tech arrived with a critical post-op patient, so I stayed to help in ICU. The next time I looked at the clock, it was after eleven and cooking dinner was no longer an option. Then, just as I was getting ready to leave, the poor Boxer arrested again, and there was no response to the second round of CPR.

So as I dragged my poor aching body home, I had to admit that all that hard work and giving up my chance at a hot meal had all been for nothing. When I arrived at the house, I sneaked in on tip toes, as silently as I could, to avoid disturbing anyone. I just couldn't make myself put on a good face after the day I'd had. I had no doubt that there was a good reason why we couldn't have pets at the house, probably someone was allergic or by decree of the landlord, but tonight I just couldn't pretend that it was okay with me. I had no one but myself to blame for not realizing sooner that I couldn't keep Max at the apartment, but deep down I was inconsolably sad and irrationally mad.

I crept up the stairs, let myself in, flung open my substantial closet door and stood in front of the almost empty expanse, hoping to somehow conjure up clothes clean enough to wear tomorrow so that I could just be done with this stupid day. I picked up my black pants from the closet floor, gave them a shake and decided that they'd be good enough, and chose to wear my clean Purdue T-shirt and hoped it would be sufficiently hidden under my lab coat to be unidentifiable as a T-shirt.

I stumbled over to my rug, starting to shake as I wrapped myself in my comfort quilt, and collapsed onto my sleeping spot. And then I started to sob. At first copious tears poured down my face as I cried for the Boxer we had just lost, and then for the cat whose leg was broken in questionable circumstances, and then for Roman who was poisoned with an equally questionable story. And then I cried for me. The flood of tears slowed but the harsh sobbing continued. I had been given what I so desperately wanted and needed, people to love and care about, who might someday love and care about me, and given a dog to love and protect who had done nothing but love and trust me, even though he had no reason to believe in the goodwill of humankind. Now I would have to choose between them, walk away from one. The pain wasn't just that I would lose one; I didn't think that I could make myself do it. I just couldn't lose either one and survive the experience. I pulled the quilt up over my head and rolled up into a tight little ball trying to keep from shattering into a million pieces.

Then I started crying for the pain of last year, knowing beloved Professors and classmates were turning away from me, acting angry and disappointed in me but never knowing why. I only heard about the lies Justin had been telling about me long months after I had allowed my mentors' palpable disappointment in me to dissolve my confidence. I simply didn't understand what I was doing wrong, and I couldn't begin to fathom what question I could ask that would give me the information I needed.

And then I cried because not only was everything Justin said about me a lie, everything he said to me was an even bigger lie. He not only didn't love me; he had to have hated me to get so much pleasure from inflicting such torture on me. He had been visibly proud of himself for tricking me out of applying for the intern matching program. But why? Was it to simply give himself one less competitor, or was it merely to take something wonderful away from me? I cried and shook and cried some more until I couldn't breathe through my stuffed up nose, but every time I paused and caught my breath another sob would escape until I was utterly wept out and physically wiped out as well. I lay there limply, struggling to breathe through my mouth and making an odd wheezy whining sound on every expiration.

At last I could lie there quietly, but as my breathing calmed I started to hear other noises. It seemed to be coming from my closet: footsteps and something being moved around, and something jiggling or ringing, then some more steps and then a door being closed and a latch catching. Oh my God. With both closet doors open there must be the thinnest of barriers between the back of Dag's and my closets. What did he hear? If I had any emotional ability to respond, I would have suffered from the worst humiliation knowing he heard me lose control, but I had nothing left. So I just rolled to my side and plunged into the dreamless sleep of the hopeless.

Chapter Eleven

I woke up thinking about my Dad. He always said that there was a solution to every problem but warned that sometimes you have to give up your ideal plan and accept a different resolution, might even have to consider an odd or unusual answer. In a crisis he'd say it was unrealistic to hold out for the perfect plan if it's one of the worst days of your life. Maybe I could pay someone to keep Max, or maybe board him over at The Doggy Dude Ranch? It would cost more money than I had, but every day we made it through together gave me more time to contrive a better solution.

I shamefully put on my less than pristine pants and less than professional T-shirt and walked over to the hospital already wearing my lab coat to hide them as much as I could. It was a quiet day in ER, and everyone working seemed subdued so I tried to keep my head down and mouth shut until I knew the lay of the land. It was clear that this was an excellent Veterinary Hospital, and everyone here wanted to do what was best for the pets and their families, but how everyone in this large group got along as individuals while still holding each other's medical practices to high standards seemed to be beyond my ability to understand.

Little Oreo, the cat with the broken leg, was transferred to the surgery department for his fracture repair, but I was able to get reports on him as the day progressed. Thank goodness his surgery went well! I was worried about the home situation we would be returning him to, but there was nothing I could do about that; unfortunately, it wasn't against the law to creep me out. Midafternoon a lady called to inquire whether the Tates had brought Oreo to us and allowed surgery, and while we couldn't tell her anything due to the privacy rules, the phone call made me think that I was right about there being more to this poor kitty's story.

Max was responding well; he would eat whatever the techs gave him so now we had to be careful not to overtax his previously abused GI tract. He had already gained weight, and his skin seemed to be healing normally, without the delay that we could have expected with his neglect. I ran over to the merchandise area of the training center and bought him a rubber chew toy. I couldn't put any rich treats in it to make it irresistible so he didn't seem too interested in chewing on it yet, but when I took him into the exercise pen before I left for the day, he carried it outside with us. The techs told me that when they took him outside, he would sniff and wander around like a normal pup, but when I went out with him he always stayed right next to me. This trip he walked by my side but seemed to be inexplicably proud of himself for having his toy, and carried his tail held high, curved over his back, and had a little bounce in his step, which just made him even more adorable, if that was even possible.

The news for Rex was mixed, his most worrisome test came back negative for the zoonotic disease Brucella, so that was great news! Dr. Vincent spoke with Mr. Kaye and together they decided that the quickest way to provide pain relief and get a definitive answer was to neuter Rex as soon as possible, get a direct culture and submit the tissue to the Purdue Pathology Lab. Even though I didn't get a vote, I agreed with their plan and was curious about what the pathologist would discover. Rex was certainly a case I would never forget, for so many reasons!

Plans were made for the Saturday night intern dinner; Stretch promised to give me a ride so that was one obstacle out of the way. The Doctors were taking us to the country club so I would have to shuffle my meager wardrobe pieces around and try to make a suitable outfit. Maybe I would put my hair up in a fancy twist and hope that it would make me more presentable.

I walked back to my apartment with my feet dragging, afraid to get home this early and be forced to spend the evening confronting my personal problems. What was I going to do about Max and my increasingly desperate financial situation? I couldn't take extra paid shifts at any of the hospitals in our complex until I had been there ninety days, and while I would be willing to pet sit or clean out cars or anything else respectable that anyone needed, I wasn't sure it was appropriate.

I tried to sneak into the house again, but I did want to check my mailbox. I think Phil felt sorry for me because he often gave me mail addressed to occupant, I assume just so that occasionally I would get to open something other than just my utility bills. The only personal mail that I had ever received here was my invitation for the Fall Fantasy charity banquet in Fort Wayne that Lainey's Dad had somehow intercepted and sent on to me. One of the prestigious service awards presented at the fundraiser was sponsored by Daniel Garrison, the CEO of one of the largest companies in Fort Wayne, but it was named in honor of my mother so I usually tried to attend. This year I would never be able to overcome all the financial and practical roadblocks to attending, so sadly I'd have to miss out. As soon as I clicked the mailbox door shut, Mei's door opened, and then Phil's door opened directly after that.

"Hey, Katie girl, you're home early," Phil said warmly. "How's Max?"

"He's doing unbelievably well," I replied. "Thanks for asking."

Mei came over and stood next to me, and Phil asked, "Do you have a minute? Can we talk to you?"

"Sure," I replied hesitantly. I should have been brave and let him off the hook and tell him that I already knew I couldn't bring Max home. But I selfishly welcomed even five more minutes of peace before I heard the finality of the distressing words so I kept my mouth shut.

I followed Phil into his apartment and was surprised to see Dag and Ethan already sitting in the living room, although they both stood up when I walked into the room. Phil had the seating; loveseat, recliner, and overstuffed comfy chairs, arranged in a circle, and he indicated with a sweep of his arm I should pick my spot. One of the overstuffed chairs was the only spot of color in the room, a bright turquoise blue, and I picked it because it was so huge I could curl up in it for what was sure to be an uncomfortable intervention of some kind.

My housemates sat down and smiled at me, but no one spoke until Phil said, "We can tell that you're going through hard times."

They all nodded and Phil said, "And we're not the type of people who want to pry. We have our own secrets," and all four vigorously nodded again, and he continued, "and we appreciate each other's space, but we'd like to find a way to help you."

"I really screwed up," I admitted. "And it can't be fixed. I just have to start over."

"We'd like to help you start over," Phil said.

I looked at them one at a time, and the matching looks of care and concern tore off the patch I had applied to my emotional self-control. And as the tears started to fall silently I asked incredulously, "Why?"

They looked at each other in confusion and Ethan started crying with me, but no one answered. Finally Mei said, "You need help, and we need to help people."

I looked at them with disbelief, and in retrospect each of my questions was ruder than the one before, and asked, "I have no time and no money; how will I pay you back?"

"Pay back?" Phil asked a little stiffly. "How did I pay you back for saving my life?"

"You don't pay someone back for something like that," I assured him. "I was just at the right place at the right time."

Dag spread his arms in a kind of emphatic 'that's our point' gesture and said, "And we just happen to be here when you need help."

"I don't want to take advantage of your good natures," I replied, impatiently dashing the tears off my face. "If I have to take advantage of someone, I don't want it to be people who're as good to me as you all are."

Ethan wiped tears off his face as well and said, "I don't think bad people will help you."

Dag laughed out loud, and agreed, "He has a point."

I nodded, and then tried to shake off my feelings of fear and distrust and past pain, at the same time struggling to put any of it into words that anyone but me would understand.

"Were you shaking your head yes or no?" Dag asked rhetorically, laughing good naturedly as he patted me on the shoulder.

"All of us have suffered through some kind of harsh times and the resultant starting over process," Mei stated. "And one way that we make sense of our trauma is to use the strength and wisdom we developed through our experiences to help others. Some call it being a wounded healer."

I nodded with understanding and Mei continued, "And yes you are expected to pay it back, but odds are it will never be paid back to the four of us; it'll be paid back to some unknown people in the future. What some people call paying it forward."

Ethan nodded vigorously and added, "At different times Uncle Phil has helped each of us, but it was you who got to save him. I really wished it had been me, to pay him back for all he's done for me."

Dag agreed, "I wished it was me, too."

"I think we need to ask Kate what help she needs," Mei said in her quiet calm voice. "I don't appreciate people deciding what I need without listening to me about how I feel. Some of what people have unilaterally done to 'help' me have been the absolute worst thing for me in the situation."

Ethan nodded in agreement and said, "It's why I don't usually like people to help me either. They just want to show off what they can do better than I do. They never want to help me learn how to do it."

I smiled gratefully and said with trepidation, "My biggest problem is not having a place for Max. I can't make myself leave this house and the four of you, but I can't abandon Max. I need you and he needs me."

They all grinned in unison, even Mei who rarely gave anything but the gentlest of smiles, and Phil said, "That's easy, we already took a vote, and Max is officially the new house dog," and then continued emphatically, "the one and only house pet."

Relief flooded through me, but I couldn't completely believe or accept what I was hearing.

"I'd like you to teach me how to take care of him so I could watch him sometimes," Ethan said.

"I would so love your help, Ethan," I replied. "I work really long days sometimes."

Dag added, "You and I can work something out so you can safely use my fenced yard for him."

"That's settled then," Phil said. "What else do you need?"

I smiled and replied, "That's all I need. I can handle everything else."

"Okay," Phil said skeptically. "We've come up with a few ideas of our own. May we run them by you?"

"Sure," I agreed.

Mei pulled out a yellow legal pad with a neat list on it and said, "Dag, you go first."

"My Grandmother has a sectional couch she wanted to give me, but I prefer the leather one I already have. So now she wants to give it to you because I happened to mention it's the exact brown color that Max will be when his hair grows back in. I can borrow Phil's truck and Ethan and I can move it. Is that okay with you?" Dag asked.

"That would be great," I accepted thankfully.

"I have a practically new mattress and box springs that someone abandoned at the apartments, can we get that for you too?" Phil asked.

"The internship just lasts one year. After that I may have to move, and you'll get stuck with it again," I said.

"That's okay," Phil replied. "I deal with people leaving stuff all the time; it's part of my job."

"Thank you all so much," I said, stretching my legs out and getting ready to escape to my room. "That's all so generous."

Mei continued, "We have a couple more things."

I settled back into the chair and, starting to feel a little dazed, said, "Okay."

They exchanged brief looks and Mei said, "Maybe just one more?"

I nodded and she continued, "Can we buy you a few supplies, like they're house warming presents?"

I attempted a smile, but started crying again and couldn't answer. They all stood up, thanked me for letting them help, and then walked me to the door. I felt overwhelmed as I trudged upstairs but deep inside me, right alongside my monsters born of pain, a lovely magical creature born of gratitude came into being.

Chapter Twelve

My shifts for the rest of the week in the ER flew by in a flash, and I was beyond happy at the way everything was working out. My attitude and returning confidence made the work pressures, unpredictable cases, and offbeat clients seem more like fun challenges. It was enjoyable working with the other Interns and even Quickcut because they were all acting super sweet to each other, I assume so they wouldn't be the one to get blamed for the past problems. Dr. Vincent was his very best gregarious self and, best of all, nobody died in ICU!

Max was responding spectacularly, acting comfortable and energetic even as his pain meds were weaned away, and even better he was eating like I do when there's free food. I spent as much of my down time with him as I could and had even started to teach him simple commands. Now whenever one of the techs even barely rustled the packaging reaching in for a tasty treat to sneak a pill down another patient, Max would promptly sit down and whine for a treat of his own! His wounds were healing well, and I planned to bring him home as soon as I removed his drains, possibly on Monday.

I rushed home Saturday after my shift to get ready for the big dinner out and discovered that the house guys must have been working hard in my absence because I had furniture! The sectional couch was so beautiful and in such pristine condition I wondered if they had fibbed to me about Dag's grandmother and had bought me a new couch. Phil's turquoise oversized chair completed the arrangement and a note pinned to the chair explained that he had originally bought the chair to bring some color into his living room but had been inordinately irritated by its brightness ever since the day it arrived. There was a soft knock at the door, and I opened it to Dag and Ethan, both grinning and excited to see my reaction.

"I love it!" I gushed. "It's so perfect; you sure you didn't buy me a new couch?"

"Nope!" Dag denied adamantly, showing me the pile of brightly colored pillows and throws he was carrying. "Nana sent these too because now they don't match her new décor."

"And when Uncle Phil saw the turquoise in the pillows he said," Ethan paused for dramatic effect with a mischievous glint in his eye, then grinned and continued, "he said he could dump that dreadful turquoise chair on you because it matched."

Both men laughed and I joined them while I protested, "I love that chair! It's not the least bit dreadful!"

"You like the accessories?" Dag asked.

"I do! I love the bright colors, but I don't recognize the patterns. Where are they from?" I asked.

"India," he replied. "At least the pillows are."

India, I thought to myself; that would explain Dag's jet black hair, large expressive eyes, and maybe his hard to categorize beautiful brown skin. Heritage from some other continent would have to explain his brilliant blue eyes however, and his chiseled facial features seemed to reflect an Asian legacy more than anything else. I would have loved to ask him more about it but I had learned the hard way that while it's fine to discuss for hours possible combinations of breeds that might have contributed to an individual dog's genetic makeup, it was not socially acceptable to do so for a human.

Reading my mind, Dag asked, "It's killing you isn't it?"

I considered pretending I didn't know what he was talking about, but I just couldn't be anything but open and honest with him so I replied, "Yep," and grinned up at him.

"What?" Ethan asked, bewildered.

"She wants to know about my ethnic background," Dag replied.

"Me, too!" Ethan said. "Can she play the game with us?"

"She can," Dag replied. "There's a hundred dollar reward for the first person that can come up with the origins of all of my great grandparents!"

"All eight are from different countries!" Ethan added.

"Hmm," I said. "Do you tell us when we get one right?"

"I don't confirm, but I will occasionally deny," he said laughing again.

"So one ancestor is Indian?" I asked.

"Which kind?" he asked with a teasing tone and a slight change in his expression.

"Ahhh, as in from India or a Native American?" I asked, more to myself than to him, but closely watched his face as he tilted his head and arched his eyebrows, and I jumped on his reaction and exclaimed, "Both!"

He looked at me with admiration and, while neither confirming nor denying, insisted, "I'm never playing poker with you!"

Ethan looked back and forth between us and then mouthed, "Both?" at me and I shrugged and then nodded. Ethan announced, "I'm halfway to the hundred dollars!"

"What about the bed?" Dag asked.

"I haven't even looked," I said, then spun and bolted for the bedroom. The bed was simple, just a mattress and box springs on a low frame, but looked just as immaculate as the sofa.

"Wonderful," I raved and felt grateful for everyone's generosity, but then looking at the pink shag rug now arranged next to the bed, I felt some shame at how I had been sleeping.

Ethan and Dag seemed to pick up my mixed emotions and were looking awkwardly around the room instead of at me so I impishly exclaimed, "The crime scene cleaners did a great job on the mattress!"

They were both silent for a second and then Dag laughed so loudly that he startled Ethan. I watched the realization of what I was implying spread over his face until Ethan grinned and said, "I get it!"

"Thank you so much for all of this," I said exchanging a meaningful look with Ethan and then with Dag. "I'm so grateful. But now I have to get ready for dinner with the boss. Or bosses, I'm not sure who's who in that zoo! And with my extensive wardrobe it might take me awhile to find something to wear."

"Where you going?" Dag asked as I walked them to the door.

"The Country Club," I replied.

"Oh, I should have grabbed some of my sister's castoffs for you when I was home," Dag lamented.

"Issa's a model!" Ethan explained.

"Cool!" I said. "But no thanks; they might make me pay for my dinner if I looked like I could afford it."

The men exited laughing, and I ran to the bathroom to put my hair up and apply some makeup, if I hadn't forgotten how to do it during these last couple of months of spending all my time at work. Despite my joke, there was no 'choosing an outfit'; my black pants were the dressiest of my three pair, and I had one fitted, slightly dressy cream jacket. And the only top to wear under the jacket was the nicest thing that I had ever owned, an ivory silk camisole with a golden dragon hand painted on the front with its tail wrapping artistically around to the back. Lainey's dad had brought matching tops back from China for us when we were in college, and he told us he had chosen gold for 'his two Purdue golden girls'. If you looked really closely at the dragon's eyes however the shirts were customized. The dragon's eyes on Lainey's were black and gold volleyballs while my dragon had slightly aqua blue eyes like mine, and the Veterinary symbol, the staff of Asclepius with the Veterinary V, meticulously painted in the pupil opening.

I had never worn it before, except briefly in pictures, because it was so precious to me I was afraid of ruining it, but had packed it for the aborted weekend trip to see Lainey that fateful day because she had begged me to. I truly had nothing else to wear, but when I put it on it was thin enough and cut in such a way that my black bra, my only bra, showed through and stuck out in all the wrong places. I started to stress out at the setback, but as I stared at the mirror the downstairs buzzer rang announcing Stretch's arrival. I took a deep breath and said, "Screw it," under my breath, reached up under the camisole and whipped the bra off. I buttoned both jacket buttons, prayed that I didn't get too hot at dinner, but rejoiced that my gorgeous golden dragon still stared out of the deep v of the jacket. I grabbed my sparkly gold heels by their straps and ran downstairs bare footed.

Stretch and Taren were waiting for me on the porch and seemed to be in cheerful moods. We joked around all the way to the country club about the different ways Dr. Drama was going to torture us at dinner, but we were pleasantly surprised when we got there that he seemed to be committed to a genial host persona. Quickcut and Melanie were already seated, and Dr. Drama made a big show of escorting us to our seats at a large round table and ordering wine and appetizers for the table. Dr. Tolliver was wearing a beautiful red dress and seemed much more relaxed and engaged than she was at the hospital; she and Dr. Blackwell were laughing like two schoolgirls about something as we joined them. Dr. Drama encouraged Dr. Blackwell to tell some of her stories, warning us that they were all parables in disguise and telling us to take an important lesson away from each one. Except then he started harassing her as soon as she spoke her first word and never let her finish a story without interrupting multiple times, until it was impossible to tell what the original lesson might have been. She took it well, harassing him right back, and between their horsing around and the wine, the dinner seemed less like a prelude to an inquisition and more like an opportunity to get to know them and each other better.

When the eating part of dinner wrapped up Dr. Blackwell took over the direction of our conversation and asked, "Stretch, what's going on over at the apartment?"

He looked unhappy at being put on the spot but then answered, "We're all sorry we let apartment problems affect our behavior at the hospital, but I think we have it straightened out now."

Taren added, "We had some difficulty keeping the hospital hierarchy out of our home life."

"I wasn't trying to control you at the apartment just because I outrank you at the hospital," Quickcut interjected in a quarrelsome tone.

"Although all three of us thought so," Melanie responded, eliciting a loud exasperated sigh from Quickcut.

"Is it something you can work through?" Dr. Blackwell asked. "Resort to a chore chart and a few agreed upon rules covering the disagreements?"

"Kate and I should just exchange apartments," Quickcut countered, looking at me with a threatening glare, just daring me to object to his plan.

I glanced away initially, afraid of the confrontation, but then thought of Max and looked back directly at him and insisted, "No."

"What?" he responded indignantly.

"I can't," I explained. "They're letting me keep Max."

"It doesn't matter," Dr. Blackwell said. "Phil is adamant that Kate stays at the house. I already called him because a switch seemed like a logical solution to me also. Our valuable arrangement with the apartment management is all due to Phil, so whatever he says goes."

"But that makes no sense," Quickcut started to object, but Dr. Blackwell spoke over him and said, "Done deal. New topic."

"We can work through it," Stretch said, "maybe a chore chart and a quiet sign to use when we're on different shifts. But I have another concern; Kate is being left out of a lot of the Intern interactions, good and bad."

"Excellent point," Dr. Blackwell said. "I've been concerned about that too."

"Pizza and beer," Dr. Drama interjected.

"What?" Dr. Blackwell asked, puzzled.

"We should pick a night, buy them pizza and beer each week, and require them to discuss a topic assigned by, let's see, you!" Dr. Drama suggested with his typical flare as he pointed at Dr. Blackwell.

The three senior clinicians exchanged looks and then nods, but Dr. Tolliver added, "And salad. You and I will arrange for a healthy garden salad."

All three nodded again and Dr. Blackwell said, "Great plan. I'll speak to Molly tomorrow and get it started. I'm thinking Wednesday night, anyone have a conflict in their personal life?"

None of us replied so she continued, "Anyone even have a personal life?"

We all laughed and then shook our heads forlornly. Dr. Drama reached into his wallet, pulled out a stack of twenties and some kind of coupon and then handed them to Stretch saying, "Here, take the Interns to the pub and brainstorm how to make our plan work over BOGO drinks. Quickcut, stay here with us and we'll discuss leadership and how to be an effective mentor."

The four of us stood up, thanked our mentors effusively and made our escape. Melanie had ridden over with Quickcut so she climbed into Stretch's car with us. They told stories about Quickcut's behavior around the apartment and I'm sure him ordering them when and how to clean the toilets must have made them angry at the time, but the way they told the story now made it seem hilarious instead. I offered to have pizza night at my apartment, now that I had furniture, so that we could avoid Quickcut and any unwanted interference issues, and they gratefully agreed.

The bar was Saturday night busy when we got there, they even had a bouncer checking IDs at the door. I was distracted by the crowd and the noise, so I was shocked when we made it to the front of the line and I realized it was Dag!

"Looking good, Kate," he said with an amused smile at my surprise. "Hey, Randy, find these hard working docs a table."

"Thanks, Dag," I replied with a smile and introduced him to my friends.

The waiter came right over and led us to an empty table tucked into the corner with a good view of the stage. I kind of felt at home because my whole class used to go out after our professional meetings to a bar a lot like this one. I wasn't much an adventurous drinker, but I was already sweating in my buttoned up jacket so I skipped my usual beer and chose an enormous frozen drink to help me cool off. Stretch made fun of us for drinking Margaritas in an Irish pub and proudly ordered a Guinness, but promised he would have just one so he could drive us all home safely. And then we promptly forgot all about discussing, much less solving, any of our problems and just had fun. We told stories and drank and laughed and made fun of each other. We got up to dance, making some of the nearby gentleman complain that Stretch shouldn't monopolize all three ladies at his table, and when we finally collapsed back in our seats fresh drinks had magically appeared from our new admirers.

The drinks weren't cooling me off as fast as the dancing was making me hotter, so at first my liquor logic told me to drink faster and then it told me it would be cooler up with Dag at the front door. So I skipped over and hopped up onto the empty stool next to him with such enthusiasm that I almost slid off the other side.

"Well, Katie girl, looks like you're having a good time," Dag said, with another amused smile.

"I am!" I replied as I steadied myself on the high stool which seemed to be moving under me. "I'd be having a better time if I weren't so hot!"

"Why don't you take your jacket off?" he asked in a patient tone of voice.

"I can't," I said sensibly, but then wondered why I couldn't. I had a top on, even if it was a pretty revealing top, so I continued, "I guess I could."

I took off my jacket, laid it across my lap, and turned back to Dag who was looking at me with wide eyes and a sharp intake of breath. I was confused for a second, but then realized he must be admiring my dragon so I asked, "Don't you just love my dragon? He was hand painted in China."

Dag choked and then chuckled and said, "Yeah, I like your dragon."

"Can you see his eyes?" I said leaning closer to him. "Can you see the Vet symbol in there?"

"I can see something," he said and leaned back. "You dropped your jacket; maybe you should put it back on."

"No, it was tooooo hot," I objected and hopped down to retrieve it, missing my landing a bit, wobbling and hitting my head on Dag's shoulder. I shook my head, tossed the jacket at Dag and trotted off, saying over my shoulder, "Be right back."

There was a line to the ladies room so I leaned up against the wall to rest my spinning head as I waited. After it was finally my turn, I came out of the stall and caught sight of myself in the mirror and couldn't believe how much skin I was showing. Intent on retrieving my jacket, I walked out of the bathroom, bounced my shoulder off the door jam, and then froze in place because even in my befuddled state I was shocked to see a couple making out right there in the hallway. I knew it was rude to stare, but I couldn't believe that they were going at it right there in plain view, but then I was ashamed of myself for watching and rushed past them, sneaking a final glance over my shoulder. In horror I realized it was Lars and Taren. They didn't even notice me, but I practically ran all the way back to Dag.

"Oh my goodness," I said as I sprinted over and grabbed his arm. Dag visibly startled and turned aggressively toward me, but then his face softened, and he smiled tolerantly at me.

"Katie?" he asked.

"What?' I asked in response.

"Oh my goodness, what?" he prompted.

"Oh, I just caught Lars and Taren making out in the hallway!" I replied animatedly. "I can't believe it."

Dag laughed, shaking his head and turning away for a minute to check an ID. Melanie walked up and asked, "Where did Stretch and Taren go?"

"Nowhere we can go," I answered, then laughed maniacally at my amazing wit.

"They left?" she asked incredulously. "They're my ride and I want to go home. Don't you need a ride?"

"No," I replied as she turned back towards our table. "I mean yes I need a ride, but no, I don't want to leave now."

I looked around me when I finished and then looked up at Dag and complained, "Talking to nobody."

He looked at me with such a sweet expression, then smiled and said, "I think you should catch that ride. I can't leave until after we close at three."

"Okay, I'll go catch them," I said jumping back off the stool, wobbling for a minute and then making my way through the crowd to what had been our table. Except now it was full of strangers.

"Come sit with us," one of them offered, then they all stood up and shifted around until I was surrounded by five or six rough looking guys staring down at me. In that split second my alcohol fed carefree boldness vanished, and I realized just how vulnerable I was. My fear must have shown and instead of embarrassing them it seemed to excite them; they looked focused and ready to explode into action just like a dog when he spots a rabbit ready to run.

I tried to back out of the circle and ran into one of them who then pushed up against me and said, "Ohhh, she likes me."

I said, "Excuse me, please," and tried to wiggle away from him as he said, "Ohhh! Now she wants to dance with me."

Then he said "Ohhh-ph," as his breath was abruptly forced out; he let out another groan as he flew away from me and fell over clutching his ribs.

"Get out of here," Dag bellowed over the music. "All of you, now."

"We're just having a little fun with her," one of the guys whined.

The biggest guy leaned aggressively toward Dag and argued, "She's practically naked."

"Which is her right," Dag said as he helped me on with my jacket, and then nestled me into him so while we were both facing the group, his left arm encircled me protectively and his right arm was held out to the side holding a short stick of some kind.

"What the fuck is your problem?" he snarled, as he whipped the stick down with a sharp crack and it lengthened into an obvious weapon. "Make me use this, and I'll have you all banned."

The aggressor wilted and whined, "Sorry, Dagger. I'd never give you trouble."

"That would be a mistake," Dag replied. "But a bigger mistake would be to ever touch a woman like that again, especially this woman."

The men started trying to appease him, speaking at the same time, insisting they were leaving, it was all just a silly joke, no reason to over react, and they'd protect me with their lives from this point forward. They gathered their belongings, and walked straight out the front door as Dag pulled me back against him and the patrons in our vicinity moved away and studiously looked anywhere but at us.

"Katie girl, you're just all sorts of trouble tonight," he said, whispering in my right ear, but his voice only sounded half amused, the other half sounded sad, almost wistful. His hand slipped down and touched bare skin on my stomach where my pants had slipped down and the camisole had floated away. His hand roamed in an increasingly larger circle under my shirt and then he tightened me into him even closer. I felt his breath on my neck, rapid and hot. He kissed me on the shoulder and I couldn't catch my own breath. I swear my heart skipped a couple of beats before resuming its pounding. In that moment I wanted him with a white hot ferocity at the same time I unexpectedly understood what I had been missing in my previous relationship. Making out in the hallway, which just minutes ago seemed silly and humiliating for Lars and Taren, now seemed tame compared to what I wanted to do with him. I wanted him without concern about what I should want or should do, and it sure didn't matter what was reasonable or smart or in any way good for me. I think it was the first time I understood how desire could be such a potent active force on a person's life. It seemed to be stronger than any other emotion, including my recent soul destroying shock and pain, and certainly more powerful than the old fashioned common sense that had long been my way of life. It was the most wonderful eye opening insight in the world and the most painful. If I had gotten myself into so much trouble without it, how much worse could I do under passion's influence?

He simply held me for a few minutes, our rapid breathing suddenly synchronized, then he kissed me on the top of my head and said, "Let's get back up front and hope your friends waited for you."

"Waited for me?" I asked, proud that my voice sounded so normal.

"The three of them were leaving, but I told them to wait," he replied with a smile. Halfway back he paused and looked at me with what appeared to be distress in his eyes and said, "My life is complicated right now and I don't want you to be hurt by any of it."

"My life is beyond complicated," I replied sadly, not knowing for sure what we were even talking about but wanting to acknowledge that I knew how messed up my life was. But then I couldn't help myself and looked up at him with a brilliant joyful smile.

He looked at me with surprise, then gave a thoughtful half smile and said, "Well, isn't this interesting?"

"Isn't what interesting?" Stretch asked as we approached.

"Life," Dag replied, as he patted my back and climbed on his stool to resume his duties. "Isn't life interesting?"

Chapter Thirteen

I woke to loud banging on my door and Ethan shouting, "Kate, the hospital called you on my phone, they need you to come in."

I dashed to the door, desperately fumbling with the locks but finally flinging it open as I cried, "Is Max alright?"

"They didn't say anything about him, they said one of the doctors is sick," he explained, handing me his phone. "You can call them back."

"Thanks," I replied as I took the phone and motioned him into the apartment. Thank goodness I was sleeping in yoga pants and a T-shirt so I was close to being decent; I was so worried about Max that I hadn't even considered how I answered the door. I got the hospital on the line and found out that Melanie had called in sick for her emergency shift. My guess is that she's even less accustomed to drinking than I am, and I wasn't feeling all that great this morning.

"I'm sorry they woke you so early on a Sunday, but I'm glad someone remembered you're my emergency contact," I said apologetically.

"I am?" Ethan asked with such a serious expression that I knew it was a big deal to him.

"I apologize, but I gave them your number just once. I promise I'll get a phone as soon as I can," I assured him.

"But now I'm helping the animals, right?" he asked.

"Absolutely!" I replied.

"Good," he said happily. "Tell them they can call me anytime they need you."

I got ready in under ten minutes and jogged to the hospital. My stomach was not happy with me, but I was lucky I felt human at all this early after drinking last night, although I was seriously formulating a plan to assault someone for their coffee. My hangover seemed minor enough that I was sure it wouldn't get in the way of performing my job. Or so I told myself as I jogged over.

I walked into chaos, and not the cool controlled kind! The Sunday morning ER shift usually starts out slowly and then as each hour passes it builds to a massive crescendo by evening. Too many fun weekend activities contain hidden dangers for pets, with trauma and GI upset leading the long list. But today the fun must have started early because all the rooms and treatment tables were already full. And then there is the universal Murphy's Law of personnel calling in sick; you'll always be short staffed on the busiest day possible.

"Thanks for coming in," Dr. Nikki, one of the full time ER Docs, said as I walked by. "Just jump in on the cases up front. I'm tied up with three major traumas back here."

Jillian, the tech working with Dr. Nikki, pointed at the treatment tables in turn and said, "HBC, HBM, HBL!"

I asked, "Hit by car, hit by motorcycle, but what is L?"

"Hell is the ER this morning," the tech said with a brief grin, then she grimaced and explained, "Lawnmower."

I finished getting my medical paraphernalia situated in various pockets and headed up front, ready to start the day, and as I walked through the near door, my technician for the day walked through the far door. Since it was Felicity, my nemesis from last week, we exchanged hostile glares. But then as we both walked toward the shelf stacked with waiting charts, it all struck me as ridiculous. She had her job: triaging the patients so that the most critical received the quickest attention and then wrangling the doctors and other technicians so that everyone else had to wait the absolute shortest time possible. My job was to let her do her job and focus on each patient as I saw them. At least that's what I thought Dr. Blackwell had tried to tell me.

So when we met at the patient records shelf I extended my hand with a big smile and asked, "Truce?" and she smiled a tepid smile back and shook my hand, then handed me a chart and said, "Room two," just as we heard a loud crash from a different room, and she exchanged the charts and amended her directive, "Room one."

We walked in to see two adults wrestling a young Shepherd who was throwing herself around the room trying to get her paws up to her face. When the owners saw us, they let go and the poor dog put her head down, opened her mouth wide and desperately tried to get her splayed paws into her mouth. Felicity grabbed her front feet and I grabbed her muzzle and tilted her head back just to get an initial peek of what she had gotten stuck in her mouth. I knew I'd have to give her a sedative or anesthesia so that I could safely remove the foreign body and at the same time explore the mouth for what damage had been done or what splinters or residue had been left. But instead I had a clear view of the stick neatly caught across the upper arcade between two teeth. I impulsively reached for the stick, my left hand holding tight on that upper jaw to protect my vulnerable right hand extending in, grabbed it and tugged it out. Felicity and I let go and the hugely relieved dog jumped up on me and exuberantly licked my face and neck. I briefly stroked the thankful dog and then nodded at Felicity who grabbed her in the typical technician restraint hug, one arm under her neck, one arm under her middle with the wiggly patient snuggled tight into her body. I examined her mouth again and there was no blood, bruising or visible damage, she had luckily managed somehow to trap it only on her teeth. I offered to do a more complete oral exam under chemical restraint, but the owners chose to watch her carefully and bring her back if she showed any sign of problems. I gave the happy dog a treat which she gobbled up and swallowed easily so I left Felicity to finish up.

Room two was a crying woman with a suffering Pit Bull stretched out motionless on the exam table. Felicity's initial notes contained some important clues to what might be wrong with Dora: she had a fever, wasn't spayed, and had been in heat four or five weeks ago. That's a common history of a serious uterine infection in a bitch called a pyometra, or pyo in hospital short hand. Dora's physical exam was consistent with my initial concerns, so I explained the testing necessary to confirm the presumptive diagnosis, but warned Mrs. Chade that we were probably looking at major surgery.

I started to inform her about the money involved, but she waved me off as she started to cry again and barely managed to gasp out, "It doesn't matter. Whatever she needs. She's all I have."

I nodded and said, "I'm going to go order those tests, and I'll be back when I have the results."

"One thing I don't understand. I've had another dog with this kind of infection, and she had all sorts of disgusting stuff draining out of her. Dora hasn't had any," the owner said almost normally, as if she hadn't just been sobbing mere moments before.

"That's one way that patients can present," I explained. "I think Dora has an even more serious condition called a closed pyometra in which the material can't drain out so it builds up inside and the body absorbs all the dangerous bacterial toxins."

"Okay," she said nodding. "Help her as quickly as possible."

Just then we both could hear the Shepherd's owner announce to the waiting room, "That Doctor is amazing! She's a miracle worker!"

"You have to perform a miracle for Dora; she's my disabled granddaughter's only friend," she said clutching my arm.

With my chest tight from the pressure and way too busy to explain that while I craved being a miracle worker, I wasn't in control of who got a lucky break with the way a stick got stuck and who didn't. I wrote orders for Dora and then let Felicity direct me to my next patient. That poor dog was the first of three vomiting and diarrhea cases, and when I had them all settled in the hospital on IV fluids, I knew why Emergency Vets dreaded the summer grilling season almost as much as they hated the days after Thanksgiving. Holidays meant that careful owners, who were ordinarily strict about their dog's diets, were distracted, which allowed dogs to get into all sorts of unusual foods. And then there are those owners who give party leftovers to beloved pets so that these precious family members aren't left out of the celebrations. And who hasn't been tempted into giving that leftover burger to the dog who had been staring at it so longingly? I know Justin and I gave into that temptation with our Golden once and thank goodness she didn't get too sick, but she did have messy diarrhea all over Justin's apartment. Which I guess in retrospect wasn't such a bad thing since it happened right before I discovered all the horrid things he was saying about me. But nothing could ever pay him back for claiming sole ownership of my beloved girl and selling her behind my back.

I walked to the treatment and laboratory area, the so called 'back' that most of us working in veterinary hospitals constantly reference, to check on Dora's blood tests. Honestly I was hoping they were delayed so that I could grab a minute to sit and rest. Even mildly hungover I lacked my usual stamina and started to worry that I wouldn't be functional by the end of my shift. Directly after having that thought, I noticed a huge cup of coffee sitting on my desk, along with a bag holding an egg sandwich with a note saying, "Sorry you had to work today, Dag," with a cute little line drawing of a girl with an ice bag on her head. I felt a spark ignite deep inside me that spread warmth and energy across my body. I was shocked at the intensity of my feelings, and surprised how the simple kindness and support recharged my vitality more than the coffee and food ever would.

But I needed all the help I could get so I took an enormous gulp of coffee and a big bite of the egg sandwich and walked over to the blood machine just in time to grab my report coming off the lab printer. Dora's results were consistent with the uterine infection I was concerned about, but the kidney values were still within normal limits which gave me hope that the dreaded kidney damage hadn't occurred yet. I'd need to get an ultrasound confirmation, but it was time to warn the owner and the surgery department that as soon as we had Dora stabilized, she would need lifesaving surgery.

The discussion about surgery went well until I told the owner that Felicity would discuss the quote, including payment options, and she started crying and begging me to do the surgery immediately as I tried to leave. I reassured her that we had to take the proper steps in the proper order for the proper amount of time, and any delay was the right thing for Dora and done only to help her. She started crying to Felicity about it being Sunday and the banks were closed and she had grabbed the wrong purse, but I snuck out before she was done with her litany.

The flood of patients through the front door had slowed down, but now we had bottlenecks at all the diagnostic and treatment stations in back so I started helping in radiology, including assisting with Dora's ultrasound. Her uterus was huge and we all started making bets about how much it was going to weigh when we got it out, the present hospital champion was a three pound uterus from a twelve pound dog, i.e. twenty-five percent of that poor dog's body was infected uterus! It may sound heartless to have competitions, but I realized early that things like crowning imaginary champions was another one of Dr. Vincent's ways of finding solace. It was horribly sad that the infection was so bad and had been going on for so long that the uterus could get that big, but it was reassuring that we had already saved a dog in even more grim condition.

Dora responded quickly to fluids and initial medications, but late in the afternoon when the surgery department was ready for her, the owner wasn't answering her cell phone. Her last words had been to do the surgery as soon as possible, and she had signed both the surgical release form and quote so I told Quickcut to go ahead and take Dora to surgery. I would have loved to observe Dora's procedure, but we were still trying to catch up with all our hospitalized patients so I had to skip it.

Max was a little put out that I wasn't spending any time with him and would fuss when I walked through his ward, but medically his recovery was so outstanding I couldn't justify the time with him. His guilt trip proved successful however when I used my only brief break to take him outside. Taren was in one of the enclosures with an ICU patient and I stood by the fence to chat with her.

"How are you feeling?" I asked.

"Perfect," she replied sarcastically but with a big smile, her dimples at their most charming. "How about you?"

"The same," I said as I rolled my eyes. "But worth it!"

"I agree!" she said. "It looked like you were having a good time with your friend Dog!"

"Dog?" I asked, wracking my muddled memory of last night's adventure.

"The bouncer?" she asked.

"Dag," I explained. "His name is Dag!"

"What's that short for?" she asked, obviously baffled.

I shrugged my shoulders and replied, "He told Dr. Drama it was short for Dagger but I don't actually know if that's true."

"What's his last name?" she asked, still trying to make it all fit.

I stopped and gave her what I'm sure was a funny look and answered, "I don't really know. Everyone at the house calls him Dag, even his postbox just says Dag on it."

"That's kind of funny," Taren said with a fake frown. "We all thought you called him Dog when you introduced him, and we loved it! We thought it was a perfect nickname for a Vet's boyfriend and I'm seriously disappointed his name isn't Dog."

I shrugged again and replied with a laugh, "He's not my boyfriend either, but I'm wishing and hoping!"

Taren laughed out loud, "Wishing and hoping! You're so funny!"

"Well, I'd better get back inside, we're getting roasted in ER," I grumbled.

"It's no better in ICU," Taren said nodding. "And Muncher here refuses to pee anywhere but in a pristinely clean cage, so I'm wasting time waiting out here with him."

An hour before the next shift was due to arrive, the rush of new patients started up again. My favorite patient of the day was the cutest fluffy mop of a teeny tiny dog named Baby who had a fishhook imbedded in her little leg. While I was carrying her to treatment to give her a touch of sedative for the removal procedure, she was incredibly nervous, but then snuggled into me when I tried to hand her off to the technician. She kept her eyes glued on my face and fought with all her might to stay in my arms, raking her long back claws down my chest as she tried to grab hold. Obviously that wasn't what made her my favorite, it was that she acted like she had fallen madly in love with me on our two minute walk! We finally got her situated and sedated, and due to the vicious barbs on the fishhook, we had to push it through and cut off the end to remove it. But after clipping and cleaning the resultant wound, we reversed her sedative so that she could go right home. When I brought her back to her family, she greeted them like we had kept her away from them for days and she raked me a second time trying to leap away from me. I reached over to show them the area they would need to keep clean, and she nipped at me from her mother's arms like I was her worst enemy. I guess she practiced the 'love the one you're with' philosophy of life, and I found it surprisingly comical. I think there may be something wrong with me; if a human treated me that way I would have been offended but with Baby I thought it was decidedly endearing.

After I left that room, I started smelling something not so fresh in my vicinity and when the odor seemed to follow me wherever I went, I checked my shoes and clothes but they were spotless. It bothered me so much that I asked the ICU tech to check my backside in case I had backed into something disgusting, but she said I was clean. Felicity called me up front for what I hoped would be my last patient of the shift, but she caught my arm as I tried to enter the exam room.

"Wait a minute," she whispered. "I'm not trying to be mean but you smell rank."

"I know!" I replied. "But I can't find even the smallest spot of anything on me."

"Did you check your pockets?" she asked.

"I didn't put anything in my pockets," I replied. "Nothing but clean medical equipment."

"Did you check your smock pockets for poop?" she persisted.

"Pockets for poop?" I repeated in confusion.

"When you carry small scared dogs, and sometimes cats, their fear makes them poop and it can drop right down into your pocket and you never know it happened," Felicity explained with a smirk.

I pulled my smock pockets open and there in my right pocket were two perfectly formed tiny poop logs, thanks to Baby I presume. I dashed to the back before I began to laugh uncontrollably and announced the incredible answer to everyone there, "Poop in my pocket! I have poop in my pocket!'"

Then I couldn't stop laughing while I tried to carefully lift the poop out without squishing it. Finally I leaned against the table, removed the offending smock and handed it to Felicity who was laughing, but had it under enough control so that she was still functional. After I calmed down, I went to the locker room to get a new smock and when I came out, Dr. Blackwell had not only arrived early for her shift; she had also taken my final patient. I thanked Felicity for sharing her brilliant insight and promised to never again forget to check my pockets for poop.

Even though I was dead tired and anxious to leave, I finished my paperwork with a smile on my face. Dora had come through surgery like a trooper and was doing well in recovery, but her owner still wasn't answering her phone, so I didn't get a chance to speak with her. Dora's uterus only weighed four and a half pounds which was less than ten percent of her body weight, nowhere near any record thank goodness.

Then I took Max for a walk for some quality bonding time before I went home. Despite all he had been through, he was basically a big clown who just wanted to play; he seemed to think every little thing I did was exceptionally fascinating and potentially a game of some kind. When I tried to wipe off his paws before we went inside, he started raising each foot in turn in a fast game of keep away and then when I got control of a foot, he tried to grab the towel out of my hand. But as soon as I huffed in exasperation, he dropped the towel and froze in place; his entire body dejectedly drooping down: head, tail, ears, like one of those old fashioned push button collapsing toy dogs. I reassured him I wasn't mad as I wiped his paws, but only after I gave him a couple of treats did his droopiness dissipate.

After I returned him to his run, I headed to the back of the kennel area to get his bag of puppy food. I wanted to carry it home with me now instead of tomorrow when I would have to deal with him as well. Just as I was about to round the corner, I heard voices from the supply room so I abruptly stopped and tried not to make any more noise.

"I still don't like her," Felicity said. "She was better today, but she doesn't have any idea of how to handle clients. She's totally out of touch with reality."

"What do you mean?" a voice I couldn't identity asked.

"She's so concerned about doing everything some mythical perfect way, but it's never practical so she takes forever," Felicity complained. "And she never says anything bad about the clients, she just makes excuses for their behavior."

"It's very scary when your pet is sick and you don't know how to help them," the other voice replied.

"Of course," Felicity said impatiently. "But you can't reward their whining or they'll just heap it on you while the waiting room fills up."

"That's harsh," the voice replied.

"Boo hoo," Felicity countered. "You're as impractical as she is. Skin cases? Just give them a steroid shot to stop the scratching. That will shut the owner up and the regular Vet can figure out the rest later. She was in there off and on for almost an hour with that case today."

"I guess I have a lot to learn," my mystery defender replied.

"People are asses," Felicity added harshly. "Learn to deal with that reality, and everything will go much smoother."

"Even some technicians are asses," the voice retorted and I almost snorted out loud in surprise. I still didn't know who it was, but I admired her courage in confronting Felicity.

But Felicity didn't even recognize the rebuke and continued in her indignant rampage, "That's right. Some of them are just as bad as Dr. Sappy Happy. I'd be happy too if I were a rich entitled Doctor with no worries."

I turned and walked away. Oh my goodness, I could think of a thousand mean things someone could say about me, or for that matter had said about me, but rich with no worries were nowhere on either list. Her attack reached deep enough to disturb multiple unhealed wounds, but there was some odd part of me that saw humor in it. As I escaped the clinic I realized that I never got Max's puppy food, but decided not to worry about it. Tomorrow I would need to beg a ride from someone to transport the large kennel that the hospital was lending me, so I'd be able to get his food home then. Maybe it's more evidence that there was something seriously wrong with me, but the expected waterfall of hurt feelings that I anticipated cascading over me on the walk home never appeared, instead the outright ridiculousness of her final insult made me want to laugh in her face. Felicity's tirade didn't seem funny enough to tell my house family about. Probably because I was embarrassed that someone didn't respect me at work and a little ashamed that I hadn't marched in there and confronted her. But I chuckled when I thought about telling the family my poop in the pocket story, hopefully they would appreciate that as much as I did.

Chapter Fourteen

"Good morning Dr. Kate," Dr. Blackwell greeted me with a warm smile as she pulled overstuffed sacks out of her SUV.

"Good morning Dr. Blackwell," I replied. "May I help you with those bags?"

"No thanks, I've got 'em and I'm heading over to primary care today," she replied with another smile.

"Why do you work at both hospitals?" I asked, hoping I wasn't being rude. "I'm struggling to make a plan for next year, so I'm curious why others have made the choices they have."

"Well, it's a complicated answer," she answered thoughtfully. "After thirty five years of practice I was physically having trouble working full time, so I went part time when we hired a new Vet for primary care. But then we ended up short staffed in ER, so I picked up some shifts there. But I won't do it again next year. It's not working out for me. We need a new plan."

I nodded and said, "It must be complicated."

"All of management is!" she said. "And it's not something most of us attending Veterinary school ever set out to do. And managing independent minded veterinarians is the worst! It's like wrangling a herd of cats! But I'm convinced that poor management directly contributes to equally poor patient care so we all have to do our best."

"Thank you for doing it!" I said spontaneously. I was so glad I didn't have to worry about any of it at this stage of my career. "Have a great day!"

"I know I will," she said grinning, with an expression that made her look like she was up to something.

All my Sunday patients were doing well and would get to go home this morning, except Dora who was struggling a bit. She had broken with horrible diarrhea last night after recovering from surgery. Her fecal sample had been massively full of roundworm and hookworm eggs, the most common intestinal parasites in dogs, so hopefully she would respond to simple treatment. While parasites can kill vulnerable puppies, some adult dogs can tolerate them without any symptoms until their body is stressed in some other way like Dora's had been. Worst news was that their presence proved that Dora wasn't being given consistent year round heartworm preventative, which would have treated the intestinal parasites at the same time. The worried overnight ER Doctor had quickly done a heartworm check which thank goodness had been negative. I hadn't ordered a heartworm test as part of the pre-op bloodwork because Mrs. Chade had assured us that Dora had recently been tested negative and was on preventative religiously. I understand that nobody wants to look like a bad pet parent, but fibs like that can really put their pets' health at risk, especially in an emergency situation.

We all worked diligently to get our paperwork finalized and releases done promptly because the hospital was on an odd schedule, seeing only emergencies this morning, because all the senior clinicians had to attend some important off site luncheon. It was odd to be so slow on a Monday morning, but it gave me a chance to go upstairs and talk to Molly about Max's bill. She greeted me with a smile but shut the office door behind me which let me know how serious it was.

"The news is mostly good," Molly said, gesturing for me to sit down. "Dr. Vincent definitely low balled his surgery charges and you weren't charged for the work you did yourself. But the best news is that the credit service that you applied for approved you for three thousand dollars!"

"That's wonderful!" I exclaimed.

"Just remember if you don't pay it off on time they charge you hefty interest. But more good news, two different anonymous donors paid some of your bill. Someone from the hospital paid for the plasma Max needed, and someone from outside the hospital dropped off two hundred and fifty dollars to help pay his final bill," Molly explained happily.

Tears stung my eyes and with emotion cracking my voice, I asked, "That's unbelievably nice of them. Who was it?"

"You do know what anonymous means, right?" Molly replied laughing.

"Yes," I admitted with a break in my voice.

"There's another problem that we need to talk about," she said with a regretful expression. "The technicians are uncomfortable not being able to call you. I understand you'll be pushed to your limit paying off Max's bill, but you need to solve the phone problem too. "

"I will," I promised. "I don't know how, but I'll do it. Today I'll make sure everyone has my friend Ethan's number for urgent problems."

"Good plan," Molly said. "I have the extra-large kennel in my SUV for Max, do you want me to give you and him a ride home tonight and deliver it then?"

"I would love that," I accepted gratefully.

"I'll come find you when I'm ready to leave, sometime around six," she said and turned back to her computer screen.

I said, "Thank you so much, Molly," as I left. I felt my problems were becoming manageable for the first time in a long time. That fact alone made a huge difference in my ability to face my issues and contemplate solutions.

When I entered the treatment area the atmosphere was almost spooky with so many people cleaning or organizing or chatting in small groups. But it didn't make me anxious like it did the first time I had a quiet day in the ER, now I knew I would more than make up for any down time the next time I was buried neck deep in cases. With surgery being my next rotation, I was searching for Dr. Drama's favorite book to study in preparation when I saw Dr. Blackwell peeking into treatment through a barely cracked door. At first I thought she was afraid to come in, but then I saw her catch the eye of Dr. Drama holding court across the room and exchange quick nods.

The door was then flung open and the most surprising thing I have ever seen or ever will see in a hospital occurred. Fast beat calypso music blared out of a handheld speaker and the entire primary care hospital group danced into the area. Dr. Blackwell led the conga line wearing a neon purple and lime green ruffled dress and a huge hat piled high with fruit, and Amelia following her in a grass skirt over a modest bathing suit with fifteen or twenty leis draped around her neck, and the rest of the line had equally wild and crazy costumes. When they had all danced into the room they started shouting over the raucous music.

"Nothing happened today!" Dr. Blackwell bellowed. "I gave all my patients their Parvovirus vaccines so none of them are deathly ill with Parvo and racking up thousands of dollars of bills!!"

Everybody in line stomped and cheered and whistled until the ER audience joined in. Then as they quieted, Amelia screamed out, "Nothing happened today, not one of my patients came in with heartworms!!! My patients are on prevention year round so they're all protected!!"

The dancing line started up again and Dr. Drama shouted, "Gastropexy! Nothing happened to any of the at-risk dogs whose stomachs I tacked down, no emergency bloat and torsion surgery for them!"

He leapt up on the table and shook his butt, rather professionally I must say, and then jumped back down and joined the dance line. Everyone took turns shouting out their joy about what didn't happen to their patients due to good wellness care, then joined the undulating line. We wove in and out of the different departments, and people alternatingly joined and dropped out of the line, sometimes participants, sometimes appreciative audience instead.

"Molly-Mom, come take our pictures!" Dr. Drama bellowed when he saw her at the door. After she took multiple shots and approached him with the camera, he grabbed her and they danced around the treatment tables with amazingly quick feet, doing a dance I think they call a two-step.

Suddenly the music changed to Celtic music and Siobhan, one of the rehabilitation technicians, danced to the front of the line and we all tried to copy her Irish dance. Everyone except Siobhan was stunningly horrible, although maybe we made up for it with our exuberance. After we danced through all the departments, the original dancers threw us mini candy bars and bid us goodbye to take their conga line to the other buildings.

I was left panting but happy, at the same time I was plagued with serious thoughts for the rest of the day. It was just that I had never thought about it before but if primary care did their wellness jobs impeccably, their prize, their big reward, was that nothing challenging, exciting, or satisfying would happen. Nobody would pat them on the back, or bring them cookies, or call them miracle workers because their dog or cat was boringly fine! I can imagine Dr. Blackwell doing the right thing day after day, week after week, year after year preventing problems, promoting wellness and educating people without anyone ever appreciating it, sadly including me. I loved being part of people's lives with their pets and envied Dr. Blackwell's relationships with people that had spanned generations of pets and their families, but I didn't know if I could be satisfied without some of the excitement of emergency work or drama of lifesaving surgery. At the same time I didn't know if I could stand an entire career filled with relentless stress. In outlying clinics Vets did almost everything in one building, true generalists, but then they had to deal with the professional isolation and lack of easy access to specialists, high tech equipment and 24 hour care. I didn't know which type of practice would be right for me, not only for next year but more importantly for an entire life long career.

Chapter Fifteen

When the senior clinicians had returned from their luncheon and appointments had started up again, the emergencies flooded in too. I saw a couple of patients and had to admit that emergency cases weren't always hot messes; it's just the harsh cases were the ones that kept me from sleeping at night and would stick forever in my memory. Then I saw Mr. Emerson's name on the next chart and my heart lurched. I sure hoped Gentleman Jiminy wasn't worse or having trouble tolerating his arthritis medicine.

But when I walked in, Mr. Emerson hadn't brought his stately geriatric; it was Dizzy, his crazy lab. She was standing quietly beside him, but wagged her tail when she saw me and immediately came over to greet me. If I hadn't met her before I would have judged her behavior as normal, but compared to the Tasmanian tornado from the last visit, she was not the same dog.

"Hi, Mr. Emerson," I said. "What's going on with Dizzy?"

"It's hard to describe, but she just isn't herself," he replied. "She's eating all her food, but she's not wild for it. She's happy to do whatever Jiminy and I are doing, but then she lays down instead of pestering us or getting into some kind of trouble. And then this morning I opened her kennel door and instead of her usual bursting out of the door like it's a starting gate at the racetrack, she didn't even get up."

My first impression was that Dizzy had some kind of minor problem, but I had just heard Dr. Blackwell tell a story about one of her own dogs. She had snuck into the clinic at night to do bloodwork because she didn't want any of her colleagues, particularly Dr. Drama, to call her a neurotic owner since her reason for checking was that her mischievous dog was being more obedient! The routine bloodwork had shown a serious blood disease, caught super early, and even Dr. Blackwell had been astonished by the news.

I did a full physical while peppering Mr. Emerson with questions, but the only abnormality I found was that Dizzy was breathing more rapidly than normal. It didn't unduly alarm me because most dogs are so anxious in the exam room that I almost always had to write panting in the space on my physical form for respiration rate. But she seemed generally subdued so anxiety made less sense. I didn't know what to recommend to Mr. Emerson so I repeated Dr. Blackwell's story and we decided to do that same general bloodwork for Dizzy and then decide about further workup.

"Whatcha got?" Becky asked when she took the sample from me in the lab.

"ADR," I replied, which is our abbreviation for 'Ain't Doing Right.' That might sound like we're making fun of the owner for bringing their pet in with vague signs, but it's said with great respect that the owner knows their pet so well and pays such close attention that they can pick up subtle changes. It may be harder to make a diagnosis at this early stage but treatment is almost always easier, patient suffering is definitely lessened and sometimes lengthy hospital stays can be avoided. Most Doctors and Technicians bring their own dogs in for workup at the ADR stage.

Dizzy's bloodwork was within normal limits, but it showed a few nucleated red blood cells. In the dog, red cells normally lose their nuclei before being released into the bloodstream. But even more alarming, when I checked her blood smear under the microscope, the normally roundish red blood cells were all sorts of odd shapes and sizes instead of being uniform. I immediately headed back to talk to Mr. Emerson.

"It's not what you want to hear," I started gently, "but you're right, something is wrong with Dizzy. I don't know what it is yet, but there are changes in her blood cells that give me specific places to check."

"Is it serious?" he asked with his lower lip quivering.

"It could be, but you caught it so early that we have the best chance to help her," I replied and I felt tears well up. I could handle my own pain without crying, but seeing Mr. Emerson's pain tore at my heart.

"What are we going to do?" he asked.

"We'll start with X-rays of her chest and abdomen, and then we'll need to do an ultrasound of her abdomen as well," I explained. "It'll take a while, so it's best to leave her with us."

"May I stay in the waiting room?" Mr. Emerson asked, looking older

113

and frailer than he had just minutes ago, repetitively petting Dizzy's head as he spoke.

"Certainly," I replied. "I'll get Dizzy situated and find out where we're in the line for Radiology, and I'll come back to give you a better idea on timing!"

Dizzy and I left first, but at the door she turned and pulled to go back to Mr. Emerson, such a different reaction from her last visit when she was happy to leave on an adventure with the tech. I spoke to her encouragingly, promising her a treat, so she brightened up and went with me, but when we got to her kennel she was breathing even harder and looked at me with sad, soulful eyes. Her color was still pinkish but it wasn't a bright enough shade for a dog who was breathing that hard.

She was first in line for X-rays, but we were going to have a longer wait for her ultrasound. I handed Dizzy's leash to Becky and started to go up front to tell Mr. Emerson about our estimated schedule, but the ICU technicians asked me to weigh in on their debate about a new protocol and by the time we had the issue resolved, Becky was already waving me into the viewing room.

Two of Dizzy's images were up on the large monitors, and I went first to the side view of her abdomen, hoping to rule out my biggest fear, a tumor called hemangiosarcoma that is seen more commonly in Labrador Retrievers and some other breeds. The outline of her spleen looked large and distorted, which didn't prove she had a tumor but it sure didn't rule it out. Thank goodness the ultrasound would be more definitive.

I shifted my gaze to the first view of her chest and loudly swore, "Oh, shit!"

I looked away, as if not seeing it would change the horrible news, but the hundreds of small pea to olive sized densities scattered across the entire lung field were still there when I looked back. Dr. Tolliver and Dr. Blackwell came up behind me and I looked at them with wounded eyes.

"Who's this?" Dr. Blackwell asked kindly.

"Mr. Emerson's dog Dizzy," I replied dejectedly.

"You mean Jiminy?" she prompted.

"No," I answered bleakly, "it's Dizzy."

"I'm so sorry," Dr. Tolliver said. "Is she the patient you put on the schedule for ultrasound?"

"Yes," I replied. "But now I have to talk to Mr. Emerson and see how much work up he wants to do."

"I think the primary tumor is in the spleen," Dr. Tolliver added.

"Me too," I agreed. "How come you both followed me in here? Did you see all the metastatic tumors from across the room?"

They exchanged glances, and then Dr. Blackwell answered with a gentle smile, "We heard you swear. Spontaneous swearing in radiology means someone was just surprised by horrific news."

"If I hear someone swear in here, I always come to see if they need me," Dr. Tolliver explained. "Anywhere else in the hospital I go get the swear jar, but I give people a pass in here."

"Please let me know what happens," Dr. Blackwell said. "I've known Dizzy since she was a puppy. In fact I'm the one that told Mr. and Mrs. Emerson that their crazy new puppy was making me dizzy!"

"So he's married?" I asked, glad that he wouldn't go through this alone.

"He lost Mrs. Emerson to cancer a few months ago," she replied sadly.

My reaction to the realization that this kind gentleman would lose his dog so soon after losing his wife was so visceral it felt like a hand reached into the core of my body and viciously squeezed, paused and then squeezed even tighter. I took a couple deep breaths to steady myself and then left the room to tell Mr. Emerson the bad news before my courage deserted me.

The waiting room was moderately full and at first I couldn't find him, but then I caught sight of him entertaining two little kids in the far corner. I walked over to the group and Mr. Emerson smiled up at me and said, "That was fast."

I hesitated as I fought for control of my voice and then said, "Let's go back into an exam room."

"My hip is bothering me a bit today. Can't you just tell me here?" he asked, totally clueless about what I was about to tell him. "I know you'll have to talk about money but you can just whisper."

I tried to smile at his little joke but must have failed miserably because the lady with the kids got a troubled look on her face and began patting Mr. Emerson sympathetically on the arm. He looked up at me with a confused expression, and then stood up hesitantly, taking my arm when I offered it for support. We walked to the closest room, and he frowned when I closed the door softly behind us, pulled the chair over in front of the screen and helped him sit down.

"I'm sorry, Mr. Emerson," I said with as much sympathy as I could exude without crying. "It's bad news."

"Oh," he exhaled the word unhappily. "Oh, no."

Pointing at the image on the screen, I explained, "All these white spots are most likely metastatic tumors, mets in medical shorthand, that have spread from a large primary tumor, probably on her spleen. There are so many and she's already struggling to breathe, so I'm not sure if we can buy her any good time with medication or chemotherapy."

"Oh," he said again. Tears welled up in his eyes and when they fell, he hid his face in his hands and sobbed softly. I rested my hand on his shoulder but didn't try to tell him any more details.

When he quieted and looked up, I handed him the tissue box and asked, "Is there anyone we can call for you?"

"No," he said desolately. "I called my daughter earlier but she hasn't called me back so she's probably in a meeting. I don't know what to do."

"May I make a suggestion?" I asked.

"Of course," he replied gratefully. "I'll do whatever you say."

"We could do the ultrasound and get better idea of how extensive the disease is," I offered. "There's a small chance it's a systemic fungal disease instead, but that's not good news either."

"So it's cancer?" he asked.

"We think so," I replied.

"Is there any hope?" he asked with his eyes locked onto mine.

"Not much," I said honestly. "That's why I don't want to spend lots of your money without talking about her chances first. But sometimes it's hard to make good decisions without knowing more facts."

"The money doesn't matter," Mr. Emerson said emphatically. "But I do need to know that I did everything I could for her, I must know that I didn't give up on her too soon. But I sure don't want her to suffer or live a shadow life, all doped up and struggling to breathe, like my wife did."

I nodded my agreement but couldn't trust myself to speak. Finally I managed to say, "Let's do the ultrasound, and if she struggles at all I'll give her oxygen for comfort. How does that sound?"

He nodded and then asked, "May I go back to the waiting room? I feel trapped in here."

"Absolutely!" I replied. "I'll walk you out. Would you like some coffee or a pop or a snack?"

"Nothing," he refused forlornly.

"You need to keep your strength up to be there for Dizzy," I prompted gently.

"Okay," he agreed as we stopped at the little hospitality bar.

The teenager with all the lab pups and experimental fashion sense was pouring a steady stream of sugar into his cup of coffee but paused to ask, "Can I get you a cup of coffee?"

"Sure," Mr. Emerson replied with a dead voice.

The teenager's face dropped and he made a circle with his hand encompassing his piercings and tattoos and asked, "Unless this bothers you?"

"Sure doesn't, son," Mr. Emerson replied and lifted his sleeve to reveal a large detailed U.S.M.C. tattoo covering his entire upper arm.

"I'm Trev," the boy introduced himself. "Let me get you that coffee."

Mr. Emerson gave a tiny smile and teased the boy, "I'm Bill Emerson and I don't take quite that much sugar."

The boy laughed and assured him, "I'll make it however you want it."

I excused myself and walked to back to treatment. I certainly knew that I would have to give people bad news as a veterinarian, but until that moment I didn't really realize that one of my responsibilities would be to outright break their hearts.

The ICU tech directed me to the Ultrasound room, Dr. Tolliver had jumped Dizzy to top of the list and was examining her already. I eased myself in to the darkened room just as Dr. Tolliver started scanning the spleen and unfortunately the tumor was so huge and so obviously surrounded by fluid that it was even easy for someone as inexperienced as me to see it. I couldn't stop my reaction and tears started to run down my face, but I forced myself to watch until the scan was complete, making sure not to sob or sniffle so that I didn't distract the people working. When she was done Dr. Tolliver handed me the box of tissues, directed her tech to put Dizzy in the oxygen cage, and then left to inform Dr. Blackwell of the findings. I thanked everyone and escaped to the far back kennel so that I could finish crying by myself and then prepare myself to help Mr. Emerson make the hardest decision that pet owners have to make.

The first thing I saw when I walked back into the waiting room was Mr. Emerson surrounded by a group of people. Trev was there, as well as the lady with the children holding a cat carrier in one hand, and another lady had her arm around his shoulders, all leaning toward Mr. Emerson who was snuggling a pudgy brown puppy in his lap. Everyone looked up as I approached and then their faces collectively fell as they registered my expression. There was no doubt in my mind that pet people were some of the most compassionate and empathetic people on earth.

The lady nodded at me as tears gathered in her eyes and she called to her children, "Time to go kids, I bet Cali wants to get home."

Trev stood up, took the wiggly puppy from Mr. Emerson and said, "I live a couple houses away from you, I can bring the puppies down to visit any time you need us. I put my number in your phone as Trev Labpup!"

"Thank you, Mr. Labpup," he replied with a sad smile. "I appreciate that you stayed with me."

"Any time," Trev replied.

Mr. Emerson turned to the woman at his side and said, "This is my daughter, Rose. Do you mind explaining everything to her?"

"I'd be happy to," I replied as I escorted them back into an exam room. "Dr. Tolliver did Dizzy's ultrasound already so I have more answers. But none of them are good."

I explained all the facts as best as I could, but after showing them pictures of the main tumor leaking blood into the abdomen and the lungs full of the spreading cancer, all hope left their eyes.

"So we have to put her to sleep?" Mr. Emerson asked, crying again.

I struggled to speak but croaked out my answer, "We can't cure this."

"When?" Rose asked. "Can we take her home?"

"I don't think we can get her home," I replied regretfully. "The oxygen is making her more comfortable but it's temporary because the tumor on the spleen is bleeding. We could buy some time for you if we could take her to surgery and remove it, but the metastatic tumors in the lungs make it hard to do that safely. They may be bleeding too, she coughed up a bit of blood in the oxygen cage."

"Can I be with her?" Mr. Emerson asked with a sob.

"Yes," I replied, and then told them everything that would happen. He and Rose nodded at each detail as I explained, but their eyes had a stunned look to them and I wondered how much they were really understanding.

Dr. Blackwell slid into the exam room and Mr. Emerson asked forlornly, "Did you hear that we're gonna lose our Dizzy girl?"

"I'm so sorry," she replied nodding. "I saw the images of her lungs."

"Such a happy girl," he said, starting to cry.

"She made me laugh every time I saw her," Dr. Blackwell agreed. "But letting her go before she truly can't breathe is the last gift we can give her."

"She deserves the best," he said, his voice gruff with emotion.

"We'll go get her so you can have a minute with her," Dr. Blackwell said with emotion but with a lot more control than I had. "I brought part of my sandwich for you to give her if you want. She may not feel like eating it but she might appreciate the offer."

Mr. Emerson laughed briefly and asked, "Did you remember my story about how she barks at my front door when I'm eating my lunch and when Jiminy and I go to see who's there, she runs back to the kitchen and eats my sandwich?"

Dr. Blackwell said with a sad smile, "I sure did."

"Thank you," he said simply but with obvious deep appreciation at her kindness.

Dizzy was glad to see Mr. Emerson and happily took a bite from the sandwich, but after just a couple minutes out of the oxygen cage, she started to breathe heavily and stopped to rest her head in his lap instead. He struggled to speak but finally whispered, "It's time."

Dr. Blackwell helped the Emersons hold their precious girl and I gave her the injection that let her slip away. We were taking care of her body for them, so I gave them a chance to give her a last kiss and then carried her to the back. I was torn between taking care of her and taking care of him, but Dr. Blackwell was much calmer so I left Mr. Emerson to her care.

After Becky and I took care of Dizzy, Dr. Blackwell found me back in the kennel area crying again and said, "It's not your turn."

"Excuse me?" I replied.

"It's not your turn to grieve, right now it's all about Mr. Emerson. As bad as it feels to us, it's all about him, his loss, his grief, his life that has a huge hole torn in it," she reminded me.

I dashed cold water across my face and vigorously rubbed it off to disguise the evidence of my crying, and tried to smile. Dr. Blackwell nodded at me and said, "That's better."

I hurried back up to the reception area and joined Mr. Emerson and his daughter in their slow progress to the front door.

"Everything's taken care of," I said with a small smile. "What a special girl she was!"

"Thank you so much for taking care of all of us today," he replied. "I think it's the shock that made it so hard."

"I think so too, it's so much harder for us when it happens without much warning," I agreed. "But easier on them."

"That's true," he said with a small smile. "It makes it hurt less to think of it that way.

Chapter Sixteen

My last afternoon appointments passed in a blur, and I felt dull and indifferent, like all my emotions were packed away under thick insulation, but I tried not to let it show in the way that I interacted with clients and patients. They deserved at least the appearance of a fresh outlook from me that was relevant to their problems and their attitude, not my left over heartbreak from another patient.

When Molly found me at the end of the day, she seemed more excited and animated about Max getting to go home than I did until Becky let him out of his kennel and he made a beeline straight for me doing his best Bambi on ice imitation. His rapidly growing, absurdly gangly legs flew here and there as he slid on the slick floors, almost wiping out a couple times but always managing to catch himself at the last minute, all the while having this profoundly goofy look on his face fixated only on me. I laughed my first real laugh since saying goodbye to Dizzy, as Becky ran behind him with a slip lead held ready, but he was always just a half step out of her reach.

"Hey, Molly, do you mind wrangling him while I get his stuff?" I asked after I had caught ahold of him.

"No problem," she replied. "After the weird day we've had, I could use some time with miraculous Max, the Zen Master."

I rushed to get his food and his bag of supplies and medications, but then I purposely slowed down when I clicked on his new blue collar and snapped on his matching leash, just so I could appreciate the feeling that Max was mine, all mine, and no one could take him away from me! He seemed to know something special was happening and hammed it up for his gathering audience, but then stopped, stood up straight and tall with his tail curved up over his back and looked at me as if he just figured out that something very substantial was up.

Becky squatted down to give him a kiss and a neck scratch and told him,

"Come back and see me, Mr. Max!"

Molly and I walked him out the side door to the parking lot, instead of the usual route out back to the exercise area, and he tensed up, but it was difficult to tell if it was with excitement or apprehension. He hesitated as if he were trying to work out a puzzle and then refused when asked to jump into the backseat of Molly's SUV. After I lifted him in, he instantly lay down, only rising part way up to peek out the window to follow my progress around the SUV to the front seat, and then he quickly sank back down, plastering himself into the upholstery in easily identifiable terror, which he maintained for the entire brief ride. I couldn't tell if it was because riding in a car was a new and therefore fearful experience for him or if it was a flashback of being dumped out of a car on his horrible abandonment day.

There was a cheerful welcoming committee waiting on the porch and they bounded out of their rockers to greet our arrival. I introduced Molly to the house crew while Dag retrieved the kennel from the back of her vehicle.

After we exchanged pleasantries, I gave her an extra warm hug and said, "Thank you so much for all your help, Molly."

As she headed to her SUV she replied, "You're so welcome. Thank you for saving Max, his rescue and rapid recovery is uplifting to everyone at the hospital. Dr. Vincent always talks about taking solace in the science, I find solace in the saves!"

Max sniffed everyone and everything he encountered from the porch steps straight through to my apartment but showed no hesitation or fear. He was as excited and inquisitive as any normal dog would be in a new environment. He had somehow maintained a general buoyant life attitude despite all that he had to face, although it was apparent car rides were not going to be his thing! I let Max off the leash and let him explore the apartment while Dag and I delivered the kennel to the bedroom. I pointed out how well the assortment of bright throws and pillows not only coordinated with the turquoise chair in the living room but with my quilt and gaudy pink rug in here as well.

"They're perfect," Dag agreed. "And now that he's grown some new fuzz I'm positive he's going to be the same multi-tone brown as the sofa."

I laughed and said, "Dr. Blackwell rescued a dog in Veterinary school named Fuzzy Brown and she says that Max is going to look like a supersized version of that dog, so when people ask me what kind of dog he is, I can answer that he's an exceptional specimen of the rare Fuzzy Brown breed!"

"He is?" Ethan asked, returning from downstairs with Phil carrying a giant dog bed with a beige cover embroidered with Max in big brown block letters.

"Nope," I replied, "just kidding."

Ethan looked at me with a furrowed brow, but I said, "Thank you all so much for the dog bed!"

"You're welcome!" Mei said. "We hope he likes it!"

"I'm sure he'll enjoy it!" I said. "I love his name on it! Oh, guess what? My friends at the hospital all thought that Dag's name was Dog!"

"That's funny," Phil said. "Big Dog?"

"Bad Dog?" Dag asked.

"Mad Dog?" Mei asked with an amused look on her usually impassive face and Dag loomed over her doing his best maniac impression which made her laugh out loud.

"I didn't hear any descriptive terms used," I answered, chuckling at their antics.

"We've got lots of food!" Phil exclaimed, holding up bags full of containers. "We made all sorts of party food so you'd have lots of leftovers this week!"

"So you can take care of Max instead of worrying about cooking," Ethan said normally but then continued in a severe tone of voice. "But no people food for Max, right?"

"That's right," I replied. "Once he's fully recovered I'll make some exceptions for training purposes, but right now I'm going to be rigid about feeding his prescription dog food only, not even any dog treats."

"Why would you make exceptions for training?" Dag asked with a confused look.

"More dogs lose their homes to behavior issues than are ever lost to health problems," I explained. "So sometimes we use extra special nummy treats to work on problems."

"How about allowing him up on the furniture?" Ethan asked.

"I don't know what decision I'll make in the long run, but I'm not going to allow him to get up now," I answered with a smile. "He needs some basic manners first, and he has to learn that it isn't his inherent right to be on the sofa, but I might make getting up a privilege in the future."

"Why do it at all?" Ethan and Dag asked at the same time, and then grinned at each other.

I smiled back at the men and admitted, "Because I want to! I know that someday the best part of my day will be snuggling with him on the couch! And all he'll have to do for that privilege is to wait for me to invite him up."

"Why?" Ethan and Dag asked together on purpose.

"Because maybe I'll want a special person to sit and cuddle with me on the couch someday and I don't want Max to think it's his spot that he gets to defend," I replied grimly, thinking back to a particularly sad behavior case I had seen as a student at the Purdue Behavior Clinic.

Ethan appeared upset but I didn't know if it was because he disagreed or if he was concerned about being able to remember all my rules, so I asked, "When Max is recovered enough to go to puppy class, do you want to go with me to help and to learn all this stuff?"

"Yes!" he replied excitedly. "May I?"

"Absolutely!" I said.

"Why do you have to take him to class if you already know how to train a dog?" Phil asked.

"For lots of reasons," I replied with a smile. "It's easy to know what to do, but it's hard to make yourself do it consistently, especially if you're short on time! I'll need the encouragement of the trainers and the ease of a scheduled group; in class you have all those people with their puppies trying to do the right thing, both to practice with and to provide distractions while you work, plus all that socialization for the puppy. I'm way too busy to arrange all of those experiences for him on my own. And I bet I learn a bunch of new training tricks I can pass on to owners having problems."

"That's so smart that you realize that," Mei said.

"And it's a little self-serving, it's so much less work to prevent behavior problems than it is to treat them," I said. "But I also think it'll be so much fun! What's not to love about going to class with a whole room full of puppies?"

Everyone laughed and Phil added, "The food's ready, if anyone is hungry?"

We mobbed the food set up on my counter and I was so happy that I had enough furniture for everyone to sit comfortably to eat. We laughed and gossiped and told stories, while Max happily laid on my feet, but no one seemed to think that my poop in the pocket story was all that comical. Maybe they would have to have been there watching me search in vain for the source of the odor that seemed to be following me, sniff myself all over, and ask the ICU tech to check my backside all the while I was carrying the offender in my pocket. I had worked extremely hard in college, had to get great grades even in subjects I had no interest in or aptitude for, and then again worked night and day for four years in Veterinary school where I memorized an entire library full of facts about animals, and diseases, and husbandry, and pharmacology and a hundred other subjects, but no one ever taught me to check my pockets for poop! But I guess most of my work stories would need to be saved exclusively for my hospital family who had some chance of understanding my humor. Or maybe I just needed to avoid poop stories while we were eating?

When everyone was leaving, Ethan offered, "I can take Max out at noon tomorrow."

"Thanks, Ethan," I replied, "but I have the next two days off!"

"Wow," Dag said in surprise. "I didn't think you ever got a day off!"

"I do when I have to work emergency shifts on the weekend!" I said. "But it's confusing because I often hang out at the hospital on my days off since I don't have a phone and I hate to be out of touch."

Mei put the containers of leftovers into the fridge for me, and then gave me a light pat on my arm and said, "I'm so happy Max has you in his life."

"I think I'm the lucky one," I said with deep sincerity. "He stares at me like I'm the single most extraordinary person in the entire world."

"You ARE the most amazing person in the world," Dag said, which certainly warmed my heart but I assumed he might be flirting. But then Ethan, Phil and Mei nodded their agreement, which was so unexpected that I felt my face flush in embarrassment.

"Aw, guys," I said shyly, then continued in a regular tone of voice, "I need to get Max outside! He's been in the hospital on fluids which may cause him to need some extra trips outside, so don't worry if you hear us clomping up and down the stairs in the middle of the night for a few days. Thank you all so much for the dog bed and the great food!"

"Come on over to check out my fenced yard," Dag said. "I'll show you the lock on my gate."

"Okay," I said. "I'll get my supplies!"

Max walked nicely on the leash, but was obviously torn between sticking with me and exploring the new environment. He squatted to pee, and immediately looked at me for praise. I had a couple pieces of his food, which I could never seem to remember at the hospital, so he finally got a treat for his great behavior, at the right time which was when he was actually doing it. Giving him treats when we got back inside only rewarded him for coming back inside!

"So he was housebroken?" Dag asked.

"I don't know," I replied thoughtfully. "He picked up the general idea at the hospital, but he might just be a quick study."

"Hey, I wasn't snooping, but I saw you had an invitation to the Fall Fantasy fundraiser in Fort Wayne on your counter," Dag said, seeming to be a little hesitant to bring it up. "Are you going?"

"I'd love to, but I can't figure out how to make it work," I replied with a smile so he wouldn't feel sorry for me.

"Why?" he asked appraisingly.

"Why would I love to go or why can't I go?" I retorted.

"Both," he countered with a smile.

"The food," I replied chuckling. But then added more seriously, "One of the awards is from an organization named in honor of my Mom. My brothers and I call it the Garrison award, but it's actually an award from Kat's Klowns, a service organization for the children in local hospitals.

"I know all about it," he replied grinning. "I just didn't know Katya was your Mom."

"She was the best," I said looking up at him. "I miss her."

"I remember her," he said. "Your Mom was my sister's favorite nurse when she was in the hospital fighting leukemia. And your Mom would always do some cat clowning just for me when I was visiting. She never forgot that it's hard being the brother or sister of a seriously ill child too."

"Wow," I said in amazement, laughing as I recalled my Mom's cat ears and tails that she would periodically wear for the patients. They always magically disappeared whenever a Doctor came in the room, in a wonderful conspiracy between her and her small charges. "That's unreal that you knew her."

"I can't believe it," he agreed. "And why can't you go this year?"

I sighed loudly and hated to even start, much less get into it, but finally simply stated, "Money. Ride. Uncle. Dress. Time off."

"Ha!" he half snorted. "What if I came up with a plan and promised to go with you?"

"There's eight more pages on the problem list," I replied gloomily, but then shrugged my shoulders and added, "But you can try."

He grinned and said, "Okay, I will," and started walking again.

At the gate Dag paused and said, "I don't want to make a big deal out of this, but I want you and Max to be safe when you use my yard."

"Safe?" I asked, puzzled, as I looked around the area for hidden dangers.

"I don't think you should leave him in the yard unattended," he replied. "Someone could let him out."

"Someone?" I asked, confused. "You wouldn't let him out."

"No one from work is ever supposed to come to my apartment, but if they did it could be dangerous for you or Max," he said seriously. "They're a rough crew."

"Why do you work with them then?" I asked.

"It's complicated," he said, looking at me like he was trying to force me, by the strength of his will alone, to comprehend without asking any more questions.

"I won't leave him unattended," I said reassuringly. "But I don't get it."

"And if someone is hanging around when you get here, just walk on by," he said intensely and shifted into his Dagger persona.

"Okay," I agreed. "But I'd like to understand."

"I can't explain, but I need you to promise," he insisted rather desperately.

"I promise," I replied. "And Max is a big goofball, but as he grows up his instinct will be to protect me."

"Then he and I'll have that in common," he said with a relaxed smile and shifted back to normal Dag.

After he showed me how to work the electronic gate lock, I let Max loose and we stood in comfortable silence watching the delighted dog sniff around the yard. He started to explore up the stairs, but froze a few steps up and then ran back down the minute he realized we weren't following him. He loped up to me, wagging his tail and acting pleased with himself.

"What are you doing, Mr. Max?" I asked him, cocking my head and waiting as if I expected him to answer.

Max sat down, looked up at me, and then cocked his head with his ears perked up as if he wanted to hear more.

Dag laughed, caught a strand of my hair blowing in the breeze and ran it through his fingers while he looked shyly at me. Then he laughed again and tilted his head like Max and I had just done and asked, "Do you want to do something tomorrow? We could take Max to the park."

"Sure," I replied. "That'd be fun. But I'd better warn you, riding in cars is not Max's favorite thing."

"Well, maybe the park isn't a great idea then while he's still recovering," Dag said thoughtfully. "Would you mind going on an errand with me, then we could have lunch on our way back and then take Max for a walk around here?"

"Sounds wonderful," I agreed with a wide smile. "That way I'll be leaving him alone for the first time for a short period of time instead of for an entire day."

"Sounds like a plan," he said nodding. Then he looked at me with a quirky little half smile on his face and asked, "So this possible future person cuddling with you on the sofa, who would that be?"

I giggled, more like a teenager than I would have liked, and then laughed at myself and admitted, "I might have someone in mind, but it's a smart training tactic for Max even if I thought my sofa was destined to be forever more cuddle free."

Dag snorted so I wasn't too self-conscious about giggling until he leaned down and kissed me on the lips. My surprise only caused a brief delay before I responded and kissed him back enthusiastically, and embarrassment became the last emotion on my mind.

He let me go after way too short of an embrace and said, "Thanks for walking me home."

I laughed and replied, "Any time!" and hooked Max up again for our short walk around the house.

"Noon okay?" Dag asked.

"Sure," I replied happily. Sticking with a teenage emotional theme, I felt like I was floating, not walking, as Max and I returned to our apartment and I got ready for bed. Max went easily into the kennel and eagerly took a couple pieces of his food as a treat, then he settled down as if he was pleased to be wrapping up his big day. I was sound asleep not long after that, both of us apparently feeling right at home with our new living arrangement.

Chapter Seventeen

While I was lucky Max didn't need to go out in the middle of the night like I had predicted, I was woken up just before five by a series of pitiful whines incorporated into my rather terrifyingly bizarre nightmare. As soon as I realized it was Max crying, I sprang out of bed, threw on my yoga pants and flip flops and we made it outside without our first accident.

I spent the morning doing household chores and while everything was a lot more fun, it took twice as long with Max's help. I was looking forward to spending some time alone with Dag, but I tried not to waste the whole morning obsessing about it. My feelings hovered tantalizingly between anticipation and anxiety, and I didn't have a clue how to decide what I should be feeling or doing.

I briefly agonized over what to wear, but finally decided on my jeans and my white shirt. They were my least worn items since I couldn't wear jeans to work and I avoided wearing the shirt unless nothing else was clean because I looked too washed out with the white shirt under my white lab coat. I have quirky self-esteem. My parents were wonderful and supportive, especially my very outgoing Mom, so I started life with a lot of warm praise. They died when I was twelve; my brothers and I went to live with my mother's brother, and my life completely changed. Every single thing about me, but not my brothers, seemed to offend my uncle in some way; my thick multi-toned blonde hair was always described as ghastly dirty blonde, and my aqua tinted blue eyes were nasty muddy blue. My athletic build was sometimes described as too bulky, sometimes too scrawny, and I was always too fat or too skinny depending on his mood, not ever on my body condition. So I have deep conflicted feelings and it's just one more topic I try not to think about; I don't want to give it power over me or my actions or my feelings.

Before I knew it, Dag was knocking at my door, and Max gave the cutest little "Woof?" at the sound. When I opened the door, we gave each other the once over and burst out laughing since he was also wearing jeans and a white shirt.

"Should I change?" I asked with a grin.

"Nay," he replied with an even wider grin. "I don't think that outfit will get me into any fights at least!"

I felt the heat rise up my neck and face, I'm sure I was blushing a becoming shade of dark scarlet when it reached peak effect.

"I'm sorry, Kate," he quickly apologized and enfolded me into a warm hug and just held me. I only half enjoyed it in my shame, but he held me until I relaxed into him and felt the heat fade from my face. "Too soon?" he asked as he let me go.

I slowly raised my eyes to his face and saw nothing there but admiration and acceptance with a large sprinkling of amusement. We continued exchanging our deeply meaningful, hopefully soulful, looks until the corners of his mouth twitched from the effort and his beautiful wide smile escaped and lit up his entire face as he said, "Come on; it was quite an entertaining evening."

I tried to respond with a disapproving glare, but failed miserably and finally agreed, "It was," and allowed myself to match his expression of good humor.

Max cavorted obnoxiously around us, I don't know if he picked up on the gravity of our mostly wordless exchange or if he just wanted to be a part of whatever was going on, but he settled down as soon as it was resolved.

"Let me put him away," I said as I grabbed Max's Kong toy and stuffed pieces of his special food inside it as I walked him to his kennel.

"Be a good boy, Mr. Woof!" Dag called out to Max as we left the room.

Dag's car was a cute little sports car of some kind, but when I asked about it, he said he was just borrowing it while his SUV was being worked on. I suspected it was something I should be really impressed by, but I just didn't know enough about cars to even ask the right questions. It definitely made the drive to Best Buy fun although walking into the store reminded me of shopping trips with my Uncle. He always went with me for big purchases and paid for them with his credit card. Then I would transfer funds from my trust fund account to pay him, and he always had a boatload of convoluted reasons for doing it that way. But the result was that when he claimed that he owned my phone, my computer and even my iPod, he had the paperwork to prove it. He was technically right even though he was very, very morally wrong. Three years of college and four years of professional school had decimated my trust fund, but my quality of life right now would be so much better if I just had all my stuff.

Dag looked at me quizzically and asked, "What?"

I smiled first to counter my negative expression and explained, "Flashback."

"Ha!" he laughed once loudly, but then stopped himself. "I thought that was my line."

I arched my eyebrows, asking the question that way, and he replied, "Another day and another conversation. What are you flashing back to?"

"Same old, same old family shenanigans," I replied, hoping I had told him enough snippets about my Uncle in our weekly house dinner conversations that I could avoid the deeper topic for the time being.

"Well, let's make some better memories," he said as he walked to the mobile phone counter. I was simultaneously thrilled and mortified when I thought he was going to buy me a phone, but he told the salesman, "I need the new iPhone, I'll be doing some travel and I need better international capability."

"Absolutely," the salesman replied and they entered into a rapid back and forth discussion about features and prices. I mostly ignored them as I wandered over to the pay as you go phones. Maybe just a couple more paychecks and Max's final surgery and then I would be comfortable getting one.

I circled back around to the counter just as the salesman asked Dag if he wanted to turn in his old phone for a discount and, after glancing at me with what appeared to be trepidation, Dag replied, "No, that's our next order of business. I want to wipe my old phone and get a new number for it, but leave it on my plan. And then I want you to help us figure out what portion of the bill is everything that I want with my new phone, and what's the extra cost for keeping the second phone."

"Sure, that's no problem," he replied and turned around with the phone to do the work.

Dag leaned over and said, "I wanted to surprise you, but when you mentioned the family issues I realized I should have asked you. I wasn't trying to bypass your input like your Uncle always did."

Like the other day when I expected to be overwhelmed by hurt feelings from Felicity's mean girl comments, I waited to feel manipulated by Dag making changes to my life without discussing it with me. But once again, the bad feelings never came. I guess it was all about motivation, and I trusted Dag's agenda, hidden or out in the open. Of course I had trusted my Uncle and Justin too and that didn't work out so well for me, but in my defense I trusted them despite how they made me feel, and I trusted Dag because of the way he made me feel.

"Sure it's all fun and games until I turn out to be a deadbeat about my share of the bill," I said playfully. "Then you'll have me scrubbing your apartment and washing your cars."

Dag gave me a little hug and said, "Thanks."

Only in my jumbled life does someone give me an expensive phone with a way to afford the service, but then feel like they have to thank me for the privilege of doing so. There is something so backwards about the way things happen to me, and I assume it's all my fault somehow. But to act hurt and cranky because of it? After he had done something so wonderful, so incredibly helpful, a negative reaction would be beyond twisted even for mixed-up me. Meanwhile I was going to go all in, revel in the ecstasy of having a phone again, and appreciate everything Dag was doing to help me.

When we got to the car, I wrapped my arms around him and said, "Thank you so much. This phone undeniably changes my life for the better."

He hugged me back happily, with a big grin, and we stood in the parking lot for a few minutes just enjoying the moment, until he mentioned lunch and I reacted more enthusiastically than I initially had for the phone! My Uncle cared way more for his things than he ever did for me, and I swore I would never chose things over people. But I'm going to think more about that on a different day. Today I was going to eat, be merry, and get everyone's numbers to put in my new phone.

Chapter Eighteen

I was run-walking as fast as I could manage; the bag of salad containers from last night's interns meeting was thumping my hip with every step, and the discomfort became intolerable if I tried to increase my speed. But it was blatantly obvious that I needed to get up significantly earlier now that I had Max's schedule to work around in the mornings. My days off had passed in a single tick of the clock, it seemed, and while I was thrilled to get back to work despite all the fun that I'd had, I'd hate to start the day dealing with one of Dr. Drama's outbursts or unique punishments. I would have squeaked in just on time except that I ran into, almost, Dr. Tolliver in the parking lot and then walked with her back to her car to return the containers.

"Thank you so much for the delicious salad," I gushed. "Cooking for one means I don't get any variety in my salad ingredients!"

She chuckled and agreed, "And concurrently I also got to indulge myself when I was shopping because I was sharing with you all!"

"Thanks again, Doc, but I've got to get in there!" I said, my desperation written all over my face.

She looked at her watch and said craftily, "I'll walk you in."

We walked in together and Dr. Drama was standing exactly where I thought he'd be, with his hands on his hips glaring at the empty space where Interns should be standing, all looking up at him adoringly and eagerly waiting to hang on his every word. I scooted into position as Stretch slipped into the spot next to me with a stack of surgery charts in his hands. Dr. Taren walked in from ICU carrying another stack of charts alongside the overnight ER Doctor so she was doubly protected with charts and a senior clinician. But Dr. Drama was obviously not going to waste a good tirade, and you could see his gears turning as he tried to figure out if there was supposed to be a fourth Intern on the schedule this morning or not.

Out of the corner of my eye, I saw Melanie sneaking in from the locker room with an already defeated look on her face, which broke my heart, so I decided I wouldn't let her take the brunt of his morning craziness and blurted out, "Guess what?!"

With the light from his high beam glare now focused in my direction, I continued, "I have a phone! And I want everyone to have my new number so you can call me whenever you need help of any kind."

Dr. Drama paused and then said quietly, but with a deep chill in his tone, "Right after rounds you need to go upstairs and speak with Molly. If you still have a job after that, you can mess around with your phone then."

And that quickly, my brand new feelings of confidence and delight deserted me and my old enemies of pain and fear slid back into their well-worn spots, front and center of my consciousness. I took a deep breath, smirked my fake cover-up smile and attempted to participate in rounds. As soon as Dr. Drama turned his back, Dr. Tolliver grabbed my elbow, pulled her eyebrows down into a deep V and shook her head in some kind of don't believe him mime, so while it was apparent I was in trouble, maybe it wasn't really a firing offense.

I escaped upstairs the minute rounds were over, but Molly's expression didn't stop my old enemies from constricting their excruciating grip on the back of my neck. She grabbed a chart and pointed to a table with a couple of chairs pulled up to it and asked me to close the door.

"Dr. Kate, we've had a complaint from Dora's owner, Mrs. Chade," Molly said, clearly distressed. "When she came to pick up Dora late Monday night, she refused to pay her bill because she claimed she was not informed that surgery was going to be done, that no one called for her decision, and additional tests and treatments were done without telling her. The night staff was confused because no deposit was on the books so they let her take Dora without paying."

"But she totally lied, that's not what we agreed on at all," I started to argue.

Molly held up one finger and continued, "She created quite a scene in the waiting room, accusing us of being money grubbers and liars and quacks, in front of a room full of people. So while I'm not happy about what they did, I can see why they let her go, figuring it could all be settled in the morning. Except in the morning, I found out her phone number and address were fake, and her name didn't show up in any directory I could check."

I was stunned. Mrs. Chade had played me from start to finish, and I don't know if it made me feel better or worse that the lack of a deposit means she must have conned Felicity as well. Molly glumly looked at me and waited for my explanation.

"I'm so sorry, Molly," I said contritely. "I worked very hard on Dora's case, made sure she got the exact care she needed and tried my best to communicate with her owner. But Mrs. Chade lied about everything, no one ever answered her phone when I called, she probably doesn't even have a disabled grandchild."

"What are we going to do about it?" Molly asked quietly. "Where do we get that missing money to replace the supplies we used? Medical and surgical supplies are extremely expensive. A tiny bottle of anesthesia costs hundreds of dollars!"

I shrugged my shoulders while holding out my empty hands in front of me and declared, "I don't have an extra penny."

"So we should make the good honest people like Mr. Emerson pay it with increased fees?" she asked.

"We can't do that," I replied.

"So we'll shut down services. We could stop using the oxygen cage for dogs like Dizzy who can't breathe?" she continued, offering impossible solutions. "I can sell it, use the cash to pay our bills and we just won't have that capability."

I looked at her with desperation, trying to come up with a fair way to make up for our mistake, but with the image of Dizzy's sides heaving as she tried desperately to catch her breath so clear in my mind, and with her sweet eyes asking me why haunting me every time I closed my eyes, I had to dispute that choice, "No, we can't do that."

"Well then, everyone here loves the animals. Let's sell the scavenger system for venting the anesthetic gases out of surgery, none of the Doctors or Technicians here will care about the appalling damage inhaling those gases day after day will cause them," Molly said peevishly.

"No!" I argued emphatically.

"Speaking of technicians, we can just get rid of all of our experienced technicians and those with specialized training, and hire inexperienced techs instead; that will save a lot of money," she continued her attack of terrible alternatives.

I looked at her helplessly, hot tears welling up in my eyes and slowly trickling down my face. Only then did Molly smile gently and say softly, "And so here endeth the lesson."

My eyes snapped up to hers in shock and she continued, "We have a responsibility to our patients to make sure everyone pays their fair share. We're protecting the Dizzy dogs and the Mr. Emersons of the world. If we let people cheat us, they're actually stealing from them."

"I'm so sorry," I repeated.

"The story has a partially happy ending," Molly said. "Felicity was livid that this woman took advantage of us and lied about both of you as part of her con game. She vaguely remembered another pyometra case like the one this woman described having had in one of her dogs in the past. Felicity spent her entire evening, completely off the clock, looking through all of the possible cases until she found this woman's real name and address in an old chart."

"What are you going to do?" I asked, worried I would have to be the one to confront her.

"We're going to speak to collections and to animal control," Molly replied. "It'll get worked out."

"Why animal control?" I asked, thankful it wouldn't be up to me to knock on her door.

"I have a contact there," Molly replied. "Two pyometras and no other Veterinary care on record? That could be a sign of a puppy mill full of neglect and abuse. Or maybe she does get preventative care somewhere else but vet hops as she cheats each of us in turn."

Molly smiled and said, "Don't dwell on it, you have more important things to be worrying about, but be careful in the future. And don't fixate on my examples, nasal cannulas for oxygen administration are excellent too, I chose the oxygen cage as an example because it was a new purchase and you had just used it for Dizzy."

I walked downstairs trying to figure it all out, but from the moment I stepped into the hallway serving the exam rooms, I was thrown into survival mode, my own as well as my patients, and didn't think about anything except their immediate problems.

Chapter Nineteen

Cute little Oreo, the black and white cat with the broken leg, was my first morning patient but my happiness at getting to see him again only lasted an instant, destroyed when Mrs. Tate's first words were, "He fell again."

"How did that happen?" I asked incredulously. "He's supposed to be confined. I know the surgery department helped you get a cage."

"My husband was holding him," she replied.

"And he just dropped him?" I could barely form my outrage into words that made a coherent question.

"I wasn't home," she whispered. "He texted me, but I had to wait until this morning to go back and check on Oreo. I had to sneak in when he was at work."

"Go back?" I asked in a less agitated voice.

"I was at a shelter," she said so quietly I could barely hear her. "I couldn't take Oreo."

For someone who usually says too much, never too little, I couldn't think of a single thing to say. Mrs. Tate pulled her long cascading hair back to reveal purple blotches trailing up, down and partially around her neck. I blurted out, "I am so sorry. Are you okay?"

"They have a nurse come to the shelter," she replied without really answering me. "I don't know what to do for Oreo."

"I'm going to get an X-Ray of the leg and talk to the surgeon, then we'll make a plan," I replied, as reassuringly as I could in the situation.

"I have no money," she said in her wispiest voice yet.

"I can get this much done without worrying about it, but after that we'll have to figure something out," I replied.

"I can't take Oreo with me to the shelter, and I can't leave him alone at the house with him," she insisted, emphasizing the word him when it referred to her husband as if it were the filthiest of words.

"Back home in Allen County, Animal Care and Control has a program that can help for a short period of time, and I hope someone around here has something similar. That would buy us enough time to make another plan," I replied.

"I tried to stay to protect Oreo, but I thought he was going to kill me this time," she said, starting to cry. She wiped her eyes and gave a shy half smile and continued, "When I passed out I thought I was dying. I was quite astonished to wake up."

"We're going to help both of you," I said firmly. "I don't know how yet, but it's going to happen."

"Thank you, Dr. Kate," she said. "Please take good care of Oreo. He's such a sweetie, and life hasn't been easy for him."

"I sure will," I assured her.

"I'm sorry but I parked in the employees' parking lot so no one could see my car," she confessed softly, looking at the floor.

"Smart plan," I praised. "You can wait in this room for now. If we become desperate for exam rooms, I'll find you a private place to wait where you can feel safe."

I met Felicity in the hallway, and asked, "Can you keep an eye on Mrs. Tate in Room Three? Maybe see if she wants something to drink or a magazine?"

"Make sure she pays every penny she owes," Felicity hissed. "I'm not getting in trouble for you again."

"For me?" I asked, as Felicity flounced off without replying. I'm pretty sure that getting a deposit was her job not mine, but I let it go. One problem at a time and I wasn't going to let Mrs. Chade's bad behavior change what I would try to get done for Oreo. Except then a picture of Dizzy's heaving sides made me stop and reconsider. Everyone needs to pay their fair share somehow. My own sides heaved with a huge anxious sigh and I repeated, "One step at a time," a couple of times to myself as I took Oreo's carrier to Radiology.

I ran into Dr. Drama, quite literally, at the door, which was a lot like walking into one of the cement block walls in the kennel. I bounced off of him while he barely noticed, but instead of making a huge production out of it, he acted like it was inconsequential. I apologized and he focused on my face for a minute and asked, "Now, what did I want to tell you?"

I shook my head and asked, "General topic?"

"No idea," he said and left the room. I thought about telling him about Oreo, but I decided to get the radiographs before I had to tell him. Facts helped Dr. Drama make decisions about how to help the patient which helped him cope with bad news better. I was trying to copy his coping techniques, but I think I was going to need multiple supersized coping mechanisms, just one was never going to work well enough on my thick layers of bruised and battered feelings.

When he made it to the surgery area, Dr. Drama shouted back, "I remember! Rex Kaye's Path report described a Sertoli cell tumor in that testicle with secondary inflammation. Since all of his workup was within normal limits, statistically he should be cured with that surgery."

I turned Oreo over to the Radiology technician, walked over closer to him so I didn't have to yell and said, "Thank you so much for telling me."

"Mr. Kaye wanted me to thank you specifically," he said with his eyes crinkling.

"And Mrs. Kaye?" I asked hesitantly.

"Not so much," he replied, now grinning. "I didn't want to laugh in the middle of her rant, so I stared at her ears to catch the exact moment when the steam started to escape."

I snickered at that visual and commiserated, "That must have been difficult. What should I have done differently?"

"Not laughing was harder than the surgery, that's for sure," he replied, but then added more seriously, "We have to try to get along with everyone, see things from their point of view. But we also can't let them force us to do bad medicine or scare us away from telling the truth. So you handled it fine. We all have to develop thick protective armor so that we can handle all of the crap we have to deal with, at the same time we have to keep our hearts open and receptive to people's needs and feelings."

I grinned at the 'handle all of the crap' comment and as if he was reading my mind, he said, "Unless it's in your pocket, then you can't let it go,"

Laughing out loud I said, "No one at the house thought my poop in the pocket story was the least bit funny."

"They never do," he answered. "That's why you have to have some fun with it at work. The comedy in our lives doesn't translate well."

I nodded and had turned to leave when he continued, "Except your scrub pants falling down in surgery. That's turned out to be universally hilarious whenever I tell the story!"

"Of course it is," I agreed with a regretful shake of my head. "Epic!"

The radiographs of Oreo's leg showed the news wasn't as bad as it could have been; the fall had caused one of the bone fragments to move but the alignment of the fracture repair remained adequate. Dr. Drama thought it could be treated with strict cage rest, but wanted a recheck in a week to be sure. Felicity, believe it or not, offered to foster Oreo at her house for a couple of weeks. It wasn't going to solve all of Mrs. Tate and Oreo's problems, but it gave us a place to start. When I told her about this plan for the first week, she broke down and sobbed. I wish I could have spent more time with her, but the ER was getting busy so I walked her to the back door, stood outside until she got into her car, and then went back inside to see the next patient.

When I walked into the exam room, before I could even look at the patient, his owner screeched, "It's his red rocket! Something's terribly wrong!"

"His what?" I asked calmly.

"His red rocket!" she exclaimed frantically. "It's been all day!"

I didn't have a clue what she was talking about, but she held up the panicky Jack Russel Terrier by clamping her hands around his upper body and dangling him in front of my face. That position exposed his underbelly and revealed his 'red rocket,' his obviously large painful erection. The tender tissue of the penis was dry and irritated, possibly even injured, trapped outside of its protective sheath of skin, the prepuce.

"Oh, poor puppy," I said sympathetically. I motioned for the owner to place him on the exam table and did a quick physical. When Becky stepped into the room I told the owner, "I'm sending Mooch with Becky and she's going to get him a sedative pain shot while I explain to you what's going on. Then I'll go see if this is going to be a quick little procedure or if it'll take a more elaborate plan to fix."

"Thank you so much," the owner said gratefully. "I was so embarrassed to come in, but I knew he needed help."

"Do you have a female in heat at your house or have you been using him for breeding?" I asked, my recent problem with Mrs. Kaye making me hesitate about what words to choose so that I didn't offend her.

"No," she replied thoughtfully. "He had only been outside once, just to quickly go pee, before this all started. Then he couldn't get comfortable, and kept licking down there and then started crying, and the more we fussed with it the bigger it got!"

I made myself think about the pain Mooch was in to keep myself from laughing, but then the lady must have replayed her own words and laughed out loud raucously, "Oh my goodness, I can't believe I said that! And I'm ashamed to be laughing right now when he's so miserable!"

"As soon as he's comfortable, you get to laugh all you want!" I promised. "He might have a bladder infection, or a prostate problem, or simply got his prepuce rolled up and caught inside, which trapped the penis outside, kept it from sliding back in. I'll check him out and let you know."

Not only was Mooch very relaxed from his medication, his tests were already running, and Becky had him well lubed up and ready for my ministrations. All the good nursing care prepped us for immediate success, and I was able to quickly unroll the hair and the part of the prepuce that was turned and trapped inside and then returned everything back to its anatomically correct and protected position. I swear Mooch sighed in relief but it may have been Becky and me. I trimmed the long hair off with the clippers to help keep it from happening again.

When I walked back into the room smiling, the owner asked, "So is the hot dog back in the bun?"

"You're killing me!" I said, keeping a semi-straight face with difficulty. "But he's comfortable now so you can laugh all you want. I'm not sure it's ever proper for me to."

"Why does it look like a rocket, what are those two big bumps on the sides?" she asked.

"Those are the bulbourethral glands that swell and lock the dog and bitch together during mating, what they call being tied?" I explained with a question in my voice.

"Do you see those bumps sometimes under the skin too?" she asked, nodding her understanding.

"Yep," I replied. "Sometimes people are afraid they're tumors, but they 'disappear' whenever they try to bring them to the Vet to check them out."

She nodded her head and asked, "So maybe we should get him neutered?"

"That helps, and also keeping the hair trimmed short," I said. "His prostate was normal on exam today, but neutering will prevent most future prostate problems too. I'm still waiting to check the urine specimen, then I plan to send him home pretty sleepy to keep him from getting excited.

Keep everything calm."

"Keep calm and keep the rocket from lifting off," she said with a smile and I laughed this time.

"He'll be ready to go home in about an hour," I explained. "You can run an errand or wait in the reception area."

"I'll stick around," she replied, tapping her phone. "Lots of people are waiting for an update on Facebook."

I couldn't stop wondering about how she was going to appropriately explain Mooch's problem on social media, but as soon I was called for appointments I had to let it go. I saw a couple of urgent care patients with relatively minor problems, released the still calm Mooch, and then got to sit down and actually enjoy my lunch of party leftovers. I could have run home and let Max out, but Ethan was so excited to be entrusted with the chore that I didn't want to ruin the experience for him.

Dr. Blackwell sat down with me and said thoughtfully, "I told you it wasn't your turn to grieve after we lost Dizzy, but when I had a chance to think about it, I regretted saying it. I had an epiphany that I've caused myself a lot of pain with that exact attitude over the years because it turns out it's never my turn to grieve. I sure never wanted to bring the pain home to my kids, or dump it on my pet loving friends either. And I couldn't share with non-pet people for fear that they'd use my all-time least favorite phrase, 'It's just a dog or cat,' and I might end up with one of those terrible police booking photos."

"I can see that," I said. "My friends at the house are the most compassionate people in the world, but I'm struggling with what I can share with them and what I can't."

"Ha!" Dr. Blackwell chortled. "My friends and family think I'm getting forgetful because I'll excitedly start a cool anecdote but mid story, when I remember that it has a gross or sad ending, I try to change parts of it on the fly but I never actually finish telling a story that makes any sense."

"Yes!" I agreed. "I did that this week. I tried to play it off as being ditsy from being overtired, but I think they figured it out."

"So if it's not our turn at the hospital, and it's not our turn at home, when is it our turn?" Dr. Blackwell asked seriously.

"I don't know," I replied. "But I think we have to figure out an answer. The suicide rate of veterinarians has surpassed the rate of combat Veterans."

"I'd think you were fibbing about that statistic except not only did I read that article; Dr. Vincent and I just lost a close friend to suicide," Dr. Blackwell replied.

Chapter Twenty

The intercom paged above us, "Dr. Kate to reception for a delivery. Dr. Kate to reception."

I looked at Dr. Blackwell in amazement and asked, "Delivery? For me?"

She shrugged her shoulders and said, "Go see! I need to run next door anyway."

Dag, looking ferocious in his tight black T-shirt and black 511 tactical pants, was waiting at the front desk holding a large coffee cup and as I approached, Tess, the receptionist, announced, "Dog has an important delivery."

"Thank you so much," I said, accepting the cup with glee and not even bothering to correct Tess about Dag's name. "I just finished my delicious lunch of party leftovers."

"I'm the one that brought the broccoli cheese soup," Dag bragged.

"The soup is long gone," I said. "That was my favorite."

"I'll remember that," he said with a smile, but then he spun at a crashing sound from the front door area and, without any warning, shoved me forcefully behind him.

When I saw it was Maisy struggling to hold three small carriers with an expression of abject horror on her face, I dashed past him to help her. He managed to leap frog ahead of me to grab the door and we each took a carrier from Maisy.

I got into Maisy's face and demanded slowly and simply, "What happened?"

"All the dogs," she managed to gasp. "Some are passed out."

As I headed to the closest exam room I saw two semiconscious Yorkies squashed inside and turned back to Tess and ordered, "Call a mass casualty emergency, room two."

144

Maisy shoved her carrier at me and insisted, "I have to go get the rest."

"How many dogs?" I asked, knowing she had lots of pets but with no clue to the total number, as I heard the call for help echo throughout the hospital.

"The Dobies are walking around like they're drunk, the Yorkies are sicker," she said crying.

"How many dogs are at your house?" I asked again.

"Fifteen," she replied, still calculating. "No, thirteen, Tucker is with the handler and Roman was with me and he's fine."

I looked up at Dag and he nodded yes, so I turned back to Maisy and said, "This is my very close friend Dag. He can help you."

Indecision froze Maisy until I added a comment that would seem irrelevant if you weren't a dog person, "Some people are afraid of Dobermans because of their fierce appearance."

"I'm sorry," Maisy apologized to Dag. "Please help me."

"I'm driving a large SUV. Should I follow you?" he asked her with a gentle smile.

"Yes, a second vehicle will help," she replied as she turned to follow him out.

"Wait," I said as people started converging on our room. "Quickly identify these dogs as I hand them to a caregiver."

Maisy named the dogs and then she and Dag sprinted across the reception area as I called out to Tess to pull all of the Cruse records. Dr. Tolliver entered the room, and I gave her the initial report, "Thirteen affected dogs, smaller ones are sickest, previous poisoning at this location."

Dr. Tolliver gave orders to get vitals, place IVs and draw blood for initial tests, and then turned back to me. As she spoke half of me was paying close attention to her words, but it was like I was viewing a split screen, my other half was seeing the large informational sign in our waiting room warning people about potential household poisons for pets. I looked at Dr. Tolliver hesitantly, but decided that I had to say something about my fears, so I leaned over closer to her and surreptitiously whispered, "I think her son gave her Doberman pup marijuana laced brownies. I'm afraid he might have decided to try one of the poisons from our poster. I told him the Yorkies were more vulnerable because of their size. This might be my fault."

Dr. Tolliver shook her head vigorously in disagreement with my possible culpability, but continued talking to the various helpers as they arrived so that we'd be as ready as possible when the next eight patients arrived. We didn't even have thirteen treatment tables or ICU cages, but one of the wards would have to be converted to serve as backup, and carts, stretchers, and X-ray tables would be pressed into service as well. She turned back to me and asked, "What's your best guess for poison?"

"Something a teenager could get with no trouble, that would be easy to give to a large group," I said thoughtfully. "Maybe alcohol, or prescription meds or oh my God, sugarless gum! He was snapping and popping his gum when I was trying to talk to him last time."

I followed her back to the treatment area and as she blew through the door she demanded loudly, "Get the glucometer, I need stat glucoses. Get ready to hang dextrose."

My stomach rolled with anxiety as I thought that it was much more likely that I was wrong than I was right in this guess, but I had to accept that when speed counts you must make leaps of judgement until you have the necessary facts.

Dr. Tolliver tilted her head indicating a treatment table, silently instructing me to get to work so I started doing physical exams as we waited.

Then Amelia shouted out, "33!"

"Hang dextrose on everyone," Dr. Tolliver barked. "Do it now."

Teams formed up around each patient, usually the holder was incongruously dressed from one of the support buildings, like the girl in the Hawaiian shirt from the Polynesian Pet Spa and the cowboy from the Doggy Dude Ranch boarding facility. Using the additional people as holders freed up the technicians to do what they did so well--all the highly technical skills. Amelia continued to yell out dangerously low glucose numbers as she got results, and Dr. Tolliver ran from table to table trying to respond to the most critical patients first.

My phone vibrated in my pocket and of course I planned to ignore it, but then remembered it could be Dag needing help with Maisy. It was a text from Dag which simply stated "two minutes," so I shouted to Dr. Tolliver that they were back and jogged to the front door, followed by Molly and a couple more arriving helpers.

Maisy was carrying two limp Yorkies while Dag was attempting to lead three adult Dobermans, all trying to meander anywhere except where Dag wanted to go, but we hustled the new patients to the triage area in back, shouting at Maisy to identify each one as they left. Dag and Maisy returned quickly with two more Yorkies and another Doberman, this time announcing their name as they handed off their charges, sadly practice making us efficient.

"Which of the Dobies are stable?" I asked. "As soon as she gets glucoses on them, Dr. Tolliver's going to use an emetic to make them vomit, both to get rid of as much poison as possible and to see if we can determine what they were given."

"Given? Poison?" Maisy asked, but then answered the question. "Captain, the big black and tan male, seems to be almost normal, but none of Dobermans are as sick as the Yorkies."

"Or got into?' I replied, even though I couldn't imagine how thirteen dogs could all get into something at the exact same time accidentally.

"Oh no," Maisy said. "I left Roman in his kennel at the house, I didn't ever imagine that someone did something on purpose and could come back."

"Should I go with Maisy to check it out?" Dag offered.

"Did I remember to lock up?" Maisy asked looking up at Dag in panic.

"I'll go with you," he stated forcefully, then checked his pockets and pulled out a wad of thick black exam gloves. "I have these but do you have anything to put the samples in? We'll bring you anything suspicious that we find."

I found a box of zip closure plastic bags for them to use and sent them on their way, wondering why Dag carried the gloves, which had me wondering once again why he had been wearing them the night I had found Max, but I pushed the question away as I concentrated on the more vital medical mysteries of the day.

Dr. Tolliver's calm demeanor was an incredible balm on the rest of us, and multiple ER doctors, interns, technicians and support staff soon had all thirteen dogs situated, with IV catheters placed and fluids running. Captain threw up multiple wads of what looked like gum to us, but nothing that looked like paper or foil wrappers or plastic pieces of chewed up containers. That sad fact confirmed our suspicions that the dogs had been dosed intentionally. The full blood reports confirmed the low blood glucoses, and some of the Yorkies' samples showed signs of liver damage as well. The two smallest were by far the sickest, even after the dextrose was given to combat the low blood sugar they were having seizures off and on. The tiniest one lapsed into a coma not long after arriving. Dr. Tolliver told us that she didn't expect either of them to make it, and warned us that we could lose all the Yorkies, but she continued to try every desperate measure to change this predicted outcome. At least the Dobies were doing surprisingly well, although they certainly weren't out of the woods yet since serious liver damage could show up later.

I went over to help ICU catch up with the charting, chatting the whole time with Amelia, who was sitting in the large run with Captain. She was trying to keep his IV running consistently without the use of an infusion pump. Since the critical Yorkies needed the available equipment as a priority, at least until we could appropriate more pumps from the other buildings, we were making do without pumps for the much larger, more stable Dobermans. Unfortunately for Amelia, Captain's stomach continued to be upset and as he tried to climb into her lap for comfort, he threw up a huge volume of fluid, profusely soaking her from the neck down. She turned, looking at me with wide eyes as the new technician Tabitha, passing by with a small tub of dirty water from cleaning the other large run, tripped and showered her from above, making a splashing sound as it hit the top of her head. After startling from the double drenching, Amelia continued staring at me in shock, but then grinned her bright righteous smile and proclaimed, "Livin' the dream!"

I made some kind of a loud choking noise and then started laughing so forcefully and loudly that I could barely walk over to the pile of clean towels. After I stooped down to grab a stack for her I couldn't stand up as I continued to belly laugh compulsively. I ended up having to crawl the last few steps to the run door, dragging the towels behind me. Dr. Drama loomed over both of us with his sternest expression until I gasped out, "She said, 'Living the dream.' I can't believe it."

"Incredible!" Dr. Drama bellowed. "My hero! Best use of 'living the dream' ever!"

Even Dr. Tolliver was smiling and shaking her head as she continued to cycle among the critical patients, and I'm pretty sure I heard her muttering off and on as she worked, "Living the dream!" as the evening wore on, hour after harsh hour.

Chapter Twenty-one

Dag and Maisy picked Roman up on their second trip to the Cruse house and the adorable puppy provided much needed comfort to his devastated owner as the long miserable night stretched out. They had also collected a large number of samples, of what looked like random stuff to me, but they hoped it might be some kind of clue, placing it in the bags I had sent with them. I honestly didn't know what to do with it, but Dag and Dr. Tolliver had a long discussion and decided to tape them shut and sign their names across the tape in case the contents ended up being legal evidence. After finding all the kennel's trash containers suspiciously empty, Dag had gone to the Cruse's commercial sized trash bin in the alley, collected all the bags disposed of there and unselfishly loaded the stinking garbage into his pristine SUV. Then he spent his evening valiantly digging through the entire disgusting mess out in our parking lot. Only one bag offered any clues to what had happened, but that bag was the mother lode, yielding more than ten plastic containers which at one time had each held sixty pieces of sugarless gum containing xylitol. And worse news, there was also an empty bottle that had once contained a acetaminophen pain reliever.

When Dag left at midnight he promised to check on Ethan, who was happily watching Max for me. Later he sent a picture of Max sweetly sleeping curled up on his bed with his embroidered name peeking through the center of his doggie donut. I had clung to that reassuring image as the horrific night passed, the same way Maisy had clung to Roman in the waiting room. We lost the third Yorkie just as dawn lightened the sky, and even though I was devastated I tried to keep working, attempting to get everything done before rounds so I could start this day's battle with a fresh to do list.

"Could you double check this x-ray?" I asked Dr. Drama as he walked up behind me in radiology.

149

"Look at the x-ray? Seriously?" Dr. Drama asked mockingly. "You can't see x-ray beams."

I was worn out and heartsick, and first harrumphed disrespectfully and then protested, "Oh, come on. I know the proper term is radiograph, the image that the x-ray beam produces, or since it's digital I guess image is the correct term? But it doesn't matter, our job is to communicate with our clients and they understand the word x-ray."

"I don't see any clients," he snottily snapped back, as he dramatically looked around the small room, peering under the table and then opening the trash container and carefully scrutinizing it for hidden clients by sticking his head deep inside with his butt high in the air.

I sighed again, and apologized, "I'm sorry. We just lost the third Yorkie and I'm beyond tired."

"I'm sorry too," he unexpectedly responded as he stood up. "Precise medical terminology is an important conversation to have, but it's not the right time to have it."

"Thanks," I replied. "Have I missed anything on the radiographs?"

"Everything looks to be within normal limits. You didn't really expect to find anything did you?" he asked kindly.

"No, but after we found evidence that they might have been exposed to more than one toxin, we wanted to check at least one of them to make sure there wasn't evidence of other kinds of foreign materials," I replied dejectedly. "Pennies were listed on the same poster of toxic substances as the sugarless gum and acetaminophen."

"The whole situation seems unbelievable," Dr. Drama said soberly. "What do you think happened?"

"I don't know," I replied, shaking my head disgustedly. "Maisy's husband called to tell her that he'd found their son, but neither of them ever came in overnight to check on the dogs or to comfort Maisy. Something's not right."

"That's for sure," Dr. Drama agreed pensively. "Maisy is one of my all-time favorite clients, but Mr. Cruse has changed radically over the years. He used to go to all the dog shows with her, and showed concern about their surgeries and illnesses, but then he seemed to lose all interest in the dogs."

Dr. Drama paused, as if considering whether he should say more, but then added, "Maybe lost interest in more than just the dogs."

"Awww," I said mournfully. "Oh, I hope not. It would be bad enough if her son is to blame, I hope to God her husband isn't involved somehow."

"He sure never complains about her spending gobs of money on the dogs," Dr. Drama said. "He seems to be rolling in cash all the time even though his little hole in the wall car shop never seems to be doing much business when I drive by."

We looked at each other in silent speculation as people started to gather for rounds, and then Dr. Drama metamorphosed into his typical hyperactive self, handing out immediate assignments to people as they arrived, dismissing rounds for the time being and relying on each person to individually handoff responsibilities to their replacement. The entire treatment area looked like pictures on the news after some ghastly natural disaster, except instead of pieces of shattered homes, it was medical litter, especially the wrappers from sterile items like catheters and IV lines, carelessly discarded on the floor in the mass casualty pandemonium. I started picking up the debris and tying up overfull trash bags while Dr. Drama and Molly both got mops out and focused on cleaning and disinfecting the main treatment area floor. When they were almost done, their hard work deteriorated into some kind of a race which culminated in swatting at each other's mop, ending in a loud clacking fight over the final corner.

I was chuckling at them as I worked on ferrying multiple piles of disgusting soiled laundry and trash to the utility room, but then tears sprang to my eyes as I recalled walking out to the waiting area three different times to tell Maisy her precious dog had died. I know that these losses, and being up all night, made me both sentimental and overly sensitive, but to me that was what I thought I wanted my life to be about: working hard, trying to do the right thing for the patients, caring deeply if we won or lost, but facing these harsh times with other people who did their best to face each day with courage and the will to fight to the best of their ability. But this morning I had to admit that I really and truly, but totally unrealistically, wanted to win every battle, even the impossible ones, and never, ever wanted to tell another person that three of her dogs had died in one night.

And oddly I couldn't stop missing my older brother Andrei, who was the epitome of a person who could work devilishly hard or face soul crushing adversity yet still keep a positive attitude, making you want to work with him or face that adversity by his side, because doing anything with him would be more fulfilling and more amusing than any fun activity you could imagine with people ready to whine and pout at minor inconveniences. But on his eighteenth birthday, he had stripped his room bare, loaded up all his belongings in his car, driven to the lawyer and to the bank to change every piece of paperwork, including his precious trust fund, solely into his name and then had driven out of our lives, never to be heard from again. That horrific day my younger brother Stefan and I had stayed up all night waiting to have our little birthday party for him, behind our Uncle's back as usual, but he had never come home. Then we had faithfully waited to hear from him, to hear that he was coming back to rescue us, for weeks and then months and finally years. Honestly I must still be waiting for him to remember us, but it was hidden deep inside of me, the intense feelings only activated when I least expected it. I'd catch a glimpse of a tall, muscular blonde man with a short haircut out of the corner of my eye, and my heart would leap with unbridled joy and my first thought would always be, "I knew he'd come back for me." But it was never Andrei.

I kept working as my emotions bounced from pride in my coworkers, joy at the great response of the Dobermans, compassion for Maisy, to desperate despair at our losses. But I also had a moment of clarity: the emotions I would never feel here at work would all fit under the heading of peace and tranquility. There would be little chance for harmony, serenity, security, calmness, or even quiet to be the dominant sensation. I would have to find a way to bring that into my private life because it would never flourish at this or any other Veterinary hospital. There might be glimpses of the emotion, as a groggy bitch, whose life and the lives of her puppies had just been saved by an emergency caesarian surgery, valiantly tried to clean and care for her nursing puppies even in her post-anesthesia befuddled state. Or when a recovering patient shifted from a stiff, pain filled awkward position and curled up naturally as pain was dispatched and comfort returned. Those peaceful scenes might be appreciated for a moment, but then I'd have to be on to the next challenge.

"What deep thoughts are you having?" Dag's voice, softened suitably, still startled me in my hallway reverie.

"What?" I responded guiltily and inappropriately loudly. "What are you doing here?"

He patted my shoulder and said, "Molly paid for a massive breakfast spread, and I offered to pick it up for her. You should go eat."

"I'm not hungry," I said quietly.

Dag arched his eyebrows up in obvious shock so I added, "But I'll get some coffee and I bet I feel differently when I see it."

"I can't stay, but I'd better check on you later," Dag said. "I'm concerned that you're not ravenous after working so long and hard."

I smiled just a little bit and attempted to be reassuring, "I'm just tired."

"Molly told me that they're going to try to send all the overnighters home early. Maybe we can have an early dinner together?" Dag asked considerately.

"Sounds good," I replied, even though it didn't sound that great. I'd never been able to eat when I was deeply upset, first time was my parent's death, later it was my brother Andrei's desertion, and finally Justin's betrayal, although I'd never lost weight like I had the end of my senior year when it seemed like I had been abandoned by every living being on Earth. But I sure didn't understand why I was feeling so bad right now.

"We can talk, if you want," Dag said, giving me a quick hug after glancing around to be sure we were alone. "I don't understand all the medical stuff, but I understand loving a job that rips your insides up."

I nodded and said, "I need to spend whatever time I have before I crash tonight with Max. I'm a terrible absentee pet parent!"

"Even better," he agreed, making a funny face. "I'd much rather play with the dog than talk about feelings."

I briefly laughed, as was expected, but I sincerely hoped he was one of those guys who could listen to what I was feeling and try to be there for me. I wasn't a drama queen and didn't blather on and on about my feelings, after all my main emotional role models and support in my teen years were my barely verbal brothers, but on occasion the only way I can figure out what I'm actually feeling is when I attempt to put complex emotions into words to another human being. I guess I had pretty complex feelings about my feelings, maybe too deep for anyone not living in my brain to fathom. I grimaced at my convoluted thoughts as I waved goodbye to Dag, or Dog as he now insisted everyone at the hospital call him, and wondered if he might be my equal in complexity and convolution.

Then the front door ringer chimed and then chimed again and then played an entire song of rings to announce multiple arrivals. I straightened my lab coat and regretted not dashing upstairs for a humungous cup of coffee the minute that Dag had mentioned it. I was so exhausted I felt as impaired as I did on Sunday when I had worked partially hung over. In fact I think I had just read an article that drivers were more impaired by lack of sleep than if they had been drinking. I wonder if that was true for practicing veterinarians?

My first case was an adorable red Pomeranian who was coughing so badly that both she and her owners had passed a miserable, sleepless night of their own. Her color wasn't good and I caught myself speaking faster and faster, as I tried to do my physical, make a plan, and explain it to the very worried owners before I dashed out of the room with their beloved pet. But as soon as I told them that she had a heart murmur and I could hear fluid in her lungs, they were equally anxious for me to get her immediate comfort and care.

I popped Foxy into the oxygen cage and then wrangled her into first in line for Radiology by vigorously pleading my case with Dr. Tolliver. She looked as tired as I felt. She had managed the mass casualty emergency all night so that the emergency service wouldn't grind to a halt for other patients, but today she was back on regular duty as our Radiologist. She was so skilled and experienced she could probably handle it perfectly, but I was worried whether I could; my thought process seemed to be operating on half speed and not only did my mouth feel cottony, my brain felt even worse.

I stood just outside of Radiology as the techs tried to get the images I needed; they took the right and left lateral views easily, but when they turned Foxy onto her back, she struggled and threw her body around so violently two average sized techs couldn't hold the frantic ten pounder in position.

"Do you care if we take just a DV?" Tabitha asked, wanting to know if I'd accept the sometimes easier view taken with the patient on their abdomen.

"Whatever you can get," I replied, silently apologizing to my first radiology mentor, who I still felt looking over my shoulder even when I was working alone. I was supposed to choose the best views to get the most info, not take the easiest view, but what I wanted and what I could get were two different things in practice.

"She's purple," Tabitha barked at me, startling me from my sleep deprived distracted thoughts.

I watched Tabitha let Foxy get up into a sitting position as she simultaneously connected a hose to the central oxygen supply, turned on the oxygen and held the mask over Foxy's face. She looked impatiently at me for instructions, finally prompting me by asking, "Drugs?"

"Yes, furosemide, IV," I replied, but then completely blanked on what dose to use in an emergency. I grabbed my little notebook out of my pocket, fumbled around to find the entry, and finally read off the dose to Tabitha, but my stomach flopped as I realized that I knew the dose just a couple days ago, as surely as I knew my own name. I really wasn't firing on all pistons today, maybe I wasn't firing on any at all. Doubt crept in that I had made a mistake to have stayed up all night knowing that I had to work today. Had I done what was best for Maisy and the Cruse dogs only to sacrifice the care that Foxy and her folks would receive today? It wasn't an original thought, during my last reading binge, I had also read competing articles debating whether medical errors in human hospitals were or weren't attributable to Interns and Residents lack of sleep from impossibly long shifts, a practice that was ingrained in medical education. But I hadn't really thought that the articles had any application to me and my education since I was scheduled for pretty standard shifts. It was one hundred percent my fault that I didn't wrap things up and leave last night, either on time or later in the evening, I should have done whatever it took to get some sleep and avoid this walking dead feeling.

"Doctor?" Tabitha asked.

"Sorry, Tabitha," I replied. "I should have grabbed some sleep last night. Pop Foxy back in the oxygen cage, schedule her furosemide IV every six hours while I look at the lateral radiograph and consult with Dr. Tolliver."

"Thanks, Doc," she said with a smile. "Do you want me to schedule an 'ask doc' in an hour to make sure Foxy is on the right dose of the diuretic?"

"I sure do!" I answered with a grin. "Brilliant idea."

I think the fear generated by the realization that I could have made a mistake gave enough of an adrenaline boost to my somnolent brain to spark it back into normal function. I made a plan to work up Foxy's probable heart problem, presented it for Dr. Tolliver's approval, transferred Foxy to the Internal Medicine department, and then had a great discussion with Foxy's concerned family. Foxy responded miraculously to the diuretic so by the time Dr. Tolliver and Dr. Bennet, our Internal Medicine specialist who did most of our Cardiology workups, were ready for her, she was breathing easily even out of the oxygen cage, and she cooperated for her radiographs and ultrasound even when she had to lay on her back.

"I don't know why you couldn't get good quality images on her," Dr. Tolliver said with her typical deadpan face, but by now I knew her pretty well and felt free to chuckle at what I understood was one of her understated jokes.

"Yeah, funny what being able to breath does for their cooperation," I replied with a small smile.

The day crept by painfully as I divided my time between the hospitalized Cruse dogs and working up patients entering through the emergency department. Every little thing that went wrong, from pens that wouldn't write, to lab machines giving error messages for no reason, to new techs not being able to get blood on compliant patients, irritated me almost beyond my ability to control my response. I wanted to fling the pens across the room, smash the expensive machines into smithereens on the lab floor, and scream at the top of my lungs at the techs trying so hard to learn their craft, and while I knew my reactions were beyond inappropriate, it didn't make the feelings go away. Thank goodness Dr. Tolliver sent all the overnighters home in the afternoon before I did something horrible and inexcusable. I was never so glad to escape my beloved hospital and work family as I did at that moment.

Chapter Twenty-two

As dull as I was, I was still aware enough when I arrived home to be shocked that the nameplate on Dag's mailbox now said Dog! It caught my eye because it was printed in beautiful calligraphy with a Japanese symbol on either side of it. I snapped a picture so that I could try to look up what the symbol meant, although my best guess at this point was going to be that it was the designation for dog. In my mailbox there was a note from Mei offering to make me a new name plate in the same style as the one she had made for Dag, or should she have called him Dog now? But there was no note from him explaining the reason for his name change and I was too tired to even think about it now. I did want Mei to make me a new fancy nameplate except that when choosing my Japanese symbol I might have to discuss my own name and I didn't want to face that.

Ethan was sitting in my apartment working on his laptop with a headset on, and he attempted to continue to speak seriously with whomever was on the other end of the phone call as Max cavorted around the room at my return. Max whined, crouched down low and then grinned that weird grimace of a happy but submissive puppy. I knew that I should keep my greeting low key, to help him avoid developing separation anxiety, that classic and oft recommended 'never say hello, never say goodbye' advice. But he was so loveable and my need to embrace his joy after the night I had just survived was so great, that I couldn't help myself. I bent down, reached out for him, greeting him with the high pitched voice that seems so natural to use with both dogs and babies. He gave that doggy grin again and squatted as he looked into my eyes and peed on the floor.

"I gotta let you go," Ethan said as he ripped his head set off, then apologized to me, "I'm so sorry. I just had him out an hour ago."

"My fault," I said with a smile as I dabbed up the urine with the newly designated dog cleanup towel. "Not Max's fault and certainly not your fault. That's his way of greeting me, appropriate for a puppy of his age. I did everything wrong: I bent down, I looked right at him, reached for him, and spoke in a high greeting voice. I was in effect demanding his response be to squat and pee."

We snapped his leash on and headed outside together, just to be sure he was empty, and Ethan asked as we walked, "You didn't even yell at him, you just went, 'Oh, oh' and reached for the towel. How will he learn it's wrong to pee in the house?"

"If I made a big fuss, it might convince him that he had to greet me even more dramatically next time," I replied. "I had a case where the poor puppy had been intensely punished for submissively peeing when the owner got home, so that poor puppy went so far as to flop on his back and pee straight up into the air in an desperate attempt to try everything in his doggy behavior repertoire to beg the owner not to punish him again."

"Wow," Ethan said with a bewildered look on his face. "That seems backwards to me."

"Ethan, thank you so much for all you do for him," I replied. "I may know the right things to do with him, but I'm sure not doing any of them when I spend all my time at work!"

Ethan replied gratefully, "I'm glad you trust me."

"I really do," I replied. Then I sighed and said, "I'll let you get back to work, but I'd better follow my own advice and take this cute puppy for a nice long walk!'

Back in my apartment, I sat on the floor tossing Max's chew toy, and as it bounced around unpredictably he chased it eagerly, acting like every random move it made was a cross between unbelievably magical and the funniest thing he had ever seen. He made me laugh out loud every time it happened so I guess we were equally easily amused.

Dag's arrival interrupted my hodge podge of haphazard thoughts so after jumping up to let him in, I tackled him about his confusing name change, "Hey, how come you're telling everyone you're Dog now?"

"Because everyone said it's adorable!" he replied with a grin.

"And you're not particularly attached to your name and can change it at will?" I asked.

"Yep," he replied, still grinning. "Can't you?"

I glared at him as I tried to figure out if he was calling me out on my own name deception. He didn't say anything more, leaving the opportunity to explain open in front of me at the same time he wasn't demanding an explanation. I finally said, "Kinda," in a funny, drawn out way.

He chuckled and changed the subject, "I went all out and got us a three course dinner! Crab Rangoon for the appetizer, broccoli cheese for the soup course and cedar plank salmon with vegetables for the main course!"

"Oh my goodness!" I said in shock. "You went to three different restaurants for my favorite foods?"

"I did!" he replied happily, and then part by part his face fell, as if he was slowly realizing something wasn't right. "What's wrong?"

"Nothing," I replied gently.

"Then why do you look more horrified than happy?" he asked just as gently.

"I don't know," I answered as honestly as I could. "I sure don't want to be so much trouble."

"It wasn't trouble. I wanted to do something nice. I had fun planning it, I like them too," he offered up rapid fire multiple explanations as if he were going to continue until he came up with the right answer.

"I'm sorry," I said with as much of a return to a normal attitude as possible. "I don't know if anyone has ever done something so nice for me in my whole life. I'm just stunned."

I helped him empty the bags and lay out our magnificent dinner at the counter, setting out carefully washed plastic takeout utensils at both places on folded paper towels. Then I hugged him close and whispered, "Thank you so much. This is the best meal ever."

"It makes me feel good to do nice things for you," he tried to explain again.

"I do understand," I replied. "And I'm grateful right down to the core of my being. But I'm just not used to it. I don't have any reference point to know how to react."

"Like reacting to compliments?" he asked as he continued to hold me close.

"Yeah, I guess so," I agreed. "Every time you've said something nice, it has made me feel so happy. I know I'm supposed to say thank you and move on, but the sheer surprise and amazement confuses me instead."

"Well, I predict it won't be long before you don't even notice; it'll be your new way of life," he said with a smile. "Now, come on and let's eat, I'm hungry!"

"Me too!" I agreed with a wide grin.

The next thing I knew, I jerked awake, abruptly sitting up with my arms stretched out into the air grabbing for some nonexistent handhold, and I didn't have the foggiest idea where I was or what time it was. With my heart racing, I surveyed my immediate surroundings without giving in to the impulse to jump up and bolt away, but only because I didn't know where to go. I gathered information; I was alone on my couch, covered with multiple throws, with dishes from dinner still on the counter and with Max nowhere to be seen. Nor did Dag/Dog seem to be here, at least not in the living area, but he could be back in the bedroom, which was a rather alarming thought. The sunlight peeked through the blinds in the room, but the angle of the light made it look like it was still pretty early. I remember we ate dinner, then sat down on the couch and started talking, about what? I pulled the throws off to look at what I was wearing, which were the same scrubs I had been wearing last night, only now I was barefoot. I must have fallen deeply asleep within minutes of sitting down; my last coherent thought was how great it felt to relax into the soft seat and feel the tension drain out of my body.

I stood up, stretched and then reached for my phone, but it was beyond dead, barely showing the empty battery symbol even after I stuck it on the charger. I pulled the blinds up to look out the window and discerned it couldn't be much past sunrise, so I wasn't late for work, but I still must have slept more than twelve hours straight. Then I remembered that it was Saturday and I didn't have to work until second shift. I heard the thump thump rattle of Max stirring in his kennel so I went to the bedroom door, sneaking a quick look in first to confirm that Max and I were alone in the apartment, then let him out of his kennel. I put his collar back on and hooked up his leash, slipping into my flip flops as I passed them, and then we headed out the door.

It was cool for the middle of September, and I stood with my arms wrapped tightly around my body as I waited for Max to finish up. One of the older gentlemen that I had previously seen walking the alley with Jim approached me shyly and asked, "Miss, do you want my jacket?"

"No, thanks," I refused with a smile. "Max and I are going right back in. But I really appreciate the offer."

"May I pet your dog?" he asked softly.

My first impulse was to assure him that Max was just a big sweet puppy, like the angelic advisor on one shoulder was telling me to do, but knowing that this guy was part of the group that hung out in this odd, rough area made me listen to my 'other' advisor in charge of keeping me and mine safe. That guide cautioned me from his perch on the opposite shoulder, warning me to keep quiet about Max and let people assume the worst. So I compromised and said, "Sure, but let him come to you. You never know what a dog will do if they're frightened."

"Same with people," he said, with a brief upturn of his lips, reaching his hand out to Max. "There are some teenagers hanging out back here that I hope he bites."

"I only know one of them, and he's a good guy," I added, in case he was talking about the much decorated Trev. "He takes great care of his dogs!"

"The boy with the tattoos and the puppies?" he asked, as Max walked up to his outstretched hand and gave it a thorough sniffing, then a small quick lick. "He's one of the good ones. In fact, he gave us guys first choice when he was giving away his Dad's clothes. I got this really warm jacket from him."

"That was so nice of him," I said. "Did his Dad pass away recently?"

"He died in the spring I think," he replied.

"I'm Kate," I said, and reached my hand out towards him.

"I'm Jack," he replied, pumping my hand rather enthusiastically, and Max tensed up at the movement, or at my reaction, I don't know which, but Jack let go and stepped back away from me.

"Nice to meet you," I said with a smile. "Which teenagers you worried about back here?"

"The rich kids with all their drugs," he replied with a scowl, looking at the ground first then looking up at the alley by Maisy's high privacy fence, then looking down again.

I didn't want to put him on the spot or spook him so I said, "Well, if you have any concerns, you can always tell Dag."

"I did," he replied timidly, "when he was out in the alley cleaning up."

"Cleaning up?" I asked skeptically.

"I saw him out here wearing those thick protective gloves, picking up the stuff those nasty kids had littered the alley with," he explained. "He was putting it in a garbage bag."

"Was it Thursday night?" I asked, thinking it might have been the night he was helping Maisy gather evidence.

"No," he said, glancing up to check my expression and then immediately staring back at a spot on the ground. "I saw him a couple different days."

"Good for him for cleaning up," I said with a pleasant smile in case he snuck another look at me.

"Aren't we supposed to call him Dog?" he asked.

"He told you that?" I asked. "I thought that was just at our hospital."

Jack went silent, and looked at a new spot even farther away from me, so I babbled for a minute to cover the suddenly awkward silence, "Whatever Dog wants! He seems to like the nickname even though it started as a mistake. I think it's really cute."

He still didn't reply so I said as I turned back to the house, "Well, we better get back in! Nice talking to you. Bye."

When I was just about out of earshot, I heard him say, "Goodbye, Miss."

Max was excited for his breakfast so he started pulling me towards the front door. I immediately slowed down and then stopped, only walking again when he came back to my side. When I was in a rush to get to work on time, it was hard not to give in to his bad behavior, but today I could afford to be patient and only move towards his goal when he was walking next to me. It was beginning to dawn on me that the unheralded day to day manners training was going to be a persistent pain in my butt with my crazy schedule. At the same time I surely recognized that a lifetime of pay backs was worth every minute.

I wanted to do some household chores, but it was important to make up for my crazy work week and prioritize Max. I decided I could cook a big batch of beans and brown rice to eat this week; that project wouldn't steal much attention from Max and would help me eat healthier, at least part of the time. Kroger had just had their ten for ten frozen vegetable sale, so I would have a great choice of ingredients; it was an oddly exciting realization. Then when I opened the refrigerator door, there were multiple large containers of what looked like a pasta dish, salad, and dessert, and a half loaf of bread. It certainly appeared to be the leftovers from one of our typical Thursday night dinners, which Dog and I had both missed this week, but when had they put it in there? Optimistically I decided Ethan had done it Thursday night when he was watching Max. I truly hoped I wasn't so dead to the world last night that the entire house family had paraded through the apartment while I snored and/or drooled in oblivion.

The morning passed way too quickly and then it was time to get ready to go to work, long before I was mentally prepared to go back. Something about the routine morning puttering around the apartment and playing with happy Max was so soothing and restorative that I desperately craved more of the same instead of being satisfied with my time off.

I couldn't remember if I'd told either Ethan or Dog about my second shift schedule so I texted them as I walked to work. Happily Ethan texted right back and offered to take Max out for me around dinner time. Dog texted me a few minutes later, called me Sleeping Beauty, but then instructed me to put my phone down and keep my head on a swivel, to stay aware of my surroundings and be safe, which seemed like an odd thing to say but maybe he had a point. The ugly bruises from my fall the night I found Max had stuck around an embarrassingly long time. Or maybe Dog was being brusque and critical because he was mad at me for falling asleep on him after he had gone to all that trouble to get my three favorite foods from three different places.

Chapter Twenty-three

Everything was quiet when I arrived back in ICU and the remaining Cruse dogs were all responding well, thank goodness! In fact, their charts made it clear that Dr. Tolliver had scheduled all four Dobermans to go home first thing this morning, I hope Maisy wasn't embroiled in family trouble at home and that's why they were all still here. Or maybe Maisy didn't think it was safe for even the recovered dogs to be at her house? I didn't have the slightest idea how to help her cope or solve the mystery for her, especially since Jack's comment had reinforced my fear that the horrible drugged out delinquent mob she was so worried about might be her own son and his friends.

The rest of the day crawled by as I tried to catch up on paperwork and referral letters. Anytime I lost focus, I remembered how important those letters and updates were when I was over in the primary care practice. At the same time, it was hard to rein in my adrenaline after what we had just lived through.

Max was so happy to see me when I made it home that he raced out of his kennel and started frolicking around, throwing his dragon chew toy up in the air in pure jubilation. Since Ethan left a note telling me when he had let him out I didn't even have to rush and could just enjoy the show. Ethan also left three new toys
on the counter with a another note asking if they were safe to give to Max, adding that he knew that the use of all toys, even the ones I deemed innocuous, needed to be properly supervised. I laughed at the stiff, formal nature of the note at the same time that I appreciated his commitment to keeping Max safe by thinking ahead. I frowned remembering Justin's insistence on breaking so many of the common sense animal care rules that we were being taught by the experts, from selecting unsafe toys and treats to deciding to leave Annie at home alone for sixteen hours straight. At the time I could not understand why he would take a chance at such terrible

outcomes just to spare himself a tiny bit of effort or a little money? Now I wonder if he was trying to get a rise out of me or even harsher, hurt me, by putting our archetypically sweet Golden Annie at risk just to watch my reaction? Or maybe he really was that lazy and selfish, and every terrible thing he did to anyone was simply about him? Awful pain for Annie and soul crushing worry for me? Inconsequential emotions compared to a moment's inconvenience for him.

I checked the toys that Ethan had bought for Max; all three were made with safe natural rubber materials, no toxic vinyl with PVCs or phthalates, but one of them, the ball, wasn't size appropriate for my big boy. It clearly stated it was safe for puppies, right there on the front of the package, but it wasn't safe for a huge puppy like Max; it was small enough to pass through his mouth to the back of his throat, where it could choke him and block his airway. I'd tell Ethan so he could get his money back, I knew he'd take it well; Ethan was dedicated to doing the right thing for Max.

That reminded me about taking Ethan to puppy class with us, which made me contemplate Max's next surgery. He was healing so well that I needed to touch base with Dr. Drama, maybe we could get that done this week and we'd get to start puppy class sooner. Plus I wouldn't have surgery hanging over my head! Every time someone in an exam room told me they were scared about their pet having surgery or a dental or a diagnostic procedure under sedative, I always wanted to commiserate with them and tell them I was worried about Max's upcoming surgery too, even though the risk was so miniscule. It's natural to worry, but whenever I asked people why they were so concerned when they recounted their poor pooch's dreadful reaction to a dental or other procedure, they actually described patients who were happily under the influence of their pain killing drugs. They erroneously diagnosed patients who couldn't walk right and stared weirdly off into space as having pain or illness when those patients were doing the exact opposite of suffering; they were in fact as high as proverbial kites!

It was almost midnight and I should be too tired to be stuck with these worrisome work thoughts. There was some bible verse about keeping today's thoughts about today's problems, something about evil sufficient unto today. I needed to look that up, it wouldn't be a bad motto for me to use this year. I decided to take Max out one more time, and then I could read in bed for a little bit, in hopes of winding down enough to doze off.

After a quick trip outside and with an encouraging "Hup!" I asked Max up onto the bed with me for a little snuggle time while I read. Phil allowed me to paw through his collection of police detective books and borrow any that looked interesting but I only took a couple paperbacks home with me. On ER rotation, I wouldn't have much time even for speedy fiction reading. It felt pretty perfect to be propped up on my new bed under my beloved quilt with my sweet boy beside me. I tried to ruin it for myself because, with my closet door open, all I could see was my dirty laundry tossed haphazardly on the floor. I had the strongest urge to jump up and do my chores, but it would have disturbed my comfortable puppy so I was able to resist and return to enjoying my story.

I thought I heard something odd, then Max sat up and did his adorable head tilt, first one way and then the other. Then I was sure I heard a crash from Dog's side of the closet and Max jumped to his feet facing the same spot and, with a low rumble, growled as the hair down the center of his neck rose and small scattered tuffs of hair along his wounded back rose as well. I didn't know what to do, but figured I'd better be prepared to do something and I needed my shoes on for all the somethings I could think of to do. When I was ready I stood in my closet to listen, and then ran for my stethoscope and placed it on the wall. Angry male voices became increasingly louder and closer until I pulled the stethoscope out of my ears in distress and then dropped it down in alarm at the unmistakable loud sounds of escalating physical violence. There was another crash and the wall shook with some kind of impact. I turned to run downstairs to get Phil then remembered that he and Ethan had already left for their early family gathering tomorrow in Lafayette.

The sounds continued as Max started pacing and whining and running to the door; even my happy, gregarious, love everybody puppy knew we should be doing something. It seemed like he thought I was letting our pack member down, but I was probably projecting my own feelings onto him. I snapped on his leash and then looked around my apartment for something that could be used as a weapon, like my brother had taught me so long ago, but I had so little stuff that even my quirky imagination provided no help. I didn't even own a frying pan. All I could come up with was to dump everything out of my small cross body purse, after slipping my phone into my pocket, and refill it with some cans of Mandarin oranges. I was going to be seriously angry if some lout ruined them with his hard head; I had to think very hard before splurging on canned fruit last week.

As I passed Max's too small ball toy on the counter, I had the brilliant idea to grab it and fake an emergency with Max. I could pound on Dog's door and yell for his help, cause all sorts of noise and drama, without letting on that I had even heard the fight. Max and I flew down the steps and then off the porch in one giant leap, and then raced around the house. There was a strange car in the alley, but the gate was still locked so I punched in the code and then closed it behind us, and thudded up the stairs as hard and loudly as I could and started my yelling as I approached the door.

"Help, Dog, help!!" I screamed. "I need help, Max is choking on a ball. I need you to hold him. Help me!"

I hid the ball in my right hand and then pounded both fists against the door as hard as I could. Max was jumping around on the landing, trying to figure out this new game, and I jumped up and down with him trying to make as much noise as possible.

"I've called for the Animal Control Officer to come help me, but I don't know if the officer will get here in time!" I pleaded as loudly as I could, my voice starting to crack with the abuse, but I kept embroidering my story. "I need your help! I know you're there! Help me! He's so big and strong nobody else can hold him."

Dog cracked the door open, and then he and another rough looking man practically tumbled out as I swung the door open wide with my left hand as I shoved my right hand into Max's mouth.

"Hold him," I said and maneuvered protesting Max between the stranger and Dog. As Dog grabbed Max, I pulled my hand out and yelled, "Got it!" as I displayed the neon green ball. The stranger reached over Max to grasp at Dog but then his head snapped back, seemingly magically, and then snapped back again, but this time I saw Dogs fist reach out, not like a boxing punch but like he hit him with the back of his fist. The third time he was hit it was more of a glancing blow as the man was turning and pulling away, and then he ran down the stairs, missing the last couple, tripped onto the grass and rolled a couple times before he got up. I missed what happened to him after that because Dog grabbed me by the upper arms, too tightly to be the least bit comfortable, and jerked me into his apartment.

He slammed the door shut, barely missing poor Max's suddenly drooping tail, then threw the deadbolt and dropped the security bar down with a bang. Then he got right in my face and asked harshly, "What the hell are you doing here?"

For a moment I was scared and considered sticking with my choking dog story, but as his fingers dug into my arm, I got angry instead, and leaned forward into the two inches between our faces and said, "Let. Me. Go!"

Dog immediately dropped his rough grip and moved back, holding his open hands in front of him in appeasement and said, "Fine. But what the hell were you thinking? You could have gotten hurt."

"In my apartment it sounded like you were getting hurt," I explained. "Even Max was freaking out."

"And what the hell help would you be?" he demanded.

"I could hit him in the head with my purse," I explained.

"Your purse?" he asked in utter astonishment.

"I put cans of fruit in it and it has a long strap so I could get some speed going swinging it, that would increase the force," I said meekly.

"Yeah, that would work," he said shaking his head in utter disgust.

"No?" I asked bashfully.

"I can take care of myself," he insisted, and looked so disappointed, in me I assumed, that it broke my heart. But then he closed the distance between us in a single gliding step and gathered me up into his arms, shifting this way and that to fit me into every nook and cranny of his body, maximizing our physical contact at every point, even wrapping one leg around mine. Then he aggressively kissed my hair and my shoulder, anywhere and everywhere he could reach without letting me go or pulling back. My face was tucked into his neck and it felt so comforting that I didn't want to pull back either, because I never wanted to lose that protected and simultaneously desperately wanted feeling. Not even to look at his face to start trying to make sense of his behavior. But then practical matters exerted their force because I wasn't getting enough air, so as I started to feel light headed, I pulled back to catch my breath.

I looked up at him and simply stated, "I had to try to help you."

"I know that," he said in a distinctly miserable tone of voice, but then added desperately. "But I need, more than anything else in my life, for you to be safe. And I need you to stay good and kind like you are. Because so much of my life is wretched and evil. Can you understand any of that?"

"I don't understand," I said softly. "Why can't you just quit? I can't comprehend why you keep doing whatever you are doing if it's this bad?"

"Quitting isn't an option," he said grimly, and then sighed and continued, "Or maybe it is. But sometimes you're the absolute only one, in the proverbial right place and at the right time to be able to help, to take on the problem, to fight the monsters, to protect the people you care about. And you have to believe that what you're doing is going to make a vital difference in a badly disintegrating world."

"What are you doing?" I asked very gently, hoping if I didn't demand to know this time that he would answer me.

"I can't tell you," he replied and then asked miserably, "Why did I have to meet you now?"

"What?" I asked and then completely confused, silently waited for an explanation.

When it became obvious that all I was going to get was his wretched expression, I stretched up on my tippy toes to look into his eyes to check for some sign of outright deceit, and when I found none I kissed him with new feelings of need and desire. I genuinely didn't know that I was capable of this depth of feeling and the kiss didn't quench the sensation, it started a furious feeling that started low, burning increasingly hotter, which then accelerated across my body until I swear it was engulfing my very heart. And I knew why people likened passion to fire because it felt like flames were racing across my body. He seemed to match my feelings as he clutched me closer and started kissing available skin again, pulling my T-shirt down to gain more access. We were shifting our bodies, tiny movements so that we could simultaneously maintain contact yet still get closer, fit better, make micro-adjustments to somehow become one, as if we were trying to crawl into each other's skins. I couldn't think of a word anywhere close to describing what I was feeling but I could imagine it was why people believed in magic and spells. Enchanted. I was enchanted by the feel of him, the smell of him, my need for him, and the very fact of the wonder of his existence. And it was inconceivable to me that it could be like this for me if he didn't feel the exact same way.

And then his phone rang, and it was a horrible sound, an old fashioned demanding ring, definitely not a pleasant snippet of a favorite song. Dog groaned out his displeasure, but shifted away from me to reach his phone, and after looking at who was calling and swearing vehemently, he stalked away as he answered.

"What?" he demanded harshly, paused then answered, "That fucking asswipe. He came to my house. I told you what would happen if anyone ever came to my house."

He looked at me, and rolled his eyes as he listened, then pulled his face into a cruel expression and insisted, "I'm done. There's a thousand other people who'll pay me even more."

Dog listened again, this time with a sly grin until that same transformation into viciousness right before he spoke, "Yes, you will give me all of that, you and nobody else. I'd better never see that piece of shit again or it's going to be a whole different kind of a meeting."

He ended the call and then unexpectedly grinned at me, "That worked out way better than it should have."

Maybe eventually I would ferret out all the clues in that one sided conversation, but for the time being I was profoundly confused by the words and the way that Dog's kaleidoscopic emotions and attitudes had played across his face throughout it all. Max sat next to me looking up at Dog with a befuddled but intrigued expression on his face, which I assume was a match to mine.

Dog smiled down at me, gently patted Max on the head and said, "I'll walk you two home first, but I've got to go. Now."

"No explanation?" I asked without expectations.

"Nope," he replied casually, not the least bit defensive.

He leaned over and took my face gently between his hands and kissed me softly, then asked gently, "Trust me?"

"Nope," I replied nonchalantly. But then rolled my eyes, smiled ruefully and admitted, "But I have some kind of weird faith in you."

170

Chapter Twenty-four

It took me forever to fall asleep after the evening's excitement, but then I did manage to sleep-in and recoup some of my losses. It helped that Dog had texted me at 3 A.M. to let me know he was home safe and sound; I think that was when I was finally able to transition into a deep restful sleep. Midmorning Max obnoxiously yipped his discomfort, but only after his cage rattling didn't get me out of bed to attend to his needs. Yawning and grouching at Max about still being tired, I took him for a short walk but avoided Dog's fenced in yard for the time being. His SUV wasn't on his parking pad, but I couldn't remember if it had been there last night, hidden by that jerk's car? I sure didn't want to wake Dog if there was any chance he was in there snoozing.

I didn't accomplish much the rest of the morning, but not only did I eat a healthy lunch I managed to pack a multi course dinner to take with me from all the offerings in my fridge. And no matter how my workday was going to go, slow or crazy, I was too tired to tackle any kind of exercise except plodding over to the hospital, so that was a nonexistent choice I had to make.

I was met at the hospital back door by Felicity with a lengthy call back list headlined by Maisy's three calls. But before returning any of them I had to catch up on what was going on in the hospital. I'd learned that a lot can happen in a single shift away, and jumping to return calls right away before I was totally in-the-know could be disastrous!

ICU was relatively empty; there were just two Cruse Yorkies still there and only one of them was hooked up to an IV, so I first sat down at a computer station and caught up on that entire canine family. Thank goodness Maisy had come in early and shuttled everybody else home, but it was hard not to worry about everything that was going on at her kennel. I sure hoped that her family issues were resolved, and she was certain they would all be safe.

When Maisy answered her phone, she sounded like her old self as she asked, "Do I really have to give that liver medicine on an empty stomach and then wait an hour before feeding them?"

"Sadly, yes," I said, commiserating with her. "It's the only way to make sure it'll all get absorbed."

"It's so difficult to pill so many dogs," she said sighing. "So much easier to slip it by in food."

"I know," I agreed. "If you absolutely need to, you can use a tiny bite of food."

"No, I'll just poke it down," she said morosely. "It's just one more thing I'll have to do."

It sounded like things were not alright at her house and the entire harsh workload was falling on her shoulders, but I didn't know what I could say that wouldn't make it worse. Even if all my guesses were right about her son, I sure didn't want to be the first one to accuse him.

Maisy sighed again and admitted, "I assumed they wouldn't have put it on the label if it wasn't important but I was hoping for a little good news. And I wanted to thank you again for all your help."

"You're welcome," I replied. "I really wish we could have saved them all."

"Me, too," she agreed sadly. "But I'm blessed to have all of these precious pups to help me through those losses. I also want to send a note to your friend for all his help, but I'm not even sure what his name is?"

"We all call him Dog," I said with a barely suppressed laugh in my voice. "If you address it to Dog and drop it off here, I promise to take it to the house for him."

Maisy paused for a moment, and then said in a bright voice, "Okay, that'll work," but then continued in a subdued tone, "I don't understand anything that's going on."

"Is there anything I can do to help you?" I asked, figuring it was now or never.

"I don't know what," she answered in a hopeless voice. "But thanks for asking."

I glanced around the treatment area, but no one seemed to be looking for me so I kept making phone calls until I was summoned up front. I was smiling even before I saw who it was because no one but Dog had ever brought me anything. Thank goodness he always made it so easy on me; he never expected me to be able to talk for long or to even to come up front every time.

So I was surprised that he wasn't smiling when he handed me a huge coffee, and then asked, "Can I talk to you for a minute?"

I pointed to an empty exam room, closed the door behind us and he asked, "Did you know there's some guy hanging around your parking lot?"

"No," I replied, puzzled. "But sometimes people are too anxious to wait inside, or they go outside to talk more privately on their phones."

"He was skulking around the cars and then he was definitely mean mugging me when I walked by him," Dog said.

I smiled at the mean mugging comment. How does he come up with the things he says? But then I had the chilling thought that Mrs. Tate had been afraid that her husband would catch her out in our parking lot. Thank goodness she wasn't due to come in today and Oreo was still hidden safely out of his reach. I said pensively, "I should go check him out. It might be the guy who beat up his wife and broke her cat's leg."

"No, I don't want him to see you or connect you with me," he replied firmly. "I'll check it out and encourage him to move along if he doesn't have a pet here."

"Okay," I agreed reluctantly and let him walk out without me. I would have found a window to watch what happened, except multiple people with pets walked in as he was leaving so I returned to the Doctor ready area and tried to keep my mind on my job. Before the suspense could drive me crazy, I got a text from Dog saying that a Mr. Tate had been asked to move along and never return. Which sounded like the problem was handled, except that he also told me he was picking me up at end of shift and no matter what, I was not to leave before he got there, which made it seem like it wasn't settled at all.

I would have worried about the situation more but my next patient drove all extraneous thoughts straight out of my mind. Hiss, a six year old calico cat, had been vomiting for the last three days, but multiple "I bite!" notations appeared to make up the most significant part of her history, usually right before a note stating that 'multiple parameters are unable to be assessed or evaluated.' While most owners assured me how nice their pets were, even as they were chomping their way up my arm, Carly introduced herself and then flat out told me to protect myself at all costs. I used the towel to hold on to Hiss, shifting it as I moved all over her body and keeping her face covered until the last possible minute. I looked her in the face and shifted my hands to gently open her mouth, not expecting to get an oral exam accomplished, but simply hoped to peek in and then jump away in time to avoid severe damage. I had come to terms with the fact that I was going to get hurt throughout my entire career, but I was determined not to be seriously harmed or maimed. But I felt more anxious when I was able to do a complete and thorough oral exam, even moving the tongue to check to see if a string was caught underneath it, without even an attempt by Hiss to punish me for taking such liberties with her dignity.

When I finished and stepped back, allowing Hiss to hide under the towel again, Carly said with amazement, "That isn't normal! How did you do that?"

"I wish it was something I did, or the cat friendly changes we've made here to decrease stress on cats, but today I'm afraid that she's just not feeling well enough to fight," I replied honestly.

"Oh," Carly said, disappointed. "She was plenty feisty last week! My sister's kids have been at my house for a week, so when she seemed less put out these last couple days, I thought she was getting used to them."

"Sounds weird, but I hope we have her back to feisty soon," I said with a small smile. "But I'm worried about her now, she's significantly dehydrated and she's showing pain in her abdomen. Has she gotten anything unusual to eat or have you noticed her chewing on anything?"

"No," Carly replied thoughtfully. "Nothing on the poison list, like Lilies, are even allowed in my house and I never give her any people food."

"I'm also thinking of foreign objects," I added. "Cats seem to prefer chewy textured items, but can eat all sorts of things."

"She does like to play with hair bands," she replied. "Or anything that will skitter or bounce across the floor. She'll play for hours with the kids or even by herself. She's the most hilarious cat in the world, except for when she's not!"

"I'll keep that in mind," I said. "We're going to start with bloodwork, including an additional test for pancreatitis, and x-rays of her abdomen, but she's sick enough that we'll have to get her IV started first."

"And something for her pain?" Carly asked.

"Absolutely!" I agreed. "I'll wait until her initial blood work is done so I'll have a few facts to work with before I make the choice."

"Thank you," Carly said gratefully. "I had a veterinarian tell me that there were no safe pain killers for cats."

"That used to be true, in the not so distant past," I replied. "Thank goodness things have changed for the better, although cats are still being killed by being given painkillers meant for humans or for dogs. But no use dwelling on that since today we can help Hiss. My favorite choice for cats is one that can be squirted into their mouth when they're hissing at you! My plan is to have her feeling so much better that we'll need that one!"

Carly laughed briefly as she nodded her agreement and I carefully picked Hiss up, swaddled her in the towel, the entire time holding her loosely but prepared to tighten my grip down in case the kitty bomb showed signs of detonating. I carefully handed her off to the technicians in back with a dire warning about her nature, and sat down to write up her chart.

As Quickcut walked by I called out, "I'm just starting the workup, but I have a cat with abdominal pain that might need an exploratory laparotomy surgery."

"Cool!" he replied happily, possible surgery always put him in a good mood. Quickcut wasn't one of my favorite people, but I did enjoy how much he loved surgery.

"I'll keep you in the loop," I promised.

"A chance to cut is a chance to cure!" he replied with the surgeons' famous mantra.

I got Hiss's workup completed rapidly; the results were consistent with an obstruction high in the intestinal tract and the stomach was obviously full on the radiograph, an unexpected finding in a vomiting, not eating patient. When Quickcut looked at the same area with the ultrasound he was convinced that there was foreign material clogging up the pylorus, the outflow part of the stomach. I informed Carly, she agreed to surgery and we worked quickly to stabilize Hiss in preparation. By the time I was comfortable sending her to surgery, Quickcut and his surgery team was ready for her. That entire tale may not sound that significant or awe inspiring, but it was the first time in my ER rotation that the law of synchronicity didn't ruin my well laid plans with multiple patients needing care at the exact time my patient needed help.

Surgery itself was remarkable as Quickcut opened the stomach and starting pulling out hair band after hair band after hair band until an astonishingly gigantic pile formed, and then even more unbelievable, the stomach's revealed treasures switched to erasers, some were the old fashioned triangular ones that fit on a pencil, some were bigger character shaped erasers from assorted children's movies, and then the biggest prize was a tiny doll head. I'm ashamed to admit I gasped out loud when the head was pulled out, with its long black hair streaming behind the gruesome acid etched face. Quickcut grinned at me and I laughed out loud in acknowledgment of my inappropriate response, but I was really not expecting that!

Thank goodness Quickcut could remove all the foreign material out of a single incision in the stomach. I've assisted on surgeries for cats that have eaten some kind of string or yarn foreign body which gathered up their intestines on said string, like a seamstress gathering material on a thread to make a ruffle. Those cases had to have six or eight or more intestinal incisions to remove the foreign material safely. The resultant pile of material that Quickcut removed from Hiss was so amazing that it gathered a crowd of techs wanting to take a picture of the salvage. But of course the best news was that the healthy looking gastric and intestinal tissue hopefully meant Hiss would have a quick, uneventful recovery!

Dog arrived to drive me home just as I was passing off my cases to Stretch for the overnight shift, so I had him come to the back while I was finishing up. But as soon as I saw him in the bright white light of the exam table area, I abruptly left Stretch to check Dog's bloody hands.

"What happened?" I asked as I started to reach for his hands, then caught myself and slipped gloves on first. Veterinarians are notorious for forgetting to glove up when faced with a human patient, like I had with Uncle Phil, putting us at risk for same-species blood borne diseases that we don't face with our own patients.

"I got in a little sparring earlier," he replied blandly.

"Did any of your sparring land on his mouth?" I asked with concern.

"Yeah, I think so," he replied. "Why?"

"Human bites are the absolute worst!" I answered heatedly.

"He didn't bite me," he said, acting a little offended.

"If you hit him in the mouth and your skin breaks open on his teeth, medically you have bite wound concerns," I explained. "Did you clean the wounds?"

"I washed my hands," he answered nonchalantly but looked like he wanted to escape what he obviously thought was my overreaction.

I grabbed the chlorhexidine scrub, pulled him over to the treatment sink and scrubbed the injured knuckles, copiously flushing the area with water after each scrub cycle. When I was done, I covered his abrasions with sterile bandages and apologized, "Sorry if I came on too strong, but we had to suffer through an entire lecture about bite wounds on hands and all the gruesome things that can happen, augmented with movie screen sized pictures of the infections, permanent damage and even amputations. Veterinarians need to be bite wound experts to protect our patients, our staff and ourselves."

"I believe you," Dog replied. "But this isn't the first time I've hurt my hands in a fight."

"Was it Mr. Tate?" I whispered.

Dog looked at me hesitantly, then smiled and answered, "Nah, I wouldn't put you all at risk just to give him a little payback dose of his own medicine."

"So work?" I asked.

"Sparring," he bizarrely repeated, and then asked, "You ready to go yet?"

"Give me just a couple minutes with Stretch," I replied.

"I'll pick you up out back," he said.

I finished transferring my cases, and warned the ICU nurse again that Hiss might be a whole new cat by morning. At least I hoped she would be feeling good enough to be her feisty self.

Dog and I laughed and joked on our way home and when I mentioned I was off the next two days, he offered, "Hey, want to get Max and then come over and watch some TV? I've got a bunch of stuff recorded."

"Sounds good," I agreed with a smile.

"I have a creative plan if you start to fall asleep on me again," he said with a grin.

"Sounds good," I repeated, with a whole different meaning in mind.

Chapter Twenty-five

I awkwardly carried Max's bed with me to Dog's apartment; I had decided that I needed to establish good ground rules for Max in case this was the first of many visits. As I knocked sedately on the door, in direct contrast to my last visit, I grinned, realizing that all these future encounters might be an elaborate delusion on my part. Max hopped around on the landing in excitement, I think he was anticipating another exhilarating experience and seemed a little disappointed when Dog gently opened the door and politely ushered us in. Dog took the bed from me and placed it in front of the sofa with a lift of his eyebrow to check if that was a good position. I nodded yes and he bent and kissed me warmly.

"Want a beer?' he asked with a smile.

"Sure," I replied and held up my contribution to our evening, "I have Wheat Thins and my favorite Vermont sharp cheddar cheese!"

"Cool!" he responded happily but almost shyly.

As we sat down with our snacks, he tossed a magazine to me and asked, "Want to wear this outfit to the Fantasy dinner?"

"Sure!" I agreed enthusiastically, admiring the gorgeous aqua dress with sparkling crystal accents being modeled on the front cover. "If I'm going to dream, I might as well dream big!"

He grinned and explained, "That's my sister Issa, and she's already borrowed the entire ensemble for you, no money involved."

I looked back at the picture in surprise, noticed the family resemblance, and replied without even thinking, "Oh my goodness, she's stunning! I thought you were the most beautiful human being I'd ever seen, but wow she might take the title!"

He looked at me in shock and slowly flushed, in what looked like embarrassment but I couldn't imagine why until I guessed that he thought I was calling him feminine. I tried to dig myself out of the awkward conversational pit and added, "You're not beautiful in a girly way," but was silenced by his lips on mine.

He threaded his fingers through the hair on the sides of my head, very lightly holding my head in kissing position but also sending simultaneous lovely sensations from his fingertips moving across my scalp as his lips claimed mine. Initially he kissed me incredibly softly as his fingertips kneaded deeper on my head, but then he alternated with demanding, deeper kisses at the same time he was moving through my hair with such a light touch it sent a shower of shivers up and down my spine, some rippling up and over my head. If yesterday's embrace was enchantment, today's seemed magical in a different way, almost otherworldly. I wanted more than anything to make him feel as blissful as I did in that moment, but I couldn't move even a millimeter's width away from the sensation itself so I just relaxed and lost myself in the feelings.

Max whined and ran to the door, but what he wanted only barely even registered with me, until Dog's obnoxious phone rang, smashed somewhere between us. We both froze as the phone continued to blare until Dog swore, dug it out of his pocket and looked at the screen.

"It's Phil and it's well past 10 o'clock," Dog said worriedly.

"Answer it," I said, matching his concern. Phil insisted that since he got up every day at five, ten was the magic witching hour for him, and not much would keep him up after that.

Dog answered with a curt, "Dog," and then listened for what seemed like a long time without speaking, nodding a couple of times, finally looking at me with an odd expression, a combination of a discouraged eye roll and a grimace. He ended the call by saying, "We'll be right there; Kate and Max are with me."

"What?" I asked anxiously.

"Ethan's visit didn't go well," he replied with an added growl of a wordless expletive which startled Max back onto his feet on obvious alert.

"I don't need to know Ethan's entire history, but please tell me enough so that I don't make it worse," I pleaded as we gathered up our stuff.

"I don't know much," Dog explained. "Ethan is unique, and his family is just so negative. Everyone admits he's a genius, especially with computers, but then they criticize every little thing he does."

"Sounds like a teacher I had," I said. "She sent me for evaluation when I misspelled all the words on my first ever spelling test. It turns out I had invented my very own system of spelling."

"I'm impressed!" Dog explained.

"So was the psychologist they sent me to!" I said. "But that teacher wasn't and she picked on me the rest of the year."

"Harsh," Dog said as he headed for the door. "But you might be able to help Ethan develop more confidence, or learn to cope, or something. Although not tonight if he's upset."

"Probably not," I agreed.

Phil's door was cracked open so we let ourselves in to join our other housemates gathered in Phil's living room. Ethan was sitting in one of the chairs and didn't reply or even look up when we greeted him. Mei picked up the cup of tea on the table in front of him, put it into Ethan's hands, and then guided his cupped hands up to his mouth as she encouraged him, "It's getting cold Ethan, just take a couple of sips."

Max made his rounds, receiving a soft "Good boy!" from Mei and some distracted petting from Phil, but after he attempted to get a response from Ethan for the second time, and failed just as miserably as the rest of us had, Max fixated on Ethan. He went through his complete repertoire of behaviors; first resting his head in Ethan's lap, then getting his Kong from me and dropping it on Ethan's feet, and when it was ignored, picking it up and tossing it up onto his lap, finally pushing it with his nose, accidentally jostling the tea cup Ethan was loosely holding. Ethan stirred and looked dumbly back and forth between his wet shirt and the suddenly energized dog in front of him. Max bounced up and down as he vigorously shook the drops of tea off his face and attempted to figure out how to play this new throw the tea in the air game.

The silence was excruciating but I couldn't imagine what I could say to help. I tried to catch Ethan's eye and smile at him. Everyone's grim countenance was starting to depress me and I could only imagine that our miserable expressions weren't helping Ethan in the least bit. Max cavorted aimlessly around his chair for a bit and when Ethan finally glanced at him, Max immediately went down into an exaggerated play bow, front fully lowered to the floor with his rear end up high in the air.

I chuckled and spoke in an upbeat voice, "Sorry, cute Max, but Ethan doesn't think your butt is the least bit funny."

Max held his 'please play with me' position and wagged his tail so heartily that it in turn wagged his butt high in the air.

"It's kind of funny," Ethan said softly and the rest of us laughed out loud and agreed. Max broke his pose and shoved his head forcefully under Ethan's hand, enjoyed the soft petting for a minute then danced around the room.

"What can we do to help?" I asked.

"Nothing," he whispered. "I'm okay."

"Do you want to talk about it?" I offered gently.

"No," he replied in a stronger voice.

"Okay," I agreed, and changing the subject, held up my grocery bag and asked, "Do you have any Grimm episodes? I have crackers and cheese."

"I own all the DVDs," Ethan said proudly. "I'll get them. And I have M&Ms!"

"Party!" I declared and looked at the other housemates.

Mei was already pulling out pillows and blankets from the storage ottoman as Phil stood in front of his now open refrigerator door and asked, "What does everyone want to drink?"

When Ethan returned and we were all settled, he said softly to me, "Sorry I don't want to talk."

"I totally understand," I replied. "I not only don't talk about my problems, I don't even allow myself to think about them, much less cry or grieve the losses."

"Grieve? Did someone die?" he asked sympathetically.

"No," I said hesitantly. "I lost relationships and I lost respect for people I had high regard for. Maybe they weren't deaths, but they were deeply devastating losses."

"Yes they are," Ethan agreed with feeling, and Dog nodded beside him.

"But those avoidance tactics only work in the short run," I instructed. "Not dealing with problems means they'll hang around in the background of your life and in the future they'll certainly bite you in the butt!"

Max jumped up as soon as I said "butt" and waited with anticipation, as if that were a keyword for some kind of hijinks. I laughed and shrugged my shoulders, and then we all laughed at him, unfortunately reinforcing his mistaken idea that the word butt meant group hilarity would ensue.

I turned to Ethan and shared, "My brother's advice is that the best revenge for poor treatment is to live well and be happy."

"I like it!" Ethan agreed with a little more vitality in his voice and strength in his posture. "Should we start watching season one?"

"Yes!" I replied cheerily.

After the first episode, Phil said, "Go ahead and say it."

"Say what?" I asked innocently.

"That Juliette doesn't act like a real Vet," Phil said laughing.

"That she hardly ever has to go to work except in the first season," Dog chimed in.

"And she called that guy 'an animal' like it was a bad thing," Ethan said, mimicking my voice fairly well. "Vets would never call someone an animal to denote a bad person, since the worst encounters that Vets have are with the humans!"

I laughed out loud, even though I could feel my cheeks turn a little pink at the teasing. I don't know how physicians and police officers ever cope with how unrealistically they are portrayed in television shows but I'll admit that I'm overly sensitive about fictional veterinarians!

We settled in to watch and the palpable tension in the room ratcheted down step by step until we were all yawning and snuggling down into our spots. Phil called it quits first, standing up and saying, "I'm beat! See you tomorrow, Ethan, lock up when you leave."

"I will, Uncle Phil," Ethan replied with another huge yawn. "But can I sleep on your couch instead of going to my apartment, if I still lock up?"

"Sure," he replied over his shoulder from the hallway to his bedroom.

Mei stood up too and inclined her head to Ethan and asked, "You feeling okay?"

"I'm good," Ethan replied. "I just don't fit into my family."

"Sounds like you wouldn't want to fit in," Dog said with his mad face on, standing up while he folded the blanket that we had been using. I stood up too and Max jumped off his bed to join us.

"My Uncle made sure I felt out of place, even moved my bedroom to the basement while Andrei's and Stefan's rooms stayed upstairs with his!" I said with a frown. "And he'd dismiss everything I ever said. My older brother would get so angry when he'd pick on me, but it only made it worse for both of us so I begged him to stop."

Dog gave me a side hug and told Ethan, "Call me if you need anything."

I called Max to me, hooked him up, and said to Dog, "I'm beyond tired, but I gotta get him outside first."

While Max wandered around sniffing, Dog asked, "Have you asked for the day off to go to the Fall Fantasy dinner?"

"I took both Friday and Saturday off," I answered happily. "Almost no chance of work messing up the trip that way!"

"I'm definitely planning on going with you," Dog said smiling and nodding, appearing to be agreeing with himself. "But I've already talked to my buddy, and if I'm out of town he'll go with you instead."

I looked at him in shock, "Go with a stranger? No, I'll ask Ethan or Stretch."

"Nah," he replied. "My plan is to make sure you feel protected when you're back on your home turf. No one will dare confront you if you're with either one of us."

I smiled at him and said, "With you for sure."

"In fact my buddy might be more intimidating to your family," Dog said, obviously deep in thought. "He's a Garrison."

"I love the Garrisons!" I gushed with a wide grin. "Actually, I only know Mr. Garrison. Everyone in Fort Wayne identifies him as the richest man in the city, but I think of him as a nicest man in the world! Is that how you know the Garrison family, through your buddy?"

"Kinda," he replied evasively, watching Max intently.

My little voice told me to push him for an answer, but I yawned instead and admitted, "I'm too sleepy to worry about it. Come on Max."

"I've got lots of great plans," Dog said, looking at me intently. "But I have this trip hanging over my head which could ruin them all."

"Why does it have to be you that goes?" I asked, flashing right back to inquisitor mode, while I fumbled with the lock to let us back in the main door.

Dog paused, then replied, "I speak multiple languages. And it's not easy for anyone to guess what country I'm really from, helps with international deal making."

"But if you're that irreplaceable can't you tell them when you will and won't go?" I asked pensively.

"The deal is rather fluid," he explained. "Once things start to move I'll need to jump on the moving train."

"Hmm," I said as I opened my door while still trying to puzzle out this international deal of his, this possibly nonexistent business arrangement that is.

Dog became very focused on Max, goofing around with him and his toy and ignoring me standing right next to him. He finally looked up and said,

"The absolutely last thing in the world I would ever do is to have a relationship, imply a serious commitment, share a true connection with you and then just disappear. And it could happen just like that" as he snapped his fingers, "and there's nothing I can do about it."

"I get that part," I insisted. "It would devastate me because I wouldn't understand. But if you explained it to me, I would be part of it, like families when their service member deploys. It's still difficult but they're included in the process."

"But I can't," Dog insisted. "I made these plans before I met you."

I yawned again and said, "Well, I sure hope you don't disappear overnight but I'm dead tired. See you tomorrow?"

"Maybe," he replied with a self-deprecating laugh. "One more thing to think about?"

"Maybe," I replied with an odd laugh of my own.

"Every time you talk about your brother, I think about how much I'd like the guy," Dog said. "But he pulled the exact type of disappearing act that I regard as emotionally cowardly. Something doesn't fit, and that something might be your Uncle."

"What do you mean?" I asked.

"He lied and plotted and stole from you," Dog said intensely. "He most likely did the same thing to your brother."

"But why didn't Andrei tell us?" I cried out louder than I meant to. "He didn't call or come back for us or try to prevent the same thing from happening to us."

"Didn't he?" Dog asked. "Who told you that there were no calls, insisted that no letters came, claimed that no contact was made?"

"Well, my Uncle," I replied.

"And where do you think Andrei went that day?" Dog asked.

"He always swore that he was going to join the Marine Corps the minute he turned eighteen," I answered pensively.

Dog nodded like he had an answer of sorts, but then kissed me goodnight, enfolded me into a quick bear hug and asked, "Do I have your permission to try to find your brother?"

"Sure," I replied while he looked surprised at my easy acceptance of help. But I could feel my eyes narrow as I continued, "If you stick around that is."

He barked a sharp laugh and kissed me again, "Good night funny girl."

Chapter Twenty-six

Max and I completed our morning rituals with relaxed, happy-go-lucky attitudes. I finished up by giving what remained of his fuzzy coat an extra special spruce up so that everyone at the hospital would see how well he was doing. The walk to the hospital was idyllic, an exact perfect morning mixing the warmth and brightness of summer with just a hint of the crispness of the approaching fall. Max cut across the badlands without any apparent shadows darkening his joyful demeanor. He either didn't remember the trash filled lot or only remembered his rescue and not the reason for it. I was proud of how nicely he was walking next to me until we hit the parking lot, and then he leaned his full weight into the collar and dragged me to the back door, forcing me to admit that I had to make time today to get him fitted with a head halter.

I felt like a rock star walking him around in the hospital. Everyone wanted to celebrate his phenomenal recovery and delighted animation. Amelia hugged him and her eyes glistened with tears; I didn't know what grief or stress she was dealing with, but it was apparent that Max just being Max was the exact medicine she needed to handle it.

Molly bustled up and asked, "What's Max here for?"

"I'm hoping Dr. Vincent will think he's ready for his next surgery," I replied.

"Hope so," she said. "By the way, I made those changes to your schedule with no problem."

"Thank you so much," I replied gratefully and then started to tell her about puppy class, but the intercom announced an important phone call for her and she dashed off.

"There's the guy everyone is talking about," Dr. Drama bellowed from the farthest treatment bay. "Come here and let me see him!"

Max and I bounced over and I declared, "He's doing so well!"

"My goodness, his back looks good, lots of pretty pink granulation tissue!" Dr. Drama said excitedly. "His surgeon must be a genius!"

"He is!" I agreed. "Max is eating like a champ and I swear that I can see him grow."

"He had some catching up to do," he said, then theatrically froze in place, bugging his eyes out to stare directly at him, then announced theatrically, "There! I saw it! Grew right in front of me!"

I laughed appreciatively and asked, "So, surgery soon?"

"I bet we could squeeze him in tomorrow if we don't get any crazy emergencies," he replied with a grin, but then turned away from me when Molly opened the far door and gestured frantically for him.

I scheduled Max's procedure with the surgery technicians, made sure everyone who had worked with him was given a chance to see Max, including the often unsung receptionists out front, and then we made our way out the side door. We had barely made it to the other side of the parking lot when Dr. Drama came boiling out the back door screaming for me, "Dr. Kate! Dr. Kate! Wait! I need to talk to you."

"I'm coming!" I called and attempted to walk sedately back to him and stay in control of my excited pup. But I was pulled the last few steps as Max focused all his power on getting to his always fun friend.

"Any chance you can help out in surgery today?" Dr. Drama asked intensely, as he petted Max absentmindedly.

"Sure," I agreed, "no problem. Emergency surgery?"

Dr. Drama laughed and replied, "Yes, you could say that! An emergency appendectomy!"

I asked hesitantly, "But dogs don't have an appendix?"

"I didn't say it was a dog," he responded challengingly.

I remembered Molly's emergency call and asked, "Did we get called in to assist at the zoo with a primate?"

"Nope!" he replied, proud he was stumping me. But then with a dismayed glance at his watch he appeared to remember that he was under a time restraint and rapidly explained, "No, Stretch is the patient! He's at the ER and will have surgery today sometime. But if you'll give me a hand I should be able to get through my surgery schedule in a reasonable amount of time and still get over there to check up on him."

"Sure!" I said again more emphatically. "Should I go home and get my gear or do you need me right this minute?"

"Nah," he replied agreeably. "Run home, settle the Zen Master in and come on back."

"Okay," I said, and as Dr. Drama dashed back across the parking lot, I warned Max, "We need to be quick as bunnies and get home fast!"

Max ears went up as he went on high alert and carefully scanned the badlands for his backyard nemesis, the bunnies who ran amok in his space. We jogged all the way home and straight up to Ethan's door. I raised my hand to knock but Ethan flung the door open in my face and exclaimed, "Oh thank goodness! I heard Max but not you and thought he was running around on his own somehow."

"I just got called into work. Can you let him out midafternoon?" I pleaded.

"I'd love to," Ethan said smiling. "Anything else I can do?"

"Can't think of anything. I'll text if I'm going to be late," I promised as I urged Max up the stairs.

I got ready in a flash; I had taken to keeping a 'go bag' ready, the idea and term appropriated from some TV show back in my television watching days. I grabbed extra snacks in case I was able to hitch a ride to the hospital after work, although I suspected I would be stuck at our hospital in charge of the post-surgery mop up chores so that Dr. Drama could leave. I was optimistically envisioning figurative mopping up the voluminous paperwork, but it could just as easily be literal mopping up.

When I rushed into the treatment area, the atmosphere was charged with tension and emotion. Usually cheerful Dr. Taren was crying and complained, "I shouldn't have left Stretch alone at the hospital to come to work. He practically threw me out, but it's not right for him to be there all by himself."

I rushed over to her, draped my arm around her shoulder and assured her, "Then you'll go back."

Molly joined us and sent me off with a determined assurance, "I've got this, and you'll just have to double cover ER and surgery."

I headed straight to surgery to help, but Dr. Drama bounced me back to ER explaining, "An emergency pyometra is waiting up front. Go ahead and admit it, I already have my CCL surgery patient under anesthesia."

"Absolutely!" I agreed happily. Mrs. Chade and her dog Dora might have been a management disaster for me, but medically I'd done everything correctly diagnosing and treating her uterine infection, so I should have no problems duplicating that level of care for this case.

Tess, the receptionist, was just about to lay the chart down on the counter but turned to me and asked, "You seeing the pyo?"

"I am," I replied, taking the chart from her.

The appointment tech came out of Room 2 and gave me the run down, "Princess was in heat a couple months ago, started leaving spots of blood on the floor this week, and then acted lethargic and stopped eating yesterday."

On physical examination Princess, a jet black, well-groomed Standard Poodle, seemed pale, despite yesterday's bloodwork from the referring Vet which indicated she wasn't anemic. And when I palpated her abdomen everything felt weird, but I couldn't feel any lumps or elicit significant pain. Everyone seemed to be so sure this was a pyometra case but I wasn't convinced. Thank goodness radiographs and the ultrasound would make sure we got the necessary confirmation before we sent Princess to surgery with the wrong diagnosis.

The discussion with Carly seemed to go well until I was finished and she replied, "My husband told me to skip any further testing and go straight to surgery. Doctor Vincent did the same surgery on our first dog and no one even discussed doing an ultrasound back then."

"I'm not comfortable with that," I said gently. "Further testing can prevent diagnostic errors, options we didn't always have in the past."

"Well, we're comfortable with it," she said just as gently, but still insistently. "We'd rather spend our money on treatment, not extra testing."

"Tabitha can help you get her hospital admittance forms done while I speak with Dr. Vincent," I said, plastering a pleasant expression on my face. I didn't know how Dr. Drama was going react, but I would be very concerned skipping any testing in this less than clear cut case. I told the first technician I saw to get a tiny bit of blood from Princess and run a hematocrit and make me some slides stat. Maybe if I had a few more facts and could look at the cells for myself I could dial down my concern that we were missing something.

"Is the pyo stable?" one of the surgery technicians asked, holding up a syringe. "Dr. Vincent would like to do her next. I've got her pre-op injection."

"She's stable, but I need to discuss the case with him before we do anything," I said, distress creeping into my voice.

"Can I give her pre-op shot?" she asked doggedly, staying focused on her objective of keeping Dr. Drama on schedule.

"No," I answered reluctantly. "Don't do anything until I talk to Doc."

I got ready, put on my cap and mask so that I could step into the surgery room, and then stood there awkwardly until I could ask if it were a good time for a question.

Dr. Drama looked up at me grudgingly, but nodded so I explained my concerns about the case.

He let out a huge sigh to let me know just how put upon he was feeling and said, "Interns! Always looking for zebras when you hear hoof beats. Pyos aren't just horses, they're the most common every day bay horse you'll ever see! Go ahead, look at your slides but hurry the hell up."

As I left the surgery room I could hear him muttering his displeasure and suggesting that I was the one that enjoyed creating drama around here. On the slide some of the red blood cells had abnormal shapes and sizes, sadly just like Dizzy's blood slide had shown with her cancer. I heard the centrifuge finally stop and I stared at the spun blood sample in bewilderment. I measured it twice, but Princess's hematocrit had dropped more than ten points from yesterday, dropping her down into the anemic range. No two centrifuges spin samples exactly the same way so numbers can certainly vary, but not by ten points!

I started speed walking to surgery but just as I reached the door I did a hasty about face and walked just as quickly back to the microscope. I examined the slide and the platelet numbers were low. I took a couple of deep breaths but wasn't sure what to do next. I couldn't let Princess go to surgery without further workup, but how was I going to gather enough facts without said workup to convince the owner to let me do it? What was I most afraid of? That Princess had a lack of platelets like Belle, or cancer in her spleen like Dizzy? Or maybe an immune mediated disease in which the body attacks its own red blood cells and platelets? Actually my biggest fear at this point was that a patient suffering with any of those problems whose blood might not be clotting normally could be erroneously sent to surgery and bleed to death on my watch.

"Drama Junior!" Dr. Drama roared from across the huge treatment room with his hands on his hips and his ribs puffed out in such a way I was afraid he was going to start beating his chest like a silverback gorilla. "Do I have a surgery case or not?"

"Not!" I called back firmly, but with a pronounced deferential expression on my face.

Dr. Drama stood motionless like a pissed off statue as I walked over to him, holding my slide evidence like an offering, and said, "I think Princess has hemolytic anemia, for sure the red blood cells are under some kind of attack."

"Argh!" he exclaimed in unbearable frustration. "Of course she does! Arrrrrrrrrrrrrrgh."

I stood motionless in front of him, not knowing what to say.

He sighed, dropped his arms down and then gave me an odd half side hug, saying, "By God, some pesky Intern better have checked Stretch's bloodwork just as carefully as you did before they rushed him into surgery."

"You might be able to get over to the hospital quicker now," I suggested optimistically.

"Yea, maybe. But tell me what you've done and said because I'd better take over from here with Princess and her owner," Dr. Drama said dejectedly. "It'll be hard enough for me to explain why she isn't going to have surgery."

The rest of the day passed in a blur. It wasn't horribly busy, but I was pulled in multiple directions until Quickcut showed up. He chased me back to the ER department, happy to be alone and in charge of surgery while Dr. Drama was occupied with Stretch. I helped the internal medicine technician settle Princess into her temporary home in ICU and while there were quite a few tests still pending, no cancer or enlarged uterus like in a pyometra case had been found on the ultrasound so we could celebrate those small victories. When Quickcut called for rounds at six I was shocked that my day was almost done, at the same time ecstatic to flee the hospital. As I was packing up, Dr. Drama returned and announced that Stretch was in recovery and doing well, so that news gave me the bounce of energy necessary to finish up. As I headed out Dr. Drama told me to bring Max back for surgery in the morning, after warning me that he'd be the first patient bumped off the schedule if surgery time was needed for an emergency.

Chapter Twenty-seven

Dog's backyard was quiet and his parking pad was empty, so I decided to collect my waiting puppy and grab my book and make use of the space. That way Max could run around to his heart's content and sniff every leaf and blade of grass while I blissfully escaped into someone else's story. But by the time I got back downstairs and around the house to the fenced in yard, Dog and three of the alley guys were piling out of the SUV, laughing and mocking each other as men so often do. They awkwardly stopped when they saw me, and then Dog grinned, came over and kissed me hello, on the mouth but definitely more greeting than romantic gesture, maybe with a sliver of possessiveness thrown in.

I grinned up at him, then included Jim, Jack and a third man I hadn't met yet in my greeting, "Hi, guys! Whatcha doing?"

Jim and Jack shyly walked over and shook my hand and called me Ma'am, and then introduced their friend as John, and Dog said, "I've been trying to get them to start a band and call themselves the Jays!"

"We like the name but none of us can sing or play an instrument so that stands in the way of his plan," Jack explained.

The men laughed together happily and I got the feeling it was an old joke. I joined them and agreed, "Might stand in the way of your success."

"Hey, Big Dog, where do you want the trash bags?" Jim asked as he was unloading the SUV.

"Toss it all in our dumpster except my bag, leave that one in the SUV," Dog replied. "I'll put the rakes away. Thanks for your help."

"Anytime Big Dog," John said smiling. "I'd help even if you didn't feed us."

"I wouldn't," Jack said, and they all snickered conspiratorially, again like it was an old private joke.

They finished with the trash, leaving a single small black bag for Dog, and collected their containers of restaurant leftovers from the back seat.

Then the three of them walked companionably down the alley bantering and joking again.

"Whatcha got?" I asked with a smile, sure that he was going to blow me off once again, but wanting to signal I wasn't going to get angry when he did.

"Stuff," he said with a partial shake of his head, but then looked directly at me as he reached inside the passenger's door and announced happily, "and your favorite soup."

I wasn't in the mood for playing twenty questions with him only to fail to get any real answers so I just said, "Soup for me? Awesome!"

"If you want to eat out here while Max runs around, I can sit with you for a bit," Dog offered with a sweet smile, relieved I wasn't pressuring him. "Then I have to head in to work."

"Sounds like a plan," I said with a brighter smile. "You're so good to all of us."

"They're great guys," he replied warmly. "Veterans all of them."

"You're a veteran too, aren't you?" I asked gently, then chided myself for so quickly breaking my vow to keep our brief break together pressure free.

"I am," he replied, startling me by actually answering a question.

I struggled for a topic that would reward him for the personal information by not pushing for more details, but all I could think of were additional questions about him or the guys. I concentrated on eating my soup and tossing the toy for Max. It turned into a pretty comfortable silence.

Dog seemed equally at ease until he sat up straight beside me and asked, "Do you think you have any prejudices?"

"I probably do," I answered honestly. "I don't always agree with what other people say."

Dog stiffened at the same time his face fell into a disappointed expression and he asked, "Like?"

"Like everyone's so sure Calico cats are more aggressive than other cats," I replied as I closely watched his face to figure out what he felt so strongly about. "But I don't think that it's true, and I have an article that proves my point! But most of the people I work with believe it, and adding to the confusion there's a second article that supports them. But maybe people are causing their own problems by acting tense around them?"

"Calico cats?" he asked, obviously bewildered.

"Oh, you're talking about Pitbulls aren't you?" I said as it dawned on me what he was really asking. "I know I'm much more likely to be bitten by a Chihuahua than a Pitbull, but I'm also not an idiot, I know which bite could more likely end my career. But generally I'm more careful with animals showing fearful or aggressive body language, not so much by breed."

Dog let out an exasperated breath and then explained, "No, I'm talking about people, not pets."

"Oh, sorry," I said apologetically. "That's a hard one. I'm sure not prejudiced against people who don't own pets; there's a thousand good reasons not to have a pet. But if someone is unkind to animals? Actually gets pleasure from causing them pain? Yeah, I could never trust them or believe they're good people. And now the FBI tracks animal abusers so they must have proof I'm right."

Dog shook his head sheepishly and laughed in an odd tone. I looked at him curiously as I racked my brain for what I was missing, but I just wasn't understanding whatever concept he was so concerned about.

He placed both hands on my shoulders and looked into my eyes and asked bluntly, "Do you judge people by their race or religion or education or homeless status or whatever?"

"No, I don't think so," I answered to the best of my ability. "I'm really influenced by kindness in people, if I see a stranger helping another person, I instantly want to be their new best friend. The opposite if they are being cruel, of course."

Dog sighed deeply and pulled me toward him into a stiff hug, finally resting his chin on the top of my head as I snuggled into his shoulder. It was slowly dawning on me that when I had thrown myself into my competitive pre-veterinary coursework and afterwards into the demanding veterinary school program, I had dedicated myself to one fanatical goal, becoming the best veterinarian I could be. Consequently, I had focused on this extremely narrow view of life for many long years. Dog's world view was obviously so much broader than mine was, and I couldn't begin to imagine what he had experienced out in that world, both good and evil.

"Sorry," I said softly, pulling back to look at him. "I've been living in a protected bubble for most of my adult life and I'm not fully a part of the real world yet."

"Most of me doesn't want you to ever join that world," Dog confessed and stroked my hair gently. "When I'm with you, I can forget for a bit how bleak it can be out there."

"I'm sorry," I said, and we sat there for a few more minutes without speaking until Dog started squeezing me progressively tighter which was a little unsettling until I realized he was trying to see his watch.

"I'm late," he said regretfully as he let me go and stood up. But then he grinned and exclaimed, "Calico cats! Seriously?"

Chapter Twenty-eight

Dr. Drama started the day by being a complete ass in rounds, displeased with everything and everyone. His morning monologue, instead of being his normal hilarious mix of encouragement and ridicule, was just plain mean. Dr. Tolliver stalked out after five minutes, but the onslaught continued unabated until Dr. Blackwell showed up and dragged him out, putting me in charge of rounds as they left. When we finished we awkwardly milled around until Dr. Tolliver and Dr. Blackwell came back.

"I apologize to all of you," Dr. Tolliver said sincerely. "Dr. Vincent's sense of humor loses its charm when he's upset. It's no reflection on you."

"We've been especially impressed by, and frankly incredibly happy with, this year's Intern class," Dr. Blackwell said warmly and she made eye contact with each of us in turn. "All four of you are bright, well-educated as well as well trained, kind, engaged, empathetic, honorable and passionate human beings; everything that we could want when we make the difficult decision to share our precious and much beloved patients and clients with you. But..."

"There's always a but," Dr. Drama added ominously, as he rejoined the group.

With a sideways glare at him, Dr. Blackwell continued, "But we're concerned you're the exact type of people that this job can eat alive. The statistics don't lie; we as a profession are besieged by suicide, compassion fatigue and burnout as well as problems with drug and alcohol abuse. We desperately want you to be the best veterinarians that you can be, but we don't want any of you to be destroyed in the process."

"You need to start protecting yourself early in your career, so that you'll not only still be in the profession when you're our age, but you'll be happy and healthy as well," Dr. Tolliver said, more emotional than I had ever seen her. "I was half way through my residency when I had to take a break, completely change my life and educational plans, and start all over again in a different specialty because I was totally unprepared for the constant interpersonal relationship problems. And that was even before there was such a thing as cyberbullying."

"It's the exact wonderful qualities that make you so valuable to us, that in turn make you so vulnerable to damage from the intense interactions and constant stress," Dr. Drama said dramatically, even for him, and he said it with a catch in his voice that gave proof that he was deeply feeling what he was saying. "I sum it up with one word, passion."

He looked around at us all with narrowed eyes, daring us to laugh or disagree, and continued, "You're passionate about the patients, their families, and your profession, passionate to know everything, do everything perfectly, be everything to everybody, and when that passion isn't returned or rewarded, you aren't simply disappointed you're heartbroken and feel betrayed, worse than walking in on your wife making love to the, the postman," he gave a chagrinned look toward his wife but kept explaining, "People will do the most horrific things to the pets and say the most atrocious things to you, but that isn't the only time you'll feel gutted. Your bosses, the media, social media, people at your kid's soccer game, all of them will question your motives and dedication no matter how much you do if you're not doing it for them right when they want you to do it."

"And the attacks can happen when its least expected," Dr. Blackwell added frowning.

"But you'll also need to work relentlessly to have a full, joyful life outside of work, you must be equally passionate about your family," Dr. Drama said, getting up and moving over to his wife and grabbing her face in his hands and kissing her with a loud smack. She smiled softly and for a split second, you could feel all of us fade away from their reality, and then they refocused back to the room and Dr. Drama repeated, "Passionate for your family even if sometimes you're glad they're out of town, and you can stay late at work with an interesting case without feeling torn in two directions. But know this: if you remove yourself from that dreadful pulled apart feeling, you'll fall so deeply into your work that eventually you'll drown in it."

"Family's the most important, but you must develop other interests that you can be passionate about, to enjoy and feel pleasure doing, to provide a counterweight for the heavy emotional lifting you have to do on the job," Dr. Tolliver insisted, "as well as the weight of family obligations."

"And sadly, now we have people waiting on us," Dr. Blackwell announced reluctantly.

"Let's get to work and have a great day!" Dr. Drama said encouragingly.

I immediately did get to work, but when I finally got a break and plopped down at a computer station, I stared at the clock in disbelief; this day wasn't close to being done yet. So far it had been the behavior day from hell and all my mentors' words from the morning's pep talk bounced around my brain extolling me not to let the stress wound me or worse yet, eat me alive. Neither were the best expressions to use on a day where every patient was doing their very best to maul us all.

The crowned champion of bad behavior was a Belgian Malinois whose first bite attempt was a sneak attack on Dr. Drama while he was discussing surgery with the owner, innocently raising his arm to point at a diagram on the computer screen. I was paying close attention to the explanation and almost didn't catch the flash of movement as the dog launched himself at the gesturing arm. As soon as I saw him, I stuck my chart in front of his face and screeched, "Cut it out." The chart was no real protection and my command couldn't have made sense to him, I don't even know why that particular phrase slipped out, but at least it served to distract him. After a few second's pause, it also changed his target and he came after me with a vengeance, doing his best alligator impression, complete with a gargantuan toothy grin and powerfully snapping jaws punctuating his loud barking fits.

The male owner shouted, "No," reeled the dog's leash in, and grabbed him in a head lock. Dr. Drama seized the opportunity and slipped the muzzle on, ending the confrontation as far as the owner and I were concerned.

"No, keep a close hold on him," Dr. Drama instructed pointedly, but he was too late as the pressure on the leash slacked, the dog charged me again, knocking Dr. Drama back on his way to me.

The owner and Dr. Drama came to my aid but in the time it took them to pull him off me, he had viciously driven his muzzle into my sternum multiple times, desperately trying to bite me despite the muzzle holding his mouth shut. Silver lining, I now know why medical personnel use a sternal rub as a painful stimuli on people, it hurt so badly it took my breath away. As he was being lifted off my chest, he became frantic to escape and planted his back legs on me and, with his claws held splayed out to provide grip and with tremendous power, he pushed off. Both feet raked down the front of my body from mid abdomen straight down across the tops of my thighs almost to my knees.

At the time the raking stung but didn't hurt anywhere near as much as the throbbing pain from the sternal bruising, but I was mortified, assuming the front of my clothes had been shredded. I was thrilled when I could look down and saw that my scrubs were intact, barely even dirty. But as I watched the area, parallel lines of blood started to seep through the material and I rapidly excused myself. When I made it to the locker room, dropped my pants and examined the area, the skin was broken, oozing blood from multiple scratches up and down both sides. There was scattered bruising starting to show and the left side abrasions looked deep enough that they would probably scar. Disinfecting the long wounds striped down my body hurt worse than the injury had, but I only had to bandage a couple of areas to control the bleeding before I put on a new set of scrubs.

The scientist side of me was captivated by the fact that my skin could be so traumatized while the clothing directly over the area remained intact, but while I felt rather violated I didn't feel deeply wounded. I didn't blame the dog, he was terrified and from his point of view the best defense was a decisive offense. I didn't blame the owner. None of us ever truly knows how another being will act under stress, and when his pet misbehaved he had responded immediately and appropriately. I wished it hadn't happened, the pain was increasingly difficult to bear the longer it persisted. But it didn't affect me on a more profound level, it didn't hurt my feelings or even touch them in any way, because neither the dog nor the owner's intention was to hurt me.

But oddly my day on surgery rotation did affect me in a negative way, but in a completely different respect, because I had to admit, to myself only, that I really had no interest in orthopedic surgery. I assisted on three cruciate surgeries, and while all the patients' behavior issues were controlled as soon as they received their pre-op medication, the surgery itself just wasn't my cup of tea. The first one was sort of interesting, but half way through the second one my interest faded and I know myself well enough to realize that it was never coming back. I would have given anything not to feel this way, but I had a decidedly been there, done that attitude. Physicians choosing a surgical specialty didn't have to worry about not enjoying one subspecialty of surgery, a thoracic surgeon wouldn't have to worry about being asked to do a cruciate repair. But in veterinary medicine, a referral surgeon in practice usually has to be all of those specialties wrapped into one individual. But until I had firmly made up my mind about applying for a surgical residency, I needed to fake a level of interest in it all, at least in front of Dr. Drama and the other surgeons.

Chapter Twenty-nine

"I'm back!" Dr. Drama alerted me from across the treatment room, and I jumped to my feet and headed over. "Ready for our next patient?"

"Absolutely!" I replied happily. "An abdominal exploratory from Internal Medicine right?"

"Looks like a mass on the spleen on ultrasound, but you need to keep an open mind," Dr. Drama said earnestly.

"I will," I agreed. Then I added, mimicking his voice, "We always do a complete exploratory and examine the entire abdomen."

He smiled in appreciation then asked, "Have you heard how that immune mediated poodle is doing? You know, the not-pyo dog?"

"Doing well," I bragged. "Princess is tolerating her medication and her counts have stabilized."

"Great news!" he said, and then clapping his hands rapidly asked the surgery techs, "Time to scrub?"

"Yes," the surgery tech replied. "We're a go!"

The exploratory was exactly what I needed to utterly confuse me about my future as a surgeon. From the minute I slipped my gloved hands into the abdomen, felt the warmth and subtle movement and saw the heart beat in all the arteries supplying the internal organs, especially the beautiful fan of vessels supplying the intestines, I was consumed by the magic, enthralled by the miracle of how the body worked, my state of mind oddly reminiscent of being enchanted by my feelings for Dog. And when the successful surgery was over, I had no thought that another abdominal surgery would be repetitive or boring! I felt more like I had just been released from the harness of my favorite rollercoaster at Cedar Point and I wanted more than anything to dash back into line, to feel that enticing thrill again as soon as possible. Quickcut was indeed a lucky man if he felt this way about every kind of surgery he got to do.

But by the time we were finished, I was beyond tired, physically drained and achy all over. Max's surgery was postponed so that we could squeeze in the emergency exploratory and while I still wanted it over with, it had been such a physically tough day already I was glad to be done. In fact I'd say I was dog-tired except I wasn't sure what that expression meant since most of the dogs I knew were relentlessly energetic, ready to go full speed even if just woken from a deep sleep. As I started my journey home, my feet were actually dragging enough that I scuffed the toes of my shoes a couple times as I stumbled out of the building. But when I heard someone yell "Bitch!" I summoned enough oomph to turn around and greet whichever comrade it was, assuming it was one of the other interns joking around with me.

But he wasn't a comrade, and he certainly wasn't in any kind of a jocular mood as he bore down on me from across the parking lot. Mr. Tate, with a black and blue face and split lip, fixed his one working eye on me and charged across the parking lot, fanatically zeroed in on my position. I suddenly had lots of energy and started backpedaling, tugging Max with me, who after briefly resisting began fearfully pulling backwards as well, wrapping himself around my legs trying to simultaneously maneuver behind me while keeping his head and eyes turned towards the now loudly cursing man.

A woman, carrying a small dog and shepherding two young children in front of her, took off in the opposite direction but loudly yelled back at the man, "Hey! Hey!" which was way more demanding than my quiet litany of "No. No. No."

As the furious man reached us, Max slunk back in front of me in full appeasement body language, groveling and yawning and licking his lips, and as I continued to retreat, I concentrated on swinging his slack leash in a wide arc, trying to drag him out of harm's way. But when Tate reached us, all I could focus on was his face monstrously distorted with rage. I hit the curb with my heel and was just barely able to hop up onto the sidewalk and lurch for the door, which was locked like it always was, but I hopelessly tugged and rattled it anyway, screaming for help. Then as I turned back to face him, still tugging at the unmoving door behind me as hard as I could with one hand and trying to swing Max to safety with the other hand, I saw Tate's arm cross his chest then whip back across, forcefully backhanding my now fully cowering dog, who screamed a high pitched cry as he sailed away from me.

The leash easily flew out of my terror weakened hand, but with that pitiful cry raw power surged through me, seemingly flowing through my feet, strengthening my muscles as it passed through, collecting in my core, and I didn't simply stand my ground; I took an aggressive step towards him. He charged me channeling an attacking grizzly bear, opening his arms and mouth wide, and spittle flew into my face with every foul curse. I didn't even think to punch or kick him; instead I threw all my weight forward and chucked him with my forearms as hard as I could into his belly, channeling some momma bear persona of my own. Off balance, he stepped back half way off the curb, wind milled his arms a couple times, and then awkwardly fell. As I heard the door open behind me, I watched his head fly back and crack loudly on the hard surface. I felt bodies surround me as I rushed to Max, who was standing with his tail and head drooping down, his ears hanging as low as I had ever seen them.

"You okay Max?" I asked softly and his tail started to slowly wag, but then he whipped his head over to peer behind me. I spun around in time to see Tate lurch to his feet, blood flying from the back of his head as he wobbled around, and then he staggered to his truck.

"Someone get his license plate," Molly yelled, slipping an arm around me, "the police are on the way."

She led Max and me back inside, both of us trembling and skittering at every sound. As petrified as I was I still concentrated on speaking in a composed voice to reassure Max, I didn't even care what nonsense words I was speaking. By the time Amelia came over with treats in her hand, Max was already settling down. Dr. Nikki jogged to our position and examined Max without even being asked, starting at the tip of his nose, carefully working her way down inch by inch and finishing by running her hand down the length of the tail. She spoke to him the entire time in a happy voice and he seemed to respond well to her exam, acting like it was some kind of weird petting ritual. She announced that he appeared to be injury free and I think I shocked her when I exuberantly hugged her in my relief.

I held my phone in shaking hands and called Dog, my excuse was to ask him to come pick us up but it was honestly because I wasn't going to feel safe until I could connect with him. But when he answered I could hardly speak at all. I finally gasped out what had happened, and he cursed loudly, then asked if we'd called the police. When I said yes he swore again and told me not to leave the hospital until he arrived, no matter how long it took him, and then he hung up on me. I burst into tears at the abrupt abandonment and looked up to see everyone staring at me, but I couldn't stop from sobbing in my disappointment.

Two police cars screeched into the parking lot, lights flashing and sirens blaring, and hope and glorious relief arrived with them. But then sudden silence and complete darkness followed, as all their lights were extinguished except a barely visible red glow from the front seats. A minute or two later both cars pulled out without anyone ever coming in to talk to us. Molly sputtered in shock and annoyance, but before she could call back to complain, two men arrived in street clothes and introduced themselves as detectives. They were both visibly armed which is all I cared about, even though it struck me as a strange response to a simple unsuccessful attack. They listened attentively to my entire story, taking notes throughout, and then I pulled the Tates' chart and gave them all of that information, but I got the impression they already knew more than we did about the man. They thanked us, checked our security precautions, accepted our offer to make use of our hospitality bar and settled into chairs sipping their coffee in our waiting room while they worked on their paperwork.

When I couldn't stand it anymore, I approached them cautiously and asked, "Can I get you anything? Help you in any way?"

"We're good," the younger detective answered. "Thank you."

"What are you doing?" I blurted out rudely, the adrenaline was wearing off which left me frazzled and on my last nerve.

"Sorry, Ma'am?" he replied questioningly, but then turned away from me and tapped his ear, looked at his partner, nodded a couple times and stood up.

"We're sorry, Ma'am," he stated kindly. "You were dragged into something bigger than Mr. Tate and all his problems. But it's over now."

"What's over?" I asked plaintively.

"Sorry," he repeated sternly, shaking his head no. "Ongoing investigation."

The older detective politely added, "Please don't discuss any of this with anyone," and then they turned and walked out.

I was beyond frustrated and was encircled by my colleagues and their confused yapping didn't help soothe my nerves. Molly was fuming enough for all of us, but I put my hand on her arm to stop her tirade and said, "I know it doesn't make sense, but I think something bigger is going on; now I can see all sorts of flashing lights over at the far side of the badlands."

We stared out the windows at the commotion and made guesses about what might be going on, but as always there was work that needed to be done so we had to turn our attentions to other concerns. I couldn't count how many intriguing conversations or interesting situations I had walked away from in the past few months because there were patients waiting. This was just one more time. But it was certainly the strangest mystery yet.

Chapter Thirty

I was afraid to leave with Max until Molly offered to drive us home.
Dog had instructed me to wait at the hospital, but I assumed he meant that
I shouldn't walk home on my own. I called Phil to make sure the house
was secure and he promised to be looking out for me, so I thought that was
plenty of precautions to take. Besides, if Dog was so concerned about me,
he would have shown up here already. Even with my weird brain, I
couldn't conceive of anything that could be more important than both Max
and I being attacked, so I wasn't all that interested in his feelings about this,
or about anything else for that matter.

Max crouched just as fearfully in the back seat as he had on his first trip
home, his claws extended over the edge trying to maintain some kind of
grip. He seemed remarkably uninterested in my reassurances and attempts
to comfort him, in such contrast to his response to Tate's brutal attack. His
fear of car travel appeared to have the strength of a full blown phobia. But
his profound joyous relief when released from the back seat was contagious
and added to my happiness of being home and welcomed by my
housemates. And not only was every porch light shining brightly but every
other conceivable house light was blazing as well. I hugged Molly, thanking
her intensely, and she promised me that she would be at this same spot the
next morning at 6:45 A.M. to pick me up!

Phil was on point, then Ethan, Mei and I, plus Max, clustered together
and moved as one awkward multi-legged organism through the lobby and
up the stairs to my apartment. We checked the bathroom and hall closet,
then they accompanied me into my room and we checked that closet
carefully too, like I was a child afraid of monsters. But I was so glad that
they did. Tate's face was plastered on the back of my eyelids, and I saw him
coming to get me every place I looked. And I had to face the realization
that he not only didn't care if he maimed or killed me, he wished for it with
all his heart. Tonight I had seen evil intent for myself, and I would never
be the same. But reassured by my friends, I was able to usher them out

with a smile, carefully lock my door and throw the security bar, order Max up onto the couch for snuggle time and find a way to deal with what had happened on my own.

After our mutual comfort time, I let Max out for a final chance to pee, stopping right next to the front porch under the brightest light, a spot I usually avoided to keep Max from killing the grass in such a visible area. But tonight I didn't care, nor did I care if I was being a coward or not, I was unnerved enough to stay as close as possible to the safety of our front door. In contrast Max was excited by the change in routine and happily cavorted on and off the stairs, in all ways seeming to be uninjured and unintimidated.

But then after collapsing in my bed, I struggled to fall asleep, exhausted but tossing and turning as a thousand thoughts and emotions tormented me. But the worst of them all condensed down to the fact that it desperately hurt my feelings that Dog hadn't even called to check on me. It felt more painful than the depressing fact that Tate had wanted to tear me into pieces with his bare hands, more painful than my bruised sternum and tender full body scratches. Dog's behavior didn't make any sense to me, especially after all the times he had reacted so protectively towards me, no matter how many times I turned it over in my mind. Max seemed restless too, but I was pretty sure he was being disturbed by my flipping and flopping around and wasn't suffering because of his most recent trauma. I concentrated on slowing my breathing down, counting as I breathed in, held my breath, and then slowly let it out. It was the pattern I had been taught to control anxiety and it usually worked to help me sleep as well, but it wasn't getting the job done tonight. As I held my breath one more time, I heard a noise from the direction of my closet, and then heard Max shift his weight and rock his kennel.

I snuck over to the previously inspected closet, opened the door, but didn't see anything out of the ordinary. I froze in place to listen and the moment I decided I was just being paranoid I heard a soft knocking on the back wall and what sounded like my name being called. I still wasn't sure, but then heard a distinct call, in a weak version of Dog's voice, crying "Help."

I scooted closer and spoke at the thin wall, "I'm here Dog. We'll be right over."

"No," he responded. "It's not safe."

"How can I help?" I asked frantically.

"What?" he asked a little louder.

"Call me," I insisted.

"Phone gone," he said, his voice fading.

"What's wrong?" I asked a little louder.

"Shot," it sounded like he said, but I couldn't believe that was right. I tugged the closet door shut behind me, then yanked on the light chain to be able to inspect the back of the closet. The lower panel of plywood was screwed in from my side, so I guessed it should be able to be removed from my side as well. I pulled the light off again, then crept to my kitchen and found the multifunctional tool that Ethan had forced on me last week. He was afraid I was unprepared for 'all of life's little disasters' without it. I snuck back to the closet, closed the door, and turned the light back on. I could hear Dog saying something, sounding weaker yet, and I said, "I'm back," and started unscrewing the first screw.

"What are you doing?" he asked much louder.

"I'm coming through the closet wall," I said in a matter-of-fact tone. I heard what sounded like a moan, but I couldn't tell if it was from exasperation or pain. I kept removing screws until just the top two were left, then I shut off the light and with difficulty, removed them. I set the panel to the side and then, on my hands and knees, scrunched down and stuck my head into his closet, then I had to twist and contort myself in the struggle to make my way through his impressive collection of shoes and boots. I finally found him by the odd sound he was making. I think he was trying to laugh, but it was combined with a harsher, moister sound that was more cough like.

"Did you say shot?" I whispered intensely.

"Yeah," he said, again with the odd undertone. "Left upper arm. And I got hit in the chest a couple times."

"Shot in the chest?" I asked loudly in shock.

"No," he hissed back. "Hit. Struck. Feels like I was kicked by a horse."

"Okay," I answered. "And you're not at the hospital because?"

"I couldn't be arrested yet," he replied unexpectedly. "I just need to make it until tomorrow, then I'll go to the hospital."

I stammered nonsense in shocked response, then calmed down enough to ask, "What should I do?"

"I need your phone and I need you to clean the wound and bandage it," he said desperately. "One day. I just need you to buy me one day. Less than a day, twelve hours. Eight hours."

"Crawl through the closets and get to my bathroom where I can turn the light on without it showing outside," I said as I helped him maneuver through the awkward opening.

Once we were confined to the windowless bathroom, I switched the light on and examined him quickly, using my stethoscope to listen to his chest. Human breath sounds aren't the same as the breath sounds of dogs and cats, due to the different shape of the chests, but under two rather spectacular bruises on his chest the breath sounds were muffled enough that I thought his lungs were bruised. But his color was good and his weak voice seemed to be more from a disturbance in his throat. Or possibly his hearing, he complained his ears were still ringing from the gunshots. His arm looked gruesome, the bullet had plowed through a long stripe of skin and muscle, but it was rather superficial and oozing more than outright bleeding. I had all sorts of wound care supplies at home for Max so I had it well cleaned and bandaged efficiently.

The bandage looked very professional until I went to apply the final layer and I only had two selections of flexible self-adherent wrap; one choice was bright pink with purple hearts and the other was royal blue with navy paw prints. I held them both out to Dog for his choice with an apologetic expression on my face.

He smiled weakly and pointed to the blue with paw prints.

Dog asked me to give him some privacy with the phone so I went and sat cross legged next to Max's kennel and spoke to my resting pup. I didn't dare let him out even though I could have used the comfort. Max was obviously fascinated by our crawling through the closet and would think it was some kind of exciting game to play. But it wasn't a game if Dog expected to be arrested. And criminal behavior wasn't something I could be any part of. But caring for him medically, giving simple first aid, seemed morally feasible to me.

I felt Dog come up to me in the dark and I asked, "How you doing?"

"Doc told me what meds to take," he replied breathlessly. "After that I'm going to lie down for a few hours, will you make sure I'm up by four?"

"I will," I agreed reluctantly, following him through the opening into his apartment. Max whined once when I left but then settled down.

"You can stay in your apartment," Dog whispered. "I'll be fine."

"No," I stated simply, and turned away from him, unwilling to discuss it.

Dog moved silently around his apartment, returning to his bedroom in plaid sleep pants and a white t-shirt and carrying a glass of water. He plopped down on the edge of his bed, drank at least half the glass, and then stiffly crawled under the covers. I eased under the covers from the other side to a confused "hey" protest from Dog.

"I'm just here to monitor you," I whispered as I gently spooned up to his back. "It's what I'd do for any other patient."

He gave a raspy chuckle then somberly said, "Thanks, Kate."

Without thinking, I blurted out, "My name is Katya and I've been called Kat my whole life."

"Kat," he said drowsily. "I like it. Dr. Kat."

"Go to sleep," I said soothingly.

"Are we telling secrets?" he asked, slightly slurring his words. Either he was beyond tired or he had taken something stronger than ibuprofen.

"We're sleeping," I replied, but even I could hear the smile in my voice.

"It was really bad tonight," he said with a deep sigh. "Tate is dead."

"Tate is dead?" I asked, horrified. "Did you kill him?"

"Me?' he asked, both surprised and offended.

My breath caught in my throat as realization swept over me. Mortified, I asked, "Was it me? Was it his head? His brain? From when I pushed him?"

"No," he replied with another sigh and a gentle, reassuring pat on my leg. "He was shot too. Live by the sword…"

"Live by the sword?" I asked quietly, but was answered by his deep regular breathing. When I tried to match his slow breathing pattern so that I didn't disturb him, it made it difficult to stay awake to watch over him. It helped that everything that had happened tonight and every word Dog had said played over and over in my mind as I tried to figure out what was going on. But the oddly shaped pieces of this Dog puzzle wouldn't fit together into any kind of recognizable picture.

Dog shifted next to me, cried out briefly in pain, then whispered, "I can hear your brain working overtime, Kat, like gears that just won't mesh," and then illustrated his meaning by making a harsh grinding noise.

"Busy day," I said. "I'm fine, go to sleep."

Dog mumbled next to me, "Sometimes I think you think too much."

"Sometimes I know I think too much," I whispered back. After a long ten count I added, "But this isn't one of those times."

Chapter Thirty-one

My phone beeped just before four a.m. causing Dog and me to sit straight up together, abruptly awake. Dog groaned, coughed, and grabbed his chest in pain and groaned again.

"Ouch," he said as he hacked again, but then smiled weakly at me. "Can you help me get cleaned up and dressed?"

"I think if I really cared about you I would say no," I said, more to myself than to him because I was already moving around the bed and helping him stand up.

We managed to get him into his black cargo pants, boots, and a formfitting black t-shirt. I tried to talk him out of the tight shirt and he illustrated all my best points by moaning and coughing as I tried to manipulate him into it. But then he pulled out a scruffy black bullet proof vest from under his bed and told me how to fasten it around him.

"Where'd you get that?" I asked suspiciously.

"From the Marine Corps," he replied.

"Seriously?" I asked incredulously. "Aren't they camouflage and have like pockets and plates?"

He sighed dramatically with his Dagger alter ego clearly glaring at me through narrowed eyes, but he demonstrated remarkable restraint as his lips visibly tightened to prevent what I assumed was a typical Dagger scathing remark from escaping.

I wasn't scared, but I felt helpless to influence his reckless behavior or to get enough information to understand why it might be necessary, so I spun away from him, crawled back through the closet and retrieved my wound care supplies. When I returned, he was trying to get a loose long sleeved knit shirt over the armor, so without speaking I helped tug it into place. I was determined not to say another word to him but, as usual, immediately had to add, "I should have changed the bandage first, now we have to pull your arm out of the sleeve."

"Nah," he disagreed, grimacing as he squeezed his injured arm directly over his wound and bandage. "It's seeping and hopefully I can get it to bleed through the outer shirt."

As soon as his words sank in and I saw the blood spreading onto his outer shirt I snapped, "Cut it out! That takes away the protection of the bandage, a wet bandage is worse than no bandage at all."

He glared again, but then took a deep breath, appearing to marshal his patience and said, "Sorry, Kat, but being visibly wounded might save my ass. I have to go. Can I keep your phone?"

"It's your phone," I replied coldly.

"I'll be fine," he said kissing me on the top of my head. "Don't go anywhere by yourself until you hear from me."

"I'll be at work," I said. I lifted my hand up to touch the side of his face gently. Tears gathered in my eyes, but for once in my life I kept my face composed and let a single tear escape and run down my face without ugly facial contortions or sobbing.

Dog looked at me so tenderly I felt like I could forgive him anything. Anything but keeping secrets. He kissed the tear mid cheek, then kissed me full on the lips, almost regretfully, and whispered, "Almost done."

"Take care of yourself," I said with a catch in my voice.

"I'll be fine," he repeated and then hesitated. He huffed with frustration, or indecision, then hauled me with him to his door and told me intensely, "Lock the door, throw the security bar, go to your apartment, replace the closet wall, and tell Phil everything when he wakes up."

"I will," I promised.

He turned to go, then turned back and said, "Call Maisy about something this afternoon."

"Okay?" I agreed tentatively. "About what?"

"Anything from your world," he said ominously, with the darkest possible expression on his face. Then he shifted his demeanor and smiled, cupping my face in both of his hands and kissing me butterfly lightly, pausing to gaze at me in such a touching way that my heart tightened in my chest. Then he vowed, "You're my tether, sweet Kat," before hustling down the stairs and disappearing into the pitch black yard. I didn't hear his car start, but I didn't hear his footsteps running anywhere either.

I stood there for a minute, trying not to feel anything at all, and put most of my energy into not feeling crushing despair. I did wonder if it was darkest just before the dawn; it seemed true as I looked out over the obscured neighborhood from my high perch. Except when I looked toward Maisy's place, there was significant light shining above fence height from her backyard and kennel area, possibly also from the house but I couldn't see that far from this angle.

I checked on Max, set the travel alarm clock for 6 am, wrapped myself in my quilt, and against instructions, I creeped back to my vantage spot on Dog's porch.,

Fear gripped me as two trucks lumbered down the alley behind the house with all their lights off. I could hear and feel them pass better than I could see them, but it seemed like they stopped somewhere behind Maisy's light infused backyard. I heard random shouts, engines starting and stopping, then saw lights flashing here and there, and it looked like multiple people were moving around the area. After a resounding crash, multiple shouts and loud curses, the trucks turned their headlights on, and then I could see large rectangular crates, most requiring two people to lift, being moved around the area and then loaded into the trucks.

Feeling safely hidden in the darkness, I continued watching the scene, looking for clues about what was going on and trying to determine if Dog was down there. I heard multiple blacked out cars move past me down the alley, then another truck rumbled by, but I was shocked when, in a coordinated attack, red and blue lights emblazoned the area from every direction, as all shapes and sizes and colors of police vehicles converged on the area from every conceivable route including over lawns and possibly through Maisey's fence.

I pictured Dog trapped in some dangerous, action movie inspired dramatic situation and then stifled a nervous giggle as I imagined my morning alarm going off on the phone he was carrying. I bet he'd wish I used something other than the theme for the old cartoon Underdog for my alarm! I felt horribly guilty for laughing as I realized that an ill-timed ring could get him killed. And that he really wouldn't care what song it played if it put him in mortal danger.

I stood up when bellowed orders from the police vehicles were met with vulgar expletives so uniquely disgusting they made me pause to figure out what they meant instead of being immediately offended by them. But when a shot rang out I scrambled back inside as quickly as I could, slammed the door, and with trembling hands twisted the lock and decisively crashed the security bar into place. I ran through the apartment, crawled through the closets, and paused only long enough to attach the screws to hold the back panel in place, then let Max out of his kennel and took him with me to hide in our old fashioned cast iron bathtub.

When enough time had passed with no more shots fired, and as Max's behavior got progressively antsy, I reluctantly left the safety of our protected space. I changed into my work clothes and took him out to pee next to the front door again. He took forever to choose a spot because he was repetitively distracted at a critical point by the pulsing light show reflected over the house and the loud voices echoing around the area. At least there were no gunshots while we were out there.

Back in the lobby I breathed a huge sigh of relief the minute Phil's door swung open. Max and I gratefully rushed into his apartment, and the entire story poured out of me in a rushing torrent of words. Phil nodded and gave encouraging one word comments, but didn't ask any questions and didn't stop what he was doing. He just shepherded me around with him as he started the coffee maker, filled a frying pan full of sausage patties, vigorously whisked eggs and added them to another large pan and finally popped bread into the toaster, pointed at it and handed me the butter and a knife. Breakfast was ready by the time that I finished my convoluted tale.

We set the table and sat down to eat before Phil asked his first question, "Are you alright?"

"I'm okay," I replied equally calmly but then oddly, I felt like crying again and teared up. "But Dog isn't."

"I don't have any answers," he admitted, but continued with a reassuring pat on my arm. "But I trust Dog and I trust law enforcement to be handling it, particularly with a big show like what's going on down the road right now. But no one is going to talk to either one of us until it's over."

"So we'll get answers when?" I asked, almost sadly.

"When those answers won't endanger anyone," he replied cryptically.

At the exact moment I decided I had to ask Phil specific questions about Dog, Phil's door flew open, and Ethan rushed in shouting, "What's going on Uncle Phil? There's a hundred cars in the alley."

"Our neighbors are having a big party and didn't invite us," Phil replied.

"Oh, Uncle Phil," Ethan protested. "That's not even funny. Something bad is happening."

"Breakfast is on the stove," Phil said evenly. "Then this house needs to concentrate on keeping ourselves safe and out of the way. Our time to help will come later."

Ethan stood statue still as he considered his Uncle's words for way longer than was comfortable for me, but Phil went back to eating so I followed his example. Ethan returned to function, walked over to the pans and served himself a plateful. He set it down then asked, "What can we do to help?"

"I haven't the foggiest idea," Phil replied, "but time will tell."

I checked the alarm clock I was carrying around with me and decided I had time to have seconds. I was trying to leave just enough time to run upstairs, grab my go bag, and run back outside and catch our ride with Molly. Parts of yesterday had grown hazy in my memory and I couldn't remember if Dr. Drama said we'd do Max's surgery today or tomorrow. But to keep Max safe for anesthesia I had to hold him off food in case it was today. Disappointing Max by not feeding him at the appointed time was much easier in Phil's apartment where he was distracted from our usual routine.

There was a soft knock at the door and Ethan got up and let Mei in. She was as serene as always and asked, "Is everyone okay?"

"We're all good," Phil said. "But Dog might be mixed up in what's going on."

"Oh," she said, checking Ethan's and my face for reactions. "He'll be fine."

Tears welled up again, but somehow it was already 6:45 a.m. so I quickly thanked Phil for breakfast, made a mad dash for my stuff and Max and I arrived at our designated pickup spot as Molly drove up.

"Wow!" she exclaimed as we climbed in. "I had to try three different ways until I made it through the roadblocks. What the heck is going on?"

"We don't know," I replied, deciding not to mention anything about Dog to work friends. "But it's something big."

"That's the Cruse house and kennel, isn't it?" she asked, concerned.

"That or right next door," I answered, trying to shed doubt on it being Maisy's house for some reason. Maybe so I could play dumb and call Maisy this afternoon like Dog had suggested.

"Maybe they caught the poisoner," Molly said hopefully, but after a brief thoughtful pause we both cracked up. As much as we personally would mount that kind of multiagency response to catch someone who poisoned our patients, it seemed unlikely it would happen in the real world.

With surprising concern for my feelings, Dr. Drama put Max first on the surgery schedule. I wasn't expecting that and was beyond grateful since it kept me from getting as anxious as I had been yesterday when I felt it hanging over my head all day. After the recent orthopedics and exciting emergency abdominal exploratory surgeries, I knew Dr. Drama was a strong, knowledgeable, and tenacious surgeon, but today with Max's reconstruction I could appreciate what an awesomely talented artist he was.

We performed the planned Z-plasty surgery; cutting, undermining and sliding his healthy skin to cover the gaping wound in the middle of Max's back. The resultant repair looked absolutely beautiful! While Max would still have a series of striped scars along his back, when his hair grew in, they wouldn't be the first thing you noticed about him. Yesterday the surgery team had taken his before pictures and at the time I had been a little offended. I sure didn't want to remember him that way. But today looking at the after pictures, I was thrilled we were documenting his remarkable transformation.

In contrast to the alligator wrestling contest of yesterday, today all of our patients were as sweet as Max, and their surgical procedures were diverse and fascinating, making the entire day loads of fun, but the work load was relentless. When we were finally finished, I was unpleasantly surprised to realize that I hadn't called Maisy even though I must have thought about doing it at least ten times. But now, with the Intern's meeting canceled, I was free to talk to Maisy as long as I wanted to, and I could relax and do it sitting down, which was quite a blessing because my feet were killing me.

Maisy answered just as I was contemplating hanging up, but she didn't sound at all like herself, saying "Hello?" with an audible cringe in her tone, as if she were bracing for me to scream at her.

"Maisy?" I asked, to be sure it was even her and when she weakly answered, "Yes?" I launched into my prepared story, "It's Dr. Kate and I've been talking to Gemma at the training center about puppy class for Max. He had his reconstructive surgery today, and I was hoping to get something going for next week or the week after."

Maisy paused and then asked, "Is Max doing okay?"

"He's doing great," I replied happily. "Sleeping it off right now! Dr.

Vincent did an incredible repair on his back. How's Roman?"

"He's doing well," she answered in a low depressed tone of voice, as if Roman was the only thing doing well in her life.

I persisted in my story and asked, "So Gemma said we needed to come up with some other older puppies that might fit into a less than classical puppy class and I thought of Roman."

Maisy started crying and I abandoned my subterfuge and asked, "What's wrong Maisy?"

"Everything," she said, alternating speaking with sobbing, but appearing to be as anxious to tell her story as I had been when I unloaded on Phil this morning. "There are police everywhere, and they made me move the dogs out of the kennel so I have them all in the house, and Meme's litter is due any day and no one will tell me anything except 'read the warrants,' and they've taken my husband and my son downtown for questioning, and my husband said it was all my fault and I had to call a lawyer but it wasn't our lawyer, it some other guy from Indianapolis."

She was sobbing so hard at this point that I couldn't understand anything else she said, but it was something to do with lawyers. When she stopped trying to speak and gave into quiet sobbing, I said, "I don't know anything about the lawyer stuff, but maybe I can help with the dogs?"

"Meme isn't in labor yet," she said, dispirited, almost as if she wished Meme was in trouble so she could deserve some help.

"Well, I was asking more as a neighbor than as a veterinarian," I said. "You may not know this, but I started my career long ago in the kennels. I can clean and disinfect with the best of them!"

Maisy gave a quiet giggle and said, "I might take you up on that in the coming days. But we're okay for tonight. Plus the police or FBI or whoever it is out there won't let me anywhere near the kennel."

"Well, let me give you my phone number," I said, trying to infuse the words with my care and concern. "Call me if there's anything I can do to help."

As Maisy was assuring me that she would call, I reached into my pocket for my phone to double check my number, realized that Dog had my phone and amended my offer, "Opps, I just realized I lent my phone to a friend. How about I text you the minute I get it back?"

"Thanks, Dr. Kate," Maisy replied.

"Everything will work out," I said confidently. "Sure don't know how, might be quite an adventure."

"An adventure?' she asked, dumfounded.

"Some people test themselves on mountains or rivers," I said with a laugh in my voice. "My brothers and I always liked to test our courage against our personal problems!"

"Ha!" she laughed in surprise. "I think I'd rather jump out of an airplane or take a zip line through the rainforest rather than face my problems!"

"Wouldn't we all?" I agreed laughing. "And I don't even like heights!"

Chapter Thirty-two

Amelia dropped me off in front of my house, and I thanked her profusely for the ride. I had decided to let Max sleep it off at the hospital so I could have easily walked home instead; the neighborhood felt safe with the pack of law enforcement vehicles still parked behind Maisy's house. But I had already arranged for the ride so I sat back and enjoyed the door to door service. Every time I thought about what was going on down the alley at Maisy's house, I got a heart fluttering anxious feeling; I was concerned about Maisy and Mrs. Tate and astronomically worried about Dog. But tormenting myself wouldn't help any of us, so I tried to push the thoughts away like I had fought to do all day.

As I was letting myself into my apartment, I heard my phone chiming and following the sound I discovered it mysteriously sitting on a napkin on my countertop. I had multiple texts from various housemates letting me know what was going on at the house and in the neighborhood, including Phil telling me he had to let Dog into my apartment so he could crawl through my closet to get into his apartment. I had forgotten to undo his security bar before I left for work! Unhappily there were no texts from Dog, but a split second before I crumpled and tossed the napkin away, I saw a message on it which read: *Getting out of town. Will be back in time for Fall Fantasy. All arranged, don't worry.* And it was signed with a little drawing of a dog's fuzzy face and three little hearts. Warmth started in the center of my body and spread out in concentric circles.

But then I berated myself; was I the most gullible person in the world to believe in Dog, to trust that he was a good guy despite all the evidence to the contrary? And to trust Dog directly after my disturbing experiences with my thieving uncle and vanishing brother and lying, cheating boyfriend? That's beyond gullible; that's idiotic and self-destructive. But I still had the

Dog inspired warm feeling deep inside and, speaking in my own defense, I wondered if maybe I was like Max, mistreated and wounded, but emotionally strong enough to give someone else a chance to treat me better? And if you're going to trust another person, what are the odds that the next one you meet will be any better or worse than the one you meet five people from now? Or a hundred people from now? I had loved and taken care of Max after he gave me a chance, and my housemates and my workmates had cared for and helped me in a thousand different ways after I trusted them.

I took a deep breath and tried to breathe all my deep thoughts away, to reorder my priorities for tonight, more specifically for right this minute. What did I need to do? Eat, shower, text Maisy my number and go to bed. And so that's exactly what I did.

Going to bed at 8 pm meant I woke up extra early, and I felt lost without Max snuggled into his kennel, so I left for the hospital as soon as I got ready. The night had passed quietly in the ER so I wasn't pounced on as I walked in, and I was able to take Max outside for a meandering walk. I even had time to sit down at the picnic table, rub his ears and talk nonsense to him, watching his ears perk up and then relax as he listened intently to my changing voice inflections. I told him I loved him, and he melted his face into my hip, then rubbed his face back and forth on my leg, in absolute adoration, I thought, until I noticed he was rubbing off the lubricating ointment, which is used during surgery to protect the patients' unblinking eyes, all over my freshly laundered scrub pants. I sheepishly laughed in response, pulled a gauze pad out of my pocket and finished wiping his face for him.

"You silly boy," I said lovingly and he bounced a little, obviously thinking about getting rowdy, but I stood up, shortened his leash and walked him back to his kennel instead. His back looked really good and I was going to do everything in my power to keep it that way.

"Hey, where you going with my patient?" Dr. Drama roared from across the treatment area. I might be jumping to conclusions, but it sure seemed that the quietest mornings brought out his craziest behavior!

We hustled over to him, Dr. Drama did Max's postop examination and declared him the picture of perfection. Now that I was used to Doc's ways, I enjoyed his exaggerated way of talking. The owners absolutely loved it. They might miss some details from his scientific discussions, but if he said their dog's recovery was spectacular and danced in joy, they never forgot that and walked out announcing the great news to everyone they saw. I let the words 'picture of perfection' roll across my mind and I knew exactly how they felt!

Dr. Drama and I were scheduled as the outpatient surgery team. It was just the kind of day I needed, getting to do exams and rechecks, a day filled with solving diagnostic mysteries, my favorite! Even if the procedure to resolve the patient's problem was one of the ones I wouldn't look forward to doing, diagnosing the problem was always a lot of fun.

Our second appointment was with Mrs. Tate and Oreo. I wanted to warn Dr. Drama that her husband had just died, but I had no idea if she'd even been informed that he was gone yet. I managed to whisper, "Family problems," to Doc right before we walked in.

Mrs. Tate greeted us solemnly and said, "Oreo is doing well and he and I are moving back home. I'll be able to take extra good care of him now."

Dr. Drama said, "That's wonderful to hear," and I cringed at his exuberant response, knowing the reason she was able to return to her home.

Mrs. Tate nodded but coolly explained, "Well, I've traded one set of problems for another. My husband was killed," and she paused as her chin quivered and then she looked at me instead of Dr. Drama and continued, "Everything's in chaos, but I'm concentrating on two things. We're safe and I have enough money to take care of Oreo. I can figure everything else out later."

"You're being very brave," Dr. Drama said with an intense look. "And we'll help you take great care of Oreo. We're going to the back for another picture of his leg, but I'll leave Dr. Kate here to chat."

"Thank you Dr. Vincent," Mrs. Tate said gratefully and after he left she added, "I don't feel brave."

"You're being remarkably courageous," I said emphatically. "Dr. Vincent and I have an ongoing competition to see which one of us is the reigning King or Queen of the Silver Lining. We never want to gloss over the harshness of the cloud, but we certainly admire people who on their toughest days can pick out a positive aspect of their situation. Today you get to wear the crown."

Tears gathered in her eyes and I handed her the tissues, then took one for myself. She sniffled a couple times then said, "I did love Ross once upon a time and we had such wonderful dreams. And while in the beginning I believed that it was all my fault that he was mad all the time, nothing I ever did made it any better. But Oreo never did anything wrong, and Ross hurt him over and over again. One day I started wondering if maybe if it wasn't my fault either. And needing to protect Oreo made me brave enough to stand up for both of us.

"I know what you mean," I agreed, but certainly didn't add that I had discovered this similar response when her husband attacked me, that my initial response had only been to escape until he hit Max and only then was I willing to stand and try to fight to protect my sweet boy.

"So you've been abused?" she asked softly.

"Maybe a bit," I admitted, for the first time in my life. "Just emotional abuse, though."

"Yeah, but people say that emotional abuse can be more painful than physical abuse," Mrs. Tate said unhappily, then paused before continuing. "But in my experience Ross was pretty darn emotionally abusive before, during and after smacking me around."

Tears filled my eyes and I said, "I'm sorry you had to go through that."

She cried a little too and whispered, "Thank you."

Dr. Drama walked in grinning, looked at us both crying, stopped short and whispered, "My worst nightmare…"

"We're fine," I assured him. "What's the news?"

"It looks stunningly good," he replied, smiling again but not quite as brilliantly. "Everything is stable and we have a beautiful callus forming. But you must still keep him strictly confined."

"I promise!" Mrs. Tate swore adamantly, then smiled a sweet smile and repeated more realistically, "I promise."

Dr. Drama left the room with a wave and Mrs. Tate added, "When Oreo's back to normal and if I get to keep the house, I'm going to foster pets for ladies in the women's shelter."

"What a great idea!" I exclaimed, partly in surprise that she could already be thinking about future plans and partly in recognition of the appropriateness of her idea. "My housemates introduced me to the idea of being a wounded healer and that would be the perfect example."

"I might become a peer counselor too," she said with a shy smile. "I always liked Psychology, but Ross never wanted me to go back to school, said it would be a waste of money."

"I'm sure he was afraid," I started to say but she interrupted me saying, "Afraid I couldn't handle it," but I finished insistently, "Afraid you could!"

She appeared bewildered but then smiled as she got it. As we left the room she said, "Thanks, Dr. Kate."

"You're so welcome, Mrs. Tate," I said warmly.

"Please call me Diane," she said timidly.

"I sure will," I promised.

I started to walk her out to her car, then realized there was no reason to and felt happy for her, knowing that she had her life back. Then I was seriously disturbed because I was feeling happy that Ross Tate was dead, but so be it. He should have lived his life differently, been the sun in her life instead of the dangerous storm cloud.

One of the hardest things I did in practice was to walk out of one room, a distinct microcosm filled with fear or pain or loss, and then walk right into the next room and immediately have to acclimate to an entirely new environment, this one maybe filled with hope or satisfaction or elation. I had noticed the phenomenon during my primary care rotation the first time I left a sad euthanasia and walked right into a happy puppy visit. Sometimes I loved the feeling of being pulled away from a heartbreaking situation, sometimes I hated the incongruity of an owner in one room complaining about a minor problem when the pet in the next room was fighting heroically simply to survive. It was never all good or all bad, but it was always a jarring sensation, like a reboot on reality.

So it was a jolt to walk into the next room and see smiling Trev with his adorable black Labrador puppy, here for a final recheck of a previous 'swimmer puppy,' a puppy with a delayed ability to walk. It took me a minute to catch the rambunctious puppy, and Trev stood back laughing the whole time, two good signs that recovery was complete although some help in corralling the pup would have been appreciated. Dr. Drama took the puppy to show off to the rehab department, leaving me to chat again. I was starting to see a pattern.

I remembered that I was supposed to be collecting participants for Max's class, so I asked, "Hey, Trev, are you planning to take Licorice to puppy class?"

"I'd love to," he said frowning. "But I ended up keeping two pups so I don't know how I'd work with both, or pay for two for that matter. My Mom has to work two jobs so she's never home to help."

"That's tough," I said thoughtfully. "My friend Ethan is attending class with me so he could help you, but I don't want to set him up to get a broken heart when class was over. Puppies are too easy to fall in love with!"

"That's what happened to me," Trev commiserated. "I choose to keep Chip, one of the brown puppies, out of Coco's litter and I'm bonded to him. But then I got even closer to Licorice because I worked with him so much because of his medical issues."

"Hey, maybe we could get Mr. Emerson to help out," I speculated. "I saw him at the grocery store and he told me that he and Jiminy were missing Dizzy desperately. They used to get frustrated with her shenanigans, but life has turned out to be dull and a little depressing without her."

"That might work," Trev said, pondering a plan. "Might be worth a phone call. But the least I can do is bring the puppies over to cheer them up sometime soon."

Dr. Drama returned grinning and pronounced the puppy perfectly recovered. The rehab techs poked their heads into the room to congratulate Trev on his hard work and he replied it was all due to them, and while they continued to trade congratulations back and forth, Dr. Drama and I left the room.

The rest of the day passed quickly but pleasantly. We worked steadily but managed to stay on schedule, and that single detail took a lot of the stress away. Amelia gave Max and me a ride home, and while I tried hard to express my gratitude as I told her goodbye, I was determined to find another way to show my appreciation. I was gathering an impossibly long list of people I needed to thank in some tangible way. More than any other time, including going grocery shopping for myself, I hated having to pinch my pennies so tightly that I couldn't easily do things for other people without considering the cost carefully. I'd see if Ethan had some kind of a recipe for something fun to bake, something using ingredients that didn't cost very much. Thinking of Ethan's baking skills reminded me it was Thursday night house dinner and I bounded up the stairs to my apartment two at a time in anticipation.

Chapter Thirty-three

As I climbed into the limousine, I was beyond excited about my Fort Wayne adventure. I hadn't heard from Dog since his abrupt departure from Noblesville a week ago, but his sister Issa had averaged three or four texts a day to me on his behalf. As the days passed, Dog's initial simple scheme had amplified into a plan including this limo ride to meet him in Fort Wayne, an afternoon of pampering and preparation at a Fort Wayne spa with Issa, another limo ride back to her suite at the downtown Marriott to change, and then the Fall Fantasy event at the Convention Center with Issa and Dog.

Earlier in the week I'd had an anxiety attack, even though Issa promised to take care of everything, because I had to look absolutely perfect if I ran into my hypercritical Uncle. Issa tried to reassure me by saying that she had scheduled plenty of time in her suite to 'get me into the dress,' which then became the most frightening part of the plan. I had been slowly gaining my weight back, which was delightful since I got to welcome my girly shape back, but I sure hoped that I didn't have too many curves for this particular dress. Studying the picture of Issa modeling the dress, I decided it wouldn't be a case of the dress being too tight to fit me as much as a case of how much of me would be left over and uncovered! When I told Issa of my concerns she replied that she was bringing plenty of double sided tape for it, so not to worry. That answer and the resultant image in my mind made me even more worried!

I snuggled into the luxurious limo seat and relaxed my head back, trying to breathe my overexcitement away without letting any of my joy and anticipation escape with it. I wanted to cherish every moment of the pampering, every step of the magical transformation of the real me into a fairy-tale Princess, and then most importantly, every minute of a formal date with Dog. I planned to revel in the heavenly Cinderella experience at the same time I knew with all my heart that if the Prince came looking for me tomorrow with an offer of a new life full of similar glitz and glamour and the need to do this every day, I would heartily refuse and run from him in terror. A vacation from my real life was a wish come true, but a life based on the same experience would be my definition of a living hell.

The limo was stocked with more amenities than I could have imagined and, while I chose simple bottled water to drink, I indulged in a fancy lemon and raspberry breakfast pastry to tame my hunger. And there was an assortment of magazines to read. What a treat! I hadn't felt free to read a nonscientific magazine since before I started Vet school and probably longer ago than that. We had made this two hour drive to and from Noblesville and the Indianapolis area many times as a family to visit relatives at Christmastime so this trip always gave me a happy holiday feeling. A couple times during the trip up Interstate 69, I felt nostalgic for my missing family and would have happily traded the glamorous limo for a well-used minivan if it meant my parents and/or brothers could have been there with me.

The limo took the Dupont Road exit, the road my brothers and I used to call Doctor's Drive after two big hospitals and numerous professional offices were built up and down its length. When we turned on Auburn Road I was sure we were heading to Panera's, but we passed it by, drove by my Dentist's new office as well, and then turned into the driveway for the DeBrand Fine Chocolates main store. What a great surprise! Except I didn't know how much chocolate I was going to be able to enjoy with such a big day to get through, maybe none at all. Dog was waiting for me out front and pointed at the front door with a big "Ta Da!"

Grinning, we locked eyes, but then he tore his gaze away, reluctantly I hoped, and spoke with the limo driver about the pickup schedule for the day. As Dog discussed the plans, he ran his fingertips up and down my backbone, bumping up and down from my mid back up to the middle of my neck, stopping right where I'm ticklish on my neck. It sent chills up and down my spine and while I continued to smile brightly and stand quietly, the sensation made me want to do a whole body shake like Max could do and then throw myself into his arms with total abandon.

As the limo pulled away, Dog turned to me and asked solicitously, "Are you all right?" and for a minute I thought he was asking if I was so overexcited to see him that I might faint or something, but then I realized that he was simply concerned that I might be apprehensive about being back in my hometown where I could run into my Uncle or Justin.

"I'm good," I said happily but then, without asking for approval from my higher brain about appropriateness, I added, "I've just missed you so much."

He gathered me close and kissed me rather passionately, I'm assuming without prior approval of his higher brain as well because he sort of jumped away and looked around guiltily as cars rushed by. We laughed together, walked into the building, and stopped inside the door to inhale the scrumptious chocolate scented air.

Dog grinned again and handed me a gift card with $100 written on it and said, "This for you."

"Wow," I managed to say. "I love DeBrand! But I don't know how much I can eat today."

Dog chuckled indulgently and replied, "I thought you might like to use it for people back home. They have individually packaged treats and even chocolate bars that say 'Thank You' on them."

"How did you know?" I said shocked at his perception, or possibly spooky mind reading ability.

"You're awfully easy to read," he said laughing. "But we need to stay on mission right now. I'll take your chocolate to Issa's suite after I drop you off, so don't worry about it sitting in the car."

I walked over to the glass case and looked at all the chocolates, first attracted to the big fancy boxes but finally decided on lots of small boxes and thank you bars so that I could include as many people as possible. Dog helped by pointing out favorites of our housemates and Issa.

Dog drove me to the Spa, and it was so nice to be able to relax and chat about inconsequential matters with him on the way. The car Dog was driving was a different car, not the cute little sports car of our first date or his usual SUV, but a sexy Mercedes of some kind. And just because I don't know much about cars it doesn't mean I couldn't fall in love with one; it was such a beautiful and luxurious ride for this Princess-for-a-day.

The only serious question I allowed myself to ask Dog was about his arm, and he bragged that it was healing so well that it had started to itch rather incessantly. I threatened him with an E-collar if he started to self-traumatize and he laughed such a clear, honest laugh that it calmed some unnamed concern deep inside me. He obviously wasn't in jail despite his prediction, but I didn't know if he had bonded out or escaped legal consequences all together. I had made a strict covenant with myself that today I wasn't going to ask about that, no matter what.

Issa greeted me effusively in the Spa waiting room and I was shocked that she was so warm and outgoing. And it turned out that for someone who made her living on her spectacular looks, she was the least superficial person I had met in a long time. And best of all she was hilarious. I laughed through the entire check-in ritual.

The only hilarity I contributed to our day was totally inadvertent. We were in the dressing room getting ready for our massages and Issa asked, "Do you need more privacy? I used to be extremely modest before I started modeling, but now I don't even think about shedding my clothes on a moment's notice."

I replied, "I'm certainly comfortable in this ladies only changing area, but I don't want to shock anyone. I was raked a little over a week ago, and I'm not totally healed yet."

Issa, and the massage therapist that had just entered the room, were stunned into silence, both of them making that perfect shocked emoji face with big round eyes and mouths open in a perfect circles. I pulled my shirt up to show them my scratches to reassure them, to prove that no matter whatever horrific thing they were imagining, my wounds had mostly healed with just a couple of the red stripes still raw.

"What did he do?" Issa asked ferociously. "Oh my God."

"By the time this happened he was just trying to get off me," I tried to explain. "Just tore me up trying to get away."

"What did my brother do?" she demanded.

"He wasn't there," I said, starting to be concerned that Issa had a problem of some kind, overreacting so emotionally to an incident I hardly thought about anymore.

"Are you okay?" Issa asked sympathetically, as the massage therapist slipped out of the room.

"I'm fine," I said extra calmly, trying to reassure the now shaking girl. I didn't even mention my still bruised sternum, since the healing scratches upset her so much.

"Did the police catch him?" she asked.

"He didn't get away," I explained. "We sedated him and everything was much easier on both of us after that."

"You sedated him?" she said with the most incredibly puzzled look on her face. "That's legal?"

"Yea," I replied, really becoming disturbed about Issa's reaction. "I'm licensed with the state and the DEA."

"Where is he now?" she questioned me insistently.

"Home with his owner," I said calmly.

"Owner?" she asked quietly, paused, then asked, "What did you say happened to you?"

"I was raked," I explained, holding my hands like claws and dragging them downwards to illustrate my words. "A dog dug his back claws into me and raked them down my body."

"Oh," she said and let out a huge breath. "I thought you said raped! I couldn't believe you could be so blasé about it."

The massage therapist walked back in holding a cup of herbal tea and box of tissues for me, wearing a very concerned expression, but when Issa tried to explain, laughter bubbled up at every attempted word. Finally she was laughing so hard tears were streaming down her face and neither of us could make out a single word she was saying. I took over the explanation until the poor therapist started chuckling as well. But Issa and I continued to laugh uncontrollably, way beyond what the situation called for and I honestly don't know why. When we calmed down enough to proceed with our much anticipated pampering, I felt more in tune with my own emotions than I had in a very long time. And more amazingly, Issa and I laughed our way through the rest of the day without accepting even one of the offers of wine or cocktails.

I let Issa make all the decisions on my hair style, nail color, and makeup and the combined effect made me almost unrecognizable; I was all big blue eyes and loose blonde curls. And when we arrived in Issa's room, she held the dress up to me in front of the mirror and, reflecting the dress's aqua hue, my eyes appeared almost other worldly.

When Issa announced that Dog was fifteen minutes from picking us up, we shimmied and draped ourselves into our dresses so that the swirling layers would not only fall correctly but wouldn't shift and expose us in unacceptable ways. I started to get nervous about a possible upcoming family confrontation, but getting taped into my dress and dealing with double sided tape that wanted to stick to every part of me except the spot I was aiming at, started me giggling nonstop, creating a formidable barrier to bad thoughts of any kind.

I held up my two earring choices and asked Issa, "Which ones?"

"Neither," she answered with a sly look. "Our borrowed accoutrements are arriving with our escort!"

"Huh?" I asked in confusion, but then Dog's distinctive knock echoed at the door. Issa threw it open wide and grinned as she watched her brother catch his first sight of me. I'd heard the expression 'seeing yourself in another's eyes' but I never truly appreciated what that meant until I saw his face. And while I'd rather be known as good or kind or smart, in that moment I saw in his eyes someone extraordinary enough it flooded me with confidence.

And while I would have argued that Dog couldn't look any better than he did in jeans and a t-shirt, the sight of him in a tuxedo was breathtaking. His studs and cuff links were sparkling aqua stones, not what I'd picture him picking for himself, so I guessed that he'd allowed Issa to choose for him too. He grinned at me then held out two large rectangular jewelers' boxes to us, then crossed his hands over, then back again and admitted, "I don't know who gets what."

Issa opened the one closest to her, then handed it to me and announced, "The Star is for Kate."

Dog stared at me appraisingly and then asked, "Kate or Kat?"

Issa frowned and said, "What?"

I grimaced and tried to explain, "My name is Kat, actually Katya after my Mom, but I started going by Kate this year." I shrugged my shoulders and admitted, "But I'm thinking of going back to Kat."

"Dr. Kat, veterinarian!" Issa said, trying it out. "I like it. Is that what we should we call you tonight?"

Without answering, I lifted up my cascading curls so Dog could securely fasten the necklace, a simple thick white gold chain holding a huge, stunningly blue stone pendent. I wouldn't know how to guess how big the gem was, but it was certainly multiple, multiple carats. I wasn't ignoring Issa's question, but I was overwhelmed by the necklace, especially the fact that once it was next to the dress, it too picked up the aqua tint, matching my eyes perfectly.

Issa handed me simple diamond earrings. Issa's ears, neck and even her beautiful ebony hair were accented in diamonds, lots and lots of diamonds, and what they lacked in size compared to the pendent I was wearing, they more than made up in numbers and the crazy ceaseless way they caught the light.

"My name is Kat," I answered solemnly.

"Then that's what we'll call you," Issa said, then looked at Dog and said, "I'll take care of it."

Dog nodded then insisted, "We'd better go. I have our entrance perfectly timed."

Chapter Thirty-four

The three of us paused at the doorway to appreciate the venue; the room twinkled with copious white lights cascading from the ceiling. And, surprisingly, being flanked by two such striking human beings didn't make me feel overshadowed, instead Dog and Issa seemed to frame me and draw everyone's eye directly to me. A hush spread across the noisy crowd, accompanied by waves of movement as people stopped conversing and turned their heads to follow our progress. It was probably the Garrison Star that garnered all the attention, but it felt like it was the way the Issa and Dog were treating me, as if the precious jewel they so prized and protected was me, not the necklace.

We slowly made our way to our table as Issa and Dog greeted multiple people along our path, but while I'm sure I must have known people there, no one registered in my dazed brain. Perhaps I was mesmerized by all the magical lights everywhere I looked; the table decorations were especially hypnotic with sparkling lights intertwined around and through gorgeous red and gold and bronze fall leaves. Or maybe I just refused to focus on anyone that might break the spell of this magical day. I would love to imagine that I passed my Uncle without a single flicker of recognition, but I knew in my heart that he was nowhere in the crowd. There was no enchantment strong enough to protect me from the horror of that presence.

As soon as we took our seats, the emcee stepped to the microphone in the middle of the head table facing the room and made brief opening remarks. Mr. Garrison, very handsome in a classic tuxedo which set off his silver hair and bright blue eyes to perfection, and his wife, in a beautiful silver embellished sari, were seated next to the podium. When Mr. Garrison stood up to say grace, he gave me a cute little wave and a big grin.

The food was wonderful, as usual not overwhelmingly fancy because, as Mr. Garrison reminded us at every one of these dinners, each choice he made was to direct as much of the budget as possible to the children's programs. But I had little appetite and just picked at it, although I somehow managed to eat most of my dessert. I fondly remembered the year that Mr. Garrison had let his granddaughter Clarissa chose the food to be served since she was the inspiration for the family's charity efforts for sick children after she beat cancer at a Fort Wayne hospital. That special year she had chosen pigs in a blanket, mac and cheese and fried green beans for her menu, and topped it all off with massive hot fudge brownie sundaes. My Uncle had effusively praised Mr. Garrison for the fun menu at the time, but had actually been so offended that he had complained about it nonstop at home for weeks.

The speakers handing out the various awards were hilarious, and I don't think it was just because I was in such a joyful mood. Everyone else was laughing as much as I was. The award for creative nursing care, the Kat's Klowns award, was presented by one of the Kat's Klowns volunteers dressed in a full feline costume that was good enough to have been in the musical Cats. A huge step up from my Mom's simple disappearing ears and tails! However, the middle aged nurse that won the award staidly walked to the podium in a plain black gown but then turned to face the crowd and showcased the sparkling cat ears perched on top of her head. The entire crowd laughed and clapped their appreciation, except for me as tears slid down my face because it so reminded me of my Mom.

As Mr. Garrison was returning to the podium, Issa reached over and fussed with my makeup, especially around my eyes, and then pinched me on the tender skin on the inside of my arm.

I immediately protested, "Hey!' and she hissed back, "Smile!" so I did just in time to see Mr. Garrison staring at me.

He gestured for me to rise as he announced, "I'm thrilled to present Dr. Kat Nikolova, our beloved Katya's beautiful daughter. She's wearing the blue diamond Garrison Star tonight to help me make an important announcement."

He paused and made a circular motion with his hand to direct me to turn and face the crowd. He left me hanging there feeling out of place, but I continued to smile as brightly as I could as multiple cameras clicked and whirled and flashed until he gestured I could sit back down. He explained that the Garrison family had voted to auction off the Star at a prestigious New York auction house to raise money for their Foundation for Children.

The assembly cheered and clapped and whistled their surprise and excitement. I was thrilled to be part of the event, but was suddenly afraid that the gem hanging around my neck was worth way more than I had imagined.

That exciting announcement ended the formal part of the evening, but instead of being able to join one of the gathering groups to chat and exclaim over the generous donation the Star would provide, Issa and I were called aside to meet with the photographer.

"Hello, Issa," the young photographer said softly. "I'm so honored to be working with you again, but let's do Kat's formal shots first, then Mr. Garrison wants pictures of the two of you together."

Issa messed with my hair and fixed my face, then helped pose me, telling me where to place my feet then actually tilting my chin and pushing my shoulder into place. She was cracking jokes the whole time so it didn't feel as intrusive as it sounds. After the photographer was satisfied with my pictures, Issa joined me and although we got a bad case of the giggles we eventually got those shots as well.

"Are we done?" Issa asked.

"Can you wait here for just a minute while I get the official okay on these?" the photographer asked and when we nodded he went over to speak to Mr. Garrison.

I kept an eye on Issa as she amused herself dancing around and twirling herself up in the lights hanging down around us. She was so engaging I was perfectly content to just stand there watching, but something else, deeper down, was bothering me, almost like I was trying to remember a word, or remember some link between two facts, like I had the answer to an unknown question in my hands but couldn't quite put it all together. And then I saw Mr. Garrison look at the pictures and look over at the two of us, then he spoke to the nurse who had won the Kat's Klown award, still wearing her little cat ears headband.

The photographer returned and handed me the headband as he said, "If you don't mind he'd like one with Kat wearing her mother's kitty ears with Issa?"

Issa fixed the headband into my hair, and we posed seriously for a few shots before we started acting up again. When he pronounced us finished, we moved off the little stage and I returned the headband to the nurse with a big hug. As I looked around for Dog and took another step away, bits and pieces of previous conversations started raining through my consciousness: Dog's sister beat cancer and her favorite nurse was my mother, Mr. Garrison's granddaughter beat cancer and her favorite nurse was my mother, the little girl Clarissa, the New York model Issa, Mr. Garrison's wife in a sari, Dog's grandmother's giving me Indian print pillows and throws. Dog knew the Garrisons? He was a Garrison.

"Is your last name Garrison?" I whispered to Issa.

"No," she said, staring at me through guarded eyes, suddenly looking just like her brother. "It's Roan like Daniel. Our mother's maiden name is Garrison."

"Daniel?" I whispered.

"Pfft," she said with a rude gesture. "Dag, Dagger, Dog, Daniel Garrison Roan; whatever stupid name game he's playing tonight."

"I never knew his name," I confessed.

"I know," she said with a disgusted huff, like a typical aggravated sister. "I screwed up. Nobody's supposed to know what he's doing or where he's at or what his name is, and I'm sick and tired of it."

I nodded my agreement and asked, "Are you worried about him?"

"Yeah," she replied. "I don't know what's with his stupid games."

I started to ask more, but then saw him winding his way over to us.

"I'm supposed to escort both of you to the hallway to meet up with the bank representative and the armored car service," Dog said, laughing.

Issa theatrically grabbed ahold of the front of Dog's tuxedo and pleaded to keep the diamonds, then reached up and whispered something in his ear as the crowd started to move past us. He looked over at me and I expected to see concern in his face but saw humor instead, his eyes crinkling at the corners as he smirked an odd smile and struggled to keep his face straight.

"You knew I'd find out if we came here together!" I exclaimed in astonishment.

He shrugged his shoulders and answered, "I didn't know Issa would blurt it out," as she punched him in the shoulder. "I was betting on Grandfather! I figured he'd introduce Issa as his granddaughter Clarissa. But I felt it was worth it to have you encircled by Garrisons for your triumphant return to Fort Wayne! Too bad my elaborate plan was such a failure, your Uncle didn't even show up."

As he guided Issa and me into the hallway I sheepishly admitted, "I forgot all about him."

The three of us laughed companionably as Dog scanned the area for the representative we were supposed to be meeting, and I apologized, "I'm sorry I'm being so weird, it's not just that the Garrisons are Fort Wayne royalty. In my family, Mr. Garrison is more like Santa Claus!"

Issa and Dog laughed together again and Issa agreed, "He is kinda magical! He's a big kid and just loves helping people. If he gets bored, he runs out and buys gas cards and then hands them out to random family members at the hospitals."

I grinned at them in response, and then I swear I felt the air go out of the room a split second before I heard the voice stridently say, "Pussy," with that heart breaking, confidence shaking, excruciatingly long pause before he finished in a softer tone, "Kat. So glad you were able to attend."

"Justin," I said in a dead voice.

Dog and Issa turned to face him with identical fierce expressions. Issa put her hands on her hips and leaned forward, Dog actually stepped towards Justin and suddenly I was terrified.

Justin had a similar reaction, stepped back and held both hands out in supplication and said, "Hey, we're all friends here."

I had come to this dinner knowing that I might have to survive an encounter with my Uncle, the man who had emotionally tortured me since I was twelve, but unexpectedly I had to face my second biggest abuser. I wanted to stay tough, to hold him accountable for treating me so horribly, but I sure didn't want to start anything that would land Dog into even more legal trouble.

"Could I have a minute alone with Kat?" Justin said in a soft conciliatory tone, looking at Issa but glancing at Dog from the corner of his eye.

"No," Dog answered firmly as Issa explained, "He doesn't move away from the Star."

Justin laughed out loud in obvious glee and said, "Ahh that makes sense. He's guarding the Star."

Dog grumbled a wordless curse and took another step forward. I put my arm across his chest to restrain him and said dismissively, "Justin, we have nothing to talk about."

"Nothing?" he asked with a shocked look on his face, which settled into a sneer. "After all we meant to each other?"

"Meant to each other?" I repeated in shock, my voice starting to vibrate with emotion. "What could I possibly mean to you that you needed to cheat on me with people I called friends? Or even worse, to trash my reputation at school, lie about me to classmates and professors, and trick me out of applying for the intern matching program? You totally humiliated me at the one place in the world that I felt accepted and appreciated!"

"What?" Justin asked, attempting an innocent and bewildered expression which was ruined by his sly smile. "I didn't lie."

"You told them in elaborate detail that I wasn't going to do an internship because I didn't think I had anything more to learn from them or the University environment. And that for me an Internship was a waste time because I wanted to make real money as quickly as possible," I retorted. "Not just random fabrications but you created a false image that was the exact opposite of who I am! You could have been equally nasty with something closer to the truth, like I needed more real world experience or I lacked confidence."

"It wasn't me," he said smugly. "It was their misinterpretation of what I said."

"It was not," I retorted. "No way would multiple people mishear the exact same thing."

"Your Uncle gave me great advice in dealing with you," Justin said quietly, his lack of emphasis almost disguising the blow he was trying to aim at me. Justin was one of the few people that I had ever told how much my Uncle's manipulative treatment had hurt me and made me doubt myself.

"Deal with me?" I asked, sounding breathless from the pain starting to grip me.

"He told me all I had to do was tell you I needed your help and you'd do whatever I wanted," he said, obviously pleased with his craftiness.

"You're just making shit up now," I said. "He didn't tell you that."

"He didn't?" Justin said with another half grin.

Now I was shaking all over but decided I could hang on to ask the most important question, "Why? Why any of it?"

"Why, what?" he asked, still attempting an innocent confused expression.

"Why didn't you break up with me, or tell me how horribly unhappy I made you, or just plain avoid me?" I asked desperately. "Why did I need to suffer? Why did you have to torment me?"

He shrugged his shoulders and held his hands out in another

protestation of ignorance, "I don't know what you're talking about. I didn't do anything, it's all those people who were supposed to be your friends, who always talked about how wonderful you were. They're the ones who hurt you by believing it all."

"Because of what you made up about me," I repeated, my voice steadily screeching up the register in my disbelief at his defense. "You discredited everything I did or said, in what had to be a carefully plotted campaign. You couldn't have fooled everyone for most of our senior year without putting an incredible amount of effort into what you did."

"They could have defended you," he replied, a slight smile staying on his lips as he spoke. "No one ever came to you to ask what was going on, did they?"

"You manipulated them!" I protested. "And it hurt all of us terribly."

Anger flared in his eyes, even though he was trying to keep his face from showing it, and he spat out his retort, "It didn't hurt me. It felt right to me."

"Right?" I sputtered. "None of it was right or fair."

Justin harshly replied, "It seemed pretty fair to me. Everyone thought you were so perfect, had to give you every stupid award they ever made. They would have crucified me if I hadn't shown them a different side to you before I got away."

"For long month after month?" I wailed. "I understand you don't care about my feelings, but how could you stand being around the constant sorrow and misery?"

"That wasn't my fault, you just kept hanging on," he said, clearly offended. "Trying to help me, trying to understand me. It was repulsive. You made me sick, always worried about every damn thing."

"Worried?" I asked in disbelief. "You can't imagine how much crushing anxiety you created by never doing what you said you'd do and by lying about every little inconsequential thing and then trying to blame it on me. Seriously, why would you bother? What did you get out of it?"

He nonchalantly shrugged again and more than anything in the world I wished I was big enough to shake the shrugs right out of him. And then I remembered Annie and a flash of anger flooded over me. I stepped toward him and demanded, "What about what you did to our puppy, our sweet innocent Annie?"

"She was more trouble than she was worth," Justin said, offhandedly.

"Too much work, I didn't want her anymore."

"But she was mine! I would have taken care of her," I protested. "Being abandoned with strangers had to have devastated her even more than it shattered me. You ripped her away from everything and everyone she knew."

"She'd get over it," he countered.

"Did she?" I begged for information. "Is she okay?"

"I assume," he replied disinterestedly. "I insisted she was totally their responsibility. I didn't even save their number."

"Why?" I asked again. "Why would you ever have wanted to hurt me like that? What could you possibly get from doing it?"

Shrugging his shoulders, Justin didn't even bother to answer. And suddenly I knew that no matter what I did or said, he would never tell me why he did any of it. Maybe because he didn't know why or maybe because at some level he knew it was wrong to enjoy hurting people as much as he did.

"Well?" I asked again, realizing that whole rotten year I had never pressured him into answering me about any awful thing he did to me, even when he didn't show up to meet me for the hundredth time. Or the time he abandoned me at a meeting, even though he had driven me there, which resulted in a ride home from a drunken classmate that could have killed us both. Or even when he tricked me into being dropped off at the wrong bar for a class celebration, where I patiently but futilely waited for him to show up for hours, getting myself into a really dangerous situation. "For once I deserve an answer that makes sense. What the hell is wrong with you?"

"Well, aren't you all full of yourself in your borrowed dress and grand necklace and scary bodyguard," he said, his voice dripping with distain. "I'm not impressed. Never was. Your Uncle was right about you, too sensitive for the real world."

"Leave her alone, ass-hat!" Issa ordered ferociously as Dog lurched forward, his face practically unrecognizable with his lip lifted into an almost canine looking snarl. Issa jumped protectively in front of Dog and, shifting back and forth a couple of times to block his forward motion, continued, "You don't want to start this shitstorm. Everyone thinks we Garrisons are too nice to even notice that someone's just a big fucking bully. But know this: we always defend our friends. Step away from her before we make you step away."

Justin had the oddest expression suddenly plastered across his face, half offended that anyone could speak to him in that disrespectful way, since he obviously thought he was the most perfect being occupying the exact center of the known universe, and half terrified because Issa had evoked the power of the Garrison name.

Just as the emotional charge of the encounter ratcheted into the unbearable range, the bank representative and his guards from the armored car service approached us and we had to turn our backs on Justin to conduct our business. Dog and Issa pressed up close to me on both sides, effectively closing ranks, as we greeted the gentlemen courteously and then divested ourselves of the beautiful jewelry. Issa said a personal goodbye to each piece as she placed it carefully in the custom holder, but she did it in such a humorous way that it made the men smile and deflected any attention away from me in my sudden emotionally fragile state. Dog checked the paperwork to make sure the Star was headed to New York for the auction while the collection Issa wore was taken back to the bank vault. It gave me time to concentrate on my antianxiety breathing exercises.

When we turned to walk back to Issa's suite, I was shocked to see Justin still standing there. He had a look on his face that I had never seen before, a diminished look, an odd deflated air about him, like his confidence had been shaken to the core. That hopeless, bleak expression moved me in a way that no past bad behavior could erase and, despite the fact that he had relished hurting me in the past, I could never enjoy hurting anyone, not even him, no matter how much they deserved it.

I said to him softly, "I finally understand why you did such shameful things to me. It must have been very difficult when I told you I loved you at the same time I didn't act like I really did. I know now that I never wanted you like a woman should want a man, never craved being with you like a person with passionate feelings would. But I promise you I was absolutely not lying to you, I had simply never felt those kinds of feelings for anyone and had no clue that I was missing something that essential. My understanding changed when I met Daniel and discovered what passion and desire feels like. It must have been so painful to feel that I had never, not for a minute, felt that way about you. And every 'I love you' must have felt like being stabbed in the heart by a dirty lie."

Justin stood in place, wild eyed, shaking in his distress and moving his mouth as if he were trying to speak but no sounds were coming out. I had expected him to feel better, to feel less guilty about all the pain he had inflicted on me, but he didn't seem to be feeling the relief I was expecting. I didn't understand his reaction at all, what had I missed this time?

"You fucking…" Justin's sure to be disgusting tirade was cut short as Dog coolly wrapped a single large hand firmly around his throat.

I pulled Dog off, one finger at a time, and slowly moved him aside with steady pressure from my hip. Then I stood in front of Justin, held my hands out like claws, like I had done when I explained raking to Issa, and snapped, "The next time you try that Pussy pause Kat stupid shit I will scratch your eyes out."

He pulled his head back and started to retort, but I held my hand up in the classic stop position and continued, "Not your turn to speak, you took your turn for a whole year, all of it behind my back. You will never speak to me or about me again, or I'll let him come back for you."

Dog and Issa had shocked expressions on their faces, oddly touched with admiration perhaps, possibly even pride. When I looked at them with panic, they each grabbed an arm and hustled me down the hall, but I turned and shouted over my shoulder, "IN THE MIDDLE OF THE NIGHT!"

"Oh my goodness, girl," Issa said as the elevator doors shut behind us, astonishment written across her face. "I can't believe how badly you just eviscerated him. I thought you were one of those too nice to defend yourself people."

"What?" I asked, confused. "Oh, the scratch his eyes out comment? I don't have any idea where that came from, it totally surprised me too."

With a half-smile, Dog said, "I think she meant emasculate not eviscerate."

"Huh?" I asked quietly, trying to remember exactly what I had said.

"Never once felt passion for him?" Dog tried to explain.

"Well, I didn't and had no clue it was missing," I said sadly.

Dog hugged me warmly but tried to explain, "I love hearing that, but I can't imagine he did."

"I thought he must be feeling so bad for all those nasty things he did to me. I was trying to let him off the hook," I said. "I didn't want him to feel so guilty because now I understood why he was driven to do it."

"He didn't feel guilty," Issa insisted firmly. "He wasn't driven to do anything. He hurt you because he wanted to."

"His actions speak for themselves," Dog said gently. "It absolutely doesn't matter why. There's no excuse for doing what he did."

"No excuse at all," Issa said, kissing my cheek. "But we love you for thinking that way."

Dog leaned down and kissed my other cheek. "Well, it all worked out. You may have been trying in some upside down Kat way to be kind, but I think you gave him exactly what he deserved."

Chapter Thirty-five

It hurt my heart to leave Issa; I felt more connected and bonded to her in a single day's acquaintance than to almost anyone I'd ever met. But at the same time I was looking forward to having Dog to myself for the two hour drive to Noblesville. And while I wanted to return to my earlier feeling that this day was a complete vacation from real life, I craved information about what was going on with Dog, including his connection to all the upheaval in our neighborhood. I couldn't decide which feeling to go with so I started our trip by staying quiet and smiling a lot, eventually bouncing in my seat to the upbeat music.

Dog finally broke the ice by saying, "I had the best time today."

"I did too," I agreed enthusiastically. "It was truly magical. Thank you so much for everything you arranged. And paid for! But even more for letting me know about our family connection."

"I wish I could tell you everything," he said regretfully. "But I can't. I promise you that I'm trying to do the right thing."

"I have to ask one question," I said fearfully; afraid of making him angry and equally afraid of the answer itself.

"Sure," he replied, suddenly sitting stiff and tense next to me.

"Why didn't you rush to protect us the night Tate attacked Max and me?" I asked somberly.

"Oh, sweet girl," Dog said forlornly. "I. Am. So. Sorry. First I had to stop the police response to your attack from ruining all the hard work we had done to set up that raid on Cruse's organization at the kennel. And then Cruse caught me on my phone and smashed it to pieces."

"Are you a police officer?" I asked quietly.

"No," he admitted reluctantly.

"Will I ever know the whole story?" I asked

"You know how you had that dance party at work to show appreciation for wellness care?" he asked. "To appreciate nothing happening because you did the right preventative care?"

"Yeah?" I replied quizzically.

"If things work out right," he explained, "nothing will happen. And you'll hear nothing about it."

"Never?" I asked, confused.

"Never," he replied.

Dog nodded and went silent for long minutes, appearing to be mulling something over, then finally attempted to explain, "I thought Cruse and his son were a couple of insignificant criminals who might traffic some weed or a stolen car occasionally, so I was desperately trying to ignore them while I stayed focused on my own plan. But luck would have it, I kept getting thrown in with them! First the Jays were all worked up about the drug dealing in the alley, demanding I collect the evidence every time they found something. John stood guard over a dirty syringe for hours one day just so no child could get hurt by it."

"Awww," I said, with concern. "Is that why you were always wearing those black gloves and cleaning up the alley?"

"Yeah, I was collecting and turning over evidence to someone I served with in Afghanistan. He's in law enforcement now," Dog explained. "Then you asked me to help with Maisy's dogs at the very kennel where her husband was storing stolen weapons. And Tate, what a fuckup he was, had to be sampling his own product. After I kicked him out of your parking lot, he went straight to Cruse and threatened him, because he thought Cruse had ordered me to follow him. So over and over again I kept getting dragged back in."

"Because?" I asked calmly.

Dog shook his head regretfully and continued, "Cruse and his son turned out to be part of an unbelievably grisly organization who would traffic anything, or anyone, if you paid them enough money. And by the way, they poisoned their own dogs so they wouldn't make a fuss when Cruse was forced to hide his inventory in the kennel."

"Rat bastards!" I swore shaking my head in disbelief. "Can't believe they did that to the dogs or to Maisy; she'll be beyond traumatized when she finds out that part."

"So I'm here in the Indy area just killing time, walking around trying to mind my own business and when I meet someone new?" Dog asked shaking his head disagreeably. "I'm trying to decide if they're a run of the mill asshole or they're deeply and dangerously evil. In stark contrast, you're trying to decide how you can best help everyone you meet, or at least somehow ease their suffering."

"So you think I'm naïve and foolish?" I asked with tears filling my eyes.

"No!" he replied forcefully. "Not at all. I want to be around it. I cling to it. I want to be a part of it. My sacrifices only makes sense if there are still people like you to be doing it for. If there aren't good, kind, fair people at home to protect, there's simply no reason to keep fighting."

I sighed deeply and said, "It must be tough," and then sat in silence for a minute. I realized I had no choice but to let it go. Changing the subject, I added brightly, "Thank you so much for helping me get those thank you gifts!"

"I knew you'd love that," he replied happily.

"You do seem to understand me," I said. "More than I understand myself sometimes."

"I've noticed that you put an incredible amount of energy into judging yourself, working to be your most perfect self," Dog said sympathetically. "Especially at work. I worry that such an all-consuming dedication might actually consume you in time!"

"You sound like Dr. Drama," I said with a smile, but I silently admitted that I did think about work from the minute I woke up in the morning to the minute I went to bed, constantly evaluating if every little choice about anything was conducive to making me the best, most competent practitioner I could be.

Dog smiled and asked, "I do? You'd think he'd love and promote that kind of obsessive devotion."

I nodded and agreed, "Yeah, he gives mixed messages. He demands the obsession, but is simultaneously concerned about it!"

Dog agreed, "Maybe I am like him. I admire you for it, but worry about you at the same time."

"A speaker once advised us to aim for 'good enough', not perfection," I said ruefully. "And sometimes I play bad mind games when I'm struggling with rude or mean spirited people. I pretend I'm you and imagine what you'd say and do to people like Tate!"

"Ha! Well, I sure don't have to be polite like you do!" he granted.

I laughed, but replied earnestly, "We choose to be polite because being any other way would end up standing in the way of good care for the animals."

Dog had a serious look come across his face as he continued, "I have a confession. I did a tap dance all over Tate's face. I only lied because I didn't want you to think I was acting as your personal avenger. Tate threatened Cruse in front of me, and I needed to ingratiate myself with his organization. But I didn't shoot him. It was some crazy guy in Cruse's gang that shot us both."

Then his stridently ringing phone interrupted us, once again. He answered, immediately frowned, and then rolled his eyes dramatically and hung up.

"No," I whimpered plaintively. "Not THE phone call."

"No," he replied. "Not THE phone call, but a change in plans nevertheless."

I replied by shaking my head, but I was still smiling so Dog turned his attention back to his phone, called the house and asked, "Hey, Phil, I know its late but are you feeling good enough for an adventure?" then paused and asked, "Can you or Mei meet us up at Gas City to pick up Kat?" finally saying, "Thanks! Hate to do this to you but I need to get back to Fort Wayne A.S.A.P," and hung up.

"Gas City!" I exclaimed. "The infamous transfer point for people with family in Fort Wayne and Indianapolis!"

"I'm sorry," Dag said grimly.

"Is everything alright?" I asked, matching his expression.

"Yes," he replied. "Should only take a few days to clear up," gave another big sigh, and added, "although it probably means THE phone call will come soon though."

"Rats!" I exclaimed, then matched his eye roll with one of my own.

"I wish you could tell me everything that happened, especially with the Cruses," I said regretfully. "And why."

"You know 'that guy' who's explaining in detail all the spectacular things he did on his secret military missions?" Dog asked, with narrowed eyes observing me carefully.

"Yeah?" I encouraged him softly.

"If he's trained well enough to do all those spectacular things?" he said somberly. "Then he's trained well enough to keep his mouth shut."

I nodded my understanding and after a short period of thoughtful silence, we joked around the rest of the way to Gas City, totally pretending that we hadn't been having a serious discussion just moments before. But waiting in the parking lot, Dog said starkly, "I'm not like Justin in any way, not even one iota."

"I know that," I assured him. "But am I the same girl that kept hanging on, trying harder, never once considered giving up, no matter how idiotic I was being."

"You're not exactly the same woman," Dog responded, his inflection halfway between a statement and a question. "And now you're done with him?"

"I'm done," I said emphatically. "And I did learn something important at the end of it all. When I'm done, I'm absolutely and totally done!"

"Good," Dog said with a smile, then his face fell and he added seriously, "Don't give up on me."

"I won't," I promised. "I still want to be a reliable person, just not a stupidly loyal person."

"I'm not saying I won't make mistakes," he said softly. "I left my Mom at Target once because I forgot we went shopping together."

I laughed out loud and reassured him, "I know Justin's offenses all sound so trivial one by one, but it was so much more, it was the sum of a thousand lies and disappointments."

"Intent matters," Dog said seriously. "Justin intended to harm you."

"Yea, he did. In retrospect, his actions seem so carefully crafted," I agreed. "But in the midst of it he just seemed pathologically selfish. I'm trying to accept that I'll never understand why hurting me made him feel so good."

"I think you'd have to be equally fucked up to understand," Dog said with an insolent grin.

I laughed and it looked like he was going to continue our conversation, but Phil's car pulled up with all three housemates waving madly out the windows. The trip home flew by as I told them all about my escapade and described everything I did and wore in exquisite detail.

I slept in on Saturday, but by late morning I had written short thank you notes to accompany my little chocolate gifts. I left my housemate's gifts on their mailboxes and then walked over to the hospital. I didn't expect to find everyone I had to thank on duty on a Saturday, but I figured it would actually be easier if I could leave them on their desks in their absence. I felt a bit like a calendar confused Easter Bunny sneaking around making my deliveries, and I hopped pretty high when Dr. Drama and Dr. Tolliver discovered me creeping around their office. But they weren't angry. They seemed genuinely excited by the chocolates.

"Thanks, Dr. Kate," Dr. Drama mumbled with his mouth full. "They're delicious! You can appreciate me with these anytime you want to!'

I gave him a wide smile and started to say that I wished I could afford more, but I caught myself before I detracted from the gesture, making it all about me and my money struggles, and said instead, "I'm glad you like them. Whatcha doing here on your day off?"

"We're meeting with Dr. Blackwell after her shift, for a planning committee meeting," he replied.

"Cool," I said. "Anything fun on the horizon?"

"Yes!" Dr. Drama said. "We're just starting the process, but we're beyond excited about our latest purchase."

"What's that?" I asked, excitedly visualizing the latest super cool surgery equipment that might be coming to our hospital.

"We bought the empty lot next door!" he said with a wide grin.

"What? Why?" I asked in dismay. As far as I was concerned the badlands were the most worthless piece of property I'd ever had to walk across, while bulldozing it over and putting another building there would make me feel even more claustrophobic and confined on our busy corner.

"We're not leaving it like that," Dr. Tolliver protested. "We'll do it in stages, but we're going to make it into a lush garden, with bird feeders and benches, and eventually hedges for privacy."

"A sanctuary!" Dr. Drama insisted.

"No tech allowed," Dr. Tolliver said adamantly as Dr. Drama cringed, and she continued pointedly, "You're the one that found all that evidence that being in a natural no tech setting will recharge our brains."

"But no phones?" he pleaded with her.

She looked at me and said, "This is why we need to have a meeting!"

I smiled and said, "I'd love to help when the time comes to dig in the dirt!"

"We'll take you up on it," Dr. Drama said, exchanging a look with his wife. "In fact we've been meaning to talk to you about your plans for next year. First, I want to assure you that if you want to apply for a residency, surgical or any other, both of us will happily write you glowing recommendations. But you seem unsure about which specialty would be the right choice for you. And it seems like you're struggling with some personal problems. Am I right?"

"You're dead-on," I replied honestly. "And I don't want this to come out all crazy needy, looking for compliments, but why would you both write me a recommendation?"

They exchanged looks then Dr. Drama said simply, "We all admire your knowledge base, your work ethic and your compassion for pets and people. But what's unique is that you're so dang dogged."

"Doggy? Dog like?" I asked in astonishment.

"I said dogged," Dr. Drama insisted. "You're persistent."

"Relentless," Dr. Tolliver added. "You seem so nice and sweet, but you don't let go of what you think is right. It's a quality that will bear the test of time."

"Thank you," I said, starting to feel overwhelmed by the profundity of the compliment. I pushed it aside for the time being, sure I would return to revel in the statement tonight before I went to sleep, perhaps return to it every night for the rest of my life.

"So what are you planning?" Dr. Drama asked.

"I feel like if I just had enough time working in the practice world, I'd not only recover my confidence and focus, I'd make all the right decisions for my life," I said passionately. "I had a very specific dream for my future, but it turns out that my real life doesn't mesh with that vision."

"I never would have had my crisis in the middle of my medicine residency if I had used my Internship year as an exploratory year," Dr. Tolliver said solemnly. "But I stubbornly stayed on the course of action I set for myself as a freshman Vet student and never once considered reevaluating my plan; I trapped myself."

"We'd like to offer you a job here for next year," Dr. Drama explained. "We'd be willing to customize it to fit your needs as long as you'd cover Dr. Blackwell's emergency hours."

"Be an Emergency Vet?" I asked, confused about the offer.

"Call it an exploratory year," Dr. Drama said, nodding at his wife to give her credit for the term. "Dr. Blackwell suggested you might want to be half time Primary Care and half time Emergency Services, but I'd welcome you part time in the Surgery Department if you're interested in that."

"I'm overwhelmed," I said, trying to do some measured breathing without looking weird by making it apparent. "It sounds like it could be perfect for me."

"And it would be a real job with a real paycheck," Dr. Tolliver said smiling.

I grinned and said, "That would be a relief!"

"Why don't you think about it and we'll meet with you next week," Dr. Tolliver suggested.

"If the answer is yes, we can hash out the details," Dr. Drama said. "If the answer is no, we'd be happy to brainstorm with you to make a plan."

"Thank you," I said appreciatively. "Lots to consider."

Dr. Blackwell walked into the office, stuffing her worn lab coat into her tote, and said, "Hey Dr. Kate, I saw a gorgeous picture of you in the Fort Wayne newspaper this morning."

"You did?" I asked in astonishment.

"Yeah, wearing some famous jewel that's going to be auctioned off for sick kids?" she said. "But the article identified you as Kat, not Kate."

"Cool!" I said. "Can't wait to see it! And how hard would it be to change my name from Kate back to Kat around here?"

"Not too hard," Dr. Blackwell said speculatively.

"We're not buying you new uniforms," Dr. Drama insisted bluntly. "But I bet I could remove the extra e embroidered on your smocks and leave no trace I'd ever done the surgery."

We chuckled together and agreed to talk about it next week. But I was already pretty sure I'd be staying, and staying as Dr. Kat.

Chapter Thirty-six

As soon as we left the house, I started worrying that I'd forgotten something I needed for Max's puppy class. Then I reviewed a recent conversation with Dog about overthinking my every move, and he was right, even when I was perfectly prepared, I felt way more anxiety than excitement for almost everything, at work and at home, including activities originally planned to be fun. In a few short months, I had somehow replaced anticipation and joy with concern and obligation, but I refused to keep doing it. So I tried to ignore my anxious inner voice and only pay attention to my enthusiastic one.

Max was happy to go for a walk, but was splitting his focus between where we might be headed, the special treats he could smell in my pocket, and checking to be sure that Ethan was coming with us. Ethan was nervous about the class; he had been reading everything he could find about dog training, but was having trouble sorting out all the different opinions. He had found some articles that indorsed horrifyingly punitive tactics, and I had to assure him that nobody recommended those methods any more. Even Dr. Blackwell, who had been taught those terrible techniques when she was in school in the 1970's, was adamant that they were overly harsh and actually created more behavior problems than they ever solved.

Halfway down the alley, we came up on Trev standing with Licorice's and Chip's leashes wrapped tightly around his legs, and he laughingly called out, "Help me Doc, the pups hog tied me."

I handed Max's leash to Ethan, untangled the Labs' leashes, walked Chip away from his brother and said, "So you decided to try to bring two by yourself after all?"

"Well, actually Mr. Emerson is driving over and he'll meet us at class," Trev replied with a smile. "Mr. Emerson and I are going to co-own Chip, but he's mainly going to be his pup and live at his house. I'm going to be in charge of keeping him well exercised since that's so difficult for both Mr. Emerson and Jiminy."

"Brilliant!" I exclaimed. "Perfect solution. I don't want to steal the trainer's best lines but under exercised puppies and dogs are at the root of many behavior problems. Of course it has to be puppy appropriate exercise, you don't want to trade behavior problems for bone problems!"

Trev nodded his agreement, but then the pups tried to entangle us again so we spaced ourselves out and kept moving toward the training center. A minute later we heard a distinctive high squeaky voice call out from behind us, "Hey, wait for me."

Maisy and Roman floundered down the alley towards us and while she looked pale and her outfit was not as crisp as usual, Maisy was still wearing heels and a dress. I smiled warmly at her, but struggled to know what to say. Trev filled my awkward pause by introducing himself and his puppies, and then I was able to join in and introduce Ethan.

Trev exclaimed somewhat regretfully, "Wow! Your pup is perfect on the leash!"

"I started working with Roman the day I got him," Maisy boasted. "But then life got so crazy that he's been neglected the last couple weeks. Every single day I plan to do better, but until I can hire some kennel help I run out of time doing chores before I ever get to him."

"I'm looking for a part-time job," Trev replied shyly.

Maisy immediately announced, "You're hired!"

Trev appeared shocked and didn't answer, I assume from being on the receiving end of Maisy's glares and looks of suspicion one too many times in the past. It was obvious to me that he had no clue what had just happened at Maisy's kennel or that her son and husband were involved.

Maisy's face fell into an exaggerated frown, but after her expression froze like that briefly, with visible effort she lifted her mouth into a tenuous smile and explained, "I'm sorry Trev, if I've been rude in the past. I had no reason. I've only seen you treat people and animals kindly."

Trev turned bright red and replied, "Thank you."

As we neared the training center, Maisy insisted, "I'm serious about hiring you."

Trev replied, "I'm serious about accepting!"

Mr. Emerson limped over from the parking lot and after introductions, asked, "What do you think of our puppy plan Doc?"

"I believe you're brilliant," I stated emphatically. "Best thing for the puppies!"

"Trev has the energy," Mr. Emerson said grinning. "I have the time and the dollars."

"That's like Ethan and me," I explained. "I may have the book knowledge, but I practically live at the hospital!"

"We should form a neighborhood puppy club," Mr. Emerson said. "Like those babysitting co-ops they have, only for puppies. It could help us all out!"

"Absolutely! Sign us up!" I agreed with a smile as we entered the training building.

The area enclosed for the indoor agility course was huge, but a much smaller area for our class was blocked off with a short fence. Two pups were already there, a fuzzy white terrier mix of some kind that pulled at his leash and barked at us defiantly and a shy little black and white pup that was being held encircled in her owner's arms, partially hidden in the owner's ample bosom.

Gemma made a few general remarks, instructed us how to interact with the pups and then we let them off their leashes for playtime. The labs started chasing each other and rolling around, then they each picked up one of the toys scattered across the floor and shook them in front of the other puppies, trying to entice them into a game of keep away. Within a few short minutes Roman joined in their roughhousing, while Max picked up a toy and trotted around with it by himself, instantly relinquishing it to Chip the minute he reached for it. The little black and white pup hid under the folding chair his owner was sitting in, but watched the ongoing games with growing interest.

Max picked up an abandoned toy, and when the white terrier rushed him and launched himself up into the air to grab it, Max stretched his neck and head up as high as he could to keep it away. But when the pup persisted, jumping at him and biting at his front legs and then finally grabbing his lip, Max yipped, dropped the toy, and tried to retreat under the unoccupied chair next to the hiding black and white pup. Only Max was so much bigger that he couldn't begin to fit under it and ended up wearing the chair over his back, thoroughly frightening himself. Gemma and I rescued Max from the chair and tried desperately not to react, but finally I couldn't help myself and stood there belly laughing out loud. Ethan glared at me and tempted Max to him with one of our extra special treats, then sent him back to play, just like we were supposed to do.

We went through a couple more exercises and then we practiced having the pups settle down while Gemma briefly covered a couple more topics. When she spoke about ways to help prevent separation anxiety, I paid particularly close attention because I really had to work on this aspect of my behavior. I'm such a touchy feely person, it was hard for me not to initiate lots of petting and holding before I left Max, mostly for my own comfort. But to a puppy's way of feeling, I was essentially promising to stay with him for some pack activity, like hunting in the wild, thus becoming unintentionally cruel and creating anxiety when I abruptly abandoned him instead. But as engrossed in the topic as I was, I still noticed Dog framed in the entryway and I went deaf to what Gemma was saying.

Dog's face was alert but serious as he scanned the room and I was taken aback, once again, by how striking he was, like a work of art. I had heard people, men especially, described as having chiseled features, or a sculpted profile or a molded brow, but I had never really known what they were attempting to describe. Until now. The light played off the planes and angles of his face and he looked like marble carved by a master craftsman.

He caught my eye and smiled gently, at my expression of admiration I think, and held my gaze for a few seconds, then gestured with his head for me to come outside with him. I tapped Ethan's shoulder and whispered to him to take over with Max, but when I turned back toward Dog, he held up his hand with thumb and baby finger extended up to his ear in the classic call me pantomime. Confused, I started to reach for my phone, but then his stricken face froze me instead, as I suddenly understood what he was trying to say. The phone. The phone call had come and he was leaving.

I jogged over to him, previously warned that he would have to respond immediately when the call came, no time for big farewells to any of us. So if we only had a couple of minutes I was going to bless the fact that we got to say goodbye at all instead of wasting time regretting what we couldn't share. In the flash of time it took me to cross the expanse of the training area, I oddly thought about separation anxiety in people. Should I keep my cool, greet him sedately, send him away with a friendly hug and cool kiss to make it easier for him to leave? Should I protect him from my despair, my fear, my feelings for him, and my regret of all that we hadn't had a chance to share yet? Would that be best for him? Would it be best for me?

As soon as I reached him and the door closed behind us, I dismissed those thoughts with a muttered "No!' and committed to giving him the most intensely excruciating anxiety I could manage to elicit, all at the very thought of being away from me. I wrapped my arms around his neck and pulled him close to me, wiggling here and there to meld us together, to be as close as I could make it. He made a low gasp, in an odd combination of surprise and hurt, then I kissed him goodbye without restraint or thought of future heartbreak, I tried to physically communicate the depth and breadth of my every loving thought and passionate feeling. And then I made him be the one to break it off and gently push me away.

Now he didn't look like art anymore, his face had softened and he appeared both vulnerable and exposed. I glared at him and forcefully ordered him, "You come back to me."

"With my shield or on it," he promised intensely.

"What??" I asked, totally confused once again.

"I'll come back to you or die trying," he starkly explained as my heart clenched in my chest and he effectively schooled me on exactly how one creates life altering separation anxiety.

Made in the USA
Lexington, KY
02 February 2019